Advance Praise for *The Vavasour Macbeth*

"[*The Vavasour Macbeth*] re-creates life at the 16th century court of Queen Elizabeth via a 20th century murder mystery.... Casey peppers his imaginative novel with tidbits on the development of writing in the Elizabethan era... Each of the central protagonists is a well-drawn character. And the author's prose is elegant, with evocative imagery.... An engaging read with a plethora of captivating literary and historical details wrapped in a contemporary whodunit."

—Kirkus Reviews

Also by Bart Casey

The Double Life of Laurence Oliphant

The Wonder Seekers of Fountaingrove
(with co-author Gaye LeBaron)

Anne Vavasour and Sir Henry Lee:
Discovering a Tudor Love Story (ebook)

the Vavasour Macbeth

BART CASEY

Post Hill
PRESS

A POST HILL PRESS BOOK
ISBN: 978-1-64293-131-0
ISBN (eBook): 978-1-64293-132-7

Cover art by Cody Corcoran

The cover design includes photographs of portraits of Anne Vavasour and Sir Henry Lee, courtesy of The Worshipful Company of Armourers and Brasiers, London.

Post Hill Press
New York • Nashville
posthillpress.com

Published in the United States of America

To Marilyn, Matthew,
Lauren, and Michael

NOTE

Like Shakespeare's plays, which
have five acts, the story of
The Vavasour Macbeth unfolds
in five parts.

Each part begins with a short
visit to the Elizabethan and
Jacobean world of Anne Vavasour,
and then moves on to events in
modern England.

This is because the destinies
of Anne Vavasour and her modern
descendant Margaret Hamilton,
are closely intertwined.

Prologue

Yorkshire, 1579. Anne Vavasour was bred for this, and now she was ready. Tomorrow she would leave home to take up her place at the court of Queen Elizabeth, where all successes flowed from Her Majesty's good graces.

At sixteen, she was pretty enough, and a decade of dancing, riding, and country living made her shapely and graceful. But that was not what men noticed when they met her. It was her smile that stopped them. It lit up her face, from the point of her chin to the top of her brow, with her eyes sparkling. Then she'd speak with the wit and wisdom of a princess—in Latin, Greek, French, Italian, or even English. And when their eyebeams crossed, she held them in thrall.

She had practiced all this with the friends and neighbors who visited the house in Wiltshire where she had been tutored from the age of six. Sir Henry and Thomas Knyvet, her uncles, invested in the finest teachers and dancing masters for the family children. Since Thomas was a Groom of the Privy Chamber for Queen Elizabeth, he was well fixed to place his relations at court as they came of age.

The Knyvets' prize pupil was Anne, their sister's daughter, and they groomed her to be a kindred spirit for the Queen. Her curriculum was guided by the precepts of Roger Ascham, who had been a tutor to Princess Elizabeth and Lady Jane Grey. Master Ascham wrote these down in *The Schoolmaster*, published in 1570, just in time for

Anne's schooling. As a result, she was taught with kindness, not fear, and was encouraged to shape her own ideas. True to plan, Anne became self-confident and assured. She mastered English first, and then the most important old and new foreign languages. She loved poetry as well as philosophy, history, and literature. She also learned embroidery, music, dancing, archery, and hunting.

In the late autumn of 1579, Anne was packed to travel down to London from her parents' house in Yorkshire. Everything was arranged for her to become a Gentlewoman of the Bedchamber in the Queen's innermost circle.

On this, her last evening at home, Anne sewed together a new, blank commonplace book to record her thoughts at court, and looked through the passages she'd written in her old commonplace book during school.

They were still good words to live by, she thought. But what was to become of her now?

A.V. Anne Vavasour, her booke.
Ad maiorum Dei gloriam.

The pastimes that be fit for comely gentlemen

Therefore to ride comely, to run fair at the tilt or
ring; to play at all weapons, to shoot fair in bow,
or surely in gun; to vault lustily, to run, to leap,
to wrestle, to swim; to dance comely, to sing, and
play on instruments cunningly; to hawk, to hunt;
to play at tennis, and all pastimes generally, which
be joined with labour, used in open place, and on
the day-light, containing either some fit exercise
for war, or some pleasant pastime for peace, be not
only comely and decent, but also very necessary for
a courtly gentleman

—*Master Roger Ascham*

Nec species sua cuique manet, rerumque novatrix
Ex aliis alias reddit natura figuras

No living species remains the same,
New-making nature changes all into new forms

—*Ovid,* Metamorphoses, *XV:252–53*

Forsan et haec olim meminisse iuvabit

Perhaps one day it will help to remember even these
things

—*Virgil,* Aeneid, *I:203*

Πριν να εξετάσουμε άλμα

Look before you leap

> *—Aesop, "The Fox and the Goat"*

Herod, the king, in his raging,
Charged he hath this day,
His men of might in his owne sight
All yonge children to slay.

> *—Mysterie Playe of Coventry*

On a Maiden-head

Lost Jewells may be recovered, virginity never.
That's lost but once, and once lost, lost for ever.

> *—Anonymous*

PART ONE

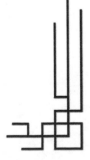

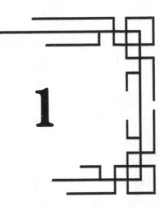

The sleeping villagers didn't know their history was about to come alive again. It was Bank Holiday Monday, the last day of August 1992. The ancient church of St. Mary and its adjacent vicarage basked in the early morning sun under a bright blue dome of sky just north of London.

"It doesn't seem the kind of day to be mucking about in damp tombs," Vicar Hamilton said aloud to the picture of his dead wife atop his chest of drawers as he dressed. "But there's no going ahead without sacrifice. No gain without pain, dear Delia."

Delia Howard had married him less than six months after he took up his post as vicar back in 1966. At first, it was something of a scandal. He was the bright young new vicar, and she was the daughter of the local gentry who had lorded over the town for the past five hundred years. But any disapproval vanished as for more than twenty-five years the two of them double-handedly kept the parish vibrant and relevant in an England where most churches were only embarrassing remnants of a medieval fantasy. The youth program flourished, with skiffle bands banging guitars and tambourines to the tunes of Cliff Richard, Tommy Steele, the Beatles, and the Stones. The married-couples ministry kept many local couples together past bumps in the road. And the Al-Anon and Nar-Anon groups countered the new realities with hope.

With everything that was going on, it was only fair to expect some trouble, and this morning Vicar Hamilton was putting on his old plaid shirt and stained work trousers to face down another challenge.

Over the last few weeks of summer, the Mothers Morning Out group he started had morphed into a proper child-care program. It was yet another of his quixotic efforts to keep the church front and center for the parish. Now the old church was making a real connection with young families in the town, giving mothers a place to get together and have their tots intermingle. The future of our parish, thought the vicar. Two groups now—about twenty-five babies—and new faces at the Sunday service as well. He had even gotten approval from the bishop to advertise for a program director, and now the CVs were flooding in for interviews with the playschool committee. That would mean even more commotion in the church office.

Inside the old church, the Lady Chapel was now sectioned off sacrilegiously, with portable red-gray office dividers between the rounded Norman arches. Green linoleum sheets covered the stone floors. Blackboards on wheels lined up in front of the tables and small chairs clustered below the ancient stained-glass windows and wall memorials to eighteenth-century benefactors.

In front of the altar with the fourteenth-century statue of Our Lady and Baby Jesus—the most famous relic of the church—a brown-cloth Brunswick billiards table was pushed in as a barrier to block the children of the crèche. The beauty and innocence of that stone carving had preserved it even through the rough days of the English Civil War, when New Model Army soldiers smashed ornaments in churches all around the country—but not that one. Now the danger was from the children of the town. And they had just made their first serious assault on the past two days before.

On the Friday afternoon of the long weekend, something went wrong in the loo next to the tearoom on the old porch of the church. Later the workmen found a disposable nappy had been stuffed into the toilet, which kept it running. And so a steady stream of cold water overflowed unseen and unheard all night, seeping onto the stone floor, under the walls, and down into the burial vaults below.

By the time Andrew James, the verger who took care of the church, found it Saturday morning, several burial vaults were flooded with water covering the old coffins and remains. Worst off was the largest vault in the nave, which had been sealed since the 1840s. Also wet was the small vault in the Lady Chapel—the final resting place of so-called Lady Anne, an Elizabethan bene-factor of the old church and an ancestor of Mrs. Hamilton herself, the vicar's late wife.

Now that side of the family had almost died out, thought the vicar. His daughter, Margaret, was the last of that bloodline now, but there was no sign of her settling down yet.

Well, the flood canceled Lucy Worthington's Saturday after-noon wedding service—at least for a stormy hour or two. Her father and the best man turned up early at the vicar's door, red-faced and livid with rage in their gray morning coats. But they calmed down when the vicar came up with Plan B, moving the service to Roman Catholic St. Luke's just across the green. Father O'Brien was very decent about lending the hall to his pagan Prot-estant neighbors on such short notice, thought the vicar.

Actually it worked out quite well, thanks to the Catholics' new central air-conditioning and the bright light coming through their newer stained glass windows. And Vicar Hamilton prob-ably wouldn't have gotten the extra two-hundred-pound cheque from Mister Worthington if the bride's father hadn't felt guilty about his earlier display in the hall of the vicarage.

The Catholics were very up-to-date—but the Protestants had the history, and that's just what the vicar would be dealing with today.

He reached for the silver-topped hairbrush on his dresser and gave three brisk strokes to smooth his yellow-white hair from left to right. Then he let his eyes move across the lace to the other dresser against the bedroom wall there, now holding his wife's treasures and keepsakes. On the top was a small cluster of her favorite photos of their daughter. There was Margaret around age eight, with her chums in school uniforms collecting donations for Bangladesh, already showing signs of a fierce determination to raise awareness of the wrongs in the world and intervene person-ally to set things right. What a commotion those young girls had made marching up and down the high street after school and on weekends, he remembered. Then there was a snapshot taken a few years later in her games uniform for field hockey, with one of her signature smiles, in spite of the cuts and gashes on each leg. Next to that, another photo showed her as a young teenager volunteering behind the counter in the Oxfam shop in the village, fighting world poverty. And then there was his wife's favorite portrait of herself, taken five years ago, standing together with Margaret who was just back from her university year abroad immersing herself in her beloved France. One never knows what moments turn out to be the height of happiness, he thought. But then the kettle whistled and he had to hurry downstairs.

From the kitchen window over the sink, he could see hoses running out the side door of the church, across the vicarage garden, and down into the drain at the side of the road. There was a steady purring from the petrol-driven pump working away beneath puffs of gray smoke.

He saw the carefully planned flower beds were in their full glory. Each planting was a different specimen, placed according to its natural height, and blooming at just the right time of the year with its neighbors—Delia's grand scheme. And the thick turf of the lawn, wet with dew, was bursting with life, now greener than green—emerald really, and soft and deep as a down duvet.

It was a shame they'd have to dig across the lawn and the beds to put in a drainage line from the troublesome church addition, but they had to prevent another flood from happening if one of the children again stuffed up the toilet. The vicar planned to draw a map showing where each plant sat so they could restore it all later. At least they wouldn't be digging across the churchyard, disturbing all those graves as well. There were enough spirits stirred up already down in the vaults. And the lawn would grow back, thick as ever by next spring, God willing.

Seven o'clock. Just time for a quick cup of tea before Verger Andrew and the workmen came back, the vicar thought.

Well, it was better to have a playschool in the chapel and a tearoom on the porch than no one in the church at all.

~

Ten minutes later, Vicar Hamilton joined Verger Andrew and the village plumber at the side of the pavement where the pump and hoses were hooked up. "Let's see what's gone on down there," said the vicar, ending his words with a sigh. And God preserve the old church's foundation, he prayed silently to himself.

They turned off the pump, restoring the morning calm to the fresh air, and walked inside the church, stepping over the hoses.

The afternoon before, masons had opened up the floor in two parts of the church. First they had freed up several large slabs of Purbeck marble in the nave atop the burial vault extending out from the old thirteenth-century wall of the church. It had been very hard to pry the slabs up from where they had been sealed over a century and a half before, but the workmen finally succeeded in shifting them, and now they were angled widthwise across the narrow opening in the floor.

The slabs were also part of the ceiling of the vault below. At first, only coal-black water could be seen down there, settling roughly two feet below the opening—so it was impossible to tell just how wide and how deep was the vault. No record of the room's measurements remained in the otherwise meticulous church archives—only the dates of interments through the years until its final sealing in 1845, with the notation that it was then full.

A few hours later, the vicar had leaned over and shone a hand torch around. Then he could see the water was lower by at least four feet and several objects were piercing the surface at different heights and angles.

Now this morning, the plumber lowered down a miner's lamp, testing the air and illuminating the damp and debris. All clear. There was only a wet and musty smell—very similar to things that sit in a basement too long—and no whiff of any decay from decomposition, as one might fear. That had all disappeared long ago. The three men angled a ladder down into the space, and when it hit the floor only about five inches of its base was covered by the receding water.

Finally, Vicar Hamilton could see the chaos of mortality. Dozens of caskets and iron coffins were stacked up in piles of four or five on top of one another. The coffins at the top were newer than the ones below and were covered with fragments of faded purple velvet. They were lined with hundreds of brass studs. Brass or golden coffin handles jutted out, embellished with the heads of cherubim. Centered on the top of one perched a coronet from which the velvet or ermine had disappeared, leaving six silver orbs protruding on long stems from the edges of a crown.

The coffins below were in worse shape. The wooden end panel of one had fallen off onto the floor, revealing a coal-black leaden shell inside. The lead explained why the other coffins were crushed like accordions: they had been broken by the terrific weight above. Most were sized for adults, but around the edges

of the stacks was a circle of small boxes. A few were the reposi-
tories of funerary organs from embalming, but most were the
doleful remains of infants and small children—sad reminders of
high hopes unfulfilled. Here they rested, awaiting the resurrection with their elders.

"Another hour or so of pumping and she'll be empty," said
Andrew. "Then we'll go down and have a look 'round before we
set up fans to dry out the damp."

Around the corner, in the Lady Chapel, was a second hole,
this one in the plain stone floor just in front of the memorial to
Lady Anne. Vicar Hamilton went over and looked down at the
words carved on a stone slab lying akimbo to this much smaller
hole: "Vavasour," the family name, and then *Constantia et
fide*" just below. He translated the Latin to himself: "Constant
and faithful"—a very good motto indeed, for both the living and
the dead. There hadn't been nearly as much water here as in the
larger vault, but it had still had a bit of a soaking. Bending down
to try to see into the hole, he felt dizzy, so he straightened up
slowly, deciding to take a closer look later.

The vicar turned to Verger Andrew and said, "Well, there
are several centuries of our village history down there. And my
dear wife's ancestors as well." Then his profound musings were
interrupted by the sounds of the workmen restarting the pump
in the nave.

~

Stephen didn't recognize it at first. A noise...a bell...a buzzer...
repeating...and staying there...coming back...again and again.
Go away!

He turned over onto his back and opened his eyes, squinting.
Light was streaming in to his bedroom—the morning was incredibly bright, hard to focus. And still the ringing.

Oh Christ! It's the phone.

Up now on two elbows he looked across the bed. Miranda was still sleeping, one arm cocked up, hand back under her head—a fetching, but almost ludicrous pose while asleep—her mouth slightly open, her left breast and nipple peeking out from under the covers. She could sleep through a train wreck, he thought.

One giant effort and he stretched over her, carefully pushing himself up to not wake her. He grabbed the phone just as he saw the clock: 0740, and it was a bloody Bank Holiday Monday morning as well.

"Hello!"

Just the dial tone. Damn!

He put the receiver back in the stand and sank back into the bed, closing his eyes. Back to sleep, or up now? The light was so strong.

No use for it—he was awake. Pushing off the blankets, he angled himself up to sit on the side of the bed.

Stephen's bedroom was crammed full with books—some new but the vast majority old, booty bought over the last ten years from secondhand bookstores all across Britain. Smallish ones were lined up in double rows on the wide shelves of the bookcases that were his bedside tables. Other larger ones were stacked up in piles about three feet high along the walls, festooned with discarded neckties.

In his front room, a large bookcase with glass doors held his treasures. What would be old and obscure books for almost anyone else were vibrant and alive with delights for Stephen: old leather backs, many crumbling but still dignified and proud of their frequent use. And some important ones, like his Third Folio of Shakespeare, printed in 1664. That one had come to him from his late father, along with the edition of Chaucer's *Canterbury Tales* printed by William Morris at his Pre-Raphaelite Kelmscott Press. A smaller bookcase held his sixteen-volume set of the *Oxford English Dictionary*.

By the bay window looking out over the common garden and courtyard of the apartment complex, Stephen's ancient refectory table was also piled with books, computer equipment, cigarette packs, and a circular rack with six or seven well broken-in pipes.

Just next to this, on the wall was a map of Switzerland and Italy with pins marking the spots from Geneva to Naples he planned to visit the following spring, following in the footsteps of Byron, Keats, and the Shelleys. He used his holidays to make history come alive by visiting the places where great events happened. In fact, planning the trips was almost as good as going, since it kept his enthusiasm growing all through the winter. And what Englishman wouldn't want to end up in Italy in the spring?

Here and there a tennis racquet and sports bag challenged the books along the walls. And one corner was consumed with cricket gear: kit bag, gloves, bats, batting pads, and a set of wickets and bails, with one wicket jauntily wearing his tricolor club hat of white, purple, and black.

Higher on the walls, Stephen also had a few prints of the buildings and deer park around his Oxford alma mater, Magdalen College (pronounced "maudlin"), plus a poster from a favorite show at the Tate Gallery and, most important, two framed pages from a medieval manuscript with lovely gold-leaf illumination, his graduation gift from his parents over four years ago.

Just below all of that, on top of the glass-doored bookcase, was his favorite photo of his parents. They smiled at the camera from their rented chairs on the sandy Riviera beach in front of the Hotel Martinez in Cannes—he called it his *carpe diem* reminder to seize the day before adversity strikes, just as it had struck them soon after.

And also, with pride of place so he saw it from his table, was a small framed poster from the Schools County Cricket Tournament two years before, signed by all the boys on his winning team. Stephen had been their coach and also had just become their unlikely headmaster at St. George's School in the village, just as he was today.

He stood up naked from the bed, stretched, and tiptoed across the archipelago of abandoned clothing he and Miranda had slipped out of six or seven hours before, and headed toward the hall and the loo. He looked a sight in the mirror, with his thick brown hair askew and standing in spikes. He splashed his face with cold water and then patted down his head.

I'll just put on the kettle before I take a shower, he thought. The kitchen was a tight space opening off from the front room, but it and the bath were kept almost hospital clean by Mrs. Case, who came in to tidy and take the laundry once a week. She applied most of her attentions to the kitchen and the loo, having been forbidden to rearrange much of anything else in the place. Since Stephen never cooked, the kitchen was always standing at attention for him to make a quick cuppa or heat up some takeaway.

Kettle on now. And then the phone again.

Stephen walked into the front room and sank into the sofa next to the other telephone. The fabric was scratchy against his bare skin.

"Hello?" Of all people, it was Vicar Hamilton from St. Mary's Church.

"Stephen, hello. Sorry to call so early on a holiday...but there's something really quite extraordinary I want you to take a look at." The vicar paused, but then moved ahead excitedly in the silence. "This morning I've had workmen over about some flooding in the vaults and among all the rubble and mess I've found two chests full of old papers. I can't quite make out the writing, but I'd say sixteenth or seventeenth century from the little I know—you can tell me after you see them—and most still in very good shape. They were buried right in the Vavasour vault underneath the Lady Chapel—my late wife's relatives, you know. Quite amazing, wouldn't you say?"

"Papers?" asked Stephen, the haze quickly lifting. "You mean books and so forth?"

"No. Actually, these are handwritten papers. Some seem to be letters with fold lines, salutations, signatures, and such. Other sheets seem to be lists and poetry—quite an assortment. And a few other things, like a few journals and an embroidered bag. Anyway, I thought you could take a look and help me understand what we've got here. Can you come over and take a look?"

"You mean to say these are original manuscripts?" Stephen said, with his voice pointedly rising into the phone.

"Yes, it seems so. I've moved most of them. But some are still down in the vault and rather damp—so I'd like some help getting them out before the workmen take over. Can you come straight over?"

"Sure...of course! I'll be right over. Fifteen minutes. Cheers."

Manuscripts from the tombs, Stephen thought. Seems too fantastic for words. I wonder how were they protected, and how would they have lasted? Well, probably only old inventories, wills, deeds, and so forth. Really nothing much else was ever saved from those centuries except for legal documents that seemed to have unquestionable value to their owners. They would be astonished to find out those had only questionable value today. We'd see the personal jottings and keepsakes as the real treasures, but hardly anything like that survived. Well, maybe he's got the dates wrong. I'll have to wait until I see them. Bloody fantastic!

Getting ready for the shower, he went back into his bedroom. Oh Christ...Miranda! And she'd wanted to spend the Bank Holiday together.

"Miranda, Miranda love, wake up. It's morning." He gave her a gentle touch on her upraised arm, and she brought it right down.

"Hmmmmm," she exhaled, turning away on to her side, still deeply asleep.

Stephen didn't date much. He had tried a few girlfriends after Margaret, the vicar's daughter. None really clicked, but Miranda was the one he was with the most. She was just the reverse of himself, unschooled, lowbrow, and incredibly lively and saucy. He had often thought she lived with an intensity that had eluded him. Maybe he had passed too much of his life inside, spending too much time planning, working, and thinking while Miranda was seizing the day and dancing on tabletops. That's why he always had fun and felt drawn out when he was with her—and last night had been lived to the fullest, as much as he could recall. He remembered belting out song after song down at the annual County Cricket Club dinner, the best one being an old ballad where you went round the room with everyone adding their own bawdy four-line verse before the chorus. His last one had been pretty good, but Miranda had left them all blushing, if he remembered right—which wasn't at all a sure thing this morning.

Well, I better just leave her. No need to ruin her lie-in this morning and I'll leave her a note on the sofa. Besides if I woke her, it would be harder to just go off over to the church.

So Stephen hopped in and out of the shower, into his clothes, and down the stairs to where his aged yellow Mini awaited, parked across the street. He literally hurdled across the small hedge separating the entry of the apartments from the pavement beyond, and then skipped between parked cars to his own.

Amazing what that call did, he thought. One minute I'm probably headed for a hangover, and now I'm hopping around like a fool. Adrenaline, I suppose, or maybe just buried treasure.

And so he drove off toward St. Mary's.

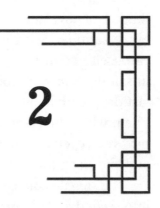

2

Stephen wound his Mini through the quiet streets at the edge of the village, coming out onto the main thoroughfare of Station Road. Going down the hill, he passed from neat rows of detached houses with their private trees and gardens to streets of plain and smaller semidetached ones, then row houses, and then the British Rail station, with its gingerbread station house with red geraniums bobbing from window boxes. After that came the shops, leading one after another farther down the hill, until finally Station Road ended at the bottom with the pub on the corner of the Oxford road.

He turned right and headed into the center of town. It was a crisp and pleasant morning, with the sunlight and deep blue sky lightening the brown and gray of the walls and pavement.

Waiting at a traffic light, Stephen gazed off across the left side of the road, where the common land began and walking paths led up and down across the picturesque heath, with miles of rolling hills and fields crisscrossed with ancient hedgerows. A group of boys was whacking a round football back and forth across a makeshift pitch, with sweaters piled on the grass as goalposts. He recognized two of them as former students of his at St. George's—free as birds, and not a care in the world, he thought.

Behind them were all the stalls and trappings of the August Bank Holiday Fair, which came to the village at the end of every summer, with its shooting galleries, tennis ball throws, carousels, bouncy castles, Ferris wheels, and one fearsomely unsafe-looking mini roller coaster. Today would be the third and last day, he thought—and the best one, with good, dry weather. Then, when the crews had packed it all up and moved on until next year, everyone in the village would know summer had ended and another autumn school term was about to begin.

The signal changed to green and Stephen started off, shifting into second and gliding past the high street banks, estate agents, bookmaker, butcher, baker, and ironmonger, until he came to the formal village green tucked away just to the left of the main road.

There the war memorial was picture perfect amid carefully maintained flower beds and winding white gravel walkways. It was different from the thousands of others dotting villages all over England with simple lists of names commemorating the village war dead. Here the memorial committee had reached higher and adorned this memorial with a life-size figure of a handsome young soldier in the Great War, helmetless, on one knee, and holding a rifle with bayonet attached, waiting expectantly for some new assault.

The statue, it had been said, looked just like the poet Rupert Brooke, his hair combed back straight from the forehead and chin raised slightly toward the future—what little future there would have been for him. More than just a written name, the poignant figure animated the sad record of the village's sons, brothers, and fathers lost in the senseless butchery of those years, dealing a blow from which many villages had never recovered.

Across from this stood the bookends to the village green, Roman Catholic St. Luke's and the vicar's Church of England St. Mary's, facing each other. St. Mary's was the ancient Norman anchor for the town, built in the early 1200s. St. Luke's looked old, too, but had really just arrived only one hundred years ago.

Stephen pulled into the driveway of the vicarage adjacent to St. Mary's and turned off the motor. This was always such an impeccably tidy place. It seemed really odd to have a confusion of hoses and pump smoke disturbing the manicured gardens between the vicarage and the old church.

A few workmen were standing beside the pump with Verger Andrew. Stephen stepped out of the car and walked over.

"Hello, Stephen," said the verger. "The vicar's just gone into the house."

"Well, looks like quite a mess. What's the damage?"

"The largest of the vaults was full up with water yesterday when we looked in," Andrew replied. "Now we've got the water out, and the foundation seems solid, praise the Lord, but there's terrible damp—and what's down there is in dreadful shape. Then the smaller Vavasour vault was not so bad. The vicar has just carried some things he's found in it up and into the house."

"Right. He just telephoned me to have a look at them, so I'm going to find him straightaway. See you in a minute."

Stephen loped with authority across the lawn and opened the hard oak door of the vicarage. Standing in the hall, he could see the corner of the best floral carpet in the lounge. He walked over, bending his head around the doorway. Everything in the room was the essence of neat propriety, he thought, as usual. Only the absence of cut flowers in the vases reminded him that Mrs. Hamilton was no longer there to breathe some life into the place.

Bookcases stood on either side of the fireplace, their shelves lined with volumes of church and county histories and sermons—riveting stuff indeed. Centered exactly over the mantle of the fireplace was the vicar's favorite painting of the martyrdom of St. Sebastian, a reproduction of a medieval work showing the strangely serene saint bare-chested and shot full of arrows. Stephen had kidded him about it before.

At the end of the room the vicar's reading glasses lay ready on a glass-topped round table next to his favorite chair, which was positioned for maximum light in front of French doors out to the terrace and back garden. That's where he reads his bible, writes his sermons, and falls asleep every evening, thought Stephen— the same pattern for the quarter century he's been here.

On the table was a cluster of small picture frames. Here was a large silver one with a decades-old wedding-day portrait of Delia, the vicar's late wife. Margaret was born less than ten months later, turning her parents' idyllic world into pandemonium. There were three or four pictures of her growing up, looking out at him with her signature smile which, even as a child, lit up her entire face. Not one of those teeth-gritting grimaces nervous people show to photographers, but something transcendent and overwhelming. Next to the smiles were school-day images of her being perhaps too rowdy at maypole dancing, judging from the distressed faces of the teachers in the background. And God help anyone who came too close to that hockey stick and tried to get in her way, he thought. And there were several newer pictures: one when she became a BBC-TV presenter; and another of her dressed in a haik, the full-body cover and veil imposed on women in Algeria by the Islamic Salvation Front in 1991. That's when Margaret went undercover for an investigative exposé on the new government's harsh treatment of women. There was also one taken just after she and Stephen became engaged.

But so much of Margaret was too hard for him to look at, and he turned back toward the hall.

"Vicar!" he called out into the stillness. "It's Stephen!"

The reply came instantly from the other end of the front hall behind him. "Stephen, yes, hello. I'm here in the kitchen."

The vicar was standing over the rectangular kitchen table, which was covered in dish towels. He was lifting out small piles of papers, some wet around the edges, from a cloth shopping bag on one of the chairs and arranging them on the towels to wick away the moisture.

"Jesus Christ," said Stephen in astonishment.

"Please, Stephen, mind your tongue. But it is quite extraordinary, isn't it? There are just so many of these. I'm going to have to start laying them out on the carpet in the lounge."

Stephen bent low over the table to focus on the papers. The old sheets were of varying sizes and cuts—most larger than the common size A4 paper used everywhere in Europe today—and they were all obviously ancient and handmade. In spite of the flooding, they were in remarkable shape, some with reddish ink and others in black, but still bright and clear, with rustlike stains on several where wax seals had lain. Mixed in were some things written on parchment, made from the hides of sheep or goats.

The vicar was most likely right about dating them to the sixteenth and seventeenth century, Stephen thought, looking quickly over a smattering of the papers. Several hands had written them. Here one was in a prim italic style, almost readable to any layman today—that's probably a woman, he thought. Things Italian had come into vogue in the second half of the 1500s in England and young ladies in the better families spent hours and hours learning and practicing the elegant new standardized script.

Most of the others were in the so-called secretary hand, the form most taught in school for writing correspondence or business and legal documents during those centuries. Its elaborate swirling lettering and irregular spellings are strange and unfamiliar to anyone today and Stephen knew that reading them would mean a tedious process of scrutinizing, deciphering, and transcribing each little mark, letter by letter, Latin or English, full word or abbreviation, and then mulling over the entire arcane concoction just to make out what it said. And often letters would be in code for privacy—just to make understanding them more of a challenge for curious servants. He'd been quite good at excavating meaning from such manuscripts at Oxford years ago—but he was out of practice now.

Everything on the table so far seemed to be letters, with easily spotted salutations and signatures, and matching papers folded up to "envelope" the other sheet in transit.

"And there's at least as much again still there at the church," the vicar said. "We'll have to go collect all that now so the workmen can get started. See if there's another shopping bag over by the icebox."

Reluctantly turning away from the tabletop treasures, Stephen found an empty orange Tyvek sack with wooden handles between the fridge and counter. It had an oversize rectangular shape made to be an exact fit with the shopping carts at the Waitrose supermarket 150 yards away.

"Yes, that'll do nicely—should be just about right for what we have to get, I should think," the vicar said as he placed the last packet from his own cloth bag onto the tabletop and drew himself up erect, stretching the kinks out in his back one by one. "Oh—and you should put on some wellies or going down into the vaults will stain your shoes."

Stephen chose from a cluster of boots in the back hall off the kitchen and sat by the table, pulling them on as he twisted around for another glimpse of the letters. "You know, vicar, you just don't see these sorts of things lying around like this. You might see printed books come up occasionally at auction—but not manuscripts. They're all locked up in collections at the British Museum or the Bodleian. And it's like going through hell to get a pass to touch them. Librarians bring you typed transcripts to look at, not the actual old originals, unless you have a damn good reason to see them. Now just look at all this. It's incredible. Priceless, too, I should think—I mean probably 'priceless,' since things like this aren't bought and sold anymore. Wealthy collectors like J. P. Morgan bought them all up at the turn of the century and now they are kept out of sight. I know from book auctions at Sotheby's that important manuscripts from this period sell for thousands of pounds—and you've got boxes full of possibilities here. They could be worth a fortune."

"Well," said the vicar, "I don't know if any of these are 'important,' but I do know a little about the lady in the tomb with them: Anne Vavasour. She's actually an ancestor on my wife's side of the family. I'll tell you when we come back with the rest of the papers. But now, let's go across to the church—I know Andrew and the men will be waiting."

In just a minute or two Stephen was watching Vicar Hamilton step around some marble slabs and onto the ladder protruding out of the large vault below the floor of the nave. The vicar moved slowly and deliberately, shifting his weight onto the rungs. "Easy does it," he said with a sigh.

The miner's lamp was suspended down into the vault, hanging about two feet below the ceiling, sending an ethereal yellow glow up into the empty church. Stephen had grown up around this church and been at choir evenings and weekends, but he had never seen the floor opened up like it was now, uncovering another world below.

When the vicar reached the floor of the vault, Stephen knelt down for a closer look. He caught his first good whiff of the musty damp smell. Just an old wet cellar, he thought.

He could make out several stacks of coffins piled atop one another, in varied stages of crushing and decay.

"Bloody hell," said Stephen, again forgetting how his cursing upset the vicar. But that one seemed to go by unnoticed.

After walking around gingerly for a few minutes, the vicar came back up the ladder. He turned to Verger Andrew and the workmen. "I think the pump has got almost all of the standing water out. Another hour or so and we should bring on the mops, and then perhaps some fans. Andrew, you go down and see what you think while Stephen and I go over to the Lady Chapel."

They left the men in the nave for the small Lady Chapel off to the side with its old memorials.

Set into one wall was a small decorative arch with the rounded figure of a marble knight reclining, arms folded across his waist and wearing what seemed to be a tunic of crusader mesh above his armored knees and feet. His figure stretched across two massive blocks of stone, both gently sloped to cradle him in sleep. No carved words remained, and the simplicity of the monument recalled the earlier thirteenth- and fourteenth-century styles, before the Italian influence of the Renaissance swept England.

The monument of his Elizabethan neighbor was much more ornate. The suggestion of a marble altar rose about three and a half feet above the floor, with its top shelf protruding about eighteen inches from the wall. Perched at either end of that were two dark marble columns reaching up and supporting a chambered floral ceiling framing the central tableau. In profile there a sculptured lady knelt in a painted red dress, ruffed collar, and white cap, with hands pointedly clasped in prayer before a lectern and an open book. Just below the effigy, two crests framed an inscribed plate. Finally, the whole structure was protected on all sides by a black wrought-iron fence, with curving rails topped with golden fleur-de-lis finial points.

"This is the memorial of Anne Vavasour," the vicar said, "our relative. The vault below it was much less damaged than in the nave, but still took in a little water."

34

The floor of the chapel had been taken up in front of the Vavasour memorial to open the vault, and three stone slabs were piled up to one side. The rubble that had been immediately below the slabs was now mounded to the side on the floor. In the hole, a short slope of shards of brick and stones led down from the base of the memorial itself and stopped at the foot of a wall of smooth firestone blocks about four feet tall. Finally, a two-foot-wide section of red bricks had been removed from the center of the wall, leaving a gaping manhole amid the blocks, which was now partially illuminated by another miner's lamp. The gate of hell, Stephen thought as he looked through the opening into the dark vault within.

Vicar Hamilton stepped gingerly down the slope exposed by the digging. He steadied himself with his left hand on the firestone blocks of the wall and shone the hand torch in his right hand through the manhole into the vault. On the edge of the damp floor inside, just within reach through the opening, Stephen could see the source of the documents: a black wooden chest, its end panel knocked off and leaning beside it, admitting a view of some stacked papers within. Most of the papers closest to the opening had already been removed to the vicarage and a second stack farther in was waiting to come out. Also, a second black box, smaller and shorter, sat next to the first, partially blocking it. Shadowy suggestions of lead-encased bodies loomed in the dim background on either side.

Peering inside the vault opening along with Stephen, the vicar said, "I thought these small cases might have held her children. But when I reached down to feel the damp on the larger one, the end panel just fell off in my hand—and that's when I saw the papers. If I hadn't touched it, we'd never have known at all. And there may be papers in the other little chest as well—I haven't tried to look inside that one yet."

Stephen stepped carefully down the slope of rubble to stand beside the vicar and look through the manhole. The larger chest was about three feet long, eighteen inches high, and the same again in width. Fashioned in black wood, it had ornate carving. "Probably ebony," Stephen said—that had been a treasured and exotic wood back in the day. The main part of the chest seemed to be still held together by heavy iron metal bands. Only the one end panel had come loose; the rest of the chest seemed to be secure.

Stephen knelt as the vicar held his torch, and then leaned forward to reach the papers at the front of the larger chest, gingerly. Holding his breath for a moment, he noticed his thumping heartbeat—and how ludicrously excited he was to be there. Pressing on, Stephen felt his fingers could shift a small stack of papers from the top into his hand. He tugged gently at them, and they slid slowly into his grasp. "I should be wearing some of those white cotton gloves they use to handle manu-scripts at the museum," he said stupidly—because of course it was impossible to get anything like that just now. He turned to the vicar and continued, "Why don't I hand small stacks to you, and you can rest them up there on the church floor. I'll put the hand torch down on the floor of the vault here, so we can see what we're doing."

The vicar handed over the torch from his right hand and rebalanced himself to be steadier on the rubble. Stephen passed him an inch-high stack of papers and the older man pivoted around to place them next to one of the shopping bags sitting higher up on the church floor.

After repeating this process a few times, Stephen and the vicar soon emptied the front stack of the larger casket. Turning to the smaller chest, Stephen reached down tentatively with both hands and grabbed its two sides. He tugged it carefully, moving it slightly forward on its four small raised feet. He picked it up—only about ten pounds, he thought—and passed it over to the vicar to take out. That left the larger, broken chest unobstructed.

"This damaged one looks very heavy," Stephen said. "I think we should just lift out the rest of the papers from the back and then get some help from the men to take it out. And perhaps we can seat a shovel underneath it to break any seal with the floor, and then drag it forward."

"All right," said the vicar.

Stephen picked up the torch and shone it squarely into the chest. At the back, some sort of scroll was perched on top of what seemed to be an embroidered bag and several bound books below. He then applied himself to taking everything else out of the chest, handing the contents to the vicar in small increments.

When this process was completed, they had unearthed a five-inch stack of oversize sheets, along with the scroll, the bag, and several hand-sewn journals. Most were bone dry, but some of the lowest ones were a bit damp.

~

Back in the vicarage with the papers and both boxes, the various surfaces of tables and floors of the kitchen, dining room, and lounge were soon covered with the damper sheets. Stephen had tried to lay them out in some kind of order so he would not lose the sequence in which they had been stacked—but such refinements had been an afterthought, and reconstructing the original order would just have to be a painstaking process later on.

Besides the loose sheets, there were the hand-bound books, all about folio size, just over 300 millimeters by 240 millimeters (roughly 12 by 9½ inches). One of these had been inside the embroidered bag, which had a long strap and seemed to be its carrying case. It was as thick as a modern bride's fashion magazine and the colors of its cover, which was also embroidered, were almost perfectly preserved. Still clear in the center of the front were the raised letters "AV," stitched in gold thread inside a circle of what might be smallish pearls or beads.

"Well, that's something different," said Stephen. "But why was the smaller vault so clean in comparison to the one in the nave? There didn't seem to be anything like as much decay, although these things are much older."

"Verger Andrew explained it to me," the vicar answered. "The difference was the marble floor in the nave. Marble traps natural condensation inside the vault, and once the humidity gathers the drops continually fall from the roof. So all that moisture was dripping onto the floor below, and over those stacked coffins. That made the wood coffins disintegrate and the lead inside corrode—so you end up with all that mess. But the Vavasour vault was fashioned completely out of the same firestone as the rest of our Norman church. It's a type of sandstone so named because it was popular for fireplaces as well. It's naturally porous and any condensation simply escapes, leaving no dew drops on the ceiling. So everything was dry—except until a modern-day toilet overflowed. That's why the papers and everything else were so well preserved."

Stephen picked up the embroidered book from the kitchen counter.

"Is it printed?" asked the vicar. "Or all handwriting? A journal perhaps?"

"It's all handwritten," said Stephen, carefully peeking between its covers. "They had things called commonplace books. We had several on exhibit back at college. People would write down clever sayings they had read or heard—or prayers or poems they'd been sent—and then send the originals on to the next person. And they would practice their handwriting, too. That's almost certainly what this is. The embroidery work and decoration were also practice sewing work by the owner—there's a famous one like this that Elizabeth, before she was queen, made as a present for Henry VIII's last wife, Catherine Parr, who was quite kind and motherly to her."

Stephen turned to another volume from the larger chest—one that was smooth to the touch. It had a plain deep brown cover, either leather or multiple sheets glued together and covered with some kind of shellac. The surface seemed dehydrated and cracking, and almost separated from the spine. It was sewn together with leather thongs. The contents looked something like lines from a play, but there were crossed out words and scribbled markings in the margins throughout. This one will be a nightmare to transcribe, thought Stephen, moving on to the other things.

Even more curious was the scroll, which turned out to be sections of handwritten pages pasted together to form a continuous length that was then rolled up into a more compact size. "I have no idea what this is," Stephen said, "but maybe a closer look will give us some clues."

"How about a cup of tea?" asked the vicar.

"Perhaps it should be champagne or brandy instead," Stephen joked, wondering exactly what it was they had unearthed.

Stephen stayed with the vicar several hours into the afternoon, as they emptied out their bags onto the carpet in the lounge and then sifted gently through what they had found.

Besides all the letters there were manuscripts of poems and journals containing what seemed to be plays or masques with annotations throughout. The commonplace book with the embroidery and another with a plain cover were sporadically dated and kept over a long period of time. From the dates in the journals and on some of the letters, it seemed that the papers constituted a family collection that started sometime in the 1570s and continued through the turn of the century into the early 1600s. The smaller box contained papers as well, but these seemed to originate later, and continued into the 1650s.

The vicar told Stephen what he knew about Anne Vavasour. "She was actually quite a character, a maid of honor in Queen Elizabeth's court along with two of her sisters. But she lost that position somehow and fell out of favor with the Queen. She had one or two children out of wedlock and was rumored to live a very long life—perhaps even into her nineties, which was unheard-of for the time. Back in the 1790s, a man named Reverend Wilson provided a detailed description of her tomb in a history of the parish he wrote."

Stephen packed up a good smattering of letters and sheets to take home for a closer look as well as the embroidered book—which he covered gently in plastic kitchen wrap for some minimal protection. He left its matching pouch behind with the vicar and promised to call in soon with a report. "Absolutely bloody marvelous!" he muttered as he walked out to his Mini and drove home.

As he put the key in his own door, Stephen suddenly remembered how he had left Miranda and realized for the first time that he had not, in fact, left her a note. There'll be hell to pay, he thought.

He opened the door and stepped in softly, looking round. "Hell-low-oh," he called, a bit too jauntily. Nothing but silence. Closing the door behind him, he walked through the front room, stuck his head into the kitchen, then the bedroom. Five o'clock. No sign. Looks like no note either. Then a quick look into the bath—and there he found it. "You shit!" scrawled in foot-high letters on the mirror in Miranda's unmistakable deep maroon lipstick, with smaller letters underneath reading "Where the fuck *are* you?"

Well, nothing broken anyway, he thought. If that's the worst of it, I guess I've gotten off easy. Actually quite understandable given the excitement, not that Miranda will get too excited about this old stuff.

Stephen sat down at the desk and swept everything littering the surface up into a short stack. Then he emptied the double-shelved bookcase to the right of his desk, stacking up his dictionary volumes in four heavy piles underneath the window. He put the much smaller books of poetry in three piles on the other side of the case. He wiped off the shelves before unpacking everything here. That's going to become the vault, he thought. I'll set out everything there in file folders and plastic slipsheets. Then at least I'll know where everything is.

Stephen spent the rest of the evening at home, starting with a nice gin and tonic and a sandwich, trying to decipher and copy out the letters and words one at a time so he could understand just what had been found.

Some of the earlier letters clearly validated Anne Vavasour's standing in the society of the day. Stephen had already recognized as a prize item one letter signed by William Cecil, Lord Burghley, chief advisor to Queen Elizabeth. Burghley's papers—all painstakingly catalogued and preserved in impressive bound-leather volumes—were the heart of the manuscript collection at the British Museum, where they were all guarded as national treasures. And now a possibly unknown original letter from the man himself was sitting on a shelf in Stephen's disheveled bookcase, perilously close to a half-empty bottle of brandy.

This was going to be a herculean task, he thought, looking over at the pile of papers still in the shopping bag, but he realized the best thing he could do was make an inventory of the trove so at least there would be a listing of everything before it fell into the hands of "experts." Even his somewhat crude record would offer protection from some of the papers going missing when the trove was out of sight. After all, the temptation to steal something so rare might be irresistible to a lowly paid clerk given such a job. Who would know? In that sense, his inventory would be a worthwhile contribution to the vicar's discovery. Stephen picked out some pages to photocopy at school tomorrow. As a first step, he thought it would be safe enough to send those off to his paleography professor at Oxford, Doctor B. H. Rowe. Rowe was an expert interpreter of old documents, as well as a pompous ass. If he learned anything from Rowe, Stephen thought he might then send a few pages to his old friend, Soames Bliforth, a college classmate who ran an antiquarian bookshop in London. Soames had been the star student when they were studying the classics and English together. He could probably decipher them in a fraction of the time it took Stephen, and also might know something about the papers' rarity and current market value.

Stephen then began one more translation on his own. Two gin and tonics later, he fell asleep in his chair.

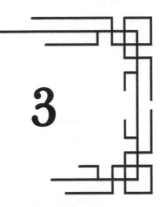

3

Stephen was headmaster of St. George's, an independent prep school for boys aged four to thirteen. From its main entrance, you could see only high gray stone walls, dense overhanging tree branches, and a darkened brass name plate. Once you ventured a few yards inside the front gate, you got a glimpse of the forbidding tower on the main building, perched on four stories of red and orange Victorian brick. Walk a bit farther on the crushed stones as the drive wound around and the lower floors presented themselves more invitingly, with large bay windows and flowering window boxes. Keep going and a wide stone staircase would lift you up through the gray stone arches and oak doors into the school itself.

Inside the lobby, you'd be in an almost holy space, more like church than a school, with light filtering through lead-paned windows to richly arched and vaulted ceilings. On the walls the names of former school captains shone like the war dead in gilded gold letters cut into the boards.

But to feel the life of the place, it was better to come onto the school grounds from the back, leaving the bordering residential streets via one of several narrow beaten pathways that ran between the stucco houses onto the school playing fields.

From the edge of the property, you'd see twenty or more acres of green lawns with occasional ancient trees circling the school. There, looking across to the graceful old main building, the boxy three-story classroom addition, and the brand-new combined gymnasium and indoor swimming pool tacked on behind, you could sense the open and generous spirit of the institution.

This Thursday late afternoon in September, three days after Stephen started sorting through the Vavasour papers, bright sunshine was turning toward twilight under a deep blue sky dotted with clouds. The sun was still hitting the tops of the school and houses but had gone for the day from the rich green turf, trimmed and rolled by the groundsmen in a pattern of alternating light and dark swaths. There was an almost magical lushness to the scene.

Stephen was working with some of the boys to help size up the next year's school cricket team. Starting in October, they would train through the winter—the difference, Stephen had learned, between a winning spring season and a losing one.

Fifteen of the twenty or so boys invited by mail weeks before were here for this optional practice. First, some jogging to get a feel for their fitness; next, simple throwing and catching; and then an hour of practice hitting and fielding.

Mister Bellamy, the senior maths master, saw them all from his study and came out to watch for a while. He was always astonished when Stephen did something like this, something clearly over and above the normal responsibilities of any head-master. But it was just like Stephen not to delegate, but to do the extra thing himself. And how many of the masters could actually get boys to show up at school a week before summer vacation was over?

Two and a half years ago, Mister Bellamy remembered, virtu-ally all of the staff were skeptics of the young man thrust suddenly into the role of headmaster and were dusting off their CVs and

44

preparing to go looking for jobs. Stephen's father, Stephen White Sr., the prior headmaster and owner of the school, died that March in a horrific car crash. His wife, the headmistress of the junior school, was driving with him and lay in critical condition at the local hospital for weeks before recovering in late summer.

As a confidant of Stephen's father, Mister Bellamy knew the school was in difficult financial straits. Mister White had even taken out a home mortgage to secure the payroll for the coming year. Enrollment was down to 300 boys from an old high of 420, the physical plant was deteriorating, academics were slipping, and athletics lackluster.

However, instead of winding things down, young Stephen rode in on a white horse and, by god, turned the whole place around. At first, some old drudges didn't think it was appropriate to be answering to such a young head, and indeed a few were soon gone. Stephen even had to triumph over his recuperated mother, who returned to work and started fighting him on virtually everything. But he stayed firm, without becoming angry, and just kept taking her through the disastrous state of the school's finances if they continued along the same path. He wore her down very shortly. She decided to retire and leave it all to him, moving down to the family's cottage in Devon, which was nearer her two girls and the grandchildren anyway. All that seemed to settle down nicely, and now his mother seemed back in his cheering section during her few visits back to the place.

And so the changes started to take hold. Stephen broke the gender barrier for teachers by bringing in Mrs. Hegarty, a young Russian woman and language wiz, to be the new French teacher—and to add a new language class, teaching her native Russian as well. He lured one of his old college friends from Oxford to head up the sciences offerings—a real scientist, for god's sake. Stephen coached the boys himself to win the Schools County Cricket trophy. Using that astonishing win, he then breathed life into the alumni association by coaxing the old boys to contribute to his expansion fund, with the result a new gym and swimming pavilion that opened last year. And now he had just concluded a merger with St. Anne's, the local girls' school, and the girls would be joining the boys in classes this year.

When that all starts, Mister Bellamy thought, we'll be up to over 500 boys and girls enrolled in a very modern coeducational enterprise. And the boys improved their scores in the examinations for entrance to elite public schools by attending extra classes in Stephen's new cramming program. Last year we sent three to Eton and Harrow, he thought. For god's sake, we even have a waiting list.

Mister Bellamy smiled to himself and went back inside, glad to see his young boss's energies were still flourishing.

~

Near the end of the practice session, Stephen and the boys were over in the nets, a row of three narrow batting cages encased in mesh so that up to three batters could swing away safely beside one another while bowlers practiced their throws. Concrete strips defined what would be the grass strip of a real pitch leading up to the batter's post, and a twelve-foot-long narrow woven mat temporarily covered the pavement to soften the bounce of the ball before it reached the batters.

Two of the nets were in action that day—with one in the middle empty for extra space. As practice drew to a close, everyone was concentrating at the side of just one enclosure where eleven-year-old Denis Juric, a new foreign transfer student hoping to make the team, was about to face off against Percival, their star fast bowler.

Along with his parents and younger sister, Juric was stuck in Britain at least for the school year, and probably longer. The family had moved into the village during the summer so Juric's father could commute to his new post at the Bosnian embassy just opening in London to represent one of the handful of new nations emerging from the disintegration of Yugoslavia. Luckily, Juric and his family were now in Britain and not in their homeland, where civil war raged. They certainly couldn't go back, Stephen thought, and the boy was desperate to fit into the strange new English world he had entered.

Stephen could sense how nervous Juric was—after all, the nets were much worse than the game. The confined space the slight boy stood in was similar to a fenced dog run. Even with a bat, batting pads, and batting gloves with rubber spikes on the backs to protect his hands, all he knew was that someone much bigger and stronger was walking back about thirty yards for a run-up to the point from which he would hurl the rock-hard red cricket ball full force directly at him—not off to the side, but *at* him—and that it would probably first land somewhere just ahead of him on the hard concrete surface, then bounce up into his front. And instead of just trying to get the hell out of the way and save himself, he was supposed to step in toward the throw, and either block it down with his bat or smash it aside as it flew by.

Juric looked unsteady as Percival started his run. The bowler was almost sprinting by the time he unwound his arm in a full-circle arc, releasing the ball with the full force of his running body and follow-through behind it. It was too much for Juric, who lost his nerve just as it bounced, pulling his arms back and up to cover his freckled face, with the ball luckily glancing off the raised bat, purely by chance.

Stephen heard a snicker or two from the onlookers. But not fatal, he thought. So he moved fast to put a pause in the action.

"Right, lads, almost time to stop now. Percival, lead the others in clearing up. Get the other mat over there and start taking the wickets and bails into the kit room. Pick up all the gear and then come right back here for the close. Leave this cage here set up for now. See if you can have it all done in five minutes. Hurry along now."

The rest of the boys broke into action, making a race of it while Stephen stepped inside the cage. Juric was in shreds, a tear just starting to form in an eye. "Now, Juric, come along—we're going to fix this up. Everyone knows this is hell itself in here. The question is, are you going to let it get the better of you? Or are you going to turn it around and have it work *for* you? Your father told me you were great with a bat or racquet and ball and I know you can do this. Come on. Let's give it a try. Ready?"

"Okay, sir," said Juric, catching a breath.

"Back in your stance. Now take a deep breath in and blow out." Stephen went round behind the boy and picked up four of the balls. Then he walked back to the open end of the cage.

"Just block these for me." He bounced an easy one onto the mat and Juric stepped into it, catching it firm in the middle of the bat, knocking it back. "Great, now forget about me and just see the ball. Don't think about where we are, or what's happening. Just keep your eyes on the ball. Find it before it ever leaves my hand, and just keep watching it, staring at it and guiding it onto the wood of your bat. Ready? I'm going to give you three in a row, so snap back after each one."

Stephen bounced the balls at the boy, rapidly, with just two seconds between each, and Juric moved forward to meet each one and then back into his stance.

"Well done," Stephen said, picking up four more balls. "Now these will be a bit faster. This time I want you to breathe in just before I bowl each, and breathe out hard as you hit. Give it a try."

Stephen stepped about ten feet farther away, and one at a time bowled three balls overhand onto the mat, each one harder than the one before.

"Try the breathing thing now. And don't take your eye off the ball. Spit your breath out as you step into it—like a karate kick or something. And I want you to be thinking, 'There is no way in *hell* I am going to let this ball by me.'"

He bowled the last one toward the boy, hard. Juric blocked it square.

Stephen began, "Now, Juric—"

"Yes, sir."

"How's it feeling?"

"Much better, sir. Sorry about before."

"Forget it. But you must put it behind you forever. You must take back lost ground. Here, let's try a few more—and this time I want to hear you say aloud as you hit it, 'There is no way in *hell* this will get by me.' And extra marks if you can say 'hell' just as you strike it. Remember—never take your eye off the ball." Stephen bowled three more balls fast and Juric sounded out the words as he smacked them.

"Stay angry, Juric."

The other boys now were coming back across the fields from the kit room and Stephen stood watching to meet them. "Come along—got to close up now. Right, line up along the side of the net here." The boys gathered quickly.

"Okay, we'll be having a 'friendly' practice match against Merchant Taylors in about a fortnight. They're big. They think very well of themselves and very little of us—very little of St. George's. So we have to be angry, and we have to be determined. We have to play for every boy in the school to put those grammar school toffs in their place."

Stephen had their total attention; he could tell they were startled to hear their headmaster speak in this manner. "So it's not going to be about you, but about all of us and our friends who aren't even on the team. We have to make a stand. So I want some spirit out there—some anger that they take for granted they can just beat us. Just like a battle for god's sake: we're David and they're Goliath. Okay, now for a final over. Percival, get ready to bowl hard—one more time, six of the best, please. Juric, give me your bat!"

Stephen went into the nets and rolled the four balls way out into the field, where Percival walked back to his mark. The boy picked up the first ball and moved farther away for his run-up, while Stephen squared up a stance in front of the wickets. "Let fire, Percival—for God, school, and country."

Stephen blocked the first one expertly, steering it over into the mesh on the left side. Amazing how fast these young teen-agers can hurl, he thought—but not near as fast as the county level he competed on.

The second ball was wide of the wicket, so Stephen stepped across over to it and smacked it baseball style with terrific force into the fencing just where the boys were, startling them and having them cover their faces, forgetting the fence.

"Right. That one was a six for St. George's. One more, Percival. Can we have a wicket this time?"

"Come on, Percival," shouted several of the boys. "Take him out, take him out."

Taking extra care, Percival sharpened his stare and aim, growing more determined. He put more spring into his run-up and was at absolute full tilt when he let it fly.

"Much better," said Stephen, barely able to block the ball down into the mat. "And again, if you can."

This time the ball was aimed true and Stephen had it true in his sights—but he let the ball take the tiny space between his bat and his leg pad, whizzing past and crashing into the three wicket stumps and hurling the two small bails skyward.

"Howzat!" shouted the boys, cheering as Stephen straight-ened up.

"That is an out, clean and full on. Well done, Percival."

The boys were excited—two of them ran out to Percival in celebration. It was quite an honor to bowl out Stephen, who they knew was a *real* cricketer and a star batsman on the county club team.

"Right now, boys, listen up. I asked Percival for one more over. That would be six balls, and he's only thrown four. So time for a final pair. Juric, come in here—and Percival, do your worst."

The boys grew still and quiet. What was going to happen?

Juric stepped in and Stephen handed him the bat and whispered. "Angry, Juric—stay angry. No way in *hell* it's going to get by you."

Juric looked very determined. Thank the lord, thought Stephen. As Stephen stepped out the front of the cage, he rolled two balls out toward Percival, who was searching his coach's face intently. "Your worst, Percival, do absolutely your worst—no holding back now. It's too important."

Juric had every fiber of his being braced behind his bat—he wasn't about to be shaken now. He didn't see Percival any longer, only the ball as it wound up around in a circle and hurtled toward him at full speed. He had taken his breath in and now forced it out through his teeth, saying "hell" as he blocked the ball squarely.

"Well done, Juric," shouted one boy.

"Bravo," said another.

"Last ball!" called Stephen, and Percival again walked way back. He ran forward and uncorked the last bowl. It had the right speed and the right length but was slightly off to the right. Moving forward with "hell" on his lips, Juric raised up his bat and hit out just as the ball went by, making contact nicely. Not a six or a four, but certainly a good chance at a run, or even two, if they ran it well.

"Hooray for you, Juric," said one, with all the boys running in to congratulate him. Percival even walked in tired and said, "Well hit!" The excitement enveloped the whole team.

Another reputation was saved, thought Stephen. Any of us can become heroes. Any of us could be atop that war memorial.

"Right," shouted Stephen above the action. "That's it for tonight. See you again at three o'clock tomorrow. Juric, come help me carry these things in and lock up."

Juric picked up the wickets and bails and threw them onto the middle of the mat with the other gear. He was glowing with the excitement. Stephen put everything else on as well and then rolled it up as a rug. "You get the other end, there," he told the boy.

He and Juric angled it out of the cage, starting off across the fields. "That was well hit, Juric. Well done."

"Yes, sir. Thank you, sir. I mean thank you very much for the second chance."

"Well, we all need a second chance at the end of the day in the nets against Percival, don't we? Important thing is to make good use of it when we get it. And you certainly did that, Juric. Snatched victory from the jaws of defeat, I should say. And will probably be a good help for us against Merchant Taylors as well."

They reached the door of the gym and put down the mat. "Right, I'll take it from here, Juric. Just let me have your pads and gloves and then go join your mates over there."

Juric unbuckled the pads from behind his legs and then ran off back to the edge of the field, where three of the lads stood waiting by the entrance to the path.

That's a good practice anyway, thought Stephen, dragging the mat through the door and into the gym.

~

Heading home, even though Stephen had walked that way a thousand times before, it all seemed a bit magical to him. That early evening September light had an extraordinary clarity, almost otherworldly in its brilliance and purity. It splashed across the dull brick and stucco housetops, reflected in the mirrored surfaces of their windows, and transformed every color in the tops of the trees into something exuberant that he noticed as if seeing it for the first time. And this evening the daylight wouldn't actually turn into darkness until well after seven. And then it would be bright again at six the next morning. These long days were so different from December and January, when it turned dark before school let out at four and the whole planet seemed to be so wet and dreary that you go mad with the gloom. Two different worlds.

Entering his flat, Stephen saw the message machine light blinking, and he pressed the Play button while he took off his jacket.

"It's Miranda. I need to talk to you—it's important. Bloody well give me a call tonight, will you?"

Not likely, thought Stephen. Hadn't seen or talked to her since the holiday. Wanted to let her cool down a bit. Then a beep and another message.

"Stephen, good afternoon. It's Hugh Rowe here. Thank you for your letter and the photocopies. I'd love to know more about what you've found, so please ring me in my office on 0345 756837. Next week I'll be there most of Tuesday or Wednesday afternoon for my regular office hours. I'm sure you remember. Thank you." Rowe had a funny way of sounding the last two words out: the first one heading down, the second one coming up. Very carefully said and yet very perfunctory as well—like he was talking to a waitress as she brought him his tea, or something.

Well, well, never mind—that's the great man himself, Professor B. H. Rowe. So he calls himself Hugh. Wonder what the "B" stands for on all his books—by B. H. Rowe. Probably Bertie or something. I wonder if he does remember me.

No more messages. Stephen walked over to his table by the window, hung his jacket on the back of his chair, and sat down. He had several sheets of the old papers on the main surface in front of him, along with a transcription work-in-progress from that morning. To the right, his bookcase held a series of organized letter files and file folders, as well as the commonplace book resting on the top shelf at the end.

Most of the day yesterday had been spent putting things in some sort of order—and there was still much more over at the vicarage. Anne Vavasour, he thought, who were you and just why did you save all of these papers?

He owed Vicar Hamilton an update, and now should be as good a time as any, he thought, dialing the vicarage and picking up his notes. The vicar answered and Stephen talked him through the highlights so far.

"Well, I'm starting to make an inventory of everything: just a simple numbering system and brief description of each item. If you wait and have an expert at an auction house or bookshop do that, it would be time-consuming and expensive, and you'd never know if anything went missing somehow."

"Very good, Stephen, if you don't mind doing it," said the vicar.

"No, I don't mind. I'm very excited to be discovering what you have here. You know, old books and such are a passion for me."

"Yes, I remember. Anything interesting yet?"

"Well, first there's that embroidered book, which does indeed seem to be Anne's commonplace book from her school days. It's very unusual for a girl of the period because she's obviously reading Latin and Greek as well as contemporary foreign languages like French and Italian. Usually a girl would be trained only in the more female arts like sewing, music, and dancing. But she even has quotes from Roger Ascham, Queen Elizabeth's own tutor. So her training was pitched very high—like a princess."

Stephen continued, "A few other things stand out. The first is a handwritten play or masque with many different handwriting styles. It looks like a group was editing it—lots of crossed out words and phrases and new sections written in the margins. I don't recognize the content: it starts with some prolonged battle scene, swords swinging and so on. I'll go deeper into it after we've got a handle on everything else. And another is a handwritten draft of *Arcadia*. That was a popular romance begun by Sir Philip Sidney around 1580. This copy is beautifully written. It must have been done by a professional scribe, and that makes sense because Sidney had copies made to circulate among friends. I haven't been able to value it, but I do know Sotheby's sold a printed first edition of *Arcadia* from 1590 for £14,000 or so in 1990, and this handwritten version should be much more, I would think.

"The last thing I'll mention is some sort of legal paper or deposition in a court proceeding between Anne and someone else. It's from about 1621 and it's all in Latin—which means it was from a church court and not a secular one. So I've sent photocopies of some pages from all these to my old professor at Oxford, and I'll let you know what he says. After that we might share copies with a rare book dealer who was mine and Margaret's classmate."

"Fancy that," said the vicar. "Delia would have been so pleased."

"Also, a lot of the papers seem to be connected to a Sir Henry Lee. So I need to find out more about him, too. I've ordered a scarce biography of him at the village library—it will come from another library on interlibrary loan, and I should have it in a week or so. Meanwhile, I'd just be careful about saying anything about the value yet. I don't think you should attract too much attention, and so on."

"Well, there already is an article in the *Village Advertiser* today," said the vicar. "You'll have to take a look at it. I'm afraid it's all about 'treasure in the tombs,' as you might expect."

"I'll look for it when I go out tonight. This is all certainly an out-of-the-ordinary experience," said Stephen.

"Yes, I mentioned it to Margaret when she called the other day. She seemed happy I had something exciting going on."

Stephen hadn't expected Margaret's resurrection on the call—he was deeply taken aback. He recovered and continued, "Well, that's the report of the hour. I'll bring these papers back on Saturday, if that's all right, and take another stack to look at."

"Very good. Thanks for the update, Stephen."

Stephen put the phone back in its cradle. Margaret is happy indeed. He sighed.

Seven o'clock.

No more work today—the morning's efforts and the afternoon practice had him a bit tired and peckish—so a quick meal out and a stop at the Village Arms for a pint or two sounded like just the ticket. Well, he thought he should give Miranda a call: no use adding fuel to the fire.

He dialed Miranda's number from memory, and after three rings the answer machine came on: "Hi, it's me. I'm not around so leave me a message—with the time, too, if you don't mind."

Stephen put the receiver back in the cradle. I'll wait—too impersonal, all this voice mail stuff. I'll catch up with her later.

He threw some water on his face, checked his wallet for cash and his ATM Barclaycard, grabbed his jacket back off the chair, and headed out into the evening.

4

"**W**ell, then the vicar hands up these bags, and they're chockful with what they picked up in the vault. And two black wood boxes. Very careful of 'em they were, I can tell you. Didn't let on a thing. And Stephen, the headmaster, is almost pissing himself with excitement, just grabbing the bags back when he comes back out of the hole and then carrying the lot off to the vicar's house."

"What was in 'em, then? Did you have a look?"

"Was there any jewelry you could see?"

"No, that's the shame of it. It all happened so fast. There was papers—but no telling what they had hid underneath. We couldn't see what they were doing when they were down there. They kept well in the back. I just know they buggered off quick. Didn't want to stop and show any else of us what they had."

A stonemason named John and his mates were hugging the rail of the bar at the Village Arms, where the flood at the church and the mysterious discovery were the topics of the day. Besides John's eyewitness account, there was the account in the *Village Advertiser*, which was spread out on the bar, with a picture of the vicar outside the church. "Flood Leads Vicar to Treasures in Tomb," read the headline. This was a lot stronger stuff than the usual zoning-board plan for a new zebra crossing or one-way system on the *Advertiser*'s front page.

The vicar was quoted downplaying the find: "Only some family papers," he said, pooh-poohing the rumors of treasure that were only natural speculation. He also said the headmaster of St. George's, Stephen White, who had studied old documents extensively at Oxford, was inventorying exactly what was there.

It all seemed very posh and suspicious. Probably it was something like gold, thought John, and not just stupid papers.

"The vicar says what they found was in a tomb belonged to his wife's own family, if you can believe it," John continued. "Well, that's very convenient, isn't it? I'm sure I'd be saying the treasure was clutched in me sainted mother's hands an' all, if it was me."

"It's not right, is it?" said one of his mates. "I mean, today his whole family's living off the public charity—vicar of the church, my arse. He's looting us...sending his daughter to Oxford and then she gets a big job on the telly while we're the ones putting our hard-earned wages in the poor box."

"I've never seen you putting wages in any poor box," said another fellow, to snickers all round. "More likely into your next pint."

"No, well, then you've never seen the inside of a church either in this life, have you, you bastard?"

At that very moment, through the walls and over in the lounge area on the other side of the pub, Stephen was sitting at one of the waitress-served tables, nursing his fourth pint and staring again at the village newspaper.

Amazing, but really true, he thought. The closer you are to any story reported in the media, the better you see all the bullshit distortion they add in to hype the facts. It's all about selling newspapers, or radio or TV or anything. He'd offered that opinion to Margaret before. Surprisingly, she'd thought the same—even though she was on the side doing the reporting. She said, "People are always surprised when they read up their own interview. They think it will come out just like they've said it...but instead it's all about what we're thinking while we're watching them talk: are they lying? ...too full of themselves...exaggerating...hiding something...you know. And that's the filter that changes things. That's us. Of course, you can do it right, or you can make it up. And, sadly, people in my business do both."

Well, here it is: the buried treasure thing has colored everything. If they only knew, Stephen thought. Truth was, neither Vicar Hamilton nor Stephen gave a hoot about money—really couldn't care less. If the vicar won the lottery, he'd give it all to the parish. And if Stephen had the winning ticket, he'd probably lose track of it in his flat, especially now that he had all those old papers. For Stephen, life was all just about teaching, history, words, and books—and he liked to help people. He had no idea about how much money he had with the house and an inheritance from his grandfather, but only that it was more than enough.

Sipping his pint, he was pondering how the language and images were loading the article in the *Advertiser*: "buried treasure from the crypt," "recovered loot," "windfall for the vicar and his daughter, Margaret, the journalist and BBC presenter," "spirited away the treasure into the vicarage," "under lock and key," "keeping tight lips," etc. Bloody inflammatory, he thought.

Stephen was just about to start reading it all over again when he looked up and saw Miranda making her entrance through the smoked-glass door of the lounge. She was stunning. So confident. Black miniskirt and close-fitting white top. A small black leather bag hanging from a long strap off her bare shoulders. A combination of good looks, fashion, fitness, and attitude, he thought. She paused as she came through the door, stacked herself onto her right heel and surveyed the scene. The Village Arms had been her home turf since schooldays. And her first words this night were a familiar "hello there" to barkeeper Jim and waitress

Mollie before taking a close look around the half-empty room and finding Stephen.

"Oh there you are, you bastard," she projected. She frowned and swanned slowly over toward Stephen's table. "Mollie, bring me my usual." Stephen could tell she had cooled down. She lowered herself smoothly into the chair across, touched her elbows onto the tabletop, and cradled her chin in her hands, leaning forward. "I read all about you in the paper. So that's where you went off to. Well, I suppose I can't compete with buried treasure—least not if you don't even wake me up to have a go." A slow blink of her lashes and then she waited.

"Miranda, I'm sorry. You were asleep and I meant to leave a note, but I forgot. The vicar telephoned me. He was in a state. He wanted me over there, and when I saw what it was I just forgot about the time completely. And it's not all this rubbish about buried treasure. It's just a bunch of old papers."

"And why didn't you call me then? I left you a message on your bloody machine. It's not an accident I'm here, you know. I had to come looking for you, for Christ's sake."

"Sorry, I did call. But you were out and all I got was the machine—"

"You know, it is a *message* machine. You talk in to it and then I can play what you say. Try that some time. Bloody hell."

Mollie arrived with Miranda's gin and tonic. "I'll have one of those, too," said Stephen, relieved the crisis seemed to have passed.

"Switching now might be bad for the head, luv," volunteered Mollie.

"Thanks. It's all right," he told the waitress. "I'll have a lie-in tomorrow. I'm not working 'til next week."

Miranda drew herself back from the table and lit a cigarette. She sent the first stream of smoke out in a long low stream of gray. "Well, what *have* you found, anyway?" she asked.

Stephen hadn't really talked about it to anyone except the vicar. He cupped his hands around his drink and looked rather distantly toward her as he remembered the scene. "When we went down into the vault, there was an old tomb from Elizabethan days—you know, 1500 or 1600—and two wooden boxes. The vicar had thought the boxes were children's coffins until the end of one came off in his hand. That revealed the papers: letters, journals, manuscripts, all in really good shape. It's really odd because it was different then—people didn't save paper the way you might now. I mean, they didn't even really make paper in England. They tried to, but no one could get it right, and so they imported it from France and Italy. And you didn't save it, you reused it. So if I wrote you a letter, after you'd read it, you might give it to the cook, and she might use it to line the baking pan. Or if you wrote something that was going to be printed—and now we're really talking rarities—then as soon as they set the type, they'd send the paper over to the binders who'd use multiple sheets of it to make the covers of a book or whatever. They would never have thought to save the original draft on the paper. That would have been too much of a waste. Sometimes they washed or bleached the ink off and then used it again—and you have all these old manuscripts where you can see two or three books that were written on top of one another. And the only people who did save paper were people doing business or law. They saved things that might be important later, like wills or deeds. No one saved ordinary letters, poetry, or things written for entertainment. But this person did save those things...or someone did for her, putting everything up in to that box. So it's really odd. Very unusual."

He took a big swallow from his glass, letting Miranda jump in, finally.

"Well, hand them over to me as you read 'em and I'll bake you some biscuits."

Stephen smiled and went on, "I'm just trying to figure out what they're all about just now. And it's very hard to make out what the hell they *are* about, what with the old handwriting and the old language. Probably will take me forever—be my life's work."

"Well, that's great, love." Miranda paused, seeming to slow things down a bit, and leaning back over the table toward him. "I'm very happy for you. But I need to talk to you about something else. Something quite important, and I'm sorry we're doing this here in the pub, but might as well, I suppose."

"Doing what?"

"I know we've never talked seriously about things...you know...like getting together or staying together for a stretch." She was looking down at the tabletop as she said the words. She seemed unusually serious now, and he searched her face for what she was trying to say.

Shaking her hair side to side, Miranda tossed her bangs away from her eyes and suddenly looked up directly into his face and eyes. Their eyebeams crossed and he started backward under her gaze. She took a deep breath and said very slowly, "The point is, lover boy, that you've stuffed me...you know, knocked me up. I'm expecting...in a family way...all of that. I'm the ma, you're the da."

He was astonished as she continued. "I guess these things happen. Well, it's happened to us. So, what d'ya think of that?"

Stephen looked down and drew back in his chair, moving away from her. She saw he was no longer surprised, but actually seemed to be turning angry as he narrowed his eyes and gazed back at her. He became cold with the silence.

"Well? Aren't you going to say something?" she asked.

Stephen picked up his glass and tossed down the rest of his first gin and tonic. He knew it was impossible for him to be the father: doctors had explained all that to him years ago. But he'd never told Miranda. What was she up to?

"That's impossible!" he hissed out at her.

"Not really, mate. Unless you were asleep in school health class. That was the one I was most awake for in me whole education," she countered.

"No, Miranda. I'm sorry, but it's bullshit."

"Bullshit? Well, you fucking bastard! I should bloody well know about what's happening to me. And it's not bullshit! I expected you to be more *caring*." Her cheeks turned as red as if a fire had lit up inside her.

"Miranda, you're either lying to me, or it's someone else's. That's all I know."

Without any pause at all, Miranda picked up her glass and tossed the contents in Stephen's face, hitting the people sitting behind him as well. Then she stood up and threw the glass on the floor, shattering it.

"You bastard," she shouted and she turned on her heel and stormed out the door.

Now all heads were turned on Stephen. Slowly he stood up and took off his jacket, hanging it on the back of his chair. He smoothed off some of the drink from his white shirt, wiping his hand across and downward. The shirt was soaked through so that his nipples were suddenly visible, dark and pressing against the damp cotton. He reached up and unslipped his tie. The man at the table behind him was also on his feet taking off his own jacket, which was splattered across the back. Looking around, Stephen saw he was the center of attention. "Sorry, everyone. Very sorry about that."

Mollie came over with several small towels and patted Stephen's front before handing one to him and another to the man aside him. She seemed to like mothering him. "Never mind, Stephen. She's always been trouble," said Mollie.

"Sorry for all the mess." His feet crunched on the broken glass as he moved away from the table.

"Just you move over there away from the glass and dry out for a while," Mollie said. "I'll take these jackets and your tie back into the kitchen by the cooker and they'll dry out faster. And here's your paper—that's still dry anyway."

"Thanks. I suppose I'll have another G and T—this one in the glass and not over my head." Stephen turned to the couple behind him. "And can I please stand you a round." Well, at least they didn't seem too upset—and they were also moving away from the broken glass.

Stephen walked over to an empty table and sat down. Minutes before, he'd felt a bit tipsy, but his drink-in-the-face from Miranda had brought back momentary clarity. Now, actually, he felt a bit sad—sad and wet—because he liked Miranda a lot, and it had all happened so fast. Too fast to really think through what to say, what to do. So he'd just let fly the first thing that came into his head. Great.

Well, she was clearly lying to him. Strange, he thought, I'd never thought of her as wanting to settle down with me before. Or maybe she wasn't lying. Maybe she had gotten pregnant and just assumed that he was the father. But there must have been another man. Now, we weren't *married* or anything. We both date other people, and neither one of us is a martyr to celibacy. And then, she couldn't have known about my not being able to have children: everything *seems* to work normally. I use condoms anyway for commonsense safety—but she would have taken that as birth control. That's understandable. I never told her—didn't seem important. I mean we were just bonking, not starting a family. Maybe I've got it all wrong with women...again.

Stephen was just halfway through his new gin and tonic—and feeling a bit drier—when in through the doors came Miranda's brother, Tony, who worked down at the village garage. He was red-faced with clenched fists. When he set eyes on Stephen, he'd found what he'd been looking for. Before Stephen could say anything—in fact, just as he was opening his mouth—Tony straightened to his full height and hit him full force in the face, catching him just to the right of his nose and square on his eye. The force of the blow knocked Stephen right off the chair and onto the floor.

"That's for fucking my sister, you bastard. Just crying her eyes out to me mum right now—got the whole house a shambles."

Tony moved in closer as if to hit Stephen again, or give a good kick, but checked himself at the last moment. "You ain't worth it, you wanker!"

Next moment, Tony had the barman in front of him.

"All right, you, out of here," Jim ordered. Come on, out the door. I'll call a copper for you if you don't move out now. You're banned here, mate. Do your drinking and your fighting somewhere else from now on. Out you go."

As the barkeeper ushered Tony out, Stephen was rolling about on the floor, his hands and arms over his face, wincing with the pain. Inside Stephen's head, the numbness was fast turning into a sharp ache. It had been quite a number of years since Stephen had been on the receiving end of any punch like that.

Mollie was having a hard night's work with Stephen—more like the trauma nurse at the hospital than a barmaid. She reentered the lounge with a towel full of ice, which she set down on the table as she helped Stephen up to a sitting position. Then Jim uprighted the chair and came over to Stephen on the other side of Mollie.

"Here. Let me have a look at that," she said, gently pushing Stephen's hands down and away from his already swelling eye. "Oh, that's a nasty one, but you'll survive. Come on up into the chair...that's it. Just like me brother after a rugby game. Towels and ice every which way." The barman grasped Stephen under his shoulder and helped hoist him up.

Stephen set his elbow on the tabletop, took hold of the towel, and lowered his eye into the ice. Slowly the pain started to be replaced by the numbness of the cold.

"Well, what next?" he winced.

"I think you've had the lot tonight, mate," Jim said. "Anyone else comes in that door after you and you'd better go and move in with Salman Rushdie."

Stephen would have smiled if he could—but he couldn't. "Right, just bring me a nightcap G and T, and I'm going to go into hiding at home. Just need to sit here for a few minutes."

"I should think you should have them look at that at hospital tonight," said Mollie. "Just keep the ice on it for an hour or two."

"Is it badly cut and bleeding? You know, I can't tell myself right now."

"Well, no. But it is swollen up pretty bad and turned a shade of deep red—must be bruising."

"Well, I'm going to give it a few minutes then. And then I'll decide. I know I'd be sitting there hours before they got to me in the emergency room, and I don't think I could take that tonight."

After about a half hour, Stephen felt well enough to stand up and go to the toilet. There, over the top of perhaps the dirtiest sink in Britain, he could make the first damage assessment with his good eye. "Bloody hell, I look a sight." It was going to get worse, too. It would be black as coal when school opened next week. Oh, what the hell, he thought. Can't do anything about that now.

After a minute he was back in the bar paying his tab and leaving five-pound tips for Mollie and Jim.

"Bless you and take care getting home. Here's a fresh towel with more ice," said Mollie.

"Thanks. Good night. And sorry about all the trouble."

Almost eleven o'clock, and now besides the pain in his eye, an overarching headache set in. Got to load up on acetaminophen before I hit the bed, he thought, or I won't last until morning.

He found the keys to his Mini in his dried jacket pocket and fumbled about with them in the lock for a while because he couldn't see much at all in the dark space of the lawn where the cars were parked between the pub and the village cricket pitch. There were people still sitting out at tables surrounding the pub, and he knew their eyes were on him. He finally opened the door and lowered himself in. He set the ice towel down on the passenger seat to his left and fit the key into the ignition. The car started up with a shake and he felt every vibration in his eye. This is going to be bad, he thought.

He shifted into reverse to back out of his space and started to lift the clutch, rolling back slowly. But suddenly there was a commotion behind him...voices...yelling...and then finally someone banging on the boot and back window. What the hell! Stephen turned his one good eye up to the rearview mirror and saw people immediately behind him, pressed up to the car. They must have been walking past, and he hadn't seen them. Now what?

He opened his door and looked back.

"Stop the car, man! You've knocked him down with the bumper. Don't move now."

Before he could get out, Stephen saw that he had apparently knocked down someone, and that others were lifting them up.

"Are you all right, Tony?"

"Aye, just a scare. Why don't you watch where you're going, arsehole?"

For Christ's sake, it was Tony Baker—the punch thrower himself. Well, he looks alive, thought Stephen, so I'm going to bugger off.

With room in front instead of behind, Stephen closed the door, shifted into first, and headed off forward out of his parking space. Last thing he saw was Tony framed in the sideview mirror shaking his fist in Stephen's dust with his friends making weak-hearted attempts to run after him. Well, I may not have hit him back, but at least I did something, thought Stephen. That's one point for me.

5

A few days after the fight at the pub, Stephen was forcing himself to spend a quiet evening at home prepping for school. He was more than annoyed at having to put the Vavasour papers aside to meet teaching obligations, but it was his own fault. As headmaster, he had made it a custom each year to be a one-day guest lecturer on the opening day of school.

In fifth-form English, they were going to read and discuss the short stories in James Joyce's *Dubliners* for a fortnight. Stephen would launch all that with a biographical talk on Joyce himself, which always went down well. It humanized the great man to tell the kids he liked to drink too much, sit down at the piano, and belt out a bevy of emotional Irish ballads. Made the old bard very approachable.

Then Stephen would kick off the new term's fourth-form Latin class. They were about to wade through weeks of translating the *Aeneid* by Virgil. He sighed, thinking how English school-masters for the last five hundred years had stood up and intoned *"Arma virumque cano"*—"Of arms and the man I sing"—to start poor Aeneas and his close friend the faithful Achates off on their heroic wanderings after the Trojan War. Actually, there was a very good reason to keep the *Aeneid*, he thought, since there was nothing like a tale of swordplay and the conflict between good and evil to get the *Lord of the Rings* generation engaged.

He liked showing the way for his teachers in a class or two as headmaster, encouraging the staff to make a strong start for the new term. Kept him in the game. But he wished he had bowed out of it this year, although it was too late now.

Over the few days just before the start of school, he had already noticed how the staff and boys helping prepare the school behaved unusually well whenever he was around them. That probably could be put down to his fearsome black eye from his pub fight, now radiant with its puffy red, yellow, and purple concentric circles. Two or three more weeks and it would be normal, he thought, but for now he might as well enjoy the mask. He tidied his papers into folders for the separate classes and slipped them into his briefcase, which was next to the chair. Now he could indulge himself again in his new passion, the Vavasour papers.

He stood up and walked over to the bookcase to his right. From the top shelf, he chose a flat leather portfolio and moved it to the desk. It was an oversize folder a Victorian artist might have kept his sketches in—just two leather covers hinged together, lined with hand-marbled Florentine endpapers inside—about the size of a large atlas when closed.

Stephen then made a detour into the kitchen to pour another glass of the red wine he'd been sipping since dinner, a very good St. Emilion, even though its label revealed it as the Waitrose store brand. He thought how librarians would bristle if they ever saw such a noxious red fluid near any old manuscript on their own premises. But for now he was alone with these scribblings resurrected from the tomb, and he could work as he wanted. He would, however, be bloody careful not to spill anything.

Back at his desk, Stephen opened the folder and lifted out the top leaf from a short stack of loose sheets. Since he had mixed up all the papers from the Vavasour tomb when he dried them out, inventories, leases, poems, and recipes were all jumbled together.

A salutation and signature proclaimed this particular page a letter. Writing was clustered in the center of the sheet and old creases showed how the edges had originally been folded and then sealed with wax for confidentiality. All that remained of the wax was a red smudge. Holding it up to the light, he could see a familiar watermark in the shape of a cooking pot—one of the most common ones found on Elizabethan-era paper.

The writing itself was in the swirling flourishes of the secretary hand. As he had explained to Vicar Hamilton, in those days it was the most common handwriting for business, literary composition, and correspondence. However, it wasn't clear whether a secretary or someone else wrote this page because the style was sloppy. That could mean the person with the pen wrote infrequently, or was too arrogant to care about clarity. Or perhaps someone wrote it very fast while taking dictation. Hopefully the content of the message would shed light on all that.

The date of "the twelfth year of the reign of Queen Elizabeth" placed the letter's date of composition around 1570. As usual, the spelling was idiosyncratic and inconsistent, rather than conforming to any set way of spelling; it was more as if the writer simply had tried to capture how the words sounded. Frequent abbreviations made some of the words hard to identify, but the general sense of the letter was clear. The writer was telling Sir Henry Lee that he was the likeliest candidate to be appointed ranger in charge of the royal estate of Woodstock, one of Elizabeth's favorite hunting properties, just northwest of London. That would indeed be a choice gift from the sovereign.

It had taken Stephen about seven minutes to get that far. Which was the pattern for all of the letters among the sheets (and there seemed to be several dozen in front of him). Understanding each would mean a laborious word-by-word transcription, working out each phrase. The next document on top of the stack in his folder, by contrast, appeared to be a poem: that would be something a little different as soon as he got to it. At least a poem should be easier, he thought, because there should be no abbreviations or attempts at code.

Stephen was using a simple inventory classification system, assigning each of the sheets a numbered identity, which he marked in soft pencil at the top right, and labeling his own sheet-by-sheet translations to match. A medium-length letter might take a half hour to transcribe, though things should move faster once Stephen became familiar with the handwriting of any individuals who were represented multiple times. However, this letter about becoming ranger at Woodstock was new. It was from someone he did not yet recognize among the find.

As a college student at Oxford, Stephen had liked this sort of work, which was called paleography. Few people could do it. England might have literally millions of unread ancient documents, but only a dwindling number of people could actually read them. Most university budgets were under pressure and recently many paid positions in paleography had been cut. The same pinch was on in the public sector, although strong pockets of skills remained at the museums and government record offices that maintained archives back to the centuries before the Norman Conquest of 1066. Fortunately, the faculty and librarians at Oxford remained strong, for the moment, and he was glad to have been given close supervision and training.

Stephen's undergraduate course at Oxford led him to a dual degree in English and classics. His focus was poetry. He especially liked the period of English writing from 1550 to 1650, when the ancient classics had perhaps their most obvious influence on what was being written and created in English. Translations from the Greek and Latin authors were popular—with some, such as Chapman's Homer, notably appearing as English verse quite different in style from the originals. That was because later Tudor and Stuart writers loved playing around with language; constructing new meters, verse styles, and rhyming schemes; and enriching them with rhetorical devices, puns, and double entendres to amuse their readers, as when Hamlet tells Ophelia "get thee to a nunnery," which could be directing her to either a convent or a brothel. They decorated their sentences the way an interior decorator styled a fine sitting room. Stephen also had a soft spot for the nineteenth-century young Romantic poets—Byron, Shelley, and Keats—because they were also worshippers of the classics, creating their own latter-day epics, cantos, and odes.

In those college days, it hadn't seemed to Stephen that his concentration in classics was an obscure, tiny backwater for twentieth-century study. The university was divided up into about forty supportive residential colleges, each with its own quadrangles, libraries, dining halls, and grounds for scholars. Magdalen College was his home. It housed about four hundred undergraduates and two hundred graduate students, and even with scores of possible concentrations, about a dozen of his fellow Magdalen undergrads were also neck deep into classics. And his classics tutor was based there as well. Besides, the rest of his studies were concentrated in the English department, one of the largest in the school. So in that small world at Oxford, he was a mainstream scholar.

After graduating, his father's prep school, St. George's, was a very good match for him as a junior teacher. Teaching his ten- to thirteen-year-old students in the upper school to love Latin and English literature suited not only his studies but also his love of books. And, since he continued playing cricket at the county level after graduating, he could also fill the role of coaching sport during spring term. What's more, from the standpoint of the school, he could be promoted to the parents as an alumnus who went on to a good public school and then became an Oxford scholar. For

Stephen, returning to St. George's and his home village gave him a welcoming base where he could happily work on a long gestating book about the Romantic poets in Italy. He had never thought he would have to step in as headmaster of St. George's after only two years. That job was his father's fate, not his.

Actually, the teaching and headmastering parts of his post-university career had gone well, but his love life was a shambles. Just after getting their degrees, Stephen and his girlfriend, Margaret Hamilton, had announced their engagement. The cadence of his life had seemed to move in such an orderly and satisfying progression: from babyhood to prep school; and then onto public school, cricket, and university. Surely next would be marriage, family, publications, and a distinguished career before the inevitable two-column obituary in *The Times*. One hundred years earlier, someone like Stephen might have had a detour into the Empire to administer a small province in India for a time. The path would generally have been the same for many Oxford grads. But that had not happened, because his fiancée was a change agent, not an order seeker. And he found that fascinating.

He thought Margaret Hamilton was the love of his life—and maybe that was still true—but apparently, for her, his love was not enough. She was even from the same village. But in their childhood its population had swollen to thirty thousand, mostly because of an influx of commuters, and they didn't know each other until they met just after their third year in college. Perhaps that wasn't so strange in England, where single-sex education still often separated upper-crust boys and girls all through childhood and adolescence, only bringing them together as young adults.

The shrill ring of his telephone interrupted his random thoughts. It was well after nine—getting a bit late for a call, he thought.

"Stephen, it's Andrew, at the church."

He recognized the voice of the parish verger and replied with surprise, "Oh, hello, Andrew."

"Sorry to call out of the blue, but I just thought you should know," Andrew continued. "I was walking home and saw all the lights on in the vicarage, so I stopped by to have a quick word with the vicar about finishing up all the repairs. There was no answer at the door, so I used my key and found Vicar Hamilton had fallen in the kitchen. I called the ambulance, because he was unconscious, and they've just taken him down to the hospital. They'll keep him there—and there's nothing for you to do now, but I wanted to call. I just called Margaret in London as well and left a message on her machine, so she'll know. Perhaps you can look in on him tomorrow there. I know you two have been as thick as thieves with all those old papers, so I wanted you to know."

"Andrew, you say he was unconscious? Did they say it was serious?"

"Well, they didn't say much. Just a fall. I thought perhaps he hit his head on the cooker on the way down. They said his breathing and pulse and such all seemed good, but they told me he would definitely be kept overnight. They'll take X-rays after he wakes up. So perhaps we'll know more tomorrow. All right? These things happen—I mean, he is getting on."

"Yes, Andrew. What a shock. But thanks very much for calling. And I will check up on him."

Stephen didn't hesitate, grabbing his jacket and keys and heading out the door. Driving, he was less than five minutes to the National Health Service hospital, a campus of stern 1960s brick and glass rectangles perched on a small hillside overlooking the village. The main door to the hospital was darkened and locked, but the lobby next to it for emergencies was bright with light, and he headed inside.

A formidable-looking nurse sat behind a desk with a glass protective window in front of her. She looked fierce, but spoke with disarming kindness, "Yes, sir. How can we help?"

Stephen asked if he could see Vicar Hamilton, but quickly had to explain he was indeed not a member of the family, just a friend. While he was rattling on, she was tapping into her keyboard and looking intently at a screen in front of her.

"Sir, he was just admitted this evening and now he's up in the intensive care ward on the fifth floor. There is a notation that he is still unconscious, but his vital signs are good. I'm afraid they wouldn't want you up there now tonight, but you can rest assured he is being well attended. You can call in again in the morning for an update. Visiting hours for that ward are ten a.m. to one p.m. and again from four to seven thirty p.m. By then he may have been transferred into a normal ward, where you can visit longer. I'm afraid that's all we can do tonight."

Stephen knew he wasn't going to get any further just then, and he thanked her and walked back out to his car.

Driving home, he thought you wouldn't think a vicar's solo evening at home would end up with a trip to hospital. *Carpe diem.*

Margaret was going to be upset.

PART TWO

London, 1579–1580. Anne Boleyn's daughter, Queen Elizabeth, knew firsthand how much damage a monarch could do.

Destruction had become the family business while she was a child. Her father, King Henry VIII, tore up centuries of tradition, dismantling the old church and parsing out abbeys and monasteries to his favorites as personal estates. Also, he beheaded her mother. Then, soon after, her half sister "Bloody Mary" made a brutal attempt at Catholic revival.

When Elizabeth took the throne, she chose instead to enforce peace over her divided kingdom. She summoned Parliament to enact a religious settlement consolidating her power both as sovereign and head of a unified Church of England, independent of Rome. She published an updated Book of Common Prayer defining the new code of worship for everyone and imposing fines on those not going to church. And all the while, she kept a close watch over all the ambitions, threats, and plots being hatched against her at home and abroad.

Close at hand, there were certainly many worthies to be managed. Her full-time court numbered twelve hundred, with each one fixed to a specific place in the great chain of being underneath her majesty. Keeping the Crown just below God and the heavens, she introduced a new nonreligious holiday, to celebrate her accession, each November 17, along with a chivalric code of court behavior based on her own ideas about the divine rights of royalty and the roles pomp and ceremony should play to honor her. She made it clear that success at court would come only to those who embraced this cult of Elizabeth, and so, around the Virgin Queen, a façade of chivalry and platonic love was acted every day in the face of more lusty realities.

Lowest in the hierarchy were the Ladies of the Presence Chamber, on call whenever the Queen was to be her most resplendent—for example, at the visits of foreign suitors to her elusive hand. They swelled the crowd with no specific duties, and had little interaction with Elizabeth.

Next, the Ladies of the Privy Chamber tended the Queen in her private rooms adjoining the Presence Chamber. These women played a subdued chorus to Elizabeth's starring role. Often they wore only vestal white as a counterpoint to the bejeweled costumes of the Queen. They walked and danced with their lady, selected the morsels for her plates, carried the dishes to her dinner table, and ate only what Elizabeth did not.

Finally were the Ladies of the Bedchamber, who were the most intimate with the Queen and also performed many arcane offices. For example, the First Lady of the Bedchamber looked after the jewels Elizabeth wore each day and made a close accounting of their transport back and forth between court and the Jewel House. The Mistress of the Sweet Coffers cleaned and scented the Queen's linens. And the Groom of the Stool made sure chamber pots were in good supply and any contents speedily removed.

Anne Vavasour was to become the most junior of the Ladies of the Bedchamber. She arrived in mid-November during the twenty-first year of Queen Elizabeth's reign, just in time for the Accession Day celebrations of November 17. With the court encamped at Whitehall for the holidays, Anne settled in to shared quarters. A small part of her hoped her kinfolk long at court would help her find her way, but mostly she just sharpened her wits and elbows and dove in to explore this strange new stage by herself.

She was fascinated by the crowded jostlings of the Presence Chamber, where so many suitors stalked the elusive queen. There, before the main midday meal, an elaborate table was laid for her majesty, but eventually only two Ladies of the Privy Chamber came out and salted plates of the choicest foods for delivery into the Privy Chamber just behind.

That's where Anne was introduced to the Queen, seated among her ladies. In a mood for testing, Elizabeth commanded her to dance a brisk galliard. Anne grasped the arm of Thomas Knyvet, her uncle and sponsor, and the pair began to pace back and forth lightly before the monarch, in time with the music from the musicians by the wall. Then the pair surprised their audience, adding a fine volte to their dance by turning their bodies together, taking two steps forward and springing high into the air before landing with their feet closely entwined in a graceful pause. It was a difficult move, done perfectly. The Queen smiled and Thomas Knyvet was well pleased. With her trial over, Anne had acquired the beginnings of a good reputation. Afterward she took every opportunity to embellish it.

Among the watchful members of the court, young Anne's arrival was a breath of fresh air. Not only had she danced full well before Elizabeth, but also she answered any prodding with a quick retort, in whatever language the jibe was put to her. She knew her books, played the virginal sweetly, and moved with vitality and grace. Though many eyes were on her now, she had the unruffled air of someone used to being looked at.

Meanwhile, preparations were under way for the Accession Day tilts. Over the past ten years, they had become the highlight of Elizabeth's most personal holiday. Overseeing the action was an older courtier, Sir Henry Lee, who also had the honor of riding as the Queen's champion.

Jousting was one great love of Tudor monarchs, combining courage and great skill. Two opposing knights with heavy body armor and helmets, and carrying wooden lances on their right sides, charged each other on horseback, riding along opposite sides of a five-foot high wall. The object was not to harm one's opponent, but to aim your lance well enough to hit the opposing knight so squarely that the lance shattered into pieces from the impact of the blow. The knight with the most rides and the most broken lances won. Several of the Ladies in Waiting were reprimanded for ogling the male courtiers as they practiced in the tiltyard, although Anne was careful enough to avoid detection. On Accession Day, it was indeed a thrilling display.

After that, the weeks surrounding New Year's Day 1580 brought many entertainments. The schoolboys of St. Paul's and their singing master acted out one of the Queen's favorite stories about Scipio Africanus defeating Hannibal's elephant army. On Twelfth Night, the Earl of Leicester's Men put on a play; apparently, it had been rescheduled from a pre-Christmas performance canceled when Elizabeth did not appear—but appear she did this night. Best of all, Anne liked the lusty tumbling of Lord Strange's acrobats on January 15, with their fantastic gyrations and contortions.

The diversions were welcome relief from the affairs of state being worked each day by the Queen's Privy

Council. There were rumors of continual conversations with France about a possible marriage alliance between Elizabeth and one of the sons of Catherine de Médicis—either Henry, Duke of Anjou or his younger brother, Francis, Duke of Alencon. Many dismissed the possibility, since the Queen, at forty-six, was much older, but then her majesty would say something that made it plain how interested she was—and that always kept the French guessing. Also, Spain was making great mischief for the council, with Papist Jesuits arriving everywhere, heightening the persecution against them. The entire country was mustering forces for defense, strengthening coastline fortifications, and raising taxes in the event of trouble—most probably from Spanish-backed rebels coming across from Ireland. Finally, although London escaped somewhat, plague was raging in cities such as Norwich, which lost a quarter of its population. At court, there was a sense of laying low, preparing for the worst, and keeping one's head down.

The list of new year's gifts made to Elizabeth in 1579–1580 showcased twenty-two offerings of jewels from her inner circle at court, one for each year of her reign. This inventory was presented in the order of the status of the giver, from earl to gentleman, and the value of each present.

Item one began with a trove presented by the Earl of Leicester, a favorite and adolescent companion of the Queen recently elevated to the post of Master of the Horse. His offering included "two bodkins of gold"—long sharp pins for ornamenting the hair—the first "a very fair table diamond, garnished about with small rubies," and the second "a very fair ruby garnished about with single diamonds." Leicester's list continued with a velvet cap, a diamond encrusted brooch, and thirty-six matching buttons. Gifts two and three were elaborate brooches and bracelets from the Earl and Countess of Oxford. Item five was a group of "twenty-four buttons of gold, enameled with white and black, with one pearl in every one," from Lady Burghley. High on the second half of the list at item thirteen was "a bodkin of gold, garnished with small diamonds," from Sir Henry Lee. The final items, numbers twenty-one and twenty-two, were gifts of lapis lazuli stone and crystal from Lady Sidney and her son, Mister Philip Sidney. After these highlights, pages and pages of less illustrious treasures and givers then followed to flesh out all the swag.

After the new year began, the 1580 Calendar of State Papers recorded the most important expenditures from the Royal Treasury, as ordered by a Crown anticipating serious trouble from Spain. For example, an important estimate was made "of the cost of keeping her majesty's whole navy being fourteen sail of ships, ready for service upon twenty days' warning." Related to this was the order for "the names of twenty-two merchant ships fit to join with the Queen's ships if needed." Another item provided Sir Henry Lee with a certificate to muster five thousand men from Oxfordshire and to deliver a full list of their captain's names, as well. Oddly, an order was recorded for the Earl of Oxford to pay two hundred pounds per year to Lady Oxford out of his rents, in case he might forget. That item was included by order of Lord Burghley, whose daughter, Anne Cecil, was Oxford's estranged wife. Also ordered by Royal Warrant was payment of "the yearly fee of twenty pounds to Anne Vavasour, Gentlewoman of the Bedchamber."

Entries in Anne's new commonplace book

From "To the Queen," a poem by Sir John Davies

What music shall we make to you?
To who the strings of all man's hearts
Make music of ten thousand parts:
In tune and measure true,
With strains and changes new.

How shall we frame a harmony
Worthy your ears whose princely hands
Keep harmony in sundry lands:
Whose people divers be,
In station and degree
Heaven's tunes may only please
And nor such airs as these.

From Philip Sidney's *New Arcadia*, describing Sir Henry Lee at jousting

(As Hardy Laelius, that great Garter-Knight,
Tilting in Triumph of Eliza's Right,
Yearly that Day that her dear reign began
Most bravely mounted on proud Rabican,
All in gilt armour, on his glistring Mazor
A stately plume of Orange mixt with Azur,
In gallant Course, before ten thousand eyes,
From all Defendants bore the Princely Prize)
Thou glorious Champion, in thy Heavenly Race,
Runnest so swift we scarce conceive thy pace.

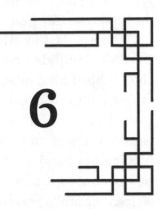

6

September, 1992. At work on the opening day of school, Stephen couldn't tell whether the boys and girls were afraid of him and his eye or simply hypnotized by James Joyce and Virgil. Probably both. But by the end of the day he'd convinced himself his classes on Dubliners and the Aeneid left them all wanting more, which was his main hope. But the administrative part of the day, dropping in on new teachers, placating parents, and addressing the newly combined male and female students of the school in the auditorium, had not gone as well as it could have. He just had too much in the back of his mind to worry about.

Finally, just after six in the evening, he was able to drive across town for the remaining hour of visiting time at the hospital to check up on Vicar Hamilton.

At the main reception desk, Stephen was disappointed to learn Vicar Hamilton was not taking any visitors. But the receptionist said there were other well-wishers keeping vigil in the waiting lobby off the men's ward on the fourth floor, if he wanted to join them. There he found Verger Andrew and Margaret alone, sitting in one corner of the fluorescent-lit room. He noticed his heart jumped a beat. He hadn't seen Margaret since the Christmas service at the church, except on television a few times—most memorably, that summer, when she reported on the arrival in France of distraught refugees from the siege of Sarajevo. At Christmas, she had waved at him from across the aisle, but didn't come over afterward. He wondered then if she snubbed him, or simply had to be with her father. Now she looked a lot less polished, leaning over the end of the vinyl sofa toward Verger Andrew's chair. In fact, she seemed quite fragile, with moist eyes and chafed reddened skin. Verger Andrew was holding her hand as they talked. They looked up cautiously as he came in, as if afraid more bad news was coming, but then a welcoming smile grew beneath Margaret's sad eyes.

He walked over to sit next to her.

"Hello, Margaret," he said, taking her hand warmly, but checking his instinct to lean over and kiss her. He sat down next to her on the sofa, leaving a gap of about a foot between them. "What's the news on your dad?"

"Well, it's not good," she said. "What's happened to your eye?"

"Oh, it's nothing. Just ran into something the other day. Looks a lot worse than it is."

Verger Andrew shared the update. "The vicar is still unconscious. The doctor says he's still strong, but it's worrying he hasn't come around yet. His breathing became irregular a few hours ago and they hooked him up to some new intravenous medicine with a mask on him for oxygen. It's all down to his head injury, they told us. Margaret's been here all day and I came over about four this afternoon. The staff didn't want us in the room the last hour or so, thought we might be in the way, although someone comes out to see us every so often." Margaret interrupted this report with a whimper.

"Oh, Margaret. I'm so sorry," said Stephen. She leaned over toward him, putting her head on his shoulder with a short sob. He felt any stiffness he was attempting to show her melt away as he hugged her. He felt no resistance from her side.

Just then, the door to the ward opened and a young Indian doctor came out. Verger Andrew introduced Stephen as "a close friend of the family," which was true enough, but it sounded strange to him.

The doctor began, "Well, I've just examined the vicar and given him some pretty strong medicine. I don't expect any more developments tonight. His breathing seems more regular, and I think all we can do now is give him some time and wait patiently. I'm having him transferred back up to the intensive care unit on the top floor, where they have more staff to keep an eye on him all night. The nurses are just changing shifts and I've made sure they have your telephone number at the vicarage, miss, and they'll call you if there are any developments—otherwise, you should just go home and rest. Then check back with us about ten tomorrow morning. We can give you any news from overnight and then take it from there. Okay?"

"Yes," said Margaret. "Is there anything I should bring for him from home?"

"No," replied the doctor. "We have everything here to keep him as comfortable as possible. It's more important just now for you to look after yourself, and get some rest. I know this is very upsetting, but don't make it worse by getting ill yourself. You can be sure we are doing everything possible for him right now, and we just have to give it some time."

"Thank you, doctor," said Verger Andrew, standing up to stretch out his stiffness from sitting so long. "We understand."

As the doctor went back through the doors to the ward, Stephen also stood up and helped Margaret up and into her coat.

"I'll let you take Margaret home, Stephen," Andrew said. "Both of you and the vicar will be in my prayers tonight."

"Thank you, Andrew. Thank you so much for coming and staying with me," said Margaret.

Outside, the twilight was darkening under a cloudy sky and the crisp air was a welcome change.

"Did you have a car, Margaret?" asked Stephen.

"No, I just took a taxi from the station. I haven't even been home yet, but I do have my key. I feel terrible I haven't been up to see him more often. I mean, I came home for Easter, but I didn't turn up all summer. I was so busy. And now all this."

"I saw you on the evening news about Sarajevo this summer, and the vicar's been telling me about how well you've been. So I guess you have been calling him often."

"Yes, that's true," said Margaret. "I call him every Saturday early evening and hear what he's planning for his sermon, and then once or twice during the week. But it's not the same as visiting, is it? Seems especially lame right now."

"I'm over there by the fence. Can I give you a ride home?" said Stephen.

"Do you mind if we just walk a bit first? I really need to clear my head."

"Of course," he said.

They walked out of the hospital car park and onto the residential streets at a stroll. "He was quite excited about all the things they found in the church—and he's said very nice things about how helpful you've been sorting through it all with him," Margaret said.

"It's been exciting for me, too. Suddenly all those quiet years in the library at Magdelan and the Bod have paid off. History coming to life from the tomb, of all things."

"I wonder if that's all been a bit too much for him," she replied. "I mean, it's been a whole new set of worries added to his plate. He told me he was up all night wondering if it might be very valuable, not that it would mean much to him. But now he's walking around with all that swirling in his head—no wonder he fell down."

"Oh, I don't know," said Stephen. "I thought it was giving him a bit of a lift." He wanted to avoid an argument with her at all costs.

"It put him into a commotion. I noticed it in our calls...." Margaret trailed off and just went silent for a while as they walked together in the dark between the streetlights.

"What is it all about, actually?" Margaret asked. "These bloody papers, I mean."

"It's about suitcase-size load of Elizabethan manuscripts—and not very ordinary ones at that. Mistress Vavasour was quite the unusual Elizabethan. She kept commonplace books with snippets of things she had read or had been sent, which isn't so odd, but she also kept letters and personal papers—and that's not normal at all. Usually you only find deeds, wills, or other legal papers as original manuscripts from the sixteenth or seventeenth centuries—things that the owners thought might have obvious value over time. Letters were kept only by people like Lord Burghley as 'state papers' and important records of who thought what or said what about government affairs. Most common correspondence simply disappeared. But this lady kept a lot of her papers and put them into her tomb. And that's how they survived over three hundred years: quite remarkable, actually. Very rare."

"Well, the lady was my mother's family, as my dad must have told you. We don't have anything to show for it, although I think my cousins have some furniture and such. But it wouldn't have been from her specifically, just from the general time period. I was always told she was the black sheep of the family—quite notorious to hear my mother tell it, although she never shared the gory details with me. Apparently, she did everything her own way. In fact, she was thrown out as a maid of honor by the Queen. I always quite liked that about her while I was growing up, especially with her tomb nearby in the church and so on. I liked that she screwed up as a young girl, but then obviously lived on to be a rich old woman. Made me think life might give me second chances, too—although I haven't seen many of those yet, damn it."

Stephen didn't know what to say to that.

By now, they had come all the way down the hill and were starting along the high street of the village. Margaret paused in front of the estate agent's window and looked over some of the photos and listings on display.

"Well, house prices are up, I see. Do you still have yours?" she asked, separating them from the common ground of the vicar's illness and adding in distance.

"Yes, and the Americans are still loving it—they even seem to finally have gotten the knack of keeping up the garden." Stephen inherited his family house after his father died. It was a large detached house and garden—completely too much for him to rattle around in alone, so he listed it with the estate agents as a rental, and an American family had been in it now for almost two years. The father commuted by train into London each day, like scores of others lining the station platform during the morning rush hour.

"I think they see it more as their house than mine, but I believe his foreign posting is ending soon and they'll be going back to the States. Nothing official, just something the wife mentioned to me when they extended the lease."

Stephen had always fantasized he would live there with Margaret and a bevy of adopted children someday, with him reading the newspaper by the fireplace in the lounge. But that hadn't happened.

"You know," Margaret said, "we probably should have a bite to eat. I didn't have anything but a roll on the train and I think the Indian would still be serving. And frankly, I don't want to go home just yet to toss and turn and stare at the ceiling."

The Cinnamon Restaurant was just behind the high street. Stephen knew it well. He and Margaret had been there often back in the day. Now he knew it more for its takeaway than its tables. In a few minutes, they were across from each other again somewhat uneasily, although with a bottle of Beaujolais, while one tandoori chicken and a lamb tikka were under construction in the kitchen.

"How has your work been going?" he asked, thinking it would be best to sink into the mundane with her tonight.

"Well, I still have nightmares about the footage on the first rumors of 'ethnic cleansing' in the former Yugoslavia. Men and boys massacred and thrown in hastily dug mass graves, with their women looking for them—and then finding them. I just don't forget that. Then, just back in June, I took on a three-week assignment about trouble in South Africa. There the horror was another massacre by a faction rivaling the African National Congress. It even seemed to have been sanctioned by the white police with over forty dead. If you're not careful, the job is like being a moth popping up around nasty candles. I mean there's no point to just spreading the news around. It seems so passive and weak compared with trying to change things somehow. I prefer the investigative side, where you're gathering evidence to make some sort of calculated point, or to reveal something people aren't aware is going on—when they damn well should be. That's quite different. I mean, the job is never boring and the pay is fantastic but you have to make sure there's some point to it. Plus, I can get very tired of all the travel on a moment's notice. So, that's me. How are you doing?"

Stephen had been staring at her as she spoke—my god, she is magnificent, he thought. He had to shake himself awake a bit to answer her.

"The kids and St. George's are fine. Everybody has had quite a shock as we merged with St. Anne's and introduced girls into

93

the mix. Now the boys and girls stand around staring at one another in disbelief. I have especially high hopes that the girls' headmistress, Mrs. Boardman, can take over much of the day-to-day running of the place. We even have a foreign student—from your Bosnia, of all places. His father works at their new embassy, just opened in Kensington. The family moved here in July and I had his parents to dinner right here in the Cinnamon."

"Really?" said Margaret.

"They're former professors at the university there. I told them to shop at Waitrose, join the tennis club for the kids, get the boy into the scouts, and so on."

"Well," said Margaret, shaking her head in disbelief, "they're the luckiest Bosnians on the planet—because the whole place is disintegrating day by day, I can tell you."

"But your father's papers have been a welcome distraction from the school for me. I've enjoyed working on them, and I thought it was a boost for your father as well—not a poison. Anyway, it's making me remember my original plan to be a writer of books and reviver of lost history. You remember? So, I'm just starting to think about all that again."

"Yes, I remember," said Margaret. "Sorry about blowing up at you for exciting my dad. I just needed to hit out at something—but it shouldn't be you."

"No worries," he said as the food arrived.

~

Later that night, after he'd dropped her off at the vicarage, Stephen knew he had been kidding himself a long time. Kidding himself about being all right alone, about getting along, about doing something totally fulfilling in this out-of-the-way village. Most of all, he had been kidding himself about Margaret. He wasn't over her. He felt so much less without her.

His thoughts wandered back to the when they started. They met while Stephen was ending his summer vacation hiking for two weeks through southern France visiting historical sites. He liked to put his own footsteps where great writers worked or great events occurred and feel the reality of centuries before more deeply. One late afternoon he was enjoying the sun outside at a café after several hours prowling around the old churches and cathedral in Poitiers. Several tables of more casual English tourists were also momentarily scattered around the same café, recovering from a day at the Futuroscope theme park nearby, and waiting for their coach driver so they could board the tour bus and continue on to stage twenty-two of their itinerary, no doubt. His countrymen were not, however, enjoying the attentions of their brusque and sullen French waitress, who seemed to have succeeded in avoiding most of them as the remaining minutes of their leisure time ticked away. When the bus driver suddenly appeared and announced their departure, most had not even received the overpriced refreshments they'd ordered. Stephen watched the farce unfold as they departed the café with a chorus of murmured insults at the expense of the French. At least they still had their money, one portly old gentleman declared.

As the bus pulled away, the French maid in question then efficiently reappeared from inside the café to tidy away the detritus of used serviettes and ashtrays in advance of a more preferred regular clientele, who soon came and filled up the places with their local French banter. Stephen thought her extremely pretty and fetching, in spite of her muttered Gallic comments on the pedigrees of the pale English patrons just removed. Her hair swung, catching the late afternoon sunlight, making her attractively backlit, as if in a film. Somehow she looked familiar. Perhaps he was watching her a bit too closely, because she felt his eyes crawling all over her. Suddenly she glared at him and stormed over, hissing *"Etes vous perdu? Pas de l'autobus, monsieur?"*

"No," replied Stephen, responding resolutely in English, at least proving he understood her. "I'm not lost and I'm not missing that coach any more than you are, mademoiselle. I'm here traveling on my own—a simple pilgrim and lover of France." She was stopped short and briefly speechless—and that's when he recognized her. He hazarded a possibly inane further comment. "I'm sorry, aren't you at Oxford?"

At first, she looked stunned, and then, unbelievably, she blushed. A shy grin stretched her lips as she seemed to recognize him. She slipped into the spare chair at his table. Then she lowered her eyes down above her reddened cheeks, like a guilty thing surprised. "Well, so much for my disguise," she said, now in the same accent as his own. "Yes, and I recognize you from college as well, now that you mention it."

That first conversation with her on the job had to be brief, but it was long enough for Stephen to realize she was a British girl acting out a real-world impersonation of a nasty French waitress. What incredible cheek to put that over. He had to find out more.

They made a date for when she stopped work at nine that night. Then they strolled around the ancient cobblestone streets of the old city as she explained herself to him. Yes, she was at Oxford in Brasenose College, and in her third year of studying English and modern languages. Her "modern" language was French, and she was finishing up her obligatory year abroad in France, immersing herself in French culture.

"I started as an au pair for a month with a wealthy family," she began. "They were willing to take a chance on an English Oxford girl while their totally French governess was on her August holiday. It was bloody ironic that my job was essentially teaching two little boys and a girl how to be French. You know, they don't treat children as we do, letting them fuss and throw tantrums and so on. The French treat kids as little adults they need to teach—not as God's gift to the world to be coddled. So, with a bit of tough love, by the time the kids are aged three or four, they can go along to dinners in restaurants without any trouble and don't have to be left at home with nanny in the nursery. Very much better," she said enthusiastically.

After that, she worked for ten months in Paris for a small independent newspaper, doing research for the journalists and helping them file the stories they either called in by telephone or sent in by telex. She would then trim and polish them to fit the available space on the page. That had been fast-paced, exciting, and totally absorbing, but she had been careful to leave the last month for some rest and recovery before heading back for her final year at college.

"That's why for the last three weeks I've been filling in as a waitress here five days a week in Poitiers. Most of the regular staff are off on their August holiday, and I was 'French enough' for the café owner to welcome me to waitressing the tourists for him—as long as I could deliver the appropriate degree of rudeness both sides of the transactions would be expecting," she finished, smiling. And, as Stephen had observed, she played that part bloody well.

They met several more evenings that week, getting on like a house on fire. After the fourth date, when they kissed good night at her door, she asked him up, and five minutes later they were all over each other. By the weekend, they were living together in the waitress's flat that Margaret was subletting. She was impulsive, sure-footed, and fearless in her passion. He had never met anyone like her in his own cautious and well-thought-out world. Then, when her month of waiting tables was over, they rented a car at the Poitiers train station and spent a few days driving around the countryside, sampling village inns and local restaurants, and getting in deeper with the newness of each other.

The first day they only got as far as the small village of Bonnes about twenty kilometers east of Poitiers on the banks of the River Vienne north of Chauvigny. Stephen knew the spot because he'd been hiking around there stalking old battlefields. He parked right on the main street of the village. She knew the town as well and she immediately swept him down to the path along the river. From there, they could see beyond the neat front façades of houses into the private back gardens on the other side of the stream, with their lush plantings and outdoor dining tables clustered up near the back doors of the sandy gray stone buildings. Looking farther out, lush agricultural fields stretched as far as the eye could see.

"It's funny," said Margaret as they strolled, "they told me in the town this river was the border between Occupied and Vichy France in World War II. You actually needed a pass to go from one side of the river to the other. Hard to believe that war would have waged all around here," she finished.

"Not too hard," said Stephen. "This is also where all the maneuvering was before the Battle of Poitiers in the Hundred Years War, when the Black Prince defeated the French king in the 1300s and took him and his youngest son back to England. Maybe that's why they don't seem to like the English very much around here. And even before, this was about where Charles Martel defeated the armies of the Caliphate in 732. If he hadn't won that, Europe might have been Muslim today. That's in Creasy—you probably know his book *The Fifteen Decisive Battles of the World*, and so on."

"No, I don't know it. You are the history wonk, aren't you," teased Margaret. "What about Julius Caesar and the *Gallic Wars*? At least I know about him from Asterix and the comics."

"Most of that was actually northeast of here—over closer to Belgium, Germany, and Switzerland. Caesar's big battle was at Alesia—we can go there on the way up to the airport, if you like.

And Asterix's village was supposedly in the northwest corner of France, right on the tip."

"Oh, really!" She laughed. "By the way, that point about hating the English is really a myth," Margaret observed. "English, American, Japanese—the French don't like anyone who doesn't at least try to acknowledge them and the fact they're standing in France. I mean, there's a big difference when you wait on people demanding an English menu and another where the tourists attempt to speak French and try to chat. Shows they respect where they are, I think. I would get so angry at the coach tourists—there are so many together they usually don't make the slightest attempt to acknowledge they are in another country. That bunch the other day just shouted out what they wanted in English at me. The real girl who's the waitress wouldn't have had a clue what they were barking at her. Germans do the same thing in German—very annoying."

Soon the path they were trodding came to an ancient bridge over the river, near a café with tables scattered outside under a spreading oak. Stephen and Margaret couldn't resist the opportunity to sit down, rest, and admire the view. The proprietor came out, and with a nod of her head, Margaret whispered out an order of ham and cheese crêpes with a carafe of *vin rouge*. Her French was pitch-perfect, as she went back and forth with the man in a rapid-fire conversation before he happily went back inside.

"He said the goat cheese they use in the crêpes comes from those goats over there," Margaret said, pointing toward small figures in a farmyard about a quarter mile away across the river. "It's like heaven here, isn't it?" The house wine was as good as most pricey labels in a London restaurant, Stephen remembered, but there it was the same price as the Badoit bottled water.

For the fifteen minutes of this reverie, Stephen was back in the warm summer of a French afternoon with his pretty new love, and not all alone in his small English flat getting ready for school the next day. But he didn't have to come back to earth with sadness or irony, thank god, because he just fell asleep in his chair.

7

Stephen drove over to the hospital after work on Thursday evening. He found Margaret pacing outside the main door, more upset than before.

"Any news?" he asked.

"Nothing good," she said, pausing a moment to light another cigarette. "I came here happy as a schoolgirl this morning. I'd convinced myself he'd be awake today—at least certainly by now. But the doctors are telling me it could go on much longer." She hissed out a cloud of blue smoke with a will.

"Did something change?" asked Stephen.

"No, it's more like nothing did change. I had to press them to cough up more details for me. Turns out they use some sort of scale—the 'Glasgow Scale,' of all things—to grade people in comas. They score whether their eyes are open, or if they respond to someone talking, or move their limbs and so on. And my dad just zeroes out on all of the bloody thing—nothing at all—naught, naught, naught. So now it's not just as simple as waking up from a fall—in fact, the only thing they're certain of is that falling didn't make any of this happen."

"How do you mean?"

"You know Verger Andrew told us he thought Dad must have gotten dizzy or something, and then hit his head falling down in the kitchen."

"Yes," said Stephen, remembering.

"That wasn't it. The wound was a blow from above—on the back of his head. And it packed a real wallop. They've even had to tell the police about it—I mean, because everything suggests an assault."

"Oh my god."

"Well, it makes sense. I mean, this all happened just after that damn article in the *Village Advertiser* about 'treasure in the tombs' or whatever."

"That's insane," said Stephen. "These papers aren't just something to steal and sell to crooks at a jewelry shop in London. But your dad's still strong, isn't he? You know, his breathing, heart, blood pressure?"

"Yes, the basics are all fine. But he's been unconscious for two full days now and all bets are off. Christ, one of the doctors even said '*if* he wakes up' to me."

She turned quiet, took another drag, and started to quiver, as if she were going to crumble in front of him. He reached over and hugged her. "Oh, Margaret," he said, and they just stood together for a long moment, holding on.

"Do you want to go up to him again now...or get something to eat?" Stephen asked finally, stepping back.

"No, not just now. And I don't want to go home either—not to an empty house—or out to a fucking pub or restaurant. I'm too jumpy."

"Well, come over to my place for a minute and have a glass of wine. I'll show you what I'm doing with your papers, and then we can get some takeaway or go out, or whatever."

"That's right," she said, snuffing out her smoke with her shoe and looking up at him. "You've gone into a flat, haven't you? I can just imagine what that looks like. Well, actually, this sounds great—'now for something completely different.'" She tossed her hair back and wiped her eyes. "Let's go," she said grasping his arm, turning her back on the hospital doors, and marching them off to the car.

~

Opening the door of his flat, Stephen was glad his cleaning lady had gone overboard for the start of school. The place was actually quite presentable. He only had to grab some clothes from chairs, throw them into the bedroom, and close that door while Margaret looked around.

"There, that's better," said Stephen, watching her take it all in.

"Nice sofa and curtains," said Margaret, smiling. "And incredibly tidy. Were you expecting some sort of inspection?"

"No," he laughed. "It's all from my family house—you, know, I took things out of storage. And my cleaning lady, Mrs. Case, just got a back-to-school wind up this week. She scrubbed, dusted, and hoovered everything in sight. Why not try the sofa and I'll get us some wine?"

Heading into the kitchen, he opened a new bottle of St. Emilion and poured two glasses. He looked into the fridge and the cabinets, but there wasn't much else to offer with the wine.

Stepping back into the living room, he began, "We're in luck. I have some of the good wine your father introduced me to—the St. Emilion from Waitrose. Before we tried it, he gave me a lecture on how you don't have to buy fancy labels to enjoy really good wine—and he was right about this one." He stopped rattling on as he saw Margaret was examining the maps he had up on the wall over by his worktable.

"What's all this?" Margaret asked, looking over the pins stuck in throughout Switzerland and Italy.

"That's me planning my next holiday adventure—for next spring, hopefully. I've pinned all the places I want to stop. I'll be following in the footsteps of Byron, Keats, and the Shelleys in the years right after Waterloo. So I'm starting with their rented villas around the lake at Geneva and then going over the Alps and down to Tuscany. I've even rented my own place outside Pisa as a base for a couple of weeks. Then, I think I'll finish up in Rome—both Keats and Shelley ended up in the Protestant cemetery there—and that's quite a remarkable place, you know. It's incredibly beautiful, even though it's a cemetery. And it's not on the tourist track."

"That's to be your own version of *Enchanted April*, is it?" she teased him.

"It's going to be in May actually, but I suppose you're right. I think I'll be on to something good—matching their writing with the settings that inspired it all. None of them are read now particularly outside of school, except perhaps Mary Shelley's *Frankenstein*. I was thinking of writing a book or long essay to make it all come alive again. I think people have forgotten their story, and it's a good one. Anyway, it would be another trip like when we discovered each other in Poitiers...when I was fresh from the battlefields."

"Actually, going back to the nineteenth century for a few weeks sounds great to me—along with a strong dose of the Italian springtime. I've had quite enough of what's going on in the world today—a break going back in time would be wonderful," said Margaret walking over to the sofa and sitting down.

Stephen put the wineglasses down on the coffee table and managed to stifle himself from inviting her to come along on his trip. It wasn't exactly the right moment to try to rekindle their romance, with her father lying comatose across town. But it would be a dream come true.

"Hmmm, the wine's great," she said. "Just the ticket."

He was happy to see a small smile start to come alive on her face.

Margaret asked, "So tell me about these papers."

"Cheers," he began. "Well, there were two boxes down in the tomb. One had older things like Anne's childhood commonplace book, and even older papers that seem to belong to a Sir Henry Lee, another courtier of the time from the generation older than Anne. He's in the documents so much I ordered his biography through the library. I just got it today and scanned it a little before I saw you at the hospital. He and your Anne Vavasour were very close, actually living together, it seems. Then the papers in the other box start off in King James's reign, sometime around 1610, and keep going until around 1650. So, all told, they cover almost a hundred years. One interesting thing in the second box was Sir Henry's will—he was very rich—and he left a substantial bequest to Anne."

"They must have been lovers," said Margaret, cutting through everything.

"I expect so. You get right to the heart of things, as usual." He was taken aback at how quickly she discovered the likely answer, while he was still pondering the possibilities.

"It's the BBC training," she said, cracking a rueful smile, "added to all those speedy 'critical thinking tools' they pounded into us in the English department at Oxford."

"The papers are quite an assortment," Stephen continued. "Most are letters—there's even one from Lord Burghley—and there's paperwork from a legal case, all in Latin—which is a bit heavy going because of the jargon. Then I've just gone through some poetry. One piece claims to be lines written by Anne together with the Earl of Oxford—it's rather romantic."

"My, she did get around."

"And then there are long pieces—I told your father about the handwritten presentation copy of *Arcadia* by Sir Philip Sidney, as well as a few masques and plays. There's also a scroll with quotes pasted together to form a long length of joined sheets.

That's one of the things I photocopied bits of and sent off to my old handwriting teacher at college, Professor Rowe—you probably didn't have him in a course because he's an Elizabethan specialist. I know that wasn't your favorite era, but I saw quite a lot of him, especially for tutorial. I also made copies of pages from the commonplace books as well as the Burghley letter— five or six pages all told—and I heard back from him in a phone message quite quickly. It was quite a shock to get such a personal response from the great man; he has a very high opinion of himself. He wanted to know more about what we'd found, and so I've planned to go over to see him on Saturday. Would you like to come?"

"Sure, if nothing's changed with my dad. It would be great— and actually my aunt is planning to visit him in the hospital this weekend, too. So she could hold the fort. I'll just want to telephone and check in every few hours."

"Okay. Then I thought later I might share those same copies with Soames Bliforth, who was in my year at Magdalen, also in my course on English and the classics. I think you met him a few times when we were going out the last year. Now he's an antiquarian book dealer in London. I thought he might be able to give us some idea of the market value today and so on."

"I do remember him. Wasn't he very posh? I think a group of us were all out for a night of pasta and wine on the town together and he ended up treating everybody," said Margaret.

Stephen smiled. "That sounds like Soames," he said. "If he thinks the papers might have significant value, then we should show the collection to experts for a proper evaluation."

"Who should see it?" asked Margaret.

Stephen thought for a few moments and said, "Well, there are the auction houses—Sotheby's and Christie's—if it's all to be sold. Or libraries and museums, although they would take a long time to research it. Or even the most authoritative book dealer working with real treasures, Maggs and Company, just off Oxford Street in Berkeley Square. And besides that, we should have a paper conservator look at it and make sure it's stored properly. Everything survived because it spent hundreds of years in a dark and cool low-humidity vault. It could really deteriorate fast if it's kept in sunlight or near boxes made of modern paper full of chemicals."

After sitting quietly for a few moments, Margaret said, "I don't think my father will be very interested in money. He'd just give all the extra cash to the church. So we'll have to draw him out on what he wants to do later...when he wakes up." She paused and choked up a bit before adding quietly, "Or *if* he wakes up."

That seemed to trigger a break in the dam of her reserve again. She started to rock gently, and tears started to run down her face. Stephen moved quickly over closer to her on the sofa and put an arm around her shoulder.

"It's all right, Margaret. I'm here for you."

"I'm sorry," she said, "but I feel as if everything is coming apart. My poor father just seems to be sleeping there in his room, and I can sit and read between the doctor visits. But then he doesn't wake up. I mean, he's not asleep—that's an illusion. He's comatose, and I don't know if he's ever going to wake up, or if I'll ever be able to talk to him again. It's all very draining. I don't know how I'd cope without Verger Andrew coming in the afternoon and then being able to see you in the evening. You're being really wonderful, you know. I do appreciate it, Stephen—it's all very upsetting."

Stephen tried to comfort her. "Margaret, he may wake up tomorrow—Christ, he might be waking up right now, for all we know. We'll just have to wait and see—and say our prayers. Your dad would like that, you know."

"Yes, I have been saying my prayers. It took me quite a while to remember all the words," said Margaret. "You're right, how he would like that. And then work has been so upsetting lately. I mean two weeks ago an artillery shell hit a crowded market in the western part of Sarajevo, killing fifteen and injuring more than one hundred innocent people. It was a flat-out tragedy—and we had to cut the story down to nothing because all the British people wanted to hear about was Charles and Diana's bloody marital soap opera—it was just incomprehensible."

"Look, you've had way too much going on. Why not just take a minute and try to calm down. All this has been an awful business, but at least it's brought us back together for a time, and we can deal with it all together, if we try."

Stephen couldn't tell if the drivel he was talking was having any positive effect or not, but in a few minutes she stopped sobbing and began breathing more easily, as she took back some control over all her emotions.

"I don't think I can eat or rest just now," she said. And then suddenly she sprung up off the sofa like a dancer. "Bloody hell, let's go over to the church and look around the tomb where these papers were. Andrew said everything is still opened up to dry. It isn't even eight o'clock yet. I could use some night air. Who knows? We might find something."

"Yes, why not?" said Stephen, again astonished at Margaret's natural impulse for action instead of reflection. Like Anne Vavasour, she did everything her own way. "Off we go," he said standing up and stretching. Actually, he was very glad for the change.

~

It was deepest twilight and almost dark when they went into the church. There was no one around this Thursday night—virtually anything would have been more important than going to church.

Stephen could see the floor of the nave had been restored to its normal condition, with the great marble slabs back in place, although the new grout was still light enough for an astute visitor to notice. Soon that would be tainted dark gray and only Stephen, Andrew, and the village workmen would be troubled by nightmares about the decaying coffins stacked on top of one another underneath the fine floor.

Around the corner, the vault under the Lady Chapel was still open, separated from the playschool by portable fluorescent orange fencing. It gave the room the feel of a roadway work site: you half-expected a man with a yellow hard hat and a reflecting vest to rise up from the floor, but of course there was no one there.

Stephen switched on his hand torch and shone it down to illuminate the entrance to the manhole on the firestone wall of the vault.

"That's where your dad and I were reaching through to take out the papers. The smaller chest was closer to the entrance, and the larger one just behind, with the end panel broken off. That's where he could first see the papers inside."

Margaret turned on her own torch, aiming it at the decorative Vavasour monument above.

"This is what I remember," said Margaret. "I always thought the bodies were inside that altar there. I didn't realize they were all under the floor. That's actually very creepy...but of course it makes sense. I remember my mother and I standing here looking at it, and her telling me Anne Vavasour was our black sheep. I always thought she couldn't be too awful because she was kneeling down there reading something. I thought she might be praying or doing her homework—I mean, how bad is that?"

"Not bad at all. And someone had a lot of money to spend on this. It's the same quality as you find for swells in Westminster Abbey. You'd have to go to some ghoulish workshop and place your order for a class A decorative monument and have it delivered and installed here. You'd also have to hire a whole troop of masons to construct the vault underneath. It probably cost more than building a house."

"And it lasted much longer," said Margaret. "The date on the top is 1612—that's three hundred and eighty years ago."

Stephen took out his pocket notebook and pen. "Margaret, can you just keep the torch shining here? I want to copy out the inscriptions. They might help me understand some of the things that are said in the papers."

At the top, underneath the word "Vavasour" and the "1612" was a brief Latin phrase, *"Christus Mihi Vita et Mors,"* which he jotted down.

"What does that say?" asked Margaret.

"Pretty normal stuff—something like 'Christ be with me in life and in death.'"

"Not very original." She sighed.

"Maybe we'll get to that underneath," replied Stephen.

On the face of the altar, under the main tableau of Lady Anne kneeling in front of her lectern, were two crests framing a brass inscription plate. Stephen turned and handed Margaret the notebook and pen. He stood carefully over the edge of the exposed vault, perilously close to falling in.

"Do you mind writing this down as I read it out? Odd it doesn't seem to be in English."

"Sure," said Margaret. "Go ahead."

The inscription was in two parts, separated by a horizontal line across the plate:

DU TRES HONORABLE CHLR

HENRY LEA CHLR DU TRES NOBLE

ORDRE DE LA JARRETIERE LE XXIIII

DE MAY AN. 1597

"I can assure you that's French," said Margaret. "It says, 'The very honorable knight'—I think that would be an abbreviation for 'chevalier' or 'knight'—'Henry Lea, knight of the very noble Order of the Garter, the twenty-fourth of May in the year 1597.'"

"Okay, then there's a poem under the line—and it bloody well is in English, Stephen said, smiling:

> If Fortune's store or Nature's wealth commends
> They both unto his Virtue praise did lend
> The Wars abroad with honour he did pass
> In Courtly Jousts his Sovereign's knight he was
> Six Princes he did serve and in the fright
> And change of state kept still himself upright.
>
> With Faith untouched, spotless and clear his fame
> So pure that Envy could not wrong the same
> All but his Virtue now (so vain in breath)
> Turned dust lie here in the cold Arms of Death
> Thus Fortune's Gifts and Earthly favours fly
> When Virtue conquers Death and Destiny.

He continued, "Then there's a shorter one below that under the name 'ANNE VAVASOUR'":

> Under this stone entombed lies a fair and worthy Dame,
> Daughter to Henry Vavasour, Anne Vavasour her name.
> She living with Sir Henry Lee for long time did dwell
> Death could not part them but here they rest within one cell.

"That's it," he said. "The crest on the left says, 'Vavasour of Copmanthorpe.'"

"Yes, that's our ancestral village in North Yorkshire," said Margaret.

"And on the right it says, 'Lee,' with *Fide et Constantia* under-neath—that would mean 'Faithful and Constant,' I suppose."

"So, it's actually a double tomb—I never knew that. And they don't even have the same name. Were they married?" asked Margaret.

"No, the biography says they were just living together, but for twenty years or more. Maybe that's why she was your black sheep," said Stephen.

"Indeed. What's inside down here? Although I suppose it must be just Anne and Sir Henry. Let's have a look."

While Stephen was righting himself from hovering precari-ously over the vault, Margaret started striding down the rubble slope toward the manhole opening.

Stephen thought there was simply no stopping her. She was absolutely fearless. No thought of corpses, vermin, spiders, or ghosts in the tomb at all.

Not even slowing down, Margaret bent down and crawled through the manhole and was suddenly crouching on her knees inside the vault, peering around. And he had shirked going in at all, just gingerly reaching in from the outside.

"Well, it's a lovely vault," she said. "It has a nice curving arch for its roof. And there are indeed two bodies inside—one on either side of the center, and one is larger than the other. They seem to be encased in some kind of silver metal and sit on top of islands of brown dust."

"That would be lead that was loosely shaped around the actual bodies. Sir Henry must be the larger one. And the dust is all that's left of the wooden outer layer that once held them. Verger Andrew said he was going to sweep all that out before it was closed back up. The ebony of the boxes didn't disinte-grate like that—it's much denser than our native woods. Finely preserved objects made of it even survive from King Tut's tomb."

"Well, they will be very tidy when it's closed up. Not even a spiderweb down here," Margaret said. "I can see why the papers survived so well. There's nothing to bother them. Just cool and dry stone."

"It's very different from the larger vault over in the nave. That was a bloody mess, and I'm glad you didn't see it," Stephen said.

"Nonsense. I'm the grizzled war journalist, remember?"

She lingered a moment, taking a last look inside.

"Actually, I'm very glad I didn't see it as well," she said, reemerging through the manhole and starting to stand up. "I see enough at work to haunt me. Help me up and let's get out of here."

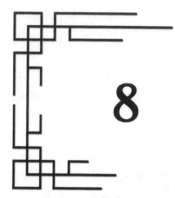

8

At nine on Friday morning, Margaret was curled up in the vinyl armchair provided for patients in her father's new room on the fourth-floor men's ward, comfortable but uneasy. She was almost hypnotized watching the regular rise and fall of his breathing and the steady flashing of the numeric scores on the screens monitoring his vital signs for the nurses. He seemed to be in a deep sleep, and not bothered by the oxygen mask and myriad tubes and needles hooked up to him. But of course that was because he wasn't sleeping. He was comatose, which actually might mean he might be more than half dead, except for these bloody machines.

"Enough of these thoughts," she said aloud, forcing herself to sit up straight and take hold of herself. He's getting great care. And he's lucky to have a private room, she thought. Or more likely it's because they know him. After all, he's here all the time for visits to patients and families. Okay. But I wish he'd wake up and visit me.

She stood up and walked over to the window. Looking down across the treetops she could see the spires of St. Mary's and the adjacent St. Luke's piercing the canopy of green. Life is going on out there—Stephen's probably in his school right now trying to manage the chaos of the living.

Her mind wandered back, conjuring up her early days with him. He was the one good thing that was happening from all this sadness with her father. She liked seeing him every day again. Back at their beginning, after a week or so ambling around France in the rental car, they ended up back in Oxford for their final year. After twelve months away out in the world of France, college was a born-again fantasy setting for Margaret, and all about Stephen being the new part of her picture.

He lived at Magdalen College, away from the Oxford town center, a sprawling hundred-acre domain of grand churchlike buildings and cloisters stretched out along the sides of its own deer park on the banks of the twisting River Cherwell, about sixty miles northwest of London. There they would stroll along the manicured walkways without disturbing the almost tame animals grazing behind the fences and take a blanket and picnic lunch down to the riverbank to study, talk, or cuddle. And she lived only minutes away at Brasenose College, which was smaller and more compact, but still the same sort of gothic castle, right in the center of town on Radcliffe Square, overlooking Stephen's beloved Bodleian Library and the round landmark Radcliffe Camera reading rooms, where they both spent so much time. And since they were both in their final year, they each had the best sort of large private rooms, where they alternated sleeping together most nights after meeting up for drinks or dinner.

She thought about their differences then, too, how Stephen was at the center of his life's ambitions at Oxford, whereas she was merely passing through to get skills she needed to go else-where—out in the world.

Only at Oxford (or also perhaps at "the other place," as they referred to Cambridge) could one find a substantial community of twentieth-century students still swept up in the everyday life of ancient Rome and Greece. Stephen had signed up for a four-year course that began with an immersion year to learn Classical Greek, of all things, so he could read works in their original language. He said it wasn't that bad, she remembered, once you got over the strange-looking alphabet. There were so many English words based directly on Greek that it wasn't that hard to figure out the meaning once you got going.

But that was all about the past, whereas what she wanted was all about the present, and beyond that hopefully some chance for improving a future which she might even be able to help shape in some small way. That's why she wanted to become fluent in her beloved French, and even learn a little Arabic and Mandarin: so she could understand what people were actually talking about and experiencing around the world today. Journalism was an obvious path for her after school, just as writing and teaching young people old literature and Latin would suit Stephen.

But actually for a long time she was fine with their differences, because *vive la difference* was a fine state of affairs for young romance. She and Stephen announced their engagement less than a year after finishing school, and that seemed natural because they were in love with each other—passionately. For a short while, he would continue to be a junior teacher by day while working on his first serious book by night; she would keep moving up from an entry-level job in London at the BBC. By god, that all sounded very fine for a start. Soon they would grow up, move away from their home village, and start an independent life together.

But after Stephen's parents were in that car crash, she became worried. She understood Stephen had to take over the school—or his family would lose all of it. And she respected how brave he was to do it for his mother, his sisters, the staff, and the kids. But somehow the doors of his compatibility started closing for Margaret.

116

Would Stephen eventually expect her to be the headmaster's wife, presiding over the new-parent tea parties, or taking charge of the junior school with the beginning students (age four to nine), just as his mother had? Margaret had lived through something like that when she was a child. Back in the 1960s, her mother was a live wire: pretty, vivacious, and talented at music, with a wonderful singing voice that could even have been a career for her if she channeled her energies in that direction. But as her father dug in to his new post as the vicar, he asked her to stop singing—because she was so good, it intimidated the parishioners he was trying to attract into the choir and the weekly life of the church. Couldn't she just be happy playing the organ during the services when they needed everyone to wake up and sing the hymns, and then help him with making his ministry work? And that was how she came to see her mother as someone who had sacrificed her own God-given talents to spend her life as an aid to her husband's selfless quest. Sometimes when Margaret came home from school in the afternoon, and when her father was elsewhere, she would sit in the lounge and listen to her mother singing and playing her piano out on the porch off the kitchen. Even as a teenager, Margaret knew her mother was exceptional at that. It was probably part of what made her father fall in love with her at the start, she was so pretty and wonderful. But then he asked Delia to lock all that away because of the damned parishioners. And Margaret wasn't going to just give up her passions and her dreams to become some kind of drudge junior headmistress in a country village. Well, at least not yet, and not for a bloody long time.

Meanwhile, she had begun hearing the siren call of adventure, which she had always wanted. Her lowly position with the BBC had just been a first step into the exotic life of journalism, and that became the path she continued along. After three months in a cubicle at Broadcasting House in London, making the tea for her seniors and buying lunch from the sandwich lady who walked through the desks, it was off on assignments—very small and local at first. She remembered her piece on the fashions at the Wimbledon tennis was a success. But soon after, the world beckoned, and she was sent over to Paris to be based at the BBC office just on the edges of the city, putting her hard-earned French persona to work.

She started to get quite a reputation at the office because she wouldn't take no for an answer when she was right. Once, when a junior editor cut an important story down to nothing because of some late-breaking society gossip, Margaret "doorstepped" him, appearing unexpectedly at the door of his apartment at nine thirty in the evening demanding he reinstate the story. He was so astonished that he relented, and she stormed back to her computer at the office to redo the scripts for the midnight deadline. The next morning her colleagues put on a mock awards ceremony for her and gave her the title *la tigresse anglaise* because she was the English tigress who had devoured the editor.

Visiting home in summer, she knew she was on the way up, and she broke off the engagement with Stephen. Now even the remote possibility of becoming the life partner of a village headmaster was just a nonstarter.

At least she cleared the air, she thought. After all, Stephen didn't die of those wounds. He didn't have the time, because he was consumed with his new life-or-death task of reviving the school. And one world crisis after another seemed to be beckoning her. So it was a soft break—if there can be such a thing—and she found herself saying "we may be back together quite soon," like some melodramatic heroine in an old movie as her train pulled away.

But they hadn't gotten back together. Not yet anyway. And other things had happened that she didn't want to reconsider just now. And didn't want to tell Stephen about yet either.

~

Across town, Stephen's day was taking a strange turn. He was in his study at work when the school secretary entered with a note. He paused and read with surprise that a policeman, Sergeant Stokes, was in the office asking to see him. That's a first, he thought.

The secretary went off to retrieve the officer and bring him down to the study. Soon they were sitting across from each other.

"So, what's this all about, sergeant?"

"Mister White, can you tell me what you were doing on Tuesday night?" asked Stokes, all business.

"Yes. I was having a quiet evening at home and prepping for my lessons this week. I picked up some takeaway and was in my flat. And then sometime after nine p.m. the verger from St. Mary's Church called me about Vicar Hamilton falling, and I went up to the hospital and tried to see him, but it was too late to visit and I came home."

"Did you happen to pass by the church and the vicarage at all earlier that day?"

"Well, no. I mean, they're quite close to the restaurant where I picked up dinner, but they are farther down the high street heading north, and that's away from my flat—farther away from the restaurant. So, no, I wasn't up around there that day at all."

"I understand you've been seeing quite a lot of the vicar lately. May I ask why?"

"I've known the vicar and his family a very long time. In fact, at one point I was engaged to his daughter, Margaret. Then, on August Bank Holiday Monday, the vicar discovered some old papers in the church—things that had been there hundreds of years—and he asked me to help him see what they were. This was all written up in the village newspaper. I'd studied old hand-writing in college, and he thought I could make out exactly what they were better than he could. So we've been seeing each other about that ever since. In fact, I was also working through some of those papers at home on last Tuesday evening staying in, as I told you."

"Would you say these papers are valuable?" asked the sergeant.

"They were papers in one of the tombs in the church. In fact, the tomb belonged to Vicar Hamilton's wife's family. And they just seem to be family papers—letters and journals and so forth—but unusually old...from the sixteenth and seventeenth centuries. So, they are certainly rare and unusual, but I'm not sure what the monetary value would be. We're still trying to work out what they are. There are quite a lot of them. Why do you ask?" Stephen was getting a little uncomfortable with the sergeant's relentless tone of questioning.

"Just a few more questions, Mister White," said the sergeant. "Can you tell me about your general financial position just now? I mean, are you in any difficulties?"

"No, thank you very much. I have this job as headmaster here and family property I inherited years ago. And I don't have many expenses—just a small flat, a Mini, and takeaway dinners. I'm sure you'd find my financial mysteries made clear at my bank manager's office, if you want. May I say I'm not comfortable with your line of questioning and must ask you to explain this intrusion here at the school, sergeant."

"And what about your eye, sir? Looks like a nasty blow."

"If you must know, that was from last Friday. I had an argument with a lout at the pub and ended up with a punch in my eye. I think several dozen people saw that, if you want to check."

"Do you know the man?"

"I know who he is: Tony Baker. He's the brother of a young woman I go out with occasionally and she and I quarreled earlier that night. He heard about that, didn't like it, and came over and punched me in the eye before I knew what was happening. We'd both had a bit to drink at the time."

"I see, sir. On another topic, may I ask if you have any jewelry or metal collectibles at your flat, or in your car, that you might have acquired recently?"

"No, sergeant. No stolen paintings either. I'm afraid I've had enough of this."

"Well, don't get too upset, sir. I wouldn't want you to have to come down to the station with me if we can finish talking here today. Why don't you just take a moment to calm yourself?"

Stephen wasn't used to dealing with the blunt yeomen of the British police force, but he agreed with Stokes that it would be better for him to just get through it all now. "All right, sergeant. What else?"

"I understand you visited Vicar Hamilton in hospital recently?"

"I actually haven't been able to see him yet after his fall. I stopped in on Wednesday and sat with Verger Andrew from the church and Miss Hamilton. She's there all day with her father."

"And then you went out to dinner with Miss Hamilton?"

"Yes, sergeant. You do certainly have your sources. We went out for a bite after visiting hours at the hospital. She'd been there all day, and then I dropped her off at the vicarage about ten o'clock."

"And then you went back to your flat?"

"Yes, sergeant. As you can see, I have a day job that starts bright and early here at St. George's. I also went by the hospital again last night and ended up spending the evening with Miss Hamilton again. We are very old friends and she is obviously quite upset by all that's happened. So we went by the church and took a closer look at the vault that was still drying out. Where I helped the vicar with those papers. Can you tell me why this is all so important now, sergeant?"

"Well, sir, this morning we were called by Verger Andrew who had discovered certain valuable items missing from the church," the sergeant explained. "There was a jeweled gold crucifix, candlesticks, and other ornaments taken from the storage chests in the vestry. It's not clear exactly when they were taken since they're not used every day. But Verger Andrew had seen the pieces in their proper places after the Sunday service the weekend before. So we're wondering whether the facts that these things have gone missing and the vicar is in hospital may be connected, d'ya see? That's why I'm here speaking with you."

Stephen was thunderstruck. "I had no idea. I don't know anything about those things from the church. I was in there on the Bank Holiday weekend to help take out those old papers with the vicar, and then with Miss Hamilton last night. Before that, the last time I was in church would have been the Christmas services last winter. I'm sure of all that. There have been a lot of workmen about in the church recently as well. I mean there was a flood there over the holiday weekend. I'm not accusing them of anything, of course. I just mean there's been lots of activity at the church lately."

"All right, sir. That should be fine for right now. Tell me, do you have any plans to go away in the near future, or travel abroad?"

"No. I mean, the school term has just started. I'm going to be right here. Miss Hamilton and I are going to Oxford over the weekend, but we'll be back Sunday evening. You're not implying I'm under some sort of suspicion in all this, are you?"

"No, sir. Just that we will be making more inquiries over the next short period and we may need to come back to you soon, if you don't mind. We're just getting started trying to sort it all out. Nothing to be too concerned about, sir. Just usual police work." Standing up, Stokes continued, "Thank you for your cooperation, sir, and I wish you a good day."

Stephen stood up and shook the sergeant's very large and puffy right hand. He opened the door of the study just as the bell rang for a change of period. The hallway filled with boys and girls as the policeman made his way out. Stephen watched as the man left, trying to recover his equilibrium after the surprise and anger that had overcome him during the interview.

What next? he thought, as he walked down to the staff break room to clear his head. This idea of the vicar's injury being part of a crime was a real worry—especially if Margaret was at risk.

~

That evening Stephen found Margaret at the hospital. There was no change in the vicar's condition. He still remained strong, but the third day of the coma was obviously making everybody more concerned and worried. Again, there was not a damn thing to do but wait. At seven thirty, they went out for a quick bite and then walked to the vicarage. Stephen came in to visit.

He had told Margaret about his interview with the sergeant at school. The whole complication of the possible burglary at the church made them both tense and edgy. Stephen took a quick walk all through the house, checking for anything amiss, while Margaret stayed in the lounge. He saw all the papers there had been organized into small stacks on the dining room table, safely out of the way, although he didn't see some of the larger journals or the case for the embroidered commonplace book.

"Margaret, are these papers here everything, or have some things been moved?" he raised his voice to ask her in the other room.

"I did put some things in the dining room buffet—the long top drawer there. I remember the embroidered bag, a journal or two, and the scroll. And a small pile of papers, too," she added. "Just wanted to get them out of the way."

"Okay, good. Everything else all looks fine," he reported as he completed his walk-through and came back into the room. "I even checked the closets." He laughed. "I think I've been watching too much television."

"Well, if I can go and report from a war zone, then I should be able to tough it out here in the village vicarage," Margaret offered, although she didn't seem as comfortable as she might have been. "I'm sure your friend the sergeant would be here in a moment's notice if we called. I mean, the police station is just about four streets away."

They both let silence hang in the room for a while, and Margaret sat down on the sofa.

"I saw some of your father's good wine in the kitchen," said Stephen. "Would you care for a nightcap glass of red—or anything else?"

"Wine sounds great," she said.

Just as Stephen started to take the foil off the bottle, the doorbell rang. "Now what? I'll get it," he called out to Margaret.

Stephen opened the door and there stood the same policeman from his school interview that morning. "Good evening, Mister White. I wasn't expecting to find you here."

Margaret appeared behind Stephen and said, "Hello, officer. What's going on?"

"I don't mean to trouble you, miss," Stokes said, "but I wanted you to know the latest developments. Mister White, you might as well hear this, too."

"Please come in," said Margaret. "Let's sit in the lounge," she said, gesturing the officer onto the sofa while she and Stephen sat in armchairs facing him.

"Regarding the items missing from the church—the altar candlesticks and so on—we have arrested a Tony Baker in the matter. We haven't charged him yet, but are holding him for questioning. There are a few circumstantial things making him a person of interest. We want to see if anything else comes out."

"Tony Baker?" said Stephen, remembering the shock of his punch the Friday before.

"I believe you know him, Mister White."

"Yes," said Stephen. "I told you we got into a fight in the pub a week ago. He gave me my black eye."

"He did say that, Mister White. An argument about his sister."

"Yes, we'd both had a bit too much to drink. I'm sure that made it easier for us to come to blows." Stephen really didn't want his dating Miranda put on the table just now, although he realized he would want to tell Margaret about it soon.

"Do you think he might also have attacked my father?" asked Margaret.

"Finding out about that is part of what we plan to talk with him about, Miss Hamilton. So I hope to have an update for you in a few days. I really don't need to take up any more of your time just now. I just thought you would like to know we have moved forward with this."

"Yes, thank you, officer," said Margaret as she stood to see Stokes off.

"Maybe they're better detectives than I thought," said Margaret after the sergeant left. "What did you fight about? Was it connected to anything else?"

Stephen had returned to the kitchen, finally getting their wine. As he entered the lounge, he began, "I don't think so, but you might as well know the story, I suppose. I had taken Tony's sister, Miranda, out a few times over the last months—and was supposed to spend the Bank Holiday Monday with her. But that's when your dad first found the papers and asked me over. And I completely forgot about her and ended being a no-show. The night of the fight we ran into each other at the pub and she made a scene. Her brother didn't like that and came over and smacked me. That's about it."

"Lovely," said Margaret. "Sounds right out of *Coronation Street*."

"Well, life in a village can be like a soap opera. But that's how it is. Then when I was taking my black eye home in my Mini, I almost ran Tony over in the car park. I didn't see him as I backed out and I knocked him down. My last sight of it all was him running after me in my sideview mirror, shaking his fist."

"Well done, you," Margaret said, smiling. "I'm glad to hear my man won the day. Let's not talk any more about all that just now."

Stephen was glad he didn't have to keep going with the saga or mention Miranda's paternity claim. He didn't want any secrets between them. But for now he was happy to have a reprieve...and to hear her say 'my man.'

Stephen said "So then, Oxford tomorrow? We can leave midmorning and have a bite to eat in town, if you like. Professor Rowe lives just nearby, in the village of Horton-cum-Studley."

"Oh, I know that one," said Margaret. "It's where they filmed *A Man for All Seasons*, about Sir Thomas More and Henry VIII."

"Really?" said Stephen, so very glad they had moved on from the saga of Miranda and Tony Baker.

He didn't realize she had steered them there. Quite frankly, she didn't want to hear about Tony's sister, nor did she want to tell him her own story yet.

After a few more minutes, Margaret finished her wine and said, "Look, a little earlier I think I was trying to sound braver than I am right now. The truth is, I'm very tired but I don't think I can relax here by myself alone tonight. . . . Would you mind staying over in the guest room? I just don't want to worry about having anything else happen now. Is that all right?"

"Sure, I can stay," he said. "Why don't you go upstairs and I'll lock up down here?"

They walked together over to the stairs. Stephen turned and gave Margaret a light kiss on her forehead. "We'll get through this, my girl. We'll just take it one day at a time."

"Thanks for staying," she said.

~

Lying down in the guest room a little later, he realized he was very tired, too. Take care of what you wish for, he thought. He wanted her back, and she's back. For a moment he wondered what she would do if he walked down the corridor and knocked on her door. He certainly wanted to...but, for Christ's sake, her father was at death's door—that's why we're here like this. She's probably praying for him to wake up. And she might be praying for me to go to sleep, too.

Damn it.

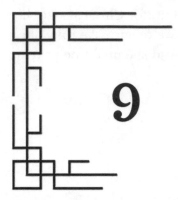

9

The next morning, they left the vicarage just before ten, planning to have lunch and a quick look around their old haunts in Oxford before seeing Professor Rowe at 2:00 p.m. It was a glorious September Saturday, and the ninety-minute drive was refreshingly free of workday hurry and traffic since most of the population was still at home and in bed. All of their challenges seemed less dire on such a fine morning, and Stephen decided to clear the air about Miranda.

"Margaret, I just wanted to tell you a bit more about the fight and the pub and all that. Since you and I have been away from each other, I've been pretty focused on my job and the school and so on, but it's not as if I haven't had a date or two in the last year or two."

"Of course I know that, Stephen," she said, watching him as he drove.

"Well, this girl, Miranda Baker, and I have gone out several times off and on. It's been a fun, social thing. She's an extrovert, very high energy and upbeat, and some times that has just been very refreshing for me...you know, to shake the cobwebs off and rejoin the living after a long week in the school. The fight was really about the disconnect between my wanting it all to be just casual and her now thinking about being more serious. And I didn't do a very good job of dealing with that conversation; in fact, I was an ass. That's why she yelled at me in the pub. The brother was just her white knight coming over to thrash me for upsetting his sister. I think I had it coming."

"You don't have to tell me all this," said Margaret, although she was so glad he'd gotten it out.

"The fact is, I'm not interested in Miranda for the long run—or anyone else new either. I'm not being melodramatic, but I wanted you to know just how it is. We don't have to go on about it...but there you are."

"Same for me, Stephen," she said. "I'm human, too. Just an entirely natural thing." She thought she'd just move everything along now. "So, tell me about Professor Rowe," Margaret shifted. "I never did come across him at school."

"Okay," said Stephen, taking a breath and relieved for the switch. "First, you'll hate him. He's an insufferable arsehole so full of himself there's no room for anyone else in the room—and if you let that put you off, then you'll miss everything else. But if you can put his manner aside (just like I am trying to put my interview with the detective aside), then you'll realize you're in the presence of a relic from an earlier generation or an earlier century—a living dinosaur—and someone that we just don't have walking around and talking to students anymore in this day and age. He is the leading British expert on all history Elizabethan and Shakespearean, as even the people who hate him would admit. When he was a young student—and he must be well past seventy today—there were still some old men at Oxford who had started their academic careers in the decades before the Great War. Teachers like Doctor W. W. Greg and Sir Edmund Chambers, who spent their whole lives pursuing some rarefied corner of scholarship, like old handwriting or the Elizabethan stage. And Rowe would have known them, admired them, and then overtaken them as the same sort of encyclopedic professor and Oxford don. So he's an anachronism—someone who just shouldn't be part of the modern world. No one thinks those areas of study are important anymore. Respected academics today study rocket science, or whatever—not the 1500s. At least, that was how it all seemed to me when I was in my tutorial with him for English and the classics."

"No, you're right. I don't remember him—but he sounds like just the sort of teacher for you," said Margaret.

"Anyway, I'd see him once a week, along with this girl who was also studying classics—Penelope something—which was actually quite useful, because he was always particularly rude to girls, or 'gels,' as he calls them. He tortured her much more than me—so watch out. I think he's much more attracted to the boys, if you know what I mean. Once he'd finished beating Penelope down into absolute silence, he'd tell us things about the sixteenth-century texts we were reading that made you think he had actually been there and known all the people writing them personally. For example, he told us that Sir Walter Raleigh had a twitch, and that's why his writing was uneven and there were so many typographical errors made by the printers who were setting his manuscripts. And this one we were reading one week was set by an apprentice at Jaggards type shop—that's why the word on the page was mysteriously "greek" when Sir Walter meant it to be "green." And Sir Walter had caught it, but thought it was so funny that the apprentice typesetter had made the mistake that he let it stay wrong, and would have a good laugh about it with his friends looking at the book. And he had even told Queen Elizabeth about it and she had had a good chuckle as well. But, not to worry, the apprentice got better later in his career, and that several other books he had set in the 1590s were much more reliable, and we could go compare the typesetter's earlier and later work from copies at the Bodleian Library—and wouldn't Penelope like to write an essay on that for next week—he'd be so interested to read what she discovered. He was, quite simply, the worst, most tyrannical teacher, and the best, most enlightening one. It was lucky we only met once a week, because you could only stand him in small doses, but then you'd end up thinking about what he had said all week."

"That's quite a story. It's going to be a challenge to stifle myself, but I'll give it a try. What photocopies did you send him?"

"I sent him a copy of the letter from Lord Burghley; I thought that would be a good start. Then others from the commonplace books...a copy of a page or two from the manuscripts of the plays or masques that were there...and finally parts of the scroll. I still have no real answer for what that is. If he paid attention to any of them, he should be able to tell us a lot."

"I was thinking we should probe him on why Anne would have kept all these papers in the first place, if it was so odd for the time. That's what seems to be a big question," said Margaret, showing her quest for the heart of a story.

"Very good," said Stephen. "I'll try to come out of the weeds for that one, too. I can't think of another good example of a trove like this one. Closest would be the surviving commonplace books. A lady called Anne Cornwallis had one with the earliest transcript of a Shakespeare poem, I remember, from about this time."

"Crikey, don't tell me Shakespeare is about to get into this?" Margaret laughed.

"No, I don't think so. But all of this was exactly at his time, you know—and in some sense, they probably all knew about one another."

"What?"

"Well," Stephen explained, "I mean, it was a very small community. On one side there was this tiny group of people who needed things written: courtiers for grand speeches, theater owners or the people putting on shows for the Queen at court or when she went around on her 'progresses into the realm,' and the few aristocrats who had playing troupes under their patronage as a kind of hobby—like Essex, Oxford, Leicester, and so on. And on the other side, watching them, and looking for jobs, was an equally tiny group of writers, all desperate to pay the rent, like Marlowe, Shakespeare, Middleton, and so on. So in that sense, they all knew, or at least knew *of*, one another."

"Hmmm. Very interesting," mused Margaret as she thought that over. "What do you think about the possible value of what we have?"

"I don't know, and I don't think Professor Rowe will be up on 'value' as far as the market prices today, if you eventually want to insure or sell them. Although I suppose he might be. But that's why I think we could send the same copies to Soames Bliforth as a next step perhaps. He was also studying with Rowe in our year and, with his used book shop in London, he should be up on the prices these days. After our meeting, we can decide if you want to do that.

"Well, this should be interesting. I'll be on my best behavior," said Margaret.

~

The village of Horton-cum-Studley, with its quaint name, sits just a few miles northeast of Oxford and is the beneficiary of an almost maniacal historic preservation. The main attraction has always been Studley Priory, a former Benedictine monastery, hotel, and sometime private home that retains all the details of its medieval and renaissance glory. Just down the road from the priory, Professor Rowe's home was an ancient white stucco cottage, replete with thatched roof, sheltering hedges, and luxuriant gardens. An elderly lady—presumably his housekeeper—met them at the front door and ushered them toward the professor's study facing the back garden, where the great man was enthroned in a leather wing chair, bathed in the best reading light, backed up against windows overlooking the terrace. Apparently many pilgrims came to call, seeking enlightenment, for the housekeeper gestured toward two smaller leather chairs and muttered, "He'll be wanting you in those little ones." As he sat down, Stephen noticed the guest seating was not only smaller than the professor's, but lower as well.

"Stephen, is it, Mister White? Yes, I do remember you, but this is not the same gel I used to see you with, is it?" He smiled expectantly at Margaret. "I think you've made quite an improvement on that score."

"Professor Rowe, may I introduce Miss Margaret Hamilton. Margaret was also in my year, but at Brasenose studying English and the modern languages at the time."

"Yes, French, actually," said Margaret standing up and walking over to the seated professor, extending her hand. The old man's hand was surprisingly small, cool, delicate, and smooth. Lots of hand moisturizer there, thought Margaret.

"You do seem somehow familiar, my dear," the professor said, continuing to look at her intently.

"Professor, you may have seen Margaret on the news," Stephen responded. "She's a journalist with the BBC and on television sometimes now. And, most important, she is the owner of all the papers I've been going through. They had been inside an Elizabethan tomb of one of her ancestors over in our village."

"Really? Well, that's fascinating, my dear. I'm very pleased to meet you. I've done some work with the BBC myself, you know, interviews about our history here and there—that's my game."

"Yes, professor. Stephen's been telling me. It's very nice to meet you—and very nice of you to let us come visit," said Margaret completing the niceties.

"This was a family tomb?"

"Yes, professor. My relative was named Anne Vavasour and her monument is dated 1654."

"Oh my dear, not *the* Anne Vavasour, surely?"

"I suppose I shouldn't be surprised you've heard of her, professor," said Margaret. "My mother only told me she had been the black sheep of our family."

"Black sheep? My gel, the colors would be more like 'scarlet woman' rather than 'black sheep.' The Vavasours were a large and prominent family at court closely connected to the Knyvets, and they placed several gels named Anne—as well as Frances and Margaret. Catholics from the north, I believe."

"Yes, the origins were around Copmanthorpe, in Yorkshire."

"Well if this was *the* Anne Vavasour, the lady was perhaps the most sought after courtesan of the age, I'm sorry to tell you. She came to court as a Gentlewoman of the Bedchamber—fittingly enough, I might say—and then was disgraced when she gave birth to a bouncing baby boy in the maidens' chamber. The scoundrel father was Edward de Vere, they said—the Earl of Oxford. And it was particularly awkward for William Cecil, Lord Burghley, because Oxford was married at the time to his daughter, who was also named Anne—Anne Cecil. The Queen sent both of the proud parents to the Tower. And a few years later, it seems the Earl of Leicester offered Mistress Vavasour money and a fortune in jewels to be set up as his mistress, but I think she declined."

"Good lord," said Margaret, hearing all of that for the first time—and from this smarmy old man, who clearly relished seeing her blush.

"Of course, she was just a teenager from the country, poor gel, albeit a pretty and well-educated one. She did rather recover, I believe. In fact, she ended up as the de facto wife of old Sir Henry Lee, the Queen's champion at the jousts. His own wife, Anne Paget, died just as he retired from court around age fifty-five or sixty, I believe, and then he and Miss Vavasour remained an item for over twenty years. It would have been salvation for her, since he was immensely wealthy and of impeccable character, and I believe they were, as they say today, 'meant for each other.' She had another child or two, and outlived old Sir Henry for another several decades. The old knight achieved a remarkable old age. I think he was eighty when he died. But the old *drab*, your ancestor, beat even that. I don't believe anyone has reported the exact details, but the rumor was that she lived to ninety years old—and that was completely unheard-of at that time. Perhaps you have her genes, dear? Though, I trust, not her inclinations."

Margaret was dumbstruck at this history. She never thought their interview would become so personal with this old git. Stephen quickly jumped in.

"Professor, I have just got hold of the Henry Lee book by Sir Edmund Chambers, so we're just on the path of discovering all of these details now. But we're not quite there yet," he said.

"Good, Stephen. The details aren't well-known—that's for sure. Old Sir Edmund wanted there to be a proper biography about one of the great yeoman gentry characters so important to Elizabeth. Not the earls and dukes and so forth, but the true gentlemen of the realm whom the Queen would count on to raise a troop of fifty men on horseback to go patrol the northern borders, for example. He chose very well with Sir Henry Lee, who was splendid in that role. Aubrey even reported he could have been a bastard son of Henry VIII."

"Aubrey?" asked Margaret.

"John Aubrey was a gossip reporter of the mid-1600s," the professor explained, "an amateur historian and provocateur. If he had been a reporter like you today, he would have written a column in one of the tabloids, my dear. Some of his reports were true, but most were probably rubbish. For example, he interviewed Shakespeare's neighbors years after the bard's death and reported Shakespeare was remembered as a butcher when a young man and always made a fine speech before slaughtering whatever poor animal he had hold of. I suppose one might say the same thing about most of the fourth estate today...with the exception of the BBC, of course."

"Of course," echoed Margaret, temporarily on her back foot.

"In any event, if Sir Henry was the King's progeny, that would have made him half brother to Edward VI, Mary, and Elizabeth. There were a lot of those so-called natural children by King Henry and the boys were all normally named Henry. That might explain how he got along so well through it all." The professor paused and then continued, "I wouldn't think too badly of poor Anne, my dear—"

"Well, no, I don't," interrupted Margaret. "Those were tough times to be a woman—like today can be—and I think she did a bloody good job fighting her corner. And believe me, I try to do the same."

"Yes indeed. She did that more than all the other gels, for certain. That's true," said the professor, noticing that Margaret was no pushover. "Everyone may have played at courtly love under the frigid glare of the Virgin Queen, but there were plenty of what we'd call sexual predators there as well, like the Earl of Oxford, who were just toying with newcomers as a way to pass the interminable time lounging around awaiting the Queen's pleasure. Anne was a victim—but the wags delighted to make it the scandal of the decade when it happened. That's why I said Anne's connection to Sir Henry was a salvation for her—and for him as well, I imagine, living on his country estates or his fine apartment on the river in London. Most of the time they were just down the road here. Henry was the Ranger of Woodstock on the Oxford road just northwest of the city—on the land where Blenheim Palace stands today."

"At least they were in a grand part of the country," said Stephen, who struggled to hold back a smile, thinking about how wonderful Margaret was at holding her own, too.

"Well," said the professor, "let me ring for Mrs. Wells and have her get us a pot of tea to calm ourselves after resurrecting Mistress Vavasour. Why don't I show you my Elizabethan garden here while she fixes the tea, and then I can give you come comments on those papers you sent me?"

~

Margaret, Stephen, and the professor stepped through the swinging doors of the terrace as the housekeeper was summoned and then retired inside to her duties in the kitchen. Stepping down onto the lush grass of the garden, the professor led them over behind a neatly trimmed shoulder-height hedgerow, revealing a small landscaped field divided into four quarters of decorative plantings behind tiny two-foot-high hedges, separated by carefully linked gravel walkways. A miniature version of the gardens at Versailles or Blenheim, Margaret thought, more scaled down to the size of garden gnomes instead of princes.

"This is a classic Elizabethan garden," the professor explained. "The clipped hedges make 'a curious-knotted garden,' as Shakespeare describes it in act one, scene one, of *Love's Labour's Lost*. Inside, sweet-smelling herbs such as chamomile, thyme, or mint are planted with flower beds of hearty perennials. Through the year, there are primroses in spring, crocuses, daffodils, wild hyacinths, and so on—and of course roses, whether red or white for Lancaster or York. I love to sit out here on that bench over there on a certain sort of day, thinking back to the familiar scenes of hundreds of years before. Clears my mind wonderfully, you know. I recommend it."

"This was a lot of work, professor. It's beautiful," said Stephen, following on the paths behind the professor and briefly taking Margaret's hand to buck her up.

"I'm afraid I cheated, Stephen," Rowe said, putting his arm around Stephen's shoulders as Margaret shuddered. "Used slave labor by my students. Had them all out here bending over and sweating in front of me. Marvelous, one of the few perks of my office."

The professor smiled as they completed the tour and turned back to go inside.

~

Mrs. Wells had left a classic tray of tea and biscuits after their twenty minutes in the garden. The professor played host. "Milk or sugar, Margaret?" he asked.

"Both, please," she replied.

"As bad as that?" Rowe gloated. "Stephen?

"Just plain, sir. Thanks." How quickly I've become the great man's student again, Stephen noted. They sipped their tea for a minute or two—it was indeed comforting and restorative.

Now let's see what the old boy thinks, thought Stephen, opening round two of the discussions. "Did you have any thoughts about those papers I sent you, professor? It was just a random selection to show the range."

"Yes, I made a few notes here. Let's see."

Professor Rowe sat back in his chair, put his teacup to the side, and placed a pair of reading glasses low upon his nose.

"Well, there was the letter from Lord Burghley. A very good signature, in his own hand as opposed to the secretary's. He was a very good friend of Sir Henry and, as noted, Lee had sent him a side of venison from the country. Probably a Christmas gift. Lee made quite extravagant presents for the Queen each year. I believe you'll find a list of them in the Chambers book when you get to it. So it's a very nice letter. But, as you can imagine, there were a lot of gentlemen sending venison to Burghley, so I think this would be something to display framed in your drawing room, Miss Hamilton—not something for a museum."

"Of course," said Margaret, making a note and regain-ing her footing as he started giving them really useful information.

"Then I find the pages from the commonplace books next. This first one must be Anne's. She wrote in the most wonderful italic hand—things Italian were all the rage just then—and it's impressive that she seems to have been on the Ascham curric-ulum, with her Latin and Greek, not the second-rate program they gave to most girls. The Knyvets had high hopes for her with Elizabeth, no doubt. The second one seems a more manly tome—probably either Sir Henry's own, or more likely some kind of gift book she had put together for him: a scrapbook of readings he liked. There's a passage by Sir Philip Sidney, who was one of Lee's friends and jousting partners. In Sidney's work *Arcadia*, there's the famous Ionian jousting scene between two knights: Philipus—that's Sidney; and Laelius—that's Lee. They were great chums. Sidney would have sent Lee his writings, and have had a scribe copy them out for him.

"And there's also a formal courtly speech inserted on the edge of the page, possibly from one of his tilts. Each of the knights at Elizabeth's tournaments would have speeches written by some academic. Then a page would climb up the stairs near the Queen and her ladies and deliver the speech while the knight waited on his horse below before riding against his opponent. I wouldn't mind seeing more pages like these. Both the commonplace books would be real 'museum pieces,' I would say."

"Anne's pages are from a book, quite finely decorated with embroidered covers, by the way," said Stephen.

"All the better. Sewing—and dancing—were essential skills for the ladies at the time," nodded the professor. "And then another photocopy seems to be a view of speeches from a masque. It doesn't seem to be a play—more of a court perfor-mance of the old school. Men with ruffled collars parading around and giving speeches about courtly love. There's a reference to an 'old knight,' for example. Sir Henry entertained the court at his estate down the road from here in 1592—they were all very happy to be out here in the country because the plague was raging in the city. He put on quite a show over two days in September, I believe. It's written up in John Nichols's books about the progresses of Elizabeth into her realm, and I believe Lord Dillon, Lee's descendant, gave a partial manuscript of the event to the British Museum just before the last war. This could be another copy of that."

Rowe continued, "The sheet in Latin is from a court case. In fact, it looks like it's a contested matter between Anne and her erstwhile husband John Finch. The ecclesiastical courts handled marital issues, so that's why it's all in Latin. Finch is probably trying to get his hands on the money Sir Henry left Anne, but I imagine Sir Henry tied it up pretty tightly so she could keep control.

"Finally," the professor said, winding down, "I didn't quite get the nature of the last thing you sent. Seems a mishmash of quotations with various reference letters and numbers separating them. Might be some kind of homemade singing sheet, I suppose. I mean, Anne and Sir Henry had lots of free time in the country. They probably created all sorts of diversions to stay sane away from court and the city. Singing would have been one of them. Might have lined up the servants into a choir, and so on. Had to do something else besides pounding away with each other at bedtime."

Well, he didn't have to finish it like that, thought Margaret. He's just trying to get a rise out of me and I will not do it.

"Yes, that last one's a bit of a mystery," said Stephen. "It's actually a copy of part of a long scroll, of all things."

"A scroll? *Really*," said Rowe, in such an affected way that he seemed to be questioning Stephen's basic intelligence. "That's a mystery indeed. Maybe I can have a look at it myself sometime, if you like."

"Yes—probably so," said Margaret, feeling it was time to get the hell out of there. Time for her to throw him her question. "Professor, Stephen has mentioned it was rare for anyone to hold on to a trove of papers like this at the time. Do you have any idea why Anne might have done that?"

Rowe pushed back a bit in his chair and raised his eyes to the ceiling, thinking. "Well, my dear, I suppose she might have been sentimental about old Sir Henry. After he died, at the start of her widow-like condition, she probably just left everything in the library at one of his houses. But after that, you're right: it is odd she would have kept them—and even been buried with them. I know the heirs of Sir Henry were in hot pursuit of her, trying to get the money. That Latin legal document is probably part of all that. Perhaps she was keeping the collection as a kind of proof that she was his soul mate, and thus entitled to the money he left her. I don't know. I'll keep thinking about that one for you—it's a good question. Shows that BBC training."

"That's wonderful, professor," said Margaret, trying to wind things up so they could escape. "It's been a real education, and we probably will want to pester you again after Stephen's finished his inventory of it all."

"Inventory, Stephen? What are you up to?" asked the professor.

"Well, sir, I'm just organizing the documents—there are well over a hundred separate items, if not more. I assign a brief reference number and then write out a description of the physical size, number of pages, condition—and of course some idea of the content.

"I'm putting what you taught me to good use, finally. I may not have your skill, professor, but I do want to get it right."

"I'm so glad to hear you say it, my boy. Very glad the spirit of the historian has been passed along to you."

They all stood up, sensing the finale. "Professor, thanks so much for seeing us," said Margaret, shaking the old man's clammy hand.

"Thank you," the professor said, in the same up-and-down pattern for the two words as he had used on Stephen's answer machine. "It's not every day treasures come back to us from the tomb."

~

"Blimey, he's a piece of work," said Margaret after she and Stephen were seated safely back in his car. "I wonder whatever became of your poor fellow student, Penelope. She probably killed herself before she got her degree."

"You're probably right. But congratulations for not letting him have it with both barrels. I do think we got some great information out of the old boy. Sorry to find out your Anne was a bit of a loose woman, but I think she seems rather wonderful. She'd have to have been, to keep Sir Henry Lee in thrall for over twenty years. It's a wonderful love story, don't you think?"

"Yes, I do," said Margaret who was really in the mood for a great love story, perhaps now more than ever.

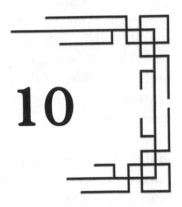

10

Very early Monday morning, Stephen left Margaret sleeping at the vicarage and slipped out from the guest room to his day job at St. George's. He had been trying to step away from most of his hands-on obligations at the school, but today there was one commitment he couldn't get out of, and didn't want to: taking thirty of his fifth- and sixth-form students on a long planned field trip to Stratford-upon-Avon.

He had the idea for this trip himself, and the plan was now to make this pilgrimage a regular yearly event at the school. For the fifth formers, it would energize their last two years at the school, and for the sixth, it would be a memorable start to their send-off year before they had to begin three or four very structured years elsewhere to lead them through the curriculum for the compulsory GCE and A-level exams that would determine where they might continue on to college. For all of them, Stephen wanted to heighten their appreciation for great literature so they wouldn't just sleep through their textbooks in the future. And what better way to open their eyes than to put them on their feet in a rehearsal room for an interactive workshop on *Macbeth* run by the country's premier acting troupe, the Royal Shakespeare Company.

Also, this was just the sort of innovative activity that had made St. Anne's headmistress, Mrs. Boardman, think that joining with the boys of St. George's might just take her own girls to a different level. She would be partnering with Stephen today as the co-leader of the trip, along with two classroom English teachers, Mister Meakins and Miss Davies, who worked with the students every day.

Mrs. Boardman was a charmingly professional lady in her late forties, who thought it was "very interesting" that her new partner in coeducation was a strapping and handsome young man not yet thirty. More important, she was impressed with Stephen for all he had achieved turning St. George's around, and for his vision of a brighter future for both of their schools. Early on, when planning the merger, she had some concerns about the disparity in salaries among the combined staff, but Stephen reworked all the numbers so the underpaid could simply be brought up to a compatible higher level—and who could complain about getting a raise? And he had also demonstrated, quite clearly, how all that could be achieved within the joint budget they had already agreed for running the school. So the business issues seemed sound, the staff and students were positively excited, and this field trip was just a taste of what might lie ahead for everyone.

Stephen drove into the parking lot at St. George's just as the first students were arriving and taking their places on the waiting motor coach for the trip. He walked over to Mister Meakins, who was by the door of the coach ticking off the names on the trip list, and started chatting about how the integration of the boys and girls seemed to be going, as seen from the front lines.

"Well," said Mister Meakins, "we have a lot less of the usual daydreaming and fidgeting among the boys. I've noticed they seem to be sitting up very straight and alert—as if someone was watching them very carefully. And they're right, because the girls can't seem to take their eyes off of them," he laughed.

"And the girls?" asked Stephen.

"They seem very comfortable. Like a pack of lionesses taking the measure of the zebras."

"My god," Stephen said with a laugh, "perhaps we should introduce a whole new set of self-defense lessons during P.E."

"Maybe the boys will be alerted to the dangers by *Macbeth*," added Mister Meakins. "I mean, the man probably wouldn't have gone through with everything without a push from his lady."

"Too true," said Stephen.

Just then Mrs. Boardman drove up, and Stephen went to greet her.

"Good morning," she said, alighting from her car.

"Yes, good morning," he replied. "We seem to have a good day for it."

"Stephen, if you don't mind, I thought you and I should go along together in my car—not yours—if that's all right?"

"Yes. You'll be glad to know I've already placed the order for a Volvo sedan for myself," said Stephen. "I'm saying goodbye to the Mini—although I'll probably just keep it in the garage in case I have some sort of crisis."

"Very good." She laughed. "The bigger one is just better for me now, sadly."

Within the next twenty minutes, the whole group had assembled and checked in, and then Stephen and Mrs. Boardman pulled out of the parking lot together in her car behind the rented coach. Once on the motorway they pulled ahead so they could arrive first, park, and announce themselves. The boys and girls smiled and waved from the coach windows as they flew by.

They arrived in the town center in less than two hours and well before the planned 10:30 a.m. start. Even though September 14 was outside the busiest tourist season, the place still seemed frantic with visitor activity. Stephen was glad Mrs. Boardman would be parking her car in a reserved visitor spot at the tiny Shakespeare Memorial Theatre car park, next to their school coach.

As they came in sight of their goal, Stephen realized whatever playbook the Shakespeare Trust had used to make the town appear Elizabethan must have been missing when they erected the red-brick Memorial Theatre back in the 1930s, according to Elisabeth Scott's winning design from a heated architectural competition. The local history captured comments ranging from "an insult to Shakespeare...like a tomb...so very ugly" to "heartwarming." Finally, after George Bernard Shaw approved, "many lesser people felt that not to do so would be rather dating." So the bold structure went forward and to Stephen, as they pulled in to the private car park, it looked like later generations had planted very large trees all around it to obscure the full effect of the rectangular austerity as much as they could. Nevertheless, it was a massive and spectacular brick and glass presence sitting in a manicured park beside the River Avon, with dozens of signature swans swimming around below the jutting balconies outside its cafeteria and vestibules.

Mrs. Boardman, Stephen, and the teachers had worked with the Royal Shakespeare Company educational staff all summer to fashion their workshop on *Macbeth*, a play that all of the students knew well. The RSC was providing a seasoned older actor as a facilitator and two younger members of the acting company to work beside the students for the whole session: Brian, who was a slim, pale, and short-haired copy of most of the boys from the school in the room (but ten years older); and Tessie, who was strikingly exotic, with beautiful ebony-colored skin, cornrowed hair, and the graceful moves of a dancer.

Filing off the coach after the journey, the boys and girls happily marched inside the vast theater and into a private area behind the main stage, where they left their things in a cloakroom. The group moved into a large rehearsal room just beside.

It was a well-lit windowless room, with a floor-to-ceiling mirror along one wall; a few folding chairs were arranged around the edges, intended for Stephen, Mrs. Boardman, and the teachers to sit and observe.

The kids stood milling around in the center of the room as the actors moved from cluster to cluster to chat and meet everyone before getting started.

Soon the older actor facilitating took charge. "Right, everyone. Welcome to the Shakespeare Memorial Theatre and our *Macbeth* workshop. I hope you've all met Brian and Tessie, our actors here to work with you today—you'll be seeing lots of them from now on. My name is John and I've been with the Royal Shakespeare Company for fifteen years, and I'll be moving us all through our paces. So now just sit down—right there on the floor—and get as comfortable as you can while I talk for a few minutes. You won't be sitting down too much today, so you might as well stretch out now and relax."

John explained the program. The RSC and their school had chosen *Macbeth* because, among other things, it had a strong juxtaposition of the leading woman's role and the leading man's role, and, as John understood it, the boy and girl students here today had only recently come together in a combined coeducational school—"so gender roles must seem very interesting to all of you. Indeed."

John went on. First he would talk through a three-minute recap of the play and then they would have an opening exercise. After that, they would break up into five groups of six, boys and girls together. Everyone was then going to focus on three key moments in the play. First, Lady Macbeth's opening scene, when she reads a letter from her husband about his success and promotion. That's when she decides she's going to get him to kill the king since the witches have promised he'll get the crown. Next, they'll move on to the scene when Lady Macbeth persuades her doubting husband to find the courage to murder the king. And finally they'll finish after the crime with the scene with all the blood.

But first, there was the opening exercise. John had everyone stand and sort themselves into two groups of fifteen. Actor Brian would take one group out of the room stage left, and actress Tessie would take the others out stage right. They were going to trot out the door and follow the actors jogging up five flights of stairs. Then they would cross over the top of the actual main stage of the theater, moving across the lighting gangway just under the roof of the soaring building, then down the stairs on the other side and back here into the rehearsal room. The idea was to get everyone's blood going, and shake any cobwebs off from the two-hour bus ride. "Now off you go," ended John.

After the kids trotted away behind the actors. John then came over to Stephen, Mrs. Boardman, and the teachers and showed them the handouts the group would be using for the first scene. The RSC had selected seventeen consecutive lines from the speech Lady Macbeth makes in her opening letter-reading scene just after she has decided to murder King Duncan. Those five sentences that had been typed out as five separate hand-outs—one for each working group of six kids. The speech was parsed out as follows:

The raven himself is hoarse
That croaks the fatal entrance of Duncan
Under my battlements.

Come, you spirits
That tend on mortal thoughts, unsex me here,
And fill me from the crown to the toe top-full
Of direst cruelty!

Make thick my blood;
Stop up the access and passage to remorse,
That no compunctuous visitings of nature
Shake my fell purpose, nor keep peace between
The effect and it.

Come to my woman's breasts,
And take my milk for gall, you murdering ministers,
Wherever in your sightless substances,
You wait on nature's mischief!

Come, thick night,
And pall thee in the dunnest smoke of hell,
That my keen knife see not the wound it makes,
Nor heaven peep through the blanket of the dark,
To cry "Hold, hold!"

The students were coming back from their stair exercise by now and John settled them into their small work groups of six each and read through the whole speech once aloud so they could hear it all together. Brian and Tessie handed out the copies along with markers.

"Right," said John. "Each group now has one of these sentences. I want each of you to read through it, and underline the words or phrase you think to be the most important on your page." After a minute he continued, "All right. Anyone care to share?"

Several hands went up and John chose a boy sitting right next to him. "All right there, what words did you choose?"

"'Direst cruelty,'" said the boy.

"Why those?"

"Because they show she is asking for the very worst—to be filled with the worst sort of cruelty so she can do something terrible."

"Okay," said John. "And your name is...?"

"James."

"Right, James, would you mind standing up now and say those words with some sort of gesture or movement that you think Lady Macbeth might use to get her point across."

The boy stood up somewhat tentatively, but with Tessie smiling, giving hints, and encouraging him, he managed to bend his arms, make his hands into fists, bend forward from the waist, and say "direst cruelty" through clenched teeth.

"That's good," said John. "Just the right idea. Now I think that was about a 'two.' Why not do it again and this time make it be a 'five.' Really go for it. Remember, she wants to commit murder."

The boy took a deep breath and spat out "direst cruelty" with real venom as he thrust his fists forward—in fact, his face turned red and he almost fell over.

"That's it. Well done," said John. "Anyone else?"

A girl in the same group thrust up her hand.

"Yes, all right. And your name is...?"

"Sarah."

"Sarah, what words did you choose from the same passage?"

"I chose 'unsex me here,'" said Sarah, shaking her ponytail off the side of her face and flicking it to the back of her head as she looked up at John.

Mrs. Boardman leaned over to Stephen and said, "Well, I think she's got everyone's attention now." Stephen nodded, looking closely at the kids, who seemed transfixed, as were the teachers.

"Right, well done," said John. "And what do you think Lady Macbeth meant by that?"

"Well, she's a woman...and I think she means she wants the gods to take all that womanness out of her, so she can do something really horrible and unnatural—like murder."

"Okay, Sarah, can you stand up now and put a gesture to that for us?"

The girl stood as all eyes in the room were fixed on her. She balanced herself evenly on the balls of her feet, closed her eyes, and raised her arms above her shoulders. And then, as she almost shouted "unsex me here," she brought her hands down, moving them in semicircles across the front of her body, then down and back out to the sides of her knees in a flowing motion, bending her knees and springing back up as she said "here."

"Brilliant," said John. "Say something about that."

"Well, I meant to show I was taking everything inside me that makes me a woman and then washing it out of me, so I would be free of all that later when I did what I had to do."

"Okay," said John. "That's excellent. Now, would the rest of your group please stand up with you here? I want you all to put together the two things that James and Sarah just said and did as we chant that full line. As you can see on your handouts, the line is 'unsex me here, / And fill me from the crown to the toe top-full / Of direst cruelty.' When you say 'unsex me here,' make Sarah's motion and then try to flow into James's gesture by the time you end on 'direst cruelty.' I'll do it along with you. Okay, let's give it a try now."

John led them, chanting the single line and going through the motions as a group. "All right, that's our 'two.' Now, let's do it again now and go for our 'five.'"

He was right: the first go was not bad, but the second one was much better—and everyone could see how the motions brought out the meaning. There was quite a lot of murmuring going on as the onlookers whispered with one another about how effective the exercise had been.

"Well, we certainly went from a 'two' to a 'four,' so now keep working with it among yourselves and take it higher. And now everyone in the other groups, get going on underlining the key words and phrases in *your* sentences and then work together on the motions. Brian, Tessie, and I will be coming 'round to you to help. So let's take time now and work on all that."

"That was very impressive," said Mrs. Boardman to her fellow teachers. "It just shows the difference between simply reading the script and acting the play."

"Yes," said Mister Meakins. "Perhaps we should actually have the students work just this way on these sorts of things in our classroom?"

"Indeed," said Stephen, very impressed at what he had just seen.

As promised, John, Brian, and Tessie walked around, sitting, standing, and coaching all of the groups. In about fifteen minutes, everyone declared themselves ready for a complete read-through of the seventeen-line speech with their accompanying gestures and movements.

Watching, Stephen thought the kids were wonderful doing this. Their inhibitions were going away and they all seemed to be really getting into it. As they read through their sentences, they punched out the key phrases and swayed rhythmically to accompany the words. The overall effect was powerful.

Stephen, Mrs. Boardman, and the teachers huddled during the first break.

"This is the way to do it," confided Miss Davies. "When we were reading through *Macbeth* in the classroom last week, it was a real struggle to keep the whole class engaged. This is so much more. I never thought to introduce the movement, gestures, and so on. Now I know what the RSC people meant when they told me they taught 'Shakespeare on your feet.'"

"Yes," added Mister Meakins. "But I think we'd be missing a trick if we just keep this for the oldest students. I think we should start this much earlier—when the kids are even more comfortable with playing and acting out."

"Very good idea, Mister Meakins," said Mrs. Boardman.

Just then, they all noticed a boy had come over to Stephen and was waiting there quietly, while the adults had been talking.

"Please, sir...Mister White," said the boy.

Stephen turned and was surprised to see young Denis Juric there, the boy from his summer cricket practice.

"Hello, Juric. How can I help?"

"Sir, we want you to come with us now. And this is Sophie," replied Juric, nodding to a girl Stephen hadn't noticed, standing just on his other side.

"Sophie. Well, hello," Stephen said to the pretty and mischievous-looking pre-teen girl, who startled him by reaching out and taking his right hand. Then Juric took his left hand and he felt totally surprised.

"Hello, sir," said Sophie. "We need you to come with us just now please. We're going to kill you."

"What?" Stephen managed to get out before the booming voice of facilitator John interrupted it all.

"Come on, Mister White," said John. "We need you over here as King Duncan. It will be just like your day job. You stroll about looking important and everyone bows to you. Come over here now and help us, will you?"

Everyone laughed and Stephen felt himself blushing, something he could never control.

The students were ready to start work on the next scene, where Macbeth has doubts but Lady Macbeth persuades him to kill the king, who is just arriving at the castle as a guest.

"You'd better get over there," laughed Mrs. Boardman, as Stephen began to understand he was being drafted into the workshop—and not just as an observer.

The class was standing in a circle in the center of the rehearsal room, with facilitator John in the middle. Stephen stood up, smiled, and the kids dropped his hands as he took off his jacket. Then Juric took his left hand, and Sophie took the right, and lifted them up high as they ceremoniously slow-marched with him toward the circle.

"All hail, King Duncan," the class boomed out.

Well, here I go to be murdered, thought Stephen. And how enthusiastic they all seem about it.

~

After that, the rest of the workshop only got better. Next, Macbeth, acted out by all the boys, delivered a soliloquy and then told his wife they were no longer going to kill the king. And then Lady Macbeth told him right back to "man up" and do the deed, and he gave in. The girls really liked that.

For the final scene, a makeup crew came in with smocks for all the students and splattered them copiously with fake blood. So when all the boy Macbeths came in with their bloody daggers and then all the Lady Macbeths went offstage to smear the king's guards with blood to frame them for the crime, the kids really put their hearts and souls into acting it all.

By three o'clock everyone was saying their goodbyes to John, Brian, Tessie, and the impressive Memorial Theatre, leaving about ninety minutes in their day for a visit to Shakespeare's supposed schoolroom, which was only a five-minute walk from the theater.

As arranged, a special tour guide was waiting for them and led them from the entry hall of the timbered old village guildhall, past a waiting queue of tourists, and upstairs into the ancient classroom where Shakespeare allegedly had been schooled. At the front, another guide was dressed in Tudor period robes and cap and stood holding a fearsome-looking cane made out of long birch twigs. He bellowed out the order for all the students to sit down and fill up the desks, holding the cane aloft as a threatened weapon.

As the man acted out his set piece with the students, he introduced himself as Shakespeare's supposed actual teacher, Thomas Jenkins, and made the point that the students would have been all boys back in the 1570s, but the curriculum would probably be familiar to each of them today. It was mostly a lot of Latin—which all of these contemporary English children had also suffered through for several years—followed by a smattering of numbers and science. The day would have started at 6:00 a.m. in the summer, and an hour later in winter, and continued on until 5:00 p.m. Everything would have been free, provided by the borough council. The old desks they sat at, covered with deeply carved initials of the former students, were all actually Georgian rather than Elizabethan, but they looked incredibly ancient as it was.

"They missed a trick with the whitewashed walls," whispered Stephen to Mrs. Boardman. "They would actually have been brownish, mixed with the mud and bush cuttings from the local fields. And the beams would have been light brown, not dark as the mock-Tudor buildings are today. Also, things wouldn't have been this clean: Shakespeare's father, John, was fined for having a large unauthorized dung hill out front."

Mrs. Boardman smiled. "And they wouldn't have had a big gift shop downstairs either," she whispered back at him, obviously very pleased with how the day had gone.

In the ground-floor shop, Stephen bought a booklet of Shakespearean insults to share with the students back at school when they were restless in class. He thumbed through it as they walked away from the guildhall toward the waiting school coach, liking Shakespeare's line "The first thing we do, let's kill all the lawyers." That's really timeless, he thought.

The visit had been a great success, both for the students and also the merger. There was no doubt Mrs. Boardman was really looking forward to working in the new partnership with Stephen and St. George's. And Stephen was hoping she might become a strong enough force to take over running the school for both the girls and the boys—which would let him escape the headmaster's job and get on with his life. Back in the car, the two chatted away happily all the way home.

PART THREE

1580–1581. Beneath the Queen, preferment at court was a fickle affair, with competition intense among those bold enough to seek it.

Top of the heap in 1580 was Robert Dudley, Earl of Leicester. His hazardous adolescent friendship with Elizabeth had secured his position for many years, though it was now showing signs of strain. At the death of Edward VI, Dudley's father, the Duke of Northumberland, led a rebellion to put Lady Jane Grey on the throne. Along with Lady Jane, Queen Mary sent the elder Dudley to death on the scaffold and imprisoned his family. That put young Robert in the Tower exactly when Princess Elizabeth was there herself, confined under suspicion from yet another rebellion. The two became the closest of friends and for many years early in Queen Elizabeth's reign he lived in the apartment next to her, sparking rumors of romance. Unfortunately, he jeopardized his position with the jealous queen by a secret marriage in 1578—which perhaps explained his lavish 1580 new year's gift to Elizabeth as a means of retaining his footing.

Just below, and momentarily coming up strong, was Edward de Vere, the 17th Earl of Oxford. His earldom was the oldest in England, and brought with it the role of the hereditary Lord Great Chamberlain of England. He came to prominence early, inheriting his title at age twelve, on the death of his father in 1562. Because of the importance of his hereditary position, he was made a royal ward and taken away from his family for formal education and training. This meant moving from his ancestral home at Castle Hedingham in Essex to the London mansion of Elizabeth's chief minister, Lord Burghley, who was also master of the court of wards. Burghley lived in the palatial Cecil House on the Strand, which had the finest private library in England. No fewer than twenty young noblemen and their tutors were lodged there for protective development. By rank, Oxford was top of the pack, and he arrived immediately after his father's funeral at the head of a troop of 140 men, all dressed in mourning black.

However, the Earl of Oxford had a very bad temper and he soon acquired, along with the great talent in music and literature he showed from an early age, a reputation for being quarrelsome and dangerous. For example, in July 1567, Lord Burghley noted in his diary that the earl had inflicted a fatal wound on Thomas Bryncknell, an undercook at Cecil House. Burghley also noted that he had successfully persuaded a jury to deliver a verdict of felo-de-se, attributing the man's death to his accidentally "running upon a poynt of a fence sword of the said earle."

When Anne Vavasour had come to court, Oxford was twenty-nine years old, well traveled, a central figure at court, and an accomplished rider in the tilts. He wrote poetry and maintained his family's own company of actors, writing comedies for them. In his capacity as Lord Great Chamberlain, he carried the sword of state in front of the Queen in ceremonial processions. He was also on the prowl, estranged from his wife, Lord Burghley's daughter, Anne Cecil, and looking for diversions.

Soon after Anne Vavasour's successful debut dancing for the Queen, Oxford and Anne could often be seen walking together. Also, from the description of her in a poem said to be written together by the couple, they also spent time at his nearby seaside estate in Essex, east of London.

And so it is not too much of a surprise to read about "a grave scandal at court" in a letter written on March 23, 1581, by Elizabeth's spymaster Francis Walsingham:

On Tuesday at night Anne Vavasour was brought to bed of a son in the maidens' chamber. The E. of Oxford is avowed to be the father, who hath withdrawn himself with intent, as it is thought, to pass the seas. The ports are laid for him and therefore if he have any such determination it is not likely that he will escape. The gentlewoman the selfsame night she was delivered was conveyed out of the house and the next day committed to the Tower. Others that have been found any ways party to the cause have also been committed. Her majesty is greatly grieved with the accident, and therefore I hope there will be some order taken as the like inconvenience will be avoided.

~

It took time for the scandal to blow over. By June, Anne had left her confinement in the Tower and slipped into anonymity to start raising her bastard son, named Edward Vere. She was helped by the de Vere family as well as the Knyvets. The Earl of Oxford was also confined in the Tower, and was banned from court for two years. The Knyvet family remained fiercely loyal to Anne, blaming Oxford for her trouble. For several years, Sir Thomas Knyvet harassed the earl, culminating in a duel in which Oxford was seriously wounded, remaining lame for life. He never did regain his favor with the Queen at court and became a sad figure, heeding the royal order to reconcile with his wife and systematically selling off all forty-five of his estates to settle debts. To avoid final embarrassment and maintain him in a style appropriate for his position, the Queen finally awarded him an annual allowance of two thousand pounds.

Meanwhile, Anne's family and friends cloaked her in the respectability of an arranged marriage to one John Finch, a sea captain often gone for months as a minor member of the Muscovy Company delegation dispatched for trade and diplomacy to the court of Ivan the Terrible, Tsar of all the Russias.

Meanwhile, living mostly by herself in England and outside the palace, Anne maintained close connections to friends at court.

She was not, by nature, a woman to spend much time alone.

From "Woman's Changeableness," a poem by Edward de Vere, 17th Earl of Oxford

If women could be fair and yet not fond,
Or that their love were firm and fickle, still,
I would not marvel that they make men bond,
By service long to purchase their good will;
But when I see how frail those creatures are,
I muse that men forget themselves so far.

Lines from Verses made by the Earle of Oxforde and Mrs Anne Vavasour

(1) Verses Made by the Earle of Oxforde

Sitting alone upon my thoughte, in melancholy moode,
In sighte of sea, and at my back, an ancyente
hoarye woode,
I saw a faire young lady come, her secret feares to wayle,
Cladd all in colour of a Nun and covered with a vaylle:
Yet (for the day was calme and cleare) I myghte
discern her face,
As one myghte see a damaske rose hid under
christall glasse:
Three times with her softe hand full hard on her left
side she knocks,
And sighed so sore as myghte have moved some
pity in the rocks:
From syghes, and sheddinge amber teares, into
sweet songe she brake,
When thus the Echo answered her to everye word
she spake:

163

(2) Anne Vavesor's Eccho

O heavens, who was ye first that bredd in me this
fevere? Vere.
Whoe was the first that gave ye wounde whose
feare I ware for evere? Vere.
What tyrant, Cupid, to mye harme usurps thy
golden quivere? Vere.

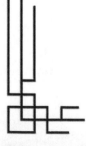

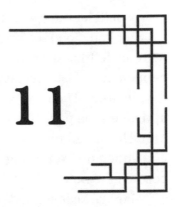

11

After the last class on Tuesday, Stephen was handed an urgent message to come to the school office. Verger Andrew had just called to leave word that Vicar Hamilton had died. Stephen should come to the vicarage as soon as he could.

He felt the reality of the loss sweep over him, making all of his everyday plans so small and irrelevant in the face of the finality of death. He already knew how it felt to have one parent die and he was so glad to still have his mother. Now Margaret had lost both. It must be the loneliest feeling in the world, he thought.

Stephen drove directly from the school to the vicarage. The vicar had never woken up, Andrew told him at the door. Margaret had sat next to her father most of the day, talking to him and reading. But sometime after noon there were erratic signals from all the bedside monitors and she ran out to the nursing station just outside. Then the medical team asked her to leave and stay in the waiting room. An hour later, the doctor came out and told her he was gone. Andrew was the first person she called and he came over to the hospital right away. She spent a few minutes with her father alone, and then they both walked home to the vicarage. She was in her father's office now, trying to reach her father's brother and her mother's cousin. Once she got them, they would let the rest of the family know.

Stephen stood looking out into the garden from the lounge, with his left hand resting on the vicar's reading chair. It had all happened so fast. His last call with the vicar had been only ten days before. Then the vicar had been so excited at Stephen's update on the papers, and as happy as Stephen had ever known him. He was all positive energy and hope for the future. Now he was gone and everything that Margaret had been dreading had become the new and bleak reality.

Margaret came into the lounge at that moment, her eyes red and her face streaked with tears. Stephen went over and hugged her. "Margaret, I'm so sorry." It was all he could get out, and yet just that had the effect of starting her to cry again. They just stood together for a minute or so, and then she calmed and came gently away to arm's length so she could look up at him.

"You know, I didn't get to say goodbye. All those machines started flashing and beeping, and they sent me out. I think they tried a few desperate things to revive him, but in the end nothing worked. I went in after and said a few things alone, even though I knew he couldn't hear me. I didn't believe it, but...he was really gone, all in just a moment. When I touched his hand, it seemed he was already starting to get cold."

Stephen just hugged her close again. Half of him wanted to console her by saying that her father didn't suffer and now would be with the God he worshipped so completely—but his better half knew he shouldn't sugarcoat the reality of this tragedy now. Not for Margaret.

After a few minutes, Stephen guided her over to the sofa and sat down with her. She was still shaking, and he turned to Verger Andrew as he held her. "Andrew, what's next? Do you know?"

"Of course, it will be up to Margaret and the family," Andrew replied. "I did, however, call the bishop's office to let them know.

Normally we'd issue a statement to the newspapers and let the townspeople know any plans for the service. We already did make a special announcement at Sunday's service about how ill he was, so the congregation is very aware. Someone will have to write an obituary notice as well and we'd place that. Then there might be some questions from the press, especially after the coverage of those papers being found. And the bishop would preside at the funeral ceremony."

"Oh god. Not the bishop," said Margaret. She couldn't stand the man's pompous self-appreciation. "I can handle the press, but not 'his lordship'—maybe my aunt can cover him for me."

They sat in silence briefly, until the doorbell rang. Andrew answered and brought in two of the village policemen to the lounge: Sergeant Stokes, whom Stephen and Margaret had already met, and his chief of the village police. "We're sorry to intrude, Miss Hamilton, at this sad time for you," said the chief. "I wanted to convey our condolences from the entire force. The vicar was always a kind and steadying force all the times he worked with us. He was a familiar face in times of trouble, ministering to many traumatized people at fires and times of family tragedies when we'd ask him to step in. I personally recall his kind visits to me two years ago when I was in hospital after my heart attack. I wasn't the most frequent face at his services, yet he stopped in to see me almost every day and we'd have a nice chat. We just wanted you to know, miss, how highly we valued him."

"Thank you very much," said Margaret. "It means so much to hear you say it."

"I also wanted to let you know about a change in the investigation of all this. It's very likely—in fact, it is certain—that the vicar's death will now be ruled 'suspicious.' That's in light of how all this began, with Verger Andrew finding him unconscious, and then the doctors thinking it was from a blow struck on his head, not just a fall, and now the robbery. Our village force will never take the lead on any investigation where a homicide may be suspected. Detectives at the county level or higher will be assigned. That will mean, at some point, that all of you here— Verger Andrew, Mister White, and you, Miss Hamilton—will surely be interviewed again, as well as everyone else who had touched the case in any significant way. That might seem redundant and very annoying, but, as you can imagine, we will want the most experienced and professional people to help us with this. We are all dedicated to finding the truth, most especially when we are dealing with the death of someone as respected and beloved as your dear father, miss. While we won't be in charge of the continuing investigation, please call me directly if you need me to intervene in any way. I would take it as an honor to help you after the vicar's twenty-five years of service to us all."

"Thank you, chief. That's a great comfort."

"We'll also be keeping an eye on your safety here while the investigation is on. Nothing intrusive. Just keeping an eye on the vicarage round the clock during our regular patrols."

"Again, thank you."

"We'll be going now, miss. You'll be in our prayers."

Then Verger Andrew walked them to the door as Stephen and Margaret sank back onto the sofa, suddenly very tired with it all.

~

The next two dull days of approaching autumn went by without Stephen or Margaret really living them. The loss of Margaret's father colored each day with a persistent ache that began on awakening and continued throughout the day.

Stephen helped Margaret with the obituaries for the *Village Advertiser*, the newspaper for the larger town nearby, and the local paper where the vicar had grown up. Stepping back to write them only underlined how Margaret's father had just disappeared in an instant from the normality of the previous twenty-five years.

When they started writing, Margaret rummaged around in her father's desk for his old CV and biography, but then just fell down onto the desk chair and cried for five minutes with her elbows propped up holding her head. Stephen just let her alone to get it out.

Verger Andrew had been right about the other logistics after the death. After Margaret placed the obituaries, she had to speak to reporters from the *Advertiser* and also to the local BBC East office in Norwich, who were now onto the case. Now the funeral was set for Friday morning, with viewings for the public on the day before at the local funeral home. Stephen would be at her side for all that.

At the funeral service, the bishop presided. The children and teachers from St. George's, where the vicar had been the chaplain, walked down the hill to fill the back of the church by 10:20 a.m., the boys on one side and the girls across the aisle. All the children were delighted at the morning off from their normal routine and the youngest were giggly in the pews. Stephen had to walk over and put the fear of God back into everyone with a stern glare. Then he returned to sit next to Margaret and her family at the front. He saw the police and the fire brigade were well represented. After the service and homily, the burial would be in the clergy's small section of the churchyard, just next to the wall of the chancel and nearest to the altar, where all the clerical bodies were placed facing east so as to be in prime position with their flock on resurrection day.

The church choir opened the service with the vicar's favorite funeral hymn, "Be not afraid, I go before you always." Margaret had heard it scores of times when her father presided. The rest seemed to proceed in a blur until the reading of Psalm 23 just before the bishop was to speak. Vicar Hamilton had always said the King James Version of it was the perfection of prayer, and Margaret knew it had the words her father would have wanted:

The LORD is my shepherd;
I shall not want.
He maketh me to lie down in green pastures;
he leadeth me beside the still waters.
He restoreth my soul;
he leadeth me in the paths of righteousness for
his Name's sake.
Yea, though I walk through the valley of the
shadow of death,
I will fear no evil; for thou art with me;
thy rod and thy staff, they comfort me.
Thou preparest a table for me in the presence
of my enemies;
Thou anointest my head with oil;
my cup runneth over.
Surely goodness and mercy shall follow me all the
days of my life,
and I will dwell in the house of the LORD forever.

Margaret had never liked the bishop, although her father seemed quite content with him as his boss. To her, he seemed to move as if standing on a kind of float, cruising down the aisle of the church, or even inside the vicarage, as if he were standing on a low cloud that lifted him along while he could turn side to side, dispensing downward benedictions with each slight dip of his hand. But that was the job, she supposed. Stephen actually felt her stiffen as the bishop ascended the stairs of the pulpit and set his hands melodramatically along the sides of the lectern, peering down on the congregation from under his ridiculous glittering miter.

The words seemed harmless and appropriate enough as the bishop remembered Vicar Hamilton's twenty-five years of leadership and service to the community, building up to the possible foul play that put him into his coma and final days. That's when the sage bishop moved on to counsel the congregation on how to behave going forward.

He abandoned his prepared eulogy and decided to ad-lib his memory of another tragic scene—the one at Enniskillen, five years before. "It was in November 1987," the bishop intoned, "that the British people were reminded of the Christian way to handle the blind and dumb adversity of an evil act. Eleven were killed and sixty-four injured by the terrorist bombing of the Remembrance Day parade in Enniskillen, Northern Ireland, and even five years later, one victim still remains in a coma. Buried in the rubble that day were a sixty-two-year-old draper, Gordon Wilson, and his daughter Marie, a nurse. Wilson held his daughter as she died; her last words were 'Daddy, I love you very much.' As Wilson told that story to the nation's hushed listeners on the BBC, he then astonished everyone by adding, 'But I bear no ill will. I bear no grudge. Dirty sort of talk is not going to bring her back to life. She was a great wee lassie. She loved her profession. She was a pet. She's dead. She's in heaven and we shall meet again. I will pray for these men who killed her tonight and every night.' Now faced with the tragedy that has befallen this village today, we must all embrace this spirit of Enniskillen."

While the hymns and Psalm 23 had the desired effect of comforting Margaret, the bishop's words on Enniskillen reignited her soul, but hardly in the way the bishop intended. Her coloring was back and she wasn't stunned or moping as just before. Stephen had his hands full just restraining her from leaping up and strangling the bishop, now suspended above them in his lofty perch. At the burial, Margaret couldn't even speak to him, which he probably put down to great grief. Luckily the plan was for her aunt from Yorkshire to step in to deliver the family's thanks for his lordship's pontification.

"Forgive the bloody murderers who hit him on his head," hissed Margaret to Stephen. "I want to cut their bloody balls off," she spat out, finally shaking off his arm. "To think that arsehole would stand up to everyone in the village and say let it all go, let's forgive the murderers and move on—what an idiot! He's campaigning for his own canonization, for god's sake. You mark my words, I'm going to get to the bottom of whoever did this and make sure they pay, all right—they'll damn well pay."

Well, thought Stephen, Margaret is back.

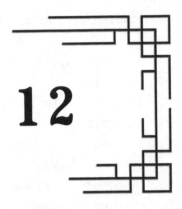

12

Margaret had not cooled down very much by the time of her interview with the new detectives Saturday.

In a light rain, she walked over to the local police station for the ten o'clock meeting with the heavyweights from the county police. Everything started out cordially enough. For the first fifteen minutes or so, she chatted over coffee with the two men interviewing her. One man was a bit older, very polished, and in a good suit, and the other was short, stocky, and a bit rougher-looking—he was quiet at the start.

Answering the first questions from the older man, she told them when she had heard the story of the papers from her father in her regular telephone calls to check in. Yes, he was very excited, and very glad that he had Stephen White, her former fiancé, right in the village to help him understand just what they were.

"And do you know how Mister White became involved with all this, Miss Hamilton?" asked the second man, the quieter detective.

"I believe my father called him right at the start...just after he had found the papers in a box in the vault. He saw they were very old, in an ancient style of handwriting, and he knew that Stephen had studied those sorts of things at Oxford. So he called him to come over. I think they actually took the rest of the papers out from the burial vault together, and then carried them up into the vicarage to dry out."

"Did your father call anyone else to come look at the papers?" continued the man.

"I don't think so. I mean, I think he wanted Stephen to help him understand what was there first—the likely dating and something of what the papers were about. And, I must say, Stephen told him they were from the precise period that he'd studied back in college, so he was obviously someone who could give my father a good answer."

"Doesn't it seem that as the vicar of the church your father should have alerted his superiors that something of such an unusual nature had been discovered?" countered the man, looking at her rather closely for her reaction.

"Well, there was the further point that the tomb these things were in belonged to a family member of ours: a direct relative on my late mother's side. So I think he was aware that it was somewhat personal to our own family. Doesn't seem very odd to me. And he certainly let Verger Andrew know what he'd found. He might have told his church secretary and superiors as well. I'm not sure of that. But he probably did. I mean, it all came out in the village newspaper soon enough." Margaret felt herself sitting up a bit straighter as she made her response.

"Actually, miss, we have heard your father kept quite quiet about the details. This seemed to provoke a degree of speculation about 'treasure in the tombs' and so on. Did he mention he was holding back about details to you?"

"No. I mean, I think he was probably waiting to hear more about it all from Mister White, who was looking everything over." She found herself choosing her words very carefully now and she felt her color changing.

"Apparently, Mister White was removing quantities of these papers from the vicarage, allegedly to study them off site. Were you aware of that?"

"I understood he was taking things home and reviewing them in the evening and in moments he had free to do so—I mean, he has a full-time job at school and the new term was just starting."

"Did your father mention he was keeping track of what was being held at the vicarage and what was being removed—some sort of list, perhaps?"

"No. In fact, I think part of what Stephen—I mean, Mister White—was doing was making up an inventory of exactly what the papers were. A descriptive record. He wanted to make sure that was in place before the papers were sent to any outside experts for review, to make sure we had a list of what was there."

"Doesn't that seem to give Mister White too much of a free hand with all this?"

"It's a question of trust, isn't it? Mister White and I were engaged. He was almost a member of our family, too, and my father was very fond of him—and vice versa."

"But that was all broken off, wasn't it?"

"Yes, but only because I—I mean we—wanted to take more time and not be so rushed right after graduating college and so on." Margaret found she was surprising herself by stretching the truth a bit.

"You seem to be very defensive just now, miss," interrupted the older detective, taking charge of the dialogue again.

"Well, I must say, I am a bit caught out by how you seem to be attacking Mister White—oh damn it, I mean, how you are attacking *Stephen*. When he's been so great about all of this, helping my father, being back with me at the hospital, and now going through all the horrors of the funeral and so on."

"I'm sorry if we seem to have provoked you, Miss Hamilton," said the older detective in an exceptionally calm voice, impervious to the way Margaret was heating up. "But, as a reporter, you must be aware of how the situation could look from another perspective other than your own at this time. Mister White has had carte blanche with what could be a very valuable trove of antique documents. He inserted himself into a position of influence with your father—who has now been the victim of what seems to be a vicious crime—and now he is suddenly back at your side during what has become a very vulnerable time for you."

"Well, it's damn well because he was so close to us because he liked my father. And because he is probably still in love with me—and me with him. If you can't see that yourselves, then you're just clueless at your jobs as detectives, or whoever the hell you are."

~

A few minutes after that, just as Margaret stormed out of the front door of the police station, Stephen sat unaware in a corridor on the other side of the building, looking at his watch and noting that it was now thirty minutes after his own interview had been scheduled to start. Comparing notes with Margaret later, they realized their time slots had been arranged to overlap deliberately so they wouldn't be able to see each other in between the interviews.

When he was finally shown into the same room where Margaret had recently exploded, the detectives were not yet fully composed. At first Stephen had thought he was on friendly ground, and happy there was a coffee there for him. But then they led him through an intense reliving of his fight night in the pub with Miranda and Tony, and even his life history, with a special focus on "Miss Hamilton."

Driving away after the session, Stephen resented how the detectives tried to make him feel like a despicable loser. Yes, he was a headmaster working with young boys in the village. No, he was not, nor had he ever been, a homosexual. Yes, he had been sleeping with Miranda when the vicar called him. Yes, later at the pub she told him she was pregnant and he insulted her. Yes, her big brother Tony then came over and punched him. Yes, he almost ran him over in the car park. Yes, back at the start of all this he helped the vicar lift the treasure from the tomb. Yes, he took the most promising items away from the vicar and back to his flat. No, he had not given the vicar a list of what he had taken. Yes, he intercepted Miss Hamilton in the waiting room where she was crying over her comatose father. Yes, he had spent every night afterward with her. No, he wasn't lurking around Miss Hamilton, spinning a foul and evil web to ensnare her with his affections. And yes, he had even taken her away to Oxford—but not to relive their happy college days.

Perhaps he should just drive over to the river outside the village, put stones in his coat pocket, and walk in to drown himself, like Virginia Woolf in River Ouse.

~

Margaret was waiting for him at the vicarage. As he parked his car, he decided there was nothing to be gained from letting himself complain to her about his rough treatment. He would just try to suck all of that up, and stay fresh.

"How was your interview?" she began with mock brightness.

"Fine, very uplifting," said Stephen. "At least they can't think that I'm hiding anything, because I'm obviously pure crap."

"Not to worry. I know from work experience that no one ever feels good after interacting with our police force—myself included. I even shouted them down when I met with them. They do deliberately try to provoke you, you know. They hope to catch you out."

Margaret told him how she had defended him. As she played back parts of her interrogation, Stephen couldn't help but think how passionate she was. Perhaps she was on her way to coming

177

back to him, he hoped. She had smashed each of the questions back at them as if she were wielding a cricket bat.

"At the end," she said, "I surprised myself—because I blurted out you were probably helping so much because you still loved me. And then I said I probably still loved you, too."

"Margaret—" Stephen began, but she cut him off.

"No, Stephen, I never went off you. You must know that. That wasn't the reason I had to stop the engagement. I can see that all now. It was just being scared about getting boxed into life in this village as a 'headmaster's wife.' I'd been looking forward to going out into the world since I was about eight, I suppose. The BBC job had just the sort of 'world orientation' I was hoping for, and it was all going so well. Then when you took over your father's place at the school—and I know you had to do it, and I respect you for doing it—but it was as if any hope of the future I'd dreamed of was going away. That's not how to go forward into a marriage, is it?"

"Well, it was a confusing and difficult time," said Stephen, trying to be as honest and open as she was. "Everything just seemed to shift at once, with my father suddenly dead and my mother so injured, and then just the bald fact that the new school term was supposed to start in September—and I was sucked in. It wasn't what I wanted either."

They just let the silence hang in the air for a few moments.

"Just so you know," Stephen continued, "I never went off you either. Meanwhile, here we are again, in the midst of another disaster. I have no idea how it will all turn out, so let's just keep going and help each other get through it. We don't have to figure everything out right now. I'm going to have another glass of wine, Margaret. Can I get you one?" he asked, heading into the kitchen. "Then I want to show you something new."

"Yes. Lovely," she answered, feeling relief at the realization she wasn't really alone anymore.

"Come into the dining room," said Stephen, putting the two wineglasses on the dining room table and walking over to grab his briefcase as Margaret came in and sat down.

"We made a joke the other day about whether Shakespeare would show up—you know, whether he knew Anne and Sir Henry. Well at least one of his *friends* may just have showed up early this morning when I was putting a little time in looking at the papers." Stephen took out a short note from his briefcase. "This note is very short and cryptic, but I think it may be signed by John Heminge, who was one of the actors in the same troupe as Shakespeare. He was also the business manager—the one who collected the money for the plays they put on at court and so on."

"Good lord," said Margaret. "What does it say?"

"It's addressed to 'Mistress Vavasour' to thank her 'for the cut that woke the Dane now pry'd back out from J.' And then there's just the signature 'Heminge.'"

"What does that mean?"

"Well, I'm not sure. Perhaps he was returning something that was attached to this note. I'm also not certain that this Heminge is the same Heminge or Heminges involved with Shakespeare. Since the actor Heminge signed contracts and leases for theaters and so on, there must be examples of his signature down at the British Museum, the National Archives, or somewhere. So I need to get down to London next week. None of the likely places are open for research on weekends, of course."

"The cut that woke the Dane?"

"No ideas yet really. I mean, I thought that the most famous Dane for Shakespeare would be Hamlet—the 'melancholy Dane'—or someone else in that play—but I can't remember any Dane getting cut and waking up. Maybe the Ghost? But then, I also have to read over that play again and check."

"Wow. Would a note like this from the actor Heminge have value?"

"I don't know about money. The man himself isn't a great celebrity today. But I do know it would fuel rampant speculation and scholarly hubbub on an enormous scale. I mean there are literally thousands of articles published each year about minutiae related to Shakespeare. It's an industry. Crazy theories everywhere, and this would throw petrol on the bonfire. Of course, I'm hoping I might find something else among your papers that helps explain the message. I still have quite a few things to wade through, but I intend to scan through everything I haven't read yet as soon as I can to see if anything jumps out."

"Very exciting."

"And I also wanted to show you that scroll Professor Rowe was asking about."

Stephen opened the long top drawer of the buffet and lifted out the scroll carefully. He put one edge of it under one of the candlesticks on the table and then gently rolled out about two feet of it in front of her, anchoring the right side under another candlestick, and with many more feet curled up to her right.

"You can see how they made this. It started with a paper sheet about a quarter of the size of the letters we have. Someone probably folded a regular sheet and cut it up. Then lines were written out on the small pages in narrow columns, and each page was pasted to the edge of the previous sheet. Then they kept adding sheet after sheet along the righthand side. So it kept getting longer, until the only way to deal with it was to roll the pasted pages up into a scroll."

"I thought scrolls were out sometime before the Middle Ages," said Margaret. "I mean, weren't they? At some point, books were the big innovation. You could stand them up along shelves and number the pages and so on—I think of scrolls more as being in Rome, ancient Greece, and Egypt, for god's sake."

"No, that's right," replied Stephen. "It does seem very odd— I've never seen anything like this at Oxford. I never did work with any scrolls at the Bodleian—I suppose they have them—but even in monasteries before the Norman Conquest, the monks were all working with books and flat sheets. And this one has several different contributors."

Stephen pointed over to the start of the scroll on the left. "You can see whoever wrote these columns here was different from the person who was writing in the middle of the third column over here. I know you probably can't make out any of the words, but you can see the swooshes and strokes are quite different. Do you see?"

"Yes. I suppose so," replied Margaret.

"And over here on the right, someone has pasted a new patch on top of what probably was an earlier text below—and that seems to be in another style of writing all together: italics. Most of the handwriting we're looking at are examples of the so-called secretary hand—but, just like today, everyone sort of makes their handwriting quirks their own, and the difference between individual writers is obvious. Also, there are queer numbers and dashes everywhere around the sections separated by the lines across the columns. And, if I rolled out the whole thing, you'd see many other styles and contributors as well."

"Fascinating," said Margaret. "Can you actually read this stuff?"

"I used to be pretty good at it at school, and it's coming back. Most people are surprised to learn just about everyone was literate in Tudor times—even in the country people did go to school and read the words for the hymns at church and so on."

"Really?" mused Margaret. "I never knew that."

"Yes, reading was widespread, but writing not so much so. We think of them going together, but not everyone who could read back then could also write." Stephen carefully lifted up one of the candlesticks and let the scroll nest back into itself so he could put it back in the buffet drawer.

"I'll get back to the scroll, but meanwhile I think it's more important for me to keep going through the papers that aren't so totally mysterious. Those I can fly through, by comparison."

Stephen paused for a minute or so, deciding whether or not to say something that was now on his mind. And why not, he concluded.

"Margaret, I know how annoying the detectives were today, with their insinuations, but I actually agree with them that you should have all of these things looked over by experts soon, and get an idea of exactly what value they have. I haven't come across any maps to buried treasure so far, and I don't really know if they are worth a lot. Great houses all around England still have family documents moldering away in their libraries, cellars, and attics, and I just don't know if these are extraordinary or not."

"Hmmm, I suppose so, although I'm not exactly hard up for money," said Margaret, now turning a little sad again, and staring off into the carpet. Stephen didn't mean to bring up anything at all about her inheritance now that her parents were both gone—that hadn't been it at all. He hurried back into the conversation.

"Within a week or so, I should have the sort of descriptive inventory that would really help any appraiser. Sure, they will want to verify it and go over it all themselves, but it would be more than just a start—it should save everyone time and money."

"Okay, you carry on with the inventory—I do know that you like that sort of thing, but I've decided to do more of my thing as well."

"What do you mean?" asked Stephen.

"I don't know about you, but I didn't think that new county detective and his friend were like Agatha Christie's Hercule Poirot—did you? More like Peter Sellers as Inspector Clouseau in *The Pink Panther*, if you ask me. I mean, I'm a bloody investigative reporter when I'm at home—usually—and I'm going to make this my new story to crack open. I can't help with those scratchings—that's your department—but I can get on the trail of all this, and probably stay miles ahead of the blessed county police. The BBC have given me weeks of what they call 'bereavement leave,' so I can sort out my family affairs. I mean, they'll appoint a new vicar and I'll have to empty everything of ours out of this vicarage and so on. But, meanwhile, I'm going into the damn office next week—and I'll get things cracking."

Stephen had no doubt that she would.

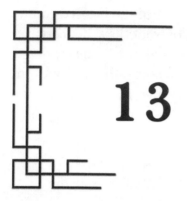

13

The last week had passed like a bad dream, thought Margaret on Monday morning as she walked from King's Cross train station to her office at the BBC. It made her feel ill to remember. Six days before, her dear father had died. She'd thought he was in the safest place on the planet—his own vicarage in the English countryside, for god's sake. And yet he ended up a victim of a vicious attack in their family kitchen, and never regained consciousness enough even to say goodbye. Now he was with her mother in heaven, he would have thought. All I want to remember is that I am going to get the bastard who did it, damn it.

There would be a lot of commotion ahead of her. The bishop was letting her keep the vicarage until the end of the year. Then a new vicar would be moving in to shepherd the village flock, and she would have to clear out. And no doubt she would now inherit her mother's house—the family seat her mother had grown up in and rented out while Margaret's dad made the vicarage their home.

That house would mean she could stay close to Stephen. He was a rock—helping her through the horror of alleged crimes, hospitals, investigations, police, and the other unthinkable complications arising. Good lord, she realized, there will be some sort of trial to live through. That will be awful...but, again, she won't be alone for that, but with Stephen, again.

Right after university, it seemed they'd be together forever. Back then, without a care in the world, she used to wander through the pages of *Brides and Setting Up Home* magazine, picking out ravishing dresses and looking at furniture, thinking how she would redecorate some big house someday. Then there would be children, even if they were adopted, and her seeing them off in their uniforms to the local schools. A doll's house life was in store for her. What a baby she was.

Of course, breaking off the engagement damn well wasn't Stephen's fault. She did that. Traded him for the supposed glory of her work—she had always wanted that. Or so she thought. But now she knew there was no point to it. She just popped up in one place, covered some bloody disaster, and then was thrown into another foreign hell where there had been a massacre, a bombing, or something.

One time, living on the edge even turned into romance, or that's what it seemed then. She was covering fighting among different factions in South Africa. It all seemed straightforward. A skirmish had happened the day before, and she and her crew were on-site, telling the story. But then, in a reversal of fortune, the victors of the night before were driven back and brought the fighting right back with them. The BBC and other press couldn't get out. For three days all the reporters were holed up in an old country hotel with the shutters nailed closed, sandbags blocking the doors, and gunshots outside. All they could do was gather down in an interior windowless room off the bar, drink, and share stories while worrying they were all about to be killed.

That was when she met David. He was covering the action for the domestic South African press. He was lovely, she thought— tall, handsome, fit, tanned, and brave. He wasn't afraid at all. He regaled her with stories of growing up on his parents' farm just to the north, in the old Southern Rhodesia. He and his sisters used to play with lion cubs on their porch—and he had photos in his wallet to prove it. He told her how he learned to conquer fear by playing "snakepit" after school. The boys would take turns standing in an actual snakepit and see who could stay the longest. The trick was just to stay still and calm because the snakes could sense movement and fear—and they would strike out at either. Eventually, he could just stand there indefinitely.

"Like a bee charmer?" she had said—and he laughed a great belly laugh. When he recovered, he said, "Yes, I guess in England I would have been a bee charmer—never thought of that." And he laughed again.

She was scared, and he was calm, and she felt much less nervous sitting very close to him as the shooting went on around the hotel. He forced the nervousness out of her by making her laugh, of all things. So when he knocked on her door one evening before they went down to the bar, why should she say no? In fact, having sex with him was a way to say yes to life instead of death—make love, not war—and the sex was great. Yes, yes, yes.

When the danger finally passed, and the press could get out, they said they would see each other soon—but they did not—just a few letters and then nothing. She hoped he was well, but it was all too simple, long ago, and now very much over.

So why should she be bothered about Stephen and his Miranda? I'm the one who set that up anyway, she said to herself, walking out on him as he had to take on that job at his father's school because I wanted adventure. Well, I got the adventure, and where am I now?

It's not my intellect or fine French-led education that are making me succeed—it's now just as important that I look good on camera. "Be sure to give a quick comb to your hair, Margaret, before you go on. And then turn to give us more of your good right side." Bloody hell.

And one day, after a shoot like that, she remembered going along with other reporters to visit a hospital. One ward was all children. She still could see the brave nine-year-old boy, now with only a left arm, trying to comfort his infant sister who lay on her back hugging the stump of her right leg that had been blown off, just the way healthy babies hugged their legs and tried to suck their toes. Those sights would never leave her.

Then she remembered a family holiday in Yugoslavia when she was about ten. The sea at Dubrovnik was lovely, and the town with its stucco and red-tile-roofed houses seemed so much more magical than the French Riviera or Italy. Magical indeed—because the magic wand of Marshal Tito held the country's six states together in a trance of unification. Now he was long gone, and all bets were off as centuries-old hatreds erupted in a misplaced frenzy of nationalism and independence. Dubrovnik itself had been under siege since the autumn of 1991. Elsewhere massacres and atrocities went on every day. And, Margaret thought, we weren't even giving those stories prime placement on the news—more likely Princess Di and Fergie. The foreign reporters hunkering down at the Holiday Inn in Sarajevo agreed they were given no coverage because their siege was rated only fourteenth on a new list of "The Worst Situations on Earth." It was ranked way behind famine in Africa, even though one of the women reporters had just had her jaw shot off.

At least Margaret heard one uplifting story about reporters visiting an orphanage, where the children were crouching around so they wouldn't be killed by the bullets coming through the windows. One of the ITN news correspondents decided to bring one of the girls there home with him to England and adopt her. And he did it. Talked her through security at Heathrow and kept her in Surrey with his family. At least that made a difference, she thought. Saving one child was worth a lot more than writing out a massacre story and sending it in to get it buried as a quick prelude to the weather on the BBC World Service news. She had to remember that.

~

Striding along, she was soon in sight of the imposing presence of Broadcasting House, the BBC's art deco "battleship of modernism," which had seemed to have been the right statement for the fast-growing broadcasting empire back in 1932, with its lofty mission to inform, educate, and entertain the nation.

As Margaret passed through the recently restored lobby toward the lifts at the back, she decided she would reach out to one of the few contacts she had inside the domestic U.K. news part of the organization. One of them was Guy Mitchell. About eighteen months earlier, Margaret became friends with him when they were "teamed" together during a weeklong BBC training program for journalists in hostile situations. Sadly, "the troubles" with the IRA had made terrorist bombings part of the U.K. beat as well as international, and they were both on the course to learn strategies for maintaining security in the field and for interacting with traumatized victims. They stayed in touch afterward as Guy sent her occasional congratulations for her stories, and she did the same.

So right after she reached her "visiting journalist" desk that morning, she left a message on his extension. She soon had an answer back that he would meet her for a coffee down in the main canteen at Broadcasting House at 11:15 a.m.—right after her call with Sarajevo.

~

The cafeteria was almost empty when she went in, and Guy soon came off the lift and waved to her as he walked over to her corner table.

"Hello, Margaret! Here for a visit?" he said, smiling and obviously glad to see her.

"Kind of," she said. "I'm actually home on bereavement leave. My father—" She paused to light a cigarette and exhaled a long first drag of blue smoke.

"Oh, I'm sorry, Margaret. I heard you were helping on Sarajevo."

"I am—but from here and not down there, thank god. It's bloody awful," she said.

"I know," said Guy, looking concerned for her.

"But it's actually about my father that I wanted to talk to you."

"Okay. What happened?" he said.

"Well, at first it seemed he just had a fall and went into a coma. But when they examined the wounds closely, the doctors and police decided it was an assault. Then he died without waking up and everything escalated into a full-scale police investigation," she explained.

"Good lord. Didn't you tell me he was a vicar?"

"Yes, that's right. But there had been a recent discovery in one of the tombs at his church—old papers that could be quite valuable—and perhaps that could have been a motive. Then there was a sensational story in the local paper—'treasure in the tombs'—and, right after that, his fall. The point is, I've met the police working on the case and I wasn't impressed. So I wanted to look into it myself as well. I mean, if he was murdered, I bloody well want to get the bastards who did it."

"Of course. And all this just happened?"

"Yes, the funeral was just last week," said Margaret. "So I called because I wanted to check out two of the people in the mix of all this. The first is a quite distinguished old Oxford professor—he got involved at the beginning when the discovery of the papers was first made. I thought there might be an obituary file started on him because he's written enough books, and given enough interviews and speeches and so forth. I also wanted to get a background check on him—which I thought would be best done from here. I was contacted by a local reporter from BBC East in Norwich about my father's death—but I didn't think they would be in a position to do something like that."

"No, they couldn't really requisition that, but we do that sort of thing all the time from here," said Guy.

"And then there's another man who's been questioned about the crime: Tony Baker. I wanted to run a check on him as well, to see if any previous criminal history turned up. That's it for now really...unless you have any ideas."

"Okay," said Guy, "it will be very easy for me to follow up with BBC East and see if they're aware of how the local investigation is going. I mean, they stay very close to the local police with regular briefings for their local radio news: robberies at convenience stores, car crashes, and so on. They should certainly know something about ongoing homicide cases. I do know the people there."

"Guy, that would be great. Maybe the police will just solve the mystery themselves—but I can't just sit by doing nothing."

"That's no problem, Margaret. I'm happy to help. And I can stay in touch with you on all this as things go along. I'll get you the obit file first thing tomorrow, if there is one. I'll let you know either way. The background checks take a few days to come back usually. Just get me the full names of the people, addresses if you can, and so on."

~

Margaret caught up with Stephen by telephone that night.

"I did get everything started on the background checks," said Margaret. "Can you just get me Tony Baker's address?"

"Sure," said Stephen. "No problem. But we had something happen at school today I wanted to tell you about; I think you may be able to help. Remember I mentioned we had a Bosnian boy at school this term?"

"Yes. Wasn't his father at the new embassy?" remembered Margaret.

"That's it. Well, there's a problem. Apparently the father—Mister Anton Juric—was called down to Sarajevo for some meetings about two weeks ago and he's gone missing. At least he hasn't been in touch with home, which is very unusual. So a week after he left, his wife went down to find him, leaving the children with an overnight caregiver. There's the boy here at my school—Denis—and a younger sister about seven or eight at the town junior school. And now that caregiver, Mrs. Quick—she's a widow here in the village—she called me this morning to say that the mother hasn't checked in with her either."

"Oh my god," said Margaret. "You can't imagine how dangerous it is down there just now."

"Mrs. Quick had called the embassy without much luck. So then I called them as well and finally got someone who told me they are also looking for Mister Juric. He went back there for meetings at the new government offices, but there was a lot of shelling aimed specifically at those buildings, so there are several people missing. In short, they didn't know much and they seemed focused on everything else. I mean, they said they'd let me know as soon as they could, but it seemed pretty crazy there."

"I have a call each morning with our team down there and can tell them," said Margaret. "But it will really help if I know exactly when they each went down—oh, and also pictures of both of them."

"Pictures?"

"Right, there's a big language issue—but if you can show pictures—especially to our team's local drivers, then we might get somewhere. Our team can copy the pictures and their drivers can show other drivers and so on and pretty soon we might know something. The network of drivers is probably the best bet. They're the ones who know what's been hit, where it's safe to go, and who's been visiting. We're all set up in the Holiday Inn down there to send and receive picture images all the time—no problem."

"I'll call Mrs. Quick and have her look around their house for good pictures of both parents."

"Okay. I'll brief everyone on the call tomorrow morning and then follow up with the photos. But this doesn't sound good, Stephen. Not good at all," she said.

~

Later that week, while Margaret was in London, Stephen finally found the guts to circle back with Miranda, whom he hadn't seen for over a fortnight. He called early and caught her in her flat. She was surprised to hear from him, but no longer angry. They agreed to meet up that evening at the Cross Keys, a quiet village pub on the high street, very different from the boisterous Village Arms, where they had staged their memorable fight night almost three weeks before.

Stephen arrived first and chose a table in the corner. At the bar, a cluster of regulars were swapping stories and paid no attention to him. Miranda came in ten minutes later and strolled over to the table, very calm. As she eased herself into the chair across from him, she stared at his damaged eye and noted, with some satisfaction, how the circles of color made him look like a raccoon.

"I ordered your usual," said Stephen, pointing to the drink he had for her.

"Not so usual for me to come in here. More likely my uncles or grandpa, I suppose. Nice eye," she said, opening her purse to find her smokes.

"Right. It's made quite an impression on the first weeks of school," he replied, relieved she had cooled off so. "Thanks for coming."

"No problem. Shouldn't be so difficult. We go back a long way."

"Look, Miranda, I want to apologize about the Bank Holiday weekend. I behaved really badly, and I wanted to explain," he said.

"Well, let me start. You know, ladies first." Miranda lit up a cigarette and blew out a slow whistle of smoke, collecting her thoughts. "Turns out I'm not pregnant. I was just late. But I didn't know all that back then. And I bloody well wasn't being with anyone else either. Just you. So what you said really gobsmacked me. It hurt. I hadn't expected anything rude like that—especially not from you."

"I'm so sorry, Miranda. I wasn't thinking, and I'd had a few drinks. But that's no excuse. But I need you to know why I was so surprised: it's something I've never told you. I know now I should have let you know all this a long time ago, but there you are. And now I'm ready to tell you."

"Just what the fuck are you going to tell me?" she said, looking quite alarmed.

"No, don't worry," Stephen said, unable to keep a wistful smile from spreading across his face. He reached across the tabletop, took her free hand, and locked eyebeams. "It's nothing too crazy—don't worry. And it all happened a long time ago, when I was a child. One spring, I got very sick with fever and the mumps. I remember spending a week or two at home on the sofa in the lounge, watching *Bill and Ben the Flowerpot Men* and Welsh folk dancing on daytime television instead of being at school or playing sports and so on. The fevers were quite hot. And then I got better and I assumed that was that.

"But a few years later—you know, around puberty, I suppose— my mother had the doctor explain to me that I wouldn't be able to have children when I grew up. All my stuff would work just as it should—and I had no idea what he was talking about then—but there wouldn't be any kids after I got married. I remember that just seemed very odd, at the time, and not too serious. I mean, I had never thought about any of that anyway. So I pretty much just went on my merry way. I mean, I was just a kid and really hadn't had any interaction with girls my age—except my cousins."

"Blimey, Stephen," said Miranda.

"So when you told me you were pregnant, I knew it couldn't be me. And that made me go off in the wrong direction. You know, thinking you must be lying or maybe you'd been with someone else. All sorts of selfish thoughts about me, and not about you— which was just awful, and it must have been something to do with the drink, because it was so terribly self-centered. Thinking back, having a gin and tonic dumped on top of me and a black eye was just what I deserved—and probably more of all that. So there it is. And I am so sorry," he concluded.

Miranda sat quietly for a minute, considering him. Then she said, "Well, I wish you'd told me earlier. I mean, it wouldn't have mattered, because I wasn't trying to catch you out and make you marry me. We were just good with each other...and good fun." She paused.

"But then, when I was late and thought I really was knocked up, I got myself thinking what a good catch you'd be. It was the first time I'd thought like that. And I thought maybe my life might be taking a turn for the better. But it wasn't. I know that now." She leaned back from the table, pushing against her chair, and pausing for a moment. "I'm just back to square one, and you seem to be back with Miss Fucking Hamilton. Hard-luck Miranda, that's me."

Stephen could see she was tearing up and felt terrible. They stayed there another half hour, moving on to good times remembered. What fun they had had. Then he made sure she knew he had nothing to do with Tony getting arrested—and that he didn't think Tony had anything to do with what had happened.

But he couldn't really disagree with her analysis. He was back with Miss Fucking Hamilton—or at least well on his way, he hoped.

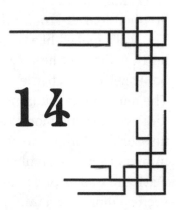

14

After lunch on Friday, Stephen was able to leave the school in the capable hands of Mrs. Boardman and board the empty midafternoon train to King's Cross. It had been a long few days away from Margaret. While she was still at work, Stephen had to get to the British Museum. He needed to sign up for privileges to use the rare book and manuscript collection so he could answer some of his questions about Anne Vavasour's papers and John Heminge's signature.

With his small overnight bag in hand, Stephen walked briskly off the train, through the main hall of the station, and came outside, just by the Euston Road. He walked westward along the pavement, past the remarkable Victorian gothic brick masterpiece of St. Pancras Station and the fenced construction site adjoining, which was planned to become the new British Library at some vague point in the future. After five minutes, he crossed the road headed south toward Russell Square and Bloomsbury, turning right onto Great Russell Street and coming up to the fenced gate in front of the museum. He asked a guard for the office, and, after a wave-through with his bag at security, he was inside thirty-five minutes before closing. Plenty of time, he thought, to get set up for his planned future visits.

Taking a number, with only one person ahead of him, Stephen looked around the grim space in the museum offices. The walls looked like they hadn't seen new paint since the war, he thought, and he meant World War Two. The metal chairs, bookshelves, and battleship gray desks were all the same vintage. The museum was running on a shoestring budget while the grandiose construction for its soon-to-be-enclosed courtyard and the new British Library were unfolding at a glacial pace. When his number came up, Stephen walked over to the Museum Privileges Desk and was surprised to take his seat across from a person who seemed more like a uniformed museum guard than a librarian.

"I'm here to request privileges for using the collections in the Manuscripts Students' Room," began Stephen. "I need access for several months as I am doing research on the Elizabethan era."

"Are you a professional researcher from an accredited university, sir?" asked the guard, seemingly happy to put up the first barrier for admission.

"No. But I'm a school headmaster, working on a tercentenary history of our school, and I need to get at some of the resources here."

"And what materials do you wish to consult, sir. Do you have your list?"

"A list? No. I need to consult your catalogues. I mean, I'll want to look at various histories of our county and the towns and so forth. And then some primary documents from the period establishing the school and its early years. That sort of thing."

"Well, sir, I'm sure you know this is a library of last resort, and we'll need to understand what you want to see here."

"Just what is a 'library of last resort' exactly," said Stephen, starting to redden slightly as he noticed the clock over the guard passing twenty minutes before five.

"It means we only allow study of materials not available anywhere else in the public or private library system, sir. Histories of counties and towns can be consulted at regular libraries open to all."

"But I need to see manuscripts such as the Burghley Papers as well."

"Those have been published in facsimile and transcription and can be studied in any good university library. There's no reason to disturb the originals. The London University Library up the road will probably have everything you'll need, sir."

"No, I need to see the actual Burghley Papers. We want to be able to describe exactly what those four-hundred-year-old-papers look like today: the texture of the papers, the watermarks and the inks, and so on...the sizes and specific appearance."

"This is for your school history?"

"We also have small classes for the students about studying old documents, and we need nuggets of information on how those all look today to keep them interested and so on." Stephen was improvising like mad as the clock ticked along.

"Then we'll need a list, sir, so we can verify what you want is available for consultation. Then the documents would be collected from storage and brought into the Reading Room."

"I don't yet know what they are, for god's sake. I need to look through your catalogues."

"The catalogues are just there, sir," said the guard as he gestured behind Stephen without looking up as he started to tidy away his things on the desk.

Stephen turned and eyed the steel metal shelving, which seemed to hold dozens of sets of well-thumbed and shabby encyclopedias.

"Those are the catalogues?" Stephen said, incredulously.

"Yes, sir. Those are the ones we have down here in the office. We need specific references to the collections before issuing any pass—at least three citations in writing."

"That's ridiculous. This is absurd." After he said it, Stephen realized stating the truth might not be the best way to deal with this man, who had stiffened and was now eyeing his impressive-looking key chain and preparing to lock up his desk.

They were alone in the room now, fifteen minutes before closing, and Stephen sprang from the chair over to the first set of shelves. The volumes seemed to be guides to various collections at random points in time. He fixed his gaze first on "Prints and Drawings of the India Office Collection, 1958 Series B," and then on "Union Catalogue of Japanese Printed Books and Serials, 1969 Series"—what on earth could he make of all this?

"Where are the catalogues for the domestic British manuscripts, officer?" asked Stephen, trying to give the man at the desk some sign of respect and contrition in his frenzy.

"On the left wall there, sir, but I'm afraid we are just about to close," intoned the man.

Stephen kept his nerve—he was good about being under pressure—and found a more relevant book about the Lansdowne Collection on the top shelf. By some stroke of wild luck, the inside listings were alphabetical by name of manuscript author, and after a few page turns he was settled on the long listing of items relating to Edward de Vere, 17th Earl of Oxford (1550–1604). Tearing out a page from his notebook, Stephen hurriedly jotted down three of the itemized listings of individual manuscript letters: one from 1572 about Oxford's reconciliation with his father-in-law, another from the same year about him desiring employment, and a third one from 1587 lobbying for promotion at court. Now there were about five minutes left to go.

As he closed the oversize book and thrust it back on the shelf, Stephen sliced open the side of his right thumb on the rough metal strut supporting the shelf. No time to deal with that now, he thought, and he leapt back over to the chair and the desk. Unfortunately, as he thrust the torn page in front of the startled man, he saw drops of blood from his thumb had gone onto the top of the page and were now falling onto the guard's leather desk pad, splashing onto its pink blotting paper and leaving deep crimson marks. "Here are the listings," Stephen said. "Sorry, I've just nicked my hand a bit—but here's what you need."

The man looked in horror down at the bloody sheet and actually wouldn't take hold of the paper.

Stephen continued, urging him on. "Officer, here is the listing, just as you requested with three citations. There will be more to come later, I'm sure, but this is all that I understand you need at this point." Unfortunately, just then another small droplet of blood hit the desk.

Stammering, the guard said, "I can give you a day pass, sir. You can use it next week."

"No, I need something longer. I'll be working all through this month and I can't keep coming in every day for new passes."

"All right, a week then," said the man, parsing out time as if he were handing out food-rationing coupons during the war.

"No, it must be something for longer." Stephen's case was supported by yet another drop on the desk.

"Six months, then."

"No, officer, I'll need at least a year," Stephen finished as he slid the paper out of his red hand and across the desk to where it touched the front of the man's chest. With three or four quick movements, the man then opened his center drawer, drew out a tan-colored annual pass, stamped the day's starting date, wrote "Mister Stephen White"—and that was that. With a short thank you, Stephen was out of the office, through the outer door where more guards stood waiting to lock up, and out into the courtyard and the fresh evening air.

What a bloody farce, thought Stephen, as he wrapped a tissue around his hero thumb, smiling at how appropriate the "bloody" part of that thought seemed. Suddenly it was all very funny—and a good story for Margaret as well.

Indeed, he kept smiling and shaking his head as he paused now to look over the items in the windows of the Museum Street bookshops before walking over to Broadcasting House, where the plan was for him to meet Margaret in the lobby at six o'clock.

~

She came into the lobby just as he arrived and they walked south into Soho for drinks among the Friday night office workers celebrating the opening bell of the weekend. Margaret wanted to go far enough away from the office to avoid the BBC crowd. After fifteen minutes, they slipped anonymously into a refreshingly normal pub called the Pillars of Hercules on Greek Street, just behind the Foyles bookshop.

After they sat down, Stephen said, "Well, I managed to set up a meeting with Soames Bliforth this weekend. We'll be meeting up for Sunday lunch at that restaurant there"—he pointed through the window—"just across the road, L'Escargot."

"Rare books and French snails?" said Margaret.

"English snails, I think—from Surrey." Stephen laughed.

Margaret loved his saga of getting the library pass, and he listened attentively to her recap of her day. She'd gotten the background check on Tony Baker. There was really nothing there: just some trouble years ago about boys breaking in to the local rugby club looking for jerseys. The kids were all let off with warnings, and there hadn't been anything since. So Tony wasn't much of a villain. She hadn't heard anything yet on Rowe.

Guy Mitchell had been talking to the local BBC East people. The police had asked them to publicize details of the things taken from the church—the jeweled crucifix, candlesticks, and other vessels, but no leads had come in. They were closemouthed about the murder investigation. And her team in Sarajevo were circulating the photos of the Jurics, but no news yet.

Stephen was happy just to sit back and listen to her talk: it was all so different from his life at the school in the village. He had missed her, and now he wanted her back the way they had been together that last year in college—before he tried to tie her down forever with the idea of engagement before she was ready. Through the whole time around her father's illness and death, he had been there to support her, by listening, hugging, holding hands, and a then quick good night kiss before he went back to his flat or slept on top of a bed in the vicarage guest room. And now he'd work with her through their investigation at her side. He had acted like the brother she had never had. Now he knew he loved her and just wanted her back as his girlfriend again. And he knew she loved him, too.

The crowd in the pub was getting a bit out of hand as the local ad agencies and record company offices emptied out, and they were shouting now just to be heard by each other, so they fled west and walked along the streets parallel to Oxford Street, finally dropping off his bag with the doorman at Margaret's smart building on Welbeck Street, just behind Selfridges. Round the corner from there was her favorite quiet Italian restaurant, the Gondola, where they could just finally talk without shouting.

"That book I ordered at the library about Sir Henry Lee...I just finished it on the train down here. I've made a lot of notes."

"Was there much about Anne in it?" asked Margaret.

"Yes, lots. As Professor Rowe told us, Henry had a full life before they settled down, but thanks to his longevity—he did die at age eighty—they did manage to squeeze in over twenty years with each other, pretty much living as man and wife, although not married."

"Wasn't that very unusual for the time?"

"Well, yes it was. And Rowe was right that she was married—or at least in a marriage of convenience after she had her baby—to a low-life sea captain. Chambers said Sir Henry paid him off. In fact, it was duly recorded in Sir Henry's household accounts."

"What? This woman as a black sheep is getting blacker and blacker." Margaret laughed. "No wonder my mother didn't tell me the details."

"Let's back up a bit, and I'll tell you," Stephen said, pouring them each another glass of Chianti. "Sir Henry Lee was very respectable, I can promise you. His mother, Margaret Wyatt, was one of Anne Boleyn's closest friends and her lady-in-waiting. It was she who held Anne's hand on the scaffold when she was executed and so on. King Henry might even have had a go at her when Anne was playing hard to get. Sounds outrageous, but it would have been normal royal behavior. King Henry often had a fling with a married woman and then rewarded the lady and the husband in question when he was done. It was his ancient droit du seigneur—the lord's privilege. So our Henry might actually have been a bastard son of Henry VIII, just as Aubrey reported. That would have made Edward, Mary, and Elizabeth his closest relatives. In fact, he might have been a lovely big brother and protector to Edward and Elizabeth," said Stephen.

"Do you think there's really a chance of that?" asked Margaret.

"I suppose there's no way to know," said Stephen. "But he did play right at the top of their society, so I'd have to say it's certainly possible. He grew up in the Wyatt household in Kent, and inherited his father's money and properties at fourteen. Then he went into the royal household as a squire to the King. Since King Henry went hunting all day immediately after breakfast and morning mass, the young man would have learned all about the manly arts of riding, hunting, jousting, and so forth—as well as poetry, languages, and courtly manners. After King Henry passed the throne on to his sickly son, Edward VI, our young Henry would have served the boy king at court, and then transitioned smoothly to serve in the court of Queen Mary and then Elizabeth. So you couldn't have ended up with a finer pedigree than his."

"But wasn't he married himself?" asked Margaret.

"Yes, but he didn't have anything to do publicly with Anne while his wife and children were alive. But they were all dead by the time he was fifty-seven, and Anne would have been about thirty years younger then, I think."

"That's long after she had her baby, isn't it?" asked Margaret.

"Yes, but he would have been aware of her earlier. Anne was a sensation when she came to court at sixteen. There was something about her that caught the eye of all the men there. She wasn't a classical beauty, so it must have been a blend of sassiness and sauciness. She was extremely well educated—as well as any person then at court, except perhaps the Queen—and simply a lot of fun to be with: a breath of fresh air. Sir Henry even had a suit of armor made for himself with the initials AV all over it; I think we can see it down at the Tower—they still have it. He also would have seen the Earl of Oxford make his move for her. Oxford was not a nice man. I think you could call him a bounder."

Stephen paused as their food came, but Margaret said, "Keep going, Stephen."

"Well, at the time of the scandal, Sir Henry was essentially the 'master builder' of the new 'cult of Elizabeth.' They established a new annual holiday celebrating the day the Queen first came to the throne—November 17—which was observed every year all over England. I think they still celebrate it at Eton and Harrow today, for god's sake. And the centerpiece of all the celebrations throughout the country was the jousting tournament run by Sir Henry. It was a kind of re-embracement of the old medieval chivalry of knights and ladies prancing about to serve the monarch. Elizabeth loved it. She made chivalry and courtly love the foundation of her reign as the Virgin Queen and Gloriana, and Sir Henry Lee personified every man's embodiment of a medieval knight; and he kept it all going, riding and winning the jousts as the Queen's champion. King James loved that, too, and very much respected Sir Henry as a well-loved hunting buddy, and as a mentor for his young son, Prince Harry."

"My god, he had quite a run, didn't he?" said Margaret.

"Yes. And when Henry had to retire as the Queen's own champion at the joust—he was then almost sixty—he was all alone. His wife had just died, and all his children were gone and he was facing a pretty lonely retirement. And that's when he scooped up your Anne. They then lived the next twenty-plus years together, between his fifteen-room apartment at the old Savoy Palace overlooking the Thames and his various estates out in the country, near where we visited Rowe. They entertained all their friends from court and even King James and his own Queen Anne, who became great personal friends of them both. There is even some compelling evidence that Elizabeth blessed their scandalous cohabitation after Henry entertained the court at Ditchley in 1592. Another reason his relationship with the Queen might have been really as a 'big brother' instead of just a loyal knight."

"That's all just amazing. So why have we never heard of them? It seems like one of the greatest English love stories. I wish I had pried more of this history out of my mother—but I suppose neither one of us was that interested at the time."

"I don't know, Margaret. I don't know. Maybe it's because we English aren't so good at love stories?"

"Hmmm. I don't know about that, Stephen," she said. "Don't give up just yet."

~

A light drizzle started as they walked around the corner to Margaret's lavish one-bedroom flat. It was just what you'd expect for someone with inherited wealth from her mother and a job as an up-and-coming television presenter at the BBC. The building, Welbeck House, had a huge marble lobby, a birdcage lift, and a liveried doorman who ran the lift for them up to her second-floor flat.

When Margaret unlocked her door and turned on the lights, Stephen saw the doorman had left his bag just inside. He realized he was quite tired from the hectic day, and actually was looking forward to sleep.

Margaret walked over to a side table and said, "Just let me check the phone here—the message light is on. Maybe there's some news from my colleagues about your Jurics?" She picked up the receiver, punched a few keys, and stood listening.

Stephen took a quick walk around. Her sitting room had a bay window overlooking the quiet Marylebone street. The space in front of it was filled with pricey overstuffed armchairs, and a long sofa, all in the same chintz fabric as the curtains. Behind the sofa was a dining table for eight, which could double as a desk if she needed to work and spread things out. Behind louvered doors, a full kitchen was hidden on the inside wall, and there was a guest loo with a sink and toilet just inside the front door. In the back, she had a lovely large bedroom, with upholstered sitting chairs and hassocks, and a complete en suite bathroom with tub and walk-in shower. It was really everything she could want—but why had he assumed he could just stay there?

It would have been better if he had taken a room at the Oxford-Cambridge Club. They both belonged to it, down on Pall Mall next to St. James's Palace. The bedrooms there were depressingly tiny, but then you could sit up late and use the desks in the grand reading rooms downstairs. There was a great bar and eating hall, with wonderful breakfasts and three kinds of marmalade on each table, if you felt like that.

Margaret hung up the phone, and said, "Well, it wasn't about the Jurics yet, I'm afraid. But it was Guy Mitchell from the office. Apparently my request for the background check on Professor Rowe ran into something big, he thinks. Anyway, I've been asked to turn up at Scotland Yard Monday morning for some sort of chat—what do you think of that?"

"Professor Rowe? Are they sure?"

"Guy is just guessing that it's about him at this point, since I did already get the report on Tony Baker. So he wants me to clue him in after the meeting, since it might be a story for the U.K. news. So there it is. Let's hope it will be progress somehow, whatever it is," she said.

"You know, Margaret, I should have booked a room at the club. I wasn't really thinking. It's a bit late tonight, but I'll do that tomorrow so I won't be underfoot here all the time bothering you."

He was eyeing the sofa in the living room somewhat uncomfortably when Margaret turned and said simply, "Well, I don't have a guest room here, so you'll just have to bunk in with me. But don't worry, I have good marmalade, too."

He was stopped in his tracks as she walked over to him, put her arms around his neck, and gave him a long and deep kiss. Energy flooded back in to him as he hugged her back tightly.

Margaret led him into the bedroom and turned down her side of the bed. Then she went into the bathroom and closed the door. Stephen was nervous, in spite of the years they had been together back in the day. He started to get undressed, taking off his shoes and socks and slipping off his trousers. He was undoing his shirt buttons when Margaret came out of the bath, completely free of her clothes. She was breathtakingly beautiful to him—and probably would have been to any boy with a pulse. She had taken what God had given her, and kept it all fit and fine. Stephen also tried to keep fit, but he was not up to her mark and he felt self-conscious as he took off his shirt and stood before her in his shorts. Margaret slipped into her side of the bed and patted the area next to her, keeping her gaze right on his eyes. He stepped over and turned down his side, and then stepped out of his shorts.

"Looking good, Stephen," she said, smiling—and she turned out the light.

They were so happy to have each other back. A terrible loss was suddenly restored for both of them.

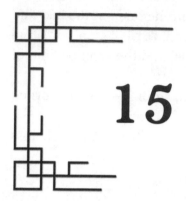

15

When they woke up on Saturday, it was a while before they could pull themselves away from each other. Life seemed all about being in love again.

They did manage to make it out of the flat just before eleven and took a taxi over to a posh shop Margaret remembered in Sloane Square. She splurged on herself there, choosing a new outfit while Stephen, perched in an armchair clearly meant to hold men captive until their mates found the right ensemble, gave thumbs-up or thumbs-down to candidates. Margaret looked radiant as she said, "I haven't bought anything like this in years" while she twirled around in front of the floor-length mirrors. It seemed like they had fallen into an old film. They walked up Sloane Street and stopped in for a lunchtime sandwich and glass of wine at the rooftop café at the Harvey Nichols store at the corner of the Brompton Road.

It was a fine afternoon, more like the middle of summer than the start of autumn, and walking and talking seemed such a delightful pleasure. They strolled along eastward from Harvey Nick's, through Green Park and even along Pall Mall, coming up to the sainted Oxford-Cambridge Club.

"Well, you must be glad not to be sleeping in a closet at the club," said Margaret, holding hands with Stephen and peering up at the club's flowery pink and white window boxes as they walked by.

"I don't know. I did see your marmalade, but no billiards table or squash court, you know," he replied.

She laughed. "I'm sure we can find something to pass the time tonight at my place."

After a few minutes, Margaret continued on, in a more serious voice. "You know, Stephen, you were great to tell me about your Miranda. I really didn't want to hear it. But I do know how normal that is."

"Margaret, we don't have to go over all that again. It's over," Stephen said, defensively.

"No, I know that. I mean I just wanted you to know you're not alone. I mean I dated someone else awhile, too."

"Oh," said Stephen, turning to look at her.

"It was while I was on assignment in South Africa. All of the reporters covering the fighting there got caught in the middle of the shooting—the two sides were moving around their positions—and we couldn't get out. We ended up locked down in a hotel, thinking we were about to get killed. And that's when it happened. I guess I thought everything was about to be over, so I had a 'battlefield romance'—or at least a fling anyway."

"Hmm," he said. "Very Hemingway and Martha Gellhorn."

"Yes, I guess so. Except they got married, and my fling finished. Nothing came of it afterward. But I just wanted you to know—so you didn't think we weren't even. Your Miranda, my David."

"David?"

"Yes. He had a name. He was from Zimbabwe and he's not in the picture. I just wanted you to know you weren't the only one who tried to go on living while we were apart."

They continued on quietly awhile but kept holding hands the whole time. Yes, Stephen thought. She was good to tell me, because I did think I was the sinner and she the saint.

"Thanks for telling me, Margaret. And you're right: all of that is over. So let's just carry on and see where we go."

Soon they found themselves at the end of Pall Mall coming into the wide expanse of Trafalgar Square. Tourists and strollers were luxuriating everywhere around the open square on the sunny day, amusing themselves watching the singers, acrobats, and sidewalk artists entertaining the crowds for tips.

"Speaking of where we go—I have an idea," said Stephen. "Let's go over onto the north side there. I want to show you something in the National Portrait Gallery. I just remembered. It's actually very relevant to our investigations, and we should see it, since we're right here."

Navigating the busy streets of the square via zebra cross-walks, Stephen led them over to the entrance of the National Portrait Gallery. They walked in, went through security, and left Margaret's shopping bag with the attendant in the cloakroom.

Stephen guided them over to the lift and up to the Tudor Gallery.

When the lift stopped and the doors opened, they were in a softly lit enclosed area, out of sight of any windows to the outside. As they followed the arrows into the Tudor section, they moved into even darker inner rooms, where it took a few moments for the eyes to adjust to the subdued light, which protected the paintings.

There were just a few small rooms in the exhibition: probably thirty pictures, very manageable for a quick stop.

"I think the Tudors were the first in England to popularize portraits," Stephen said. "I mean, of course there were earlier paintings of kings and religious scenes and so on, but it was in the age of the Tudors that courtiers, gentry, and merchants began to have their images captured as a sort of badge of notoriety. If you had the money, then you had a portrait done in your finest clothes and with your finest jewels. And as soon as one did, then all of their rivals had to as well. A handful of artists from the Continent came over to handle the volume, so a lot of these were done by the same painters."

After strolling by Henry VIII and a young Queen Elizabeth, Stephen stopped in front of a somewhat fierce-looking portrait of a young man in close-up. "Here's our Sir Henry."

"Really," said Margaret. "He's that important—I mean, to be here?"

"Yes, it was a small group at the top of the court, and even though he wasn't a duke or an earl, he was right with the top of the pack. He had this painted around 1568, at about age thirty-five, when he was coming back from various missions on the Continent. I think he had it done in Antwerp, as a souvenir. By the way, Anne Vavasour would have been about five years old at the same time."

Sir Henry stared straight out from the wall at Margaret. "He looks almost angry, or menacing. I mean, it's not a neutral pose, is it?" she said.

"No, he's sending signals. There are quite a few, actually. First, he's wearing white, gold, red, and black—those are Queen Elizabeth's personal colors. And those decorations on his sleeves—spheres and lovers' knots—are associated with Elizabeth, too. But then he's got something strange going on with that red cord around his neck that's tangled up with three golden rings on his thumb."

"What's all that about?" asked Margaret.

"I don't think they know. And he might have wanted it to be ambiguous. But it looks like he's pledging affection to a few places could be 'God, Queen, and family' or perhaps something else. Maybe he wanted it to have multiple meanings so different people would have different takeaways. And then, look here, at what's hanging next to him."

Next to Sir Henry hung a massive full-size painting of Queen Elizabeth, resplendent in a magnificent gown and jewels and standing on what appeared to be a map of England.

Margaret read out from the explanatory label next to the frame. "This says it's 'The Ditchley Portrait, produced for Sir Henry Lee who had served as the Queen's champion from 1559–90.' Good lord, there he is again. It goes on: 'It probably commemorates an elaborate symbolic entertainment Lee organized for the Queen in September 1592. Lee lived at Ditchley with his mistress, Anne Vavasour. The entertainment marked the queen's forgiveness of Lee for becoming a stranger lady's thrall.'"

"And that's one of her most famous portraits," said Stephen. She's actually standing on Sir Henry's land at Ditchley."

"Well, I'll be damned," finished Margaret.

PART FOUR

PART FOUR

1590. In the thirty-second year of the reign of Queen Elizabeth, many of her oldest advisors were gone or on their way out.

Her original favorite, Robert Dudley, Earl of Leicester, had died in 1588. And in April 1590, her well-connected secretary of state and spymaster, Francis Walsingham, followed Leicester to the grave. Lord Burghley, her principal advisor and lord treasurer, was turning seventy and was maneuvering for his second son, Robert Cecil, to first become a privy councillor and then the private secretary to the Queen.

And in the same year, Sir Henry Lee, now aged age fifty-seven, was also living through several changes.

On the personal side, his wife Lady Anne Paget Lee, was ill and about to die. Theirs had been an arranged marriage, back in the reign of Queen Mary, and they had been living separately for many years. Lady Lee always kept a low profile in her husband's affairs since her two brothers, Charles and Thomas, were Catholic agitators in exile on the Continent, scheming against Queen Elizabeth. Sir Henry buried her in an ornate marble tomb that already held their three children, all of whom had died young.

On his more public side, he retired from his role as Queen's champion at the joust, after riding with distinction at the 1590 Accession Day tilt. At the end of that tournament, as he stood before the Queen and her ladies, hidden music started to play from beneath their elevated gallery, and much to everyone's amazement, a reimagining of the Temple of Vestal Virgins, draped in white curtains, rose up from beneath the stairs in a magical and mechanical way. Stepping into the temple, Sir Henry then took off his elaborate black and gold armor, delivered his farewell retirement address, beginning "My golden locks time hath to silver turned," and presented the Earl of Cumberland as his successor as Queen's champion. Then Sir Henry clad the earl in another magnificent black and gold suit of armor and donned for himself a country cloak and cap to symbolize his rustication.

But he was not dead yet. Privately, he planned to carry on and live full-time with his latter-day love, Anne Vavasour, who had just given him a son named Thomas. From this point on, Anne and Henry were inseparable.

~

1592. Two years later, during the Queen's late summer progress northwest of plague-ridden London, Sir Henry hosted the monarch and her court for a two-day entertainment divided between the Royal Manor of Woodstock and his nearby Ditchley estate. His objective was to secure the Queen's tolerance and forgiveness for his scandalous living arrangement with Mistress Anne.

No expense was spared as he hired the best talent to write and plan the stagecraft for the spectacle. On the first day, the Queen and her courtiers became the actors in a formal masque themed around the challenges of true love. They moved from site to site around gardens transformed into an extensive set for the production. The opening action recalled a famous entertainment held for the Queen at Woodstock in 1575, seventeen years earlier. It had been a magical evening, with dinner outside under backlit trees in fine warm weather. Now in the 1592 script, the courtly participants visit a grotto filled with languishing lovers on the estate of an aging knight named Loricus (Lee) who has saved all the emblems and trappings of the earlier happy Woodstock event along with reminders of past jousting tournaments and other celebrations. Then, after a dinner break, there was an elaborate debate between Constancy and Inconstancy.

On the second day, the Queen was led to a bower where Loricus languished from the wounds of love. Her majesty, playing "a Faerie Queene," then removed the trance ensnaring him by giving her blessing and forgiveness for his love with another. The knight miraculously recovered and, to end the entertainment, a long speech in the manner of a legal document was read bequeathing "the whole Manor of Love" to Elizabeth.

The Queen was well pleased and, remarkably, Sir Henry succeeded with his objective of getting her tacit approval for his relationship with Anne. To commemorate the occasion, Sir Henry had also commissioned the famous portrait of Elizabeth regnant and standing with her feet planted on Ditchley and Oxfordshire. Painted next to her figure, a motto reads "She can take vengeance, but does not."

~

1595. Sir Henry still spent time at court. Reports from this year describe him playing cards with Queen Elizabeth while lobbying for a position as Vice Chamberlain, which he did not get. While in London, he stayed at his fifteen-room apartment in the old Savoy Palace overlooking the Thames. At court, he could have seen four plays acted by Shakespeare's troupe in the December–January festivities welcoming in 1596, or even another four acted by Edward Alleyn and the Admiral's Men in January–February.

Perhaps he and Anne occasionally crossed the river from his private boat ramp to public performances at the Rose, Swan, or Globe playhouse on the South Bank.

~

1597. With the unanimous support of his old jousting friends, Sir Henry was made a Knight of the Garter, a most unusual honor for a commoner. In a letter from this time, he mentions his eyes were getting weak and how much he loved for Anne to read aloud to him in the country. Friends at court sent them lots of things to read. Their lives seemed to be slowing down.

They would have been surprised, perhaps, to learn their story was not ending.

Lines spoken by Sir Henry Lee at his retirement as Queen's Champion

My golden locks time hath to silver turned,
(Oh time too swift, and swiftness never ceasing)
My youth gainst age, and age at youth hath spurned
But spurned in vaine, youth waneth by increasing.
Beauty, strength and youth, flowers fading beene,
Duty, faith and love, are roots and ever greene.

My Helmet now shall make a hive for Bees,
And lovers songs shall turn to holy Psalmes,
A man at Armes must now sit on his knees,
And feed on pray'rs, that are old ages alms.
And so from Court to Cottage I depart,
My Saint is sure of mine unspotted hart.

And when I sadly sit in homely Cell,
I'll teach my Swaines this Carrol for a song,
Blest be the hearts that think my Sovereigne well,
Curs'd be the soules that thinke to do her wrong.
Goddesse, vouchsafe this aged man his right,
To be your Beadsman now, that was your Knight.

Concluding speech of "The Legacy," the 1592 Ditchley entertainment

I bequeath (to your Highness) THE WHOLE MANOR
OF LOVE, & the appurtenances thereunto belonging:
Woods of high attempts,
Groves of humble service,
Meadows of green thoughts,
Pastures of feeding fancies,

Arable land of large promises,
Rivers of ebbing and flowing favors...
Fishing for dainty Kisses with smiling countenances,
Hawking to spring pleasure with the spaniels of kindness,
Hunting the deare game which repentance followeth...

—[Etc., etc. ad infinitum]

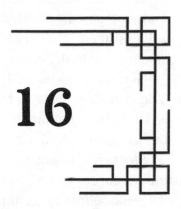

16

At twelve thirty on Sunday afternoon, Stephen and Margaret stepped from their taxi onto the pavement in Soho Square, steering clear of the empty cups and bottles by the gutter—all that remained of the boozy Friday and Saturday night crowds that filled the streets. Now there were only tidy little packs of Chinese kids walking by the garden benches, chattering respectfully on their way to weekend schools to be tutored up for Chinese high school entrance exams.

They were on time for their planned "Sunday lunch" on Greek Street with Soames Bliforth and his girlfriend, Mandy. Soames had picked the incredibly posh restaurant L'Escargot. There was no sign of Soames and his love when they arrived, so Stephen asked for "Mister Bliforth's table," and they were seated in pride of place at the front window.

Two kir royales arrived before they had a chance to place an order. The server explained, "Mister Bliforth is running slightly late, sir—he called a few minutes ago and sends you these."

"Well, I'm glad someone from our old class is making a lot of money," said Margaret as Stephen wondered how much a glass of champagne with crème de cassis liqueur would cost in a place like this. Not too many English prep school headmasters would know.

Soames and the surprising young Mandy soon arrived, sending the entire waitstaff into a frenzy, although the place was still almost empty. They were obviously regular customers—and good ones at that.

"Hello, Stephen. And Margaret, isn't it?" boomed Soames. "You're both looking as fresh as you were back at school—very perky, indeed. Let me introduce my friend, Mandy. Oh, and she did not go to Oxford, you'll be startled to learn."

Stephen's mouth fell open. Mandy was the kind of ravishingly beautiful young black girl you might see on the front cover of *Cosmopolitan* magazine, perhaps holding a whip and dressed in a leopard-print gown. Her pale eye shadow and crimson lips radiated vivacity and style.

She must be a model, Margaret thought. I mean, do I recognize her from the media somewhere?

"Mandy works right around the corner, at an ad agency. Isn't she wonderful?" said Soames, as if he were showing off a picture in a gallery.

"Really, Mandy," said Stephen. "What do you do there?" he said rather rudely to Mandy, but quite frankly unaware of his pointedness because he was totally gobsmacked and put off his guard by this apparition.

"Receptionist," said Mandy proudly, slipping into her chair.

"Yes," said Soames fondly. "I saw her through the window as I walked by and just had to go in. We've been an item since summer—and this is our favorite place for Sunday lunch, so quiet and smoothing after a vigorous Saturday."

Good lord, thought Margaret. I have led a sheltered life.

"Mandy, Stephen is a school headmaster. And you may have seen Margaret here on television."

"Really," said Mandy, landing her otherworldly eyes on Margaret for the first time, now that she just might be worthy of notice. "What show are you on? I've always fancied doing that sort of thing myself."

"Well, occasionally I'm on the news, I suppose. I'm a reporter."

"Oh," sympathized Mandy. "I never look at the news."

Somehow Stephen could believe that. He collected himself a bit and turned his attention to Soames, who smiled back and winked at him. That made Margaret smile. So he does know how outrageous she is; that's really funny. "So what you have been up to?" Stephen asked, and, quite frankly that made the three old classmates burst into laughter, and even Mandy smiled, too, as she checked her nails.

Soames was a study in stylishness, thought Margaret, right up there with Mandy. His navy and powder-blue pinstriped suit was complemented by what seemed to be a custom-made Turnbull and Asser striped shirt and a red, blue, and white regimental stripe tie, with a triangular pocket handkerchief peeping out of his breast pocket. The American BBC News producer Margaret often worked with would have said "three stripes and you're out," making some kind of baseball allusion that told the on-camera newsreaders to lose one of the stripes in their outfit before filming, or the image would start shimmering. Soames, however, actually pulled it all off. And why not? With a seventy-five-pound haircut and his tan and lean muscular frame, he could be right out of a James Bond film—and Mandy could be right there with him, too.

"Well," Soames replied to Stephen's question, "shall I give you the Sunday lunch version of a response to explain myself? I mean, it's too early for the bald truth." Soames caught them up on himself since school. He had taken a modest swath of his late father's great library and opened a used and rare bookshop not far from where they all sat. "The old man loved books—I think most of the family fortune went into them. And when it all came to me, I sold the ones I didn't want to keep, and bought others I did keep—and suddenly I realized I could open a shop and just keep doing that. I mean, they say you should do what you love, and I love the books just as much as my father did—and his father before him as well. That's worked out really well. I keep it upmarket. That's the only place the money is: I don't want to get into recycling old paperbacks or running a two-shilling lending library. More like fine bindings, travel, and exploration—even maps, atlases, old prints, and that sort of thing. Now I've become so established that a lot of the new stock just walks in the door with people wanting to sell it. At the start I had to go out looking for it: you know, at estate sales, auctions, and knocking at doors of run-down stately homes. I mean, that was good fun, but perhaps success has made me lazy. Anyway, it's still exciting. One never knows what's going to turn up!"

"Oh yes, we do know," said Stephen. "The papers we want to tell you about came from the tomb of one of Margaret's ancestors."

"Actually, it's a double tomb: my Elizabethan ancestor, Mistress Anne Vavasour, and her lover, Sir Henry Lee," added Margaret.

"Her lover?" said Soames.

"Yes, said Stephen. "There was a small flood in the church and they had to open up burial vaults to dry them. Then Margaret's father—the vicar there—found the papers. He called me because he remembered I had studied up on old handwriting at school."

"Margaret," said Soames, remembering himself and turning to lock eyebeams with her. "I am so sorry about your father. Stephen told me when he called and you have my deepest sympathies. How are you bearing up?"

"As well as could be expected, I suppose. Thank you for asking. But I am glad to be back in London and here today," she responded.

"Well," continued Soames after pausing a moment, having completed the obligatory niceties, "finding papers in an old tomb is very unusual from this period. Stephen mentioned the 1600s—correct?"

"Yes, that's right," said Stephen.

"Usually things from that time only turn up from a great house where generations have tucked papers onto a library's shelves and forgotten them. Then one day desperate descendants discover them and need to flog them to hold on to the house. That's the normal path. You get things that are somewhat damaged and dusty after centuries of neglect but the copies you sent me look rather crisp. What's the condition like?"

"They seem almost eerily new," said Stephen. "The vault they were in was made of porous firestone—as in a cathedral—so there wasn't any moisture trapped inside. And it stayed bricked up and undisturbed from the 1650s until the past Bank Holiday weekend. They were inside two ebony boxes. I was a bit suspicious of how clean they were, but the watermarks all check out with ones contemporary to their time. And I do know the handwriting styles are quite right. I sent off a set of copies to old Professor Rowe as well. We went to see him two weeks ago, and he didn't seem to have any qualms about them because of their provenance, although he didn't think too much of their value. We thought you might be a better judge of that, since you're a professional trading in that sort of thing now, and so on."

"Old Professor Rowe, you say. Yes, he'd be a good one to ask. I often get his opinion on things that come in to me. He's a walking link to that history—well, I don't know how long he'll continue to be walking, but he's certainly alive and kicking right now. What else did he say?"

"He started with a letter from Lord Burghley thanking Anne and Sir Henry for sending him some venison," began Stephen.

"Yes, he said lots of people sent him venison," said Margaret. "So I should just frame it and hang it on my wall."

"Who exactly was sent the letter. You know, whom did Burghley send it to?" asked Soames.

"It was either sent to my ancestor, Lady Anne Vavasour"—Margaret surprised herself by giving lowly Anne a title—"actually, she turned out to be not so much of a lady—or to her boyfriend, Sir Henry Lee. He was a courtier and was indeed friends with Burghley."

Stephen added, "There was a rumor that Sir Henry might have been an illegitimate son of Henry VIII, Rowe told us. And I did find that rumor mentioned in a biography of Lee written by Sir Edmund Chambers, although it's not at all clear that he was what they called the King's 'natural child.'"

"Chambers wrote a biography of him?" asked Soames. "I thought he only published about Shakespeare and the Elizabethan stage. I have those sets written by him at the shop."

"I guess it was a minor work of his. I didn't know about it either, but old Rowe did. I've just finished reading it. Chambers thought Lee should be written up as an example of the sturdy yeoman stock that kept England together: to supplement all the attention given to princes, dukes, and earls. Lee was a very wealthy landowner and well-known courtier. He's credited with starting the tradition of anniversary day jousts and tournaments for Queen Elizabeth. Lee was her 'champion' at those jousts."

"Strange, I never have heard of these people—including your Lady Anne," Soames said, turning to Margaret.

"When I was a child my mother always told me she was the black sheep of the family. Her life story told by Rowe made her sound more like she was Queen of the Bordello," said Margaret. That got Margaret another glance from silent Mandy.

"Margaret, you don't seem the right type to be the descendant of a working girl," said Soames. "I thought you a better fit as the vicar's daughter."

Soames had said that in such a gentle and joking way that the three of them all chuckled again, somewhat mystifying Mandy.

Returning to their topic, Stephen continued, "There were also longer documents: two commonplace books, a masque and play or two that were put on for some court occasions, and a scroll we can't quite figure out."

"A scroll? I thought everything was sixteenth or seventeenth century. Was there some much older artifact?" asked Soames.

"No, it's from the same time. All of the handwriting on it is contemporary to Lady Anne. Several different hands were writing on it. Small pages were pasted together onto a long scroll—must be ten or fifteen feet long. I haven't really gone over it all closely because it's a bit of a mystery and there are other things I can get on with. I'm writing out a crude inventory of all the papers; I mean, there are well over one hundred items. Perhaps you can look it over when it's finished?"

"Sure, your inventory would be very useful. I'd love to see it when you're done."

Margaret added, "We actually brought a few things for you to look at firsthand, Soames. Might you have some time to take a look?"

"Yes, wonderful. We can go over to my shop after lunch. It's just over the road near all the shops on Museum Street." Out of the corner of his eye, Soames saw Mandy shift uneasily in her chair. "I have some great brandy we could try there. You know, something for really special occasions."

"Oh, that would be lovely," said Mandy, suddenly more attuned to their conversation.

"But that's enough business for now—we can take it up again later. May I recommend you try the Surrey snails? You don't see them on the menu very often and they are great."

"No, Stephen had mentioned them to me," said Margaret. "And you *don't* see them listed like that on menus. I think the French would be horrified to see the English pushing themselves into their escargot territory."

~

True to his word, Soames's rare bookshop was just five minutes away as they strolled from the quiet of a Sunday afternoon on Greek Street, past the cinema marquees at the gaudy intersection of Tottenham Court Road and Oxford Street and down a small side street. Just before that road joined the bookshop-filled Museum Street, Soames's store was tucked into a narrow storefront, with a small-paned front shop window that looked as if it had fallen onto the ground from a movie set for Dickens's *A Christmas Carol*.

The cozy quaintness continued inside. The walls were all deep green, with white and wood trim, and walls of expensive leather-bound books glistened from the glow of the brass table lamps. There was no shop counter. Instead Soames or his store helper would sit at a large partners desk facing a brown leather chesterfield sofa, with matching chairs flanking a wide antique coffee table. Another room with more walls of books was visible behind the front room. The whole effect was one had entered the Victorian man-cave of some duke or earl who was very fond of books. It certainly seemed to be the type of shop where one could relax with a fine book and some brandy—which is exactly what they all did as they sat in the front room.

Stephen had brought his overnight case, from which he now extracted a parcel wrapped in brown paper. Carefully unfolding the paper, he revealed the embroidered commonplace book, with its pearls and the gold-threaded "AV" on the front cover medallion.

"Good lord," said Soames. He tried to calm himself somewhat and said, "That looks like Princess Elizabeth's book at the British Museum, the one she made for Catherine Parr. She copied out some inspirational work—*Mirror of the Synful Soule*, or something—in a really fine italic hand inside it."

"I don't think that was an accident," said Stephen. "Anne's family was grooming her to be a close companion to the Queen.

She even followed the same curriculum as Elizabeth did with her own tutor, Roger Ascham—you know, learning Latin and Greek and translating Virgil, Cicero, Aesop, and so on. Needlework would have been part of the program as well."

"She actually did get very close to the Queen," added Margaret, "but she got closer to the Earl of Oxford, unfortunately. And then she got pregnant, had a baby, and was thrown into the Tower."

"Margaret, that sort of story would only add to the value today. I'm beginning to really like your Lady Anne," said Soames. "May I see it?"

Stephen handed over the book to Soames, who walked over and rested it in a book cradle on his desk, gingerly looking inside.

"That's a handy thing," said Margaret.

"Yes, Margaret—one of the tools of our trade," said Soames. "It's called a book cradle and you use it for paging through old volumes without opening them too much and cracking the spine. It just holds them nicely so you can look at the pages while your hands are busy with something else, like translating or taking notes. They are essential for things like illuminated manuscripts. In fact, you probably have one somewhere in your church: your father might have used one if he was reading out prayers in a formal church service."

"Oh, that's right," said Margaret. "We do. On the altar."

"Well, you'll need one at home now, with a collection like yours. It's critical you take close care of them, you know. Condition really affects value—as I'm sure you understand. Look, I'm sorry for the lecture," said Soames, standing up again and taking another swig of brandy from his glass on the table. "You've just thrown me off my game with this." He glanced over at Mandy who looked absolutely bored to tears. "Mandy, I'm sorry. I just have to spend a little more time with this now. Shall I meet up with you over at Ronnie Scott's? There's an early set tonight at six and we can start over again with a little jazz."

"Sure, love. That makes sense." Mandy said.

She stood up, finished off her last hit of brandy, and extended her right hand, first to Stephen and then Margaret, as if she had practiced in front of a mirror with an etiquette book. "Lovely to meet you. Hope we will see each other again soon." Turning to Soames as she slipped the strap of her bag over her shoulder, she finished, "You, I'll see later." Then she pivoted and walked out the door.

~

They finished at the bookshop about an hour later and they went back to Margaret's flat. The meeting had ended on a high point, with Soames offering Margaret thirty-five thousand pounds on the spot for the collection, based on what he had seen of the commonplace book.

Margaret's immediate response was that she had to think about it. Hearing that, Soames calmed down a bit. He was a bit too excited, he said. The right thing to do was to see the whole collection, because Margaret would have to make a major strategic decision if she wanted to sell.

"Should you keep it together as a single collection, or sell parts of it off in separate lots? Map dealers have the same sort of issue when they have a rare atlas: Would the entire book be more of a treasure than its fifty maps inside sold one by one? Buyers like the University of Texas might make an astronomical bid for all the papers, since it would essentially give them an entire collection as a new credential on the academic stage. Or would individual buyers somewhere like Christie's bring more during the excitement of a bidding war? But we can talk about all that after Stephen has finished his inventory."

"Oh, I see," said Margaret. "That all makes sense."

"Well, I should have it done by the end of the week," said Stephen. "Then we can follow up with you about it—maybe next weekend?"

"Good," said Soames, reaching for his jacket. "Let me know and we'll get together then."

Much to think about indeed and what a weekend it had been: Sarajevo, the British Museum, love, fine food, wine, brandy, and a thirty-five thousand pound offer.

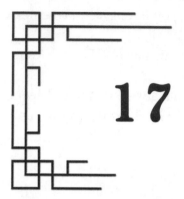

17

Monday morning, there was no drama when Stephen came to the museum with his annual pass in hand. After passing through a metal detector at initial security, he presented himself and his pass at a front desk marked Library, and he was directed up to a corner of the brightly lit top floor, where a sign declaring Manuscripts Students' Room—Private stood in the center of the outer hall. Behind the sign stood a somewhat forbidding entrance to a completely dark corridor. When he went into it, he discovered it quickly snaked to the left, and then the right, to lose all of the glare from the skylights back out in the main hall.

Entering the final windowless *sanctum sanctorum*, he noticed how the light that finally did come up in there was like early twilight. His eyes adapted to it quickly, but it underscored the fact that he was again in a world where too much light would damage the ancient materials within, as at the National Portrait Gallery with its Tudor pictures.

He stopped to read the rules posted outside the cloakroom just short of the dimly lit Manuscript Service Desk farther down the hall. First, all outerwear, jackets, and umbrellas were to be hung in one of the pale wood lockers provided there. The locker keys were imposing, oversize things, to remind you to remember your belongings, and to set off a storm of hell at the last metal detectors if you tried to leave the building with one. Second, briefcases, book bags, or satchels must also be deposited in the locker; just a single notebook or pad was allowed beyond that point. Then thirdly, and most important, no pens, markers, scissors, X-Acto knives, magnifying glasses, or such could be carried in either—all had to be left in the lockers, or preferably at home.

Stephen chose an empty locker, stripped himself of all that, and then proceeded lightly along to the service desk, which was manned by a somewhat prim and mousey-haired young woman.

It was at this point he had to explain the basic nature and scale of his project, and clarify that he wanted to see only primary material—not copies or transcriptions—because the details of the handwriting and the appearances of the paper, watermarks, and inks were all very important to his research. To the librarian, that also meant Stephen would have to be watched very carefully. Nevertheless, she speedily assigned him a numbered seat and handed over a clear plastic shopping bag to hold his notebook, eyeglasses, tissues, and whatever other approved item he wanted to carry in, all of which would be clearly visible to the staff. She also dropped a few pamphlets in the bag, which, she said, would serve as an introduction to using the collections.

Passing through what seemed to be a metal detector, Stephen finally arrived into a large study room, thirty feet wide and fifty feet long, yet strangely not claustrophobic even without any windows. The walls were white. The bookcases, desks, and chairs were all blond wood, and the wall-to-wall carpeting was light gray. The result was an unexpectedly modern look, like a Scandinavian furniture showroom. At one end of the room was a large wall clock, which was useful because there was no way to tell what time it might be by looking outside. It was a pleasant enough setting, but also, fittingly enough, it seemed as if they were all buried in a vault underground rather than sitting on the top floor of the British Museum.

This morning, the place was absolutely quiet, although about twenty scholars were dotted around the room, with open spaces for probably thirty more. Stephen's assigned study place was quite spacious, with about forty inches of desk space. There was a clutch of sharpened pencils, erasers, and a supply of manuscript call slips to be completed with name, seat number, and the catalogue number and title of any manuscript being requested. One of his pamphlets explained completed call slips were to be taken over to the Requests counter (but no more than three at a time would be accepted). Eventually, when someone had retrieved an item from the stacks within, a small light at the researcher's desk—like the Check Engine light on a car dashboard—would turn on; this meant that one or more of the requests had arrived.

Stephen soon realized the librarian had seated him in the corner of the room next to the catalogues of Elizabethan-era materials—so there was a method to their madness. He'd already brought a list of materials to request, starting with letters of Sir Henry Lee in the Burghley Papers, which were actually stored on shelves right in this room, since that collection was studied so often.

Some requests could be ready for you within an hour. Others would arrive the next day. The most obscure might take three to five days to show up because they were stored at some remote storage facility in Brighton—or even in Scotland. Stephen realized he would have to develop a strategy for his requests to be a mix of short and long-term retrievals so he could have a steady flow of things to look over. This was going to take a while, he thought. He'd probably get to know this place very well.

Stephen started by filling out call slips for the letters from Sir Henry Lee to Lord Burghley. There were quite a lot listed in the catalogue and he made separate requests for three at a time.

He was disappointed that he would have to wait to see the museum's material on John Heminge until the next week, because it had to be retrieved from deep storage, but he found out that the Theatre Archive at the Royal Shakespeare Trust in Stratford also had Heminge items in their collection. Perhaps he'd go up there.

To pass the time waiting for his first items to show up, he also filled out a call slip for one of the museum's real treasures, an old manuscript play thought to include three pages written in Shakespeare's own handwriting. As he later told Margaret, he felt as if he was asking the staff to bring the Elgin Marbles up in a wheelbarrow, but somehow they did accept his request after staring him rather closely in the eye. In fact, the librarian offered to set up an appointment with one of their Elizabethan experts to talk him through it. Perhaps Margaret could sit in with them for that.

~

Meanwhile, across town, Margaret presented herself at 9:30 a.m. at the New Scotland Yard offices in a boxlike glass and steel building buried on Victoria Street, just down the road from Big Ben. The man at the reception desk took her picture, printed it out on a laminated lapel pass for her to wear, and directed her to the lift that would take her up to the sixth floor, where she was to meet with Detective Sergeant Desmond Harris of the specialized Art and Antiquities Unit.

The sixth-floor receptionist announced her and Margaret had to wait only a minute or two before Detective Harris came out.

"Good morning, Miss Hamilton. Thanks for coming in to see me." He was a very fit, well-dressed man in his late forties with a gray suit, white shirt, and regimental striped tie. Margaret thought she looked more like a successful business executive than a policeman as he led her down the hall to his comfortable-office looking out over the rooftops toward the Houses of Parliament.

"No problem, detective. Honestly, I knew I was to come to Scotland Yard, but I did not know I was being summoned by the Art and Antiquities Unit. I hope you can tell me a little about what you do," said Margaret, seeming bemused.

"Of course, come in and sit down." He motioned Margaret to sit in one of two chairs in front of his desk, while he took the other one next to her. "I suppose the simplest way to explain ourselves is that we are that part of British law enforcement that deals with illicit trade in art and antiquities—which usually means art or other cultural artifacts which might be stolen, looted, trafficked, forged, and so forth."

"I see. And how have I fallen within your sphere of interest?" Margaret asked.

"We've been asked to join the ongoing investigation around the recent events involving your father, Vicar Hamilton. I've reviewed the local and county police reports and want to discuss all that with you. First, please let me say how sorry I am for your loss. Your father was a well-respected member of your community. The local chief wrote up quite a laudatory note for the file so everyone getting involved with this would know that."

"Oh, that's very good to hear," said Margaret, quite relieved and relaxing a bit more.

"First, I'd like to just talk through a quick recap of what's happened from your point of view—to make sure we're on the same page. Can you tell me that in your own words?"

"Well," said Margaret, "it all started with a flood in my father's church over the August Bank Holiday weekend and his discovery of old papers in one of the tombs there. That tomb belongs to an ancestor of our family who died in the 1650s. We're still trying to determine the nature and value of those papers, but there was publicity in the local paper about 'treasure in the tombs,' and so on, followed very closely by what seems to have been an assault on my father, and his resulting hospitalization and death a short while ago."

"Right, exactly what I've understood. I'm so sorry. And you are a reporter with the BBC, I believe?" asked Detective Harris.

"Yes. I work on international stories—right now it's all about the war in Bosnia—but I'm here in London now on bereavement leave. Although I still go into the office from time to time—because we're so busy and because I need to get out and about after all that's happened," she explained.

"I saw that the BBC—and presumably that's you—recently requested some background checks on various people. What's all that about?"

"I'm sure you can understand how furious and outraged I am about this happening to my father—"

"Of course," said Harris.

"Well, I'm an investigative journalist. And I suppose I just naturally started investigating it all myself. Maybe I shouldn't have, but it was just pure instinct. I don't really know the BBC staffers on the U.K. crime beat well, but I knew them well enough as colleagues to ask them for the favor of background checks on some of the people who seem to be involved in all this. It's really as simple as that," Margaret said unapologetically.

"So, I saw there was one for Tony Baker, who was held for questioning and just released."

"Oh, was he released? Yes, I did request that report. My friend who's been helping me with all this always thought Mister Baker was no villain."

"That friend would be Mister Stephen White?"

"Yes, he's a close friend of the family. In fact, he and I were engaged not too long ago. He studied classics and old documents at Oxford when we were students there and my father asked him to help us understand the papers right from the start—since he can actually read the damn things. So Stephen's been right in the middle of everything, in the most helpful way," said Margaret, deciding just to be as candid as possible.

237

"And there was a second background check requested on a Mister B. H. Rowe?"

"Yes, he was one of Stephen's professors at Oxford, an expert on the Elizabethan period and old manuscripts. Stephen sent him some photocopies of various sample papers and we went to meet with him and hear what he had to say about them."

"And you wanted a background check on him," Harris said, watching her closely.

"That was just blind instinct, I suppose. He was a bit condescending and chauvinistic with me at our meeting—and I didn't like that. So I just was angry and threw his name in as well—but I haven't heard back anything on that." Margaret added, "So I don't know if there's anything there at all."

"Okay. And where are you coming out on the papers? Any conclusions about them?"

"Well, we don't *really* know yet. We're still studying all that as Stephen deciphers the last of them. I do intend to have a proper appraisal done—but we wanted to have a good list or inventory of all that we had before turning them over to experts to value. Mister White is almost finished with that now—there are over one hundred separate items. And he knows that some of them are indeed worth quite a bit. A classmate of ours who is a book dealer in town—we met with him yesterday over lunch—made me a blanket offer of thirty-five thousand pounds for it all. But we all soon agreed that was very premature. Interesting, but premature."

"Who would that have been?" asked Harris.

"His name is Soames Bliforth. As I said, he was in our class at Oxford and studied old documents along with Mister White and Professor Rowe as well."

"I see," said the detective. "And that's where things stand from your point of view?"

"Yes, that's about it. Stephen's still trying to understand a few links from our documents to various people living at that time. But our next steps are to share that inventory Stephen is finishing with Professor Rowe and Mister Bliforth at the end of the week for final comments, and then to have a proper evaluation—whether by an auction house, a museum, or other dealers, whatever we finally settle on."

"Okay, I think I get the picture then," said Harris. "Now, Miss Hamilton, I'd like to get your agreement that we will go ahead on this together from here on—and not with you operating on your own as some kind of freelance investigator. The reason is that there are some ongoing investigations under way here already that might connect with your case, and we can't afford to jeopardize the progress we're making there. All right?"

"Well, that's a 'big ask' from you, as they say. I must be honest and tell you I won't be comfortable with that if I don't feel that we're going to make progress soon to find whoever did attack and ultimately kill my father. I'm sure you can understand that," said Margaret, refusing to simple cave in completely to this man.

"I do see that, and I can promise this case will be getting my full attention," said Harris. "And I will be partnering with the county detectives investigating the possible homicide case already underway."

Margaret sensed she could trust him but was reluctant to just close down her own thinking about how to proceed.

"Now, I do have some next steps in mind. Since you are planning to speak to Mister Rowe and Mister Bliforth about that inventory you mentioned, I would like you to take along a small recording device to capture the conversations you have."

Margaret was actually a bit shocked. "A recording device? You're not going to wire me up like some sort of TV crime drama?"

"No, it would be a small recorder either in a pocket or handbag that wouldn't look at all unlike something you might normally carry as a BBC journalist doing your job. The only difference would be that its capabilities are stronger, and it can capture a normal conversation through the walls of your clothing or bag. That's it. Also, it wouldn't have any lights or make any sounds or vibrations that might indicate it was on and recording—it would seem inert."

"Is that legal?" asked Margaret.

"Well, as a British journalist, you know you can publish secret recordings if the release is in the public interest," responded Harris. "In police work, under the Police and Criminal Evidence Act—or PACE, as we call it—there's no requirement to tell a person they are being recorded before any decision to prosecute is taken as long as doing so is 'reasonable and proportionate.' A bit of a gray area, but I would be comfortable if you did record these conversations in this case."

"Does that mean Mister Rowe or Mister Bliforth might be facing a decision to prosecute them?" continued Margaret.

"No, Miss Hamilton. You see: you yourself, me, our receptionist here on the sixth floor, and even the prime minister *might* someday be subject to a decision to prosecute—as *might* Mister Rowe or Mister Bliforth. But the point of the law is that none of us is right now. So there is no need to caution any of us about being recorded."

"Okay. Let me think about that," said Margaret. "What sort of information would you be looking for?"

"At this early stage, since the illegal antiquities trade is an international, if not global, business, we'd suggest a question or two about whether foreign parties might be interested in these papers—not just domestic buyers—and even who those parties might be, and whether Mister Bliforth or Rowe had any experience dealing with them, and so on," said Harris.

"Yes, I see, I see," said Margaret, musing. "Well, I don't think we're far enough along to ask those sorts of questions just yet. But when we get there, it would probably be all right. I'd like to speak to Mister White about this, if you don't mind. Is that all right?"

"Yes, but I must insist we go along together from this point, Miss Hamilton. Or we risk a real fiasco," said Harris, as Margaret stood up to leave.

"I do understand," replied Margaret, "and I can assure you we'll speak again very soon."

~

She spent a few afternoon hours at the office working with the Sarajevo team as the situation there was deteriorating badly. But all the while she was still processing the interview with Detective Harris in the back of her mind. After she briefed Guy Mitchell on her visit to Scotland Yard as promised, Margaret was determined to keep her four o'clock appointment at Shelter from the Storm, a charity where she volunteered occasionally with Bosnian refugee children. There she could in fact *see* that she was making a difference. Teachers and kids at a school in Hampstead had started the group to help the refugees in the neighborhood engage with the rest of the northwest London community. One day there had been a scene in the cafeteria when a new boy from Somalia suddenly broke down and went to pieces. That made everyone realize they had to *do* something. One of her old school chums had told her about it. So now they were trying experiments with outreach.

This afternoon Margaret was helping with a dancing class for children aged nine to twelve, teaching them a simple Renaissance line and round dance they would perform at the October Hampstead Heath Heritage Fair. The students were a motley crew of smiling pale English faces and slightly darker Bosnian newcomers looking a bit more worried, but also determined to fit in. Some she recognized and others were new.

Margaret knew all about the emotions in the room as she greeted them warmly and brought them gently to order. The refugee kids were slow to trust anyone, having lived through

241

shocks no one should have to endure. One or two stayed very near the door, in case they decided it was time to run.

Calming everyone down, Margaret and Mrs. Jones, the volunteer pianist, lined the children up facing one another, boy-girl, boy-girl. Margaret chose one of the older boys she'd worked with before as her own partner and when the early baroque-era music started, she demonstrated the dance routine. Following her lead, the children stepped forward and then passed one another, before retracing their steps backward to their original positions. Then each boy-girl couple grasped hands, wheeled round and round, and clapped once before sliding back into their original lines, hop-stepping all the while. Next the two facing rows moved off away from each other to make a single line and form a circle. As the circle turned, one boy and one girl would break off and move into the center, whirl each other around, and then return back into the circle, which moved clockwise and then counterclockwise, round and round. By the time they could run smoothly through the routine, it was all smiles and laughter as the children relaxed and hopped happily about with one another in time to the music.

It was wonderful to see how the music and the deliberate actions of the dance steps seemed to lift everyone's spirits and lighten the burden of everyday life from the children, at least for a time. Margaret knew atrocities and carnage might fill their dreams at night. But now her task was to help them join the community of their peers here in Hampstead—"cultural integration," they called it. And she was making a difference. In some small way, the dancing seemed to reach in deeper and help the healing.

The practice went well. Margaret was a good teacher for this. She was very kind and caring to the children, and she knew the subject because her mother had always made dancing a prominent part of her education. Besides demonstrating all the moves,

Margaret danced in the line herself, lightly springing from foot to foot while smiling and laughing with them. The boys argued among themselves about who would hold her hand. And when she dropped her song sheet, four or five of them jostled one another for the honor of giving it back to her.

Afterward, Margaret went to a small office where the young director was sitting with an older woman named Mrs. Arnold, who was called the group's "patron." Mrs. Arnold handled the interfacing with the government authorities and made sure the group had all the resources it needed. And she came in regularly to talk to parents, since she could speak their native languages and most of them couldn't communicate in English well.

After they all talked about how the kids seemed to be getting along, Margaret promised to help with a fund-raising auction during the Christmas holidays. She said she would round up as many of her BBC colleagues as possible to contribute auction items and bid themselves. She could tell Mrs. Arnold wanted to get her more involved.

Leaving to meet Stephen, Margaret felt good about her time well spent, and resumed thinking about her next moves with her "investigation."

~

Walking out of the British Museum about the same time to meet Margaret, Stephen was thinking how the museum had tidied up the past. Every random note from the tumultuous Elizabethan period entering its collection was a document in heaven. Soil had been removed and tears in the paper repaired. Then all that was probably sealed up in a clear protective sheet. That meant if a document entered the collection in 1750, Stephen could probably retrieve it tomorrow and find it in precisely the same condition as when it arrived, or even better, if it had been cleaned. Decay and disintegration were stopped in their tracks.

They met at the Pillars of Hercules again, where Stephen found Margaret sitting at a table by the front window, looking subdued. When she looked up and saw him, she smiled a bit and said, "I think you were right to study the ancient world instead of the modern one."

"How so?" he asked as he sat down next to her.

"Well, I spent the afternoon helping on Sarajevo and the tragedy there is beyond belief. Snipers are targeting the middle of downtown. Some of our team missed our call this morning because they were pinned down where they'd been filming and couldn't get back to the Holiday Inn. The snipers actually want to shoot the women and children who have to run through one "sniper's alley" just to get to the store and school, for god's sake—just to elevate the terror. I don't know how those bastards can live with themselves for doing that. Then I had another message from our team that their driver thought he'd found someone who might know about Mister Juric—so more on that soon. They also wanted to know where Mrs. Juric might have gone after checking in with the government there. Did she have some family somewhere? Where might they live? Can you check with that caregiver at their house?"

"Yes," said Stephen. "Mrs. Quick. She'll be glad to hear we're getting somewhere at least. I'm going to have to change that arrangement soon. I mean, she had no idea she was signing up for taking care of the children so long."

"What will you do?" asked Margaret.

"I was thinking of sounding out some of the parents at our school who have children about the same age, and who are in a position to perhaps take on some young houseguests for a while. I have two possibilities in mind. We'll see."

"The Jurics must have some family somewhere," said Margaret.

"Well, it's no good if the family is in Bosnia, is it? I think it would be better to just keep the kids going along with their routines in the village, don't you?"

"Yes, of course," she replied. "Especially now, while we don't know anything for sure." Changing topics, Margaret continued about her day. "My morning out of the office was much better—I liked the detective at Scotland Yard, although he seemed more interested in stolen antiquities than in finding my dad's killer. But he said he'd take the lead on that, too, and he seemed sincere. He wants us to play parts in his plan to find the killer."

"How do you mean?" said Stephen.

"Well, he said he wanted me to be on side with him, and not wander ahead on my own investigations—which I think I will be okay with, as long as he gets on with everything and starts making progress. As a first step, he asked that we go ahead and set up the meetings with Rowe and Soames to go over your inventory, as soon as you have it. One thing though: he wanted us to tape the meetings to capture everything that's said."

"What!" said Stephen. "That sounds pretty cloak and dagger, don't you think?"

"Yes—and I said I didn't feel ready for that yet. I think we just go ahead and share your inventory with each of them and then get the proper appraisal done. But anything after that, I'm okay with being on his 'team.' Because those two might just drop off the scene with us since we'll being talking with others knowing the real value, and we might never hear from them again. But if they keep prowling around, then I agree we should tape them."

"I don't know if I could pull that off," said Stephen. "I'd probably start fiddling around trying to change the tape on the machine and so on."

"Actually, it didn't seem too bad. We'd just have to carry a micro-recorder in a pocket, and it does the rest. He said it would look normal, but it would really be like a gadget from Q Branch in the James Bond films: it wouldn't need any tending and can just sit quietly in your pocket. Sounds pretty easy. He also wants to talk with you as well—you should call and arrange to see him next week."

"What was he like?"

"At least he didn't play any games or try to catch me out like the other interviews we've had. I think we must have passed some sort of test with the police. Now they think we can be part of the solution rather than suspects of some sort. He was very professional—part of the Art and Antiquities squad at Scotland Yard, of all things."

"Puts a dark cloud over everything, doesn't it?" said Stephen. "We have to be very careful now. It certainly makes me more nervous, in spite of myself. At least I should have the inventory ready to go at the end of the week. I'm just checking things against what's in the British Museum. I saw a few things today, but sadly not their Heminge material—that won't be in from storage until the end of next week probably. So I want to go up to see the Heminge things they have up at the Shakespeare Trust in Stratford as soon as possible. I made an appointment for nine thirty in the morning the day after tomorrow up there. That's the soonest they can show me. Can you come? We could drive up tomorrow and spend the night. That way we can just walk over to the appointment early Wednesday, and not have the drive before."

"Yes," replied Margaret. "They're not expecting me to be in the office all the time now. I briefed people here about how to take over for me on the calls with Bosnia. Besides, I'm totally fixated with all this now—and I need to find out if there is some sort of connection to Shakespeare," she said, pausing a moment. "Because I think that would really change the value equation for these damn papers. Shakespeare would make all the difference between a collection of family papers, and a treasure to kill for. Solving this is now the whole game for me."

18

The next afternoon, after almost two hours driving up the M40 motorway to Stratford-upon-Avon, Stephen and Margaret were glad to pass through the gates of the guest parking area at the riverside Avon Hotel. Once they checked in, they walked down a long corridor running off of the lobby to their spacious, luxurious room, with a cozy sofa and sitting area configured down at the end of the king-size bed. The bathroom was half as big as the main room and could best be described as a spa, with a tub for two and walk-in shower. Before leaving the hotel for a walk, they checked out the dining room on the other side of the lobby; it was empty at that hour but with its views of the river and tables outside on the terrace off the bar, it seemed a fine place to settle in later that evening.

They couldn't speed up their investigations, so they tried to relax and strolled from the hotel down to the riverbank just beside the Shakespeare Memorial Theatre. Turning right, they soon came to the churchyard gates of Holy Trinity Church, where Shakespeare is said to be buried. The churchyard was Disney beautiful, Margaret noted, with none of the lumpy mounds normally formed after a few hundred years of burials, like on the ground around St. Mary's, her home parish. Instead, the lawn around the stone markers was trimmed more like a golf green than a graveyard.

But the inside of the church was no modern fabrication. Stratford had been a wealthy English market town for more than a thousand years, and nothing could say that more than this church's high ceilings, stone arches, majestic cloisters, and stained-glass windows. Those windows, all given by wealthy parishioners, lined the chancel and the sides of the altar and were particularly brilliant when viewed through the dark arches of the walkways in front of them.

As several signs marking the tourist path clearly indicated, Shakespeare's grave and monument were up at the front, on the left side, nearest the altar. The somewhat odd monument to the bard was high on the side wall, behind the protective brass altar rail in front of the sanctuary. Shakespeare's painted effigy had the look of a portly deer caught in the headlights, stuffed by a bad taxidermist, and then hurriedly nailed to the wall above his own gravestone, with his wife Anne's gravestone conveniently just beside.

Margaret looked askance at the memorial. "Seems a bit odd-looking, doesn't it?" she observed.

"Well, I think the good townspeople fiddled around quite a bit with all this as the tourist trade started to grow," said Stephen. "There's a famous sketch of the memorial from the eighteenth century that shows something quite different: a workingman with his arms folded on what appears to be a sack of flour or something. Somebody changed all that into this effete-looking fat man, holding a quill pen in one hand, paper in the other, with arms resting on some kind of leather cushion. I think it was all cobbled together very quickly at some point.

"Oh," Stephen continued, "and the master supposedly wrote the verse on the floor, but it doesn't seem to be up to his usual standard," he said before reading it aloud:

"Good frend for Iesus sake forbeare
To dig the dust enclosed heare
Blese be ye man (who) spares thes stones
And curst be he (who) moves my bones."

"A bit short on the Shakespearean grandeur," said Margaret peering down at the lines carved on the slab on the floor.

"More of the mystery," said Stephen. "As you must know, there's an enormous controversy about whether or not the individual known as the 'Stratford man' actually wrote the works published under his name. All sorts of conspiracy theories have argued the true author to be the Earl of Oxford, or Sir Francis Bacon, or even Queen Elizabeth herself. It's a real circus. There are also people convinced that 'clues' are buried right here. One crazy Victorian-era American lady, Delia Bacon—no relation to Sir Francis—was actually arrested here, along with a work party of laborers she had hired, before they could carry out their plan to dig up the floor—and also bang out the memorial on the wall to find out the truth. She eventually went into an asylum—and she wasn't even the wackiest. Another story says Shakespeare's head was stolen from here by grave robbers and sold to someone for a phrenology examination. You know, to see if there was something odd about the shape of his skull that would explain his genius, and so on."

"What do you think about all that?" asked Margaret.

"Oh, I think the 'Stratford man' was the chief talent behind all those plays. But there's no truth to the belief that he wrote every word and crossed every 't.' Even today any actor will take lines and change them or write new ones if he can make it smoother for himself to say them. You could even see that in our workshop two weeks ago. The kids would change a word or two when they could say it better a different way. That's always happened."

"Well, in school we were told he did write every word, and the text was gospel," said Margaret.

"Maybe. But I think the plays were highly collaborative, and varied. I mean for every soliloquy there are thirty lines like 'Who goes there?' or 'Advance and be recognized' just before. Shakespeare would have focused on the high points—the soliloquies and so forth—not every word. And the plot and pacing. Then lots of people could have tinkered with the script, cutting it down or padding it up for any single version or performance. At least that's my best guess."

They soon left the church, heading back to the hotel along the riverside path. They paused at a dock to admire the swans, who started gathering, excited that a feeding by tourists might be in their future.

"It's a perfect evening, isn't it?" said Margaret.

As they reached their hotel, they could see the outside terraces were filling up with customers eager to have an early drink out in the fine evening weather. Stephen and Margaret sat down and ordered drinks themselves, taking in the views of the river across the street and the back of the Memorial Theater just beside.

"Excuse me," said a young man at the next table with several friends, addressing Margaret. "I think I recognize you from television."

"Make my day!" said Margaret. "You must be one of the few people in England who actually watches the BBC News then because sometimes I get to read out the stories I cover on location. That's about it, I'm afraid—not a glamorous actress, unfortunately."

"Yes, that's it. Well done, you. Over here, *we're* actually the glamorous actors and actresses, thank you very much." All his tablemates laughed. "Don't faint, or anything, but you're actually talking to the Third Soldier in our Royal Shakespeare Company's recent controversial production of *Hamlet*."

"Really? That's wonderful," said Margaret, genuinely.

"And my beautiful companion for the evening—Grace, here—was a maid to Ophelia," he continued.

"You're all well ahead of me," said Stephen. "I'm a village schoolmaster."

"Not too bad, mate. Steady pay and they say Shakespeare was a Warwickshire one as well," the young actor said.

"Why was your *Hamlet* controversial?" asked Margaret.

"It did get quite a lot of coverage—even by the BBC," said the young man.

"Sorry, I cover international events most of the time," replied Margaret.

"Oh, you do have a bad life, don't you? Well, traditionalists didn't like the fact our *Hamlet* was set in more modern times, with all the costumes either black or white Carnaby Street mod-type clothes. We all rather liked it—I mean, Shakespeare is just as relevant in a modern setting as it is in an Elizabethan one. That's one of the good things about him—the work is sort of timeless. Our lead actor was Kenneth Branagh. He was very exciting to work with, even if you happened to be Third Soldier."

Grace added, "Some reviews said it was too gloomy, as well—more like Chekhov than Shakespeare. But, I mean *Hamlet* is bloody gloomy. My lady Ophelia drowned herself, for god's sake."

"Do you like having all your work so focused on Shakespeare, or is that too limiting?" asked Stephen.

"Oh, we do other things, too," said another of the young men. "I'm Fred, by the way. We had *Volpone* by Ben Jonson a while back, and occasionally there are modern things as well. Besides, Shakespeare himself is very varied. After *Hamlet* we were all in *Taming of the Shrew* this year, so we went from gloom to acrobatic farce."

"You all must be really good to get in the Royal Shakespeare Company—even as Third Soldier," said Margaret.

Well," said Grace, "there's never a dull moment."

"Yes," Stephen offered, "I was here with my school a while back for a workshop on *Macbeth* with some of your actors. It was fantastic."

"Oh, we heard about that. Weren't you there with Brian and Tessie?" asked Fred. "They're part of our lot."

"Yes. And an older actor named John."

"I think he's mostly in the office now," said one of the other young men.

"*Macbeth* is my favorite," said Grace. "I mean, the women in it—the witches and Lady Macbeth—really run the show. Unlike *Hamlet*, where the females are all as tame as lambs. I mean, Ophelia drowns herself because stupid Hamlet doesn't seem to like her."

"It's true," said Stephen, "most of the plays have stronger men. Maybe it was the time?"

"Sorry, mate," said Grace. "Same as now, the women really ran the show. They just let the men think they were in charge. Really, most men are just clueless."

"There she goes," said Third Soldier. "She goes off like this all the time—don't you, Grace?"

"Well, I agree with her," said Margaret. "At work for me now, it's all about Sarajevo, where male snipers are shooting at women and children simply trying to get through the streets, because of some type of testosterone-fueled territorial thing. It's absolutely crazy. Any woman at all would do a much better job of running things down there."

"Too right, love," said Grace.

They carried on their good-natured chatting for a half hour—no one was in any mood to get into an argument on such a wonderful evening—until Stephen and Margaret bid the actors good night and went inside for dinner.

~

The next day, Margaret and Stephen stayed late in bed and treated themselves to a Jacuzzi. Then they ordered a room service breakfast. When the girl came to the door with the tray, Stephen greeted her wearing the fancy hotel robe from the closet and had her put the tray down in front of the sofa. Then Margaret startled the girl, appearing from the bathroom in her matching robe, with her wet hair drying underneath a turbaned towel that made Stephen think she looked like the flying nun or something.

"Oh, that looks lovely, thank you," Margaret said to the girl, who retreated quickly, closing the door.

"I bet she's had an eyeful here," continued Margaret. "This hotel looks like a movie set for naughty weekends. I don't want to think about what the staff have come across."

"I'm sure we're pretty tame," said Stephen, lifting the silver-plated lid off the toast and sitting down.

"Not too tame, I trust," said Margaret.

"No, Margaret, not at all. Coffee?"

They settled comfortably into the seating area.

After a few minutes, Margaret said, "You know, I think I'm in the wrong game. I mean, the BBC has been great. It's everything I thought I wanted, and more. But I'm starting to think it's just not right for me."

"How do you mean?" asked Stephen.

"Well, I just go to one horror show, give a riveting eyewitness report for everyone at home, and then pop up somewhere else with more of the same. And do that over and over and over. And nothing ever seems to change."

"I do see what you mean. It must be incredibly hard to deal with all that sort of reality—hard not to be damaged by it," said Stephen.

"I can tell you I feel much better when I go over to work with the refugee kids at Shelter from the Storm. After being with them

Monday night, I felt I'd made more of a difference than I ever do at work."

"Yes, I know what you mean...a little," said Stephen. "Our Bosnian boy at school with the missing parents, Denis. He was a wreck when he first came at the end of the summer—but, at the workshop here with the actors, he was doing really well fitting in with all the other kids. I think he even may be finding a first girl-friend, for god's sake. So he already seems to be healing a little, although who knows what's become of his parents and how that will all turn out."

"Yes, I haven't heard anything more from the team yet, but I know they're still on it. I gave them the name of that village you got from Mrs. Quick about where the mother was from," said Margaret. "Fingers crossed."

After sipping more of her coffee, Margaret continued, "I think that working with those sorts of people—the victims—might be better for me," said Margaret. "I don't have to make a decision right now, or anything, but that's what I'm thinking about. My own family tragedy with my dad—and my mother just before—all that makes me realize none of us has all the time in the world, so I just might do something else next year. We'll see."

~

An hour later, they went across the street to their appointment with the RSC archivist at the Memorial Theatre, whose office was in the Victorian wing attached to the back of the 1930s building.

Based on Stephen's preliminary phone call, the man had assembled a small array of Heminge memorabilia to look over. First were copies of the accounts of the Treasurer of the Chamber and Office of Revels showing payments for plays made to Heminge from 1595 to 1616. All that amounted to a very steady business, especially at the end-of-year holidays, and the players got busier as James followed Elizabeth onto the throne and wanted even more plays performed. More important, one item was a kind of receipt that had a clear signature from Heminge himself. It was an exact match with the one on the Vavasour letter, although another of his signatures there was spelled "Hemynge" instead of "Heminge."

"I don't think that's a problem," the archivist explained. "Spelling in those days was not a rigid affair. If you had more room, for example, you might add more letters, as a flourish. Even the famous six signatures of Shakespeare spell his surname differently, depending on how much space there was."

Afterward, downstairs in the lobby, the vast brick interior of the theater was quiet, with no matinee performance scheduled that day. The modern construction of the lobby, with the tallest red-brick walls Stephen had ever seen, pocketed with soaring glass windows, made for an excellent exhibition space, and the area nearest the windows was filled with display cases.

The theme of the present exhibit was theatrical ephemera, so there were lots of old programs and still photographs of famous productions, as well as wonderful costumes on display.

Ninety percent of everything was Shakespearean, but even Shakespeare would have probably approved of the three cases dedicated to Christopher Marlowe, who was certainly the leading rock star when the "Stratford man" first came to London.

They were sashaying and strolling lackadaisically through the cases when Stephen suddenly came to a halt, saying, uncharacteristically, "Holy shit."

"Stephen?" asked Margaret.

"Sorry—but come look at this. It's a bloody scroll."

There, under glass in a long case, was a scroll with at least four feet of paper extending out from it to the right. Just like the one in Anne Vavasour's papers, the length of paper had been achieved by pasting together regular-size sections edge to edge so they extended out in a continuous flow. It looked like very little of the whole thing was exposed. It would have been three or four times longer than what was being shown. Each page had a section of writing on it separated by thick lines in ink, and various symbols dotted around.

"What does it say on that card down by you?" asked Stephen.

Margaret leaned over the case. "It says this is the prompting tool used by the master actor Edward Alleyn containing all of the lines for the leading part in *The History of Orlando Furioso,* a play ascribed to Robert Greene. And it's the only surviving player's part from the time. Each of his speeches is separated from the others by ruled lines and the lines are in the sequential order for the play. The gibberish above them are the name of the character preceding each speech and the last few words of what the other actor actually says in his finish. The numbers are the act and scene. Below each clip is the name of the character who is to speak next, so Alleyn could look at them, if appropriate, or some stage direction, like 'exit left.' It's on a scroll so he could just grasp the handle and roll it out in rehearsal, rather than holding a pile of sheets, which he might drop or get out of order. Many revisions to speeches are pasted on top of the originals—so it's thick and lumpy in places."

"My god, I've never heard of such things," said Stephen.

"It also says that this contraption was an ingenious solution adopted by Mister Alleyn. Apparently, in the action, his character starts off reading from a scroll in *Orlando Furioso*, and Alleyn just kept holding this one through rehearsals to learn the lines.

"That's it," Margaret finished. "Oh, and it's here courtesy of Dulwich College. And also it says there are many more speeches for his part here on the scroll than in the printed texts of the play in 1593–94 and 1599. Those cut scenes, speeches, and dialogue—and listen to this, 'added rough clownage and horseplay to suit the tastes of a lower-class audience.' Wow."

"I can't wait to see if yours is the same sort of thing," said Stephen, "but I bet it is. I never really did scrutinize it because I had no idea what it was. It was just a mystery."

"Well, I know where it is at the vicarage," said Margaret. "I put it in a drawer of the sideboard in the dining room. It didn't seem to go with all of the papers piled up on the tabletop."

"It's probably from that masque they put on for the Queen at Ditchley," said Stephen, shaking his head and looking down at the scroll. "What luck we were going out by this exhibit."

Just blind luck.

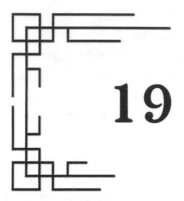

19

Back home in the village that evening, Margaret was helping Stephen scrutinize the scroll from the tomb. Now that they knew it might be a prompting tool, it didn't take long before they could decode it. After a few mysterious pages, they were astonished to arrive at familiar lines spoken by the character of Lady Macbeth in Shakespeare's Scottish play.

"These first pages of the scroll aren't in the play as we know it today," said Stephen. "It starts off here with Lady Macbeth saying goodbye to her husband as he goes off to battle for his cousin, King Duncan. In today's version, her first speech is reading a letter her husband has written her *after* that battle."

"So the battle scene was cut?" asked Margaret.

"I guess so," answered Stephen. "And then the scroll goes on to lines from another scene where Lady Macbeth is lamenting over a child she's just lost. I don't think that's in today's play either."

Margaret stood up and said, "Let me see if I've got a copy of the play in my old room." She ran upstairs and found her Penguin paperback on the shelf by her desk in her childhood bedroom.

As she hurried back into the dining room, Stephen said, "Look, here's something else. On page four of the scroll, there's the speech the kids worked on in the workshop, 'unsex me here,' and so on. But she hasn't been reading a letter before it. She's just declaring her thoughts that her husband was 'too full o' the milk of human kindness.' And those familiar speeches are written in an italic hand and pasted over some previous words underneath."

Pulling out one of the dining room chairs, Margaret said, "I'm going to count out Lady Macbeth's speeches in my old book. Why don't you do the same for the scroll?"

"Okay," he said. "Good idea."

A few minutes later, Margaret announced, "Fifty-five speeches. And most of them very short, like 'Woe, alas! What, in our house?' What have you got?"

"Well, she has eighty-five speeches on this—although more than a few of them seemed to be crossed out, especially at the beginning. That's thirty more speeches than in your paperback," said Stephen, "and a few are quite long."

"Really?" said Margaret. "Well, I think the school version I had was a proper one—you know, the real thing. I mean, I don't think they would have dumbed it down for young teenagers."

"No, I think you'd be right about that. It's probably an exact copy of the First Folio version, perhaps with a little modernization, but otherwise the same," he said. "You know all of the sources and versions of Shakespeare's plays are well documented. We've got a set of 'variorum editions' over at the school that detail any changes made version to version. I'll go over and get the one for *Macbeth* and bring it back here to look at. But I do know *Macbeth* is one of the shortest of Shakespeare's plays—almost ninety minutes shorter than *Hamlet*, for example. And the acting companies did adapt their master scripts to fit the time allowed and type of audience."

"Like Mister Alleyn and his scroll in Stratford," said Margaret.

"Exactly," said Stephen. "So I'll be back with our library's book in fifteen or twenty minutes."

~

Stephen was excited when he returned. "It looks like *Macbeth* is a special case," he explained. "Many of the other plays collected in the *First Folio* were printed up earlier in rough editions called quartos—but not *Macbeth*. The first time it ever showed up was when they put it into the First Folio, seven years after Shakespeare died. It was a later work. They know it was written after Queen Elizabeth died because it features some of King James's interests, like witchcraft, plus it was an epic of Scotland. And scholars have always thought the text of the play printed in the First Folio was cobbled together."

"How do you mean?" asked Margaret.

"Well, two songs were lobbed in that also appear in a play called *The Witches* by Thomas Middleton—the words weren't even written out. In act four, the second song is just is a stage direction saying something like 'Music and a Song. Blacke Spirits, et cetera'—using quick shorthand, as if they were too pressed for time to write it all out. And before that, in act two, the variorum notes say that Samuel Taylor Coleridge and others thought the whole scene with the drunken porter was added in by someone other than the author for comic relief—the one where the man's mumbling around at the gate complaining about strange knocking. So it looks like they typeset *Macbeth* for the First Folio directly from a promptbook cut down and tinkered with quickly for a specific performance."

"How would they know that?" asked Margaret.

"For most of the other plays, a meticulous copyist like Anthony Munday or Ralph Crane would write out everything for the typesetters, making changes and giving a consistent formatting for the stage directions and so on. But that wasn't done for *Macbeth*."

"And so the scroll has newly discovered parts of *Macbeth*," said Margaret. "That sounds amazing."

"It would be more than just amazing. There are still literally thousands of books and papers published about Shakespeare every year—I mean, he usually has his own section at any good bookstore. I think the academics would go mad for this. They would finally have something *new* to talk about. It would really drive up a bidding war at an auction, I would think."

"My god," said Margaret.

"I also found some more information on the scroll we saw up in Stratford. We just got in this new book on the Elizabethan stage by Andrew Gurr, from Cambridge University Press. It says Alleyn actually owned the play: it was dear to his heart and he always played the main role. Indeed, he took the play with him when he moved from one acting company to another. The scroll was his personal aide-mémoire for all his lines. It shows that the quarto version was seriously abridged, and there was much more to the full play, as shown by all the extra speeches on Alleyn's scroll. So that seems to be what's going on here with your scroll for Lady Macbeth."

~

Later, Margaret was in the kitchen, looking for something that could be thrown together for a light evening meal, while Stephen remained in the dining room with the scroll. He had been happy to hear that Margaret had planned a dinner meeting with Soames on Saturday. He had asked Rowe for a similar meeting, hopefully on Saturday as well, so they could complete the stage of getting their friends' input before engaging with Maggs and Company, the booksellers they had finally selected to appraise the collection, and bringing Scotland Yard into the picture.

Looking down at the scroll, Stephen noticed that several of the most important speeches made by Lady Macbeth were pasted over by bits of paper with lines written out in the same neat italic hand.

He remembered the story of italic writing infiltrating England. It started showing up from Italy around 1550 and one of its biggest fans had been Princess Elizabeth's own tutor, Roger Ascham. He was an outstanding practitioner of the form at Cambridge and also personally taught it to his royal pupil. Part of its attraction was its simplicity along with the speed with which it could be written without becoming illegible. It was also graceful and beautiful, and soon was being used for special words—like book titles or verse quotes—even when the rest of a document might still be written in the secretary hand.

Of course, the very nature of italics removed many individual eccentricities from handwriting, so all the examples of it from the sixteenth century looked very similar. But it did seem the italics on the speeches pasted over on the scroll were particularly delicate and familiar to Stephen. Or perhaps it was just the wine that he had opened a half hour before for himself and Margaret to share before dinner, which would start very soon. He was already just about through his first glass and hadn't had much to eat that day, so he could sense a light buzz.

He stood up from his place at the dining room table and walked around to the other side, where some of the Vavasour papers were piled up in a stack. He grabbed Anne's commonplace book—the earliest one, from her schooldays—brought it back over to where he had been sitting with the scroll, and opened it up.

There was Anne's excerpt from the *Aeneid* of Virgil, *"Forstan et haec olim meminisse iuvabit"*—"Perhaps one day it will help to remember these things." That's what Aeneas had said to console and rally his men after they had been thrashed by the Cyclops and shipwrecked. Anne had written the Latin out beautifully in a most prim and perfect italic hand.

His eyes drifted from the commonplace book over to the scroll, and he felt himself stop breathing. It seemed his heart even skipped a beat.

"Holy fuck," he wheezed out. "Margaret, can you come in here?" he said, almost sounding in distress.

"What is it, Stephen? Are you all right?" she asked, craning her head around the corner from the butler's corridor connecting the kitchen to the dining room.

"Just look at this," Stephen said.

Margaret came over behind his shoulder. Stephen pointed to the commonplace book quote and the pastedown on the scroll.

"Goodness," said Margaret. "The handwriting seems to be identical."

She moved her eyes from one page to the other.

"Stephen," she said. "What does that mean?"

"I think it means that Anne was involved with editing the play somehow," he said.

The two of them stood motionless, looking down at the writing on the table, realizing that everything had just changed.

~

Ultimately, their appetites reemerged about an hour later, but not their will to cook. Margaret called in a takeaway order from the Indian restaurant just down the street. And then the two of them took a break to walk down to get it.

"Well, do you have any ideas about why Anne would be writing on that scroll?" asked Margaret.

"I'm not sure. I'm still mulling it over. One thought was maybe they put on their own performance at Sir Henry's house. Remember how Professor Rowe said they might have made singing sheets for the servants and so forth. Maybe something like that?"

"Hmmm," said Margaret. "Seems like a stretch, don't you think?"

"Oh, I suppose so. It's a mystery," replied Stephen. "Part of me wants to peel up the pastedowns and see if I can make out what's written underneath, but I don't want to mangle the manuscript. We'll have to wait until it's in a conservator's hands to do that sort of thing. But meanwhile, I really want to dig in and scan everything I haven't read yet in the whole collection. This scroll and the Heminge letter are so far the only things connected to anything Shakespearean. It would be incredible if I could find something else—and that's my first priority. I certainly need to have that done before we turn over anything to Maggs, and we need to see them soon to know the value."

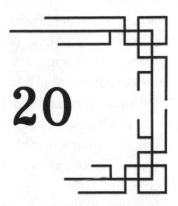

20

On Thursday morning, a much more quarrelsome couple were meeting thirty miles away in Gloucestershire. Soames Bliforth had beaten a retreat from his spacious mews house and charming bookshop in London to the refuge of his Grade II listed farmhouse in the picture-postcard Cotswold village of Upper Slaughter. Dating from about 1700, the honey-colored limestone main house and outbuildings had been lovingly maintained— mostly by the previous owners, who had doted on them for their thirty years of stewardship, and who sold it all on to Soames a few years earlier, glad to fund their retirement from their proceeds of another Cotswolds property boom. It was sheltered by lush gardens in the warmer weather and was only a short walk to the meandering banks of the River Eye or the welcoming bar of the Lords of the Manor hotel. Today, however, the house's best feature was the radiant heat rising from the floor to fend off the chill of a damp gray damp afternoon.

For this visit, Soames had not invited his iridescently hot girl-friend Mandy—although she had been several times before. She couldn't stand being so far away from the bright lights of the city for very long, and now Soames's full attention was needed for coming up with some new way to stay afloat in the sea of debts and promises that had been bankrolling his high-flying lifestyle the last few years. Selling old books and manuscripts could help address the problem, but now that his family inheritance was blown, he was, quite frankly, coming up a bit short: about half a million pounds short, in terms of his current accounts, and his creditors were turning somewhat nasty.

As it happened, Mandy did not have the exclusive rights to Soames's affections, and on this occasion Soames brought an even more unlikely lover for his planning session: the distinguished professor Hugh Rowe of Horton-cum-Studley, Oxfordshire. No doubt both Mandy and Rowe would have been shocked to learn exactly what they had in common, because neither had an inkling of the other, nor did they know the variety of their shared boyfriend's sexual tastes. But Soames was most comfortable with his choices: Mandy for outrageousness and sex; and Rowe for elite access and thefts.

His dalliance with Professor Rowe had begun right at the beginning of his university career when a few quick sex acts each week improved Soames's university grades substantially. Since he'd had already solved the problem of low grades in boarding school by warming up the beds of his resident public school masters, it had not been too much of a burden to tolerate old Rowe. However, by now, the professor was getting a bit old for sexual adoration.

But the old boy had other delights. As perhaps the nation's premier Elizabethan and Shakespearean scholar, Rowe had unquestioned access to the rarest books and manuscripts in the land—whether they were safely housed in secure premises like the British Museum, or held more tenuously in the uncatalogued libraries of decaying stately homes. In the latter premises, the owners were usually flattered to give the old boy access to their family treasures—after all, they didn't really know even vaguely what they had on all those shelves, and perhaps the great man could help enlighten them?

Most were content to welcome Rowe into their mansions midmorning and settle him down comfortably in their libraries. They usually wouldn't disturb him until lunchtime, and perhaps again for tea, when he might be able to tell them more about their own treasures. That sequence might continue for a day or two, and then the old boy would be gone, happily pursuing his research for some new bestselling book. It was usually very useful for these owners too, because Rowe would have left them with two very valuable things: first, a short list of treasures they should consider selling, in the highly unlikely event they ever needed to raise money; and second, an introduction to a trusted London book dealer named Soames Bliforth, who could be counted on to give them top prices.

Of course, what they didn't know was that several unlisted treasures from their collection also left along with Professor Rowe. In the early days, stealing them was simple as burying items in the lower regions of his briefcase, but after one or two embarrassments of near discovery, Rowe adopted another clever plan.

Sometime before, Soames directed his Saville Row tailor to add what he called manuscript pockets to several of his own jackets and coats. For the jackets, this meant the addition of a flap across the inside back panel just below the shoulders. The flap could be lifted up to reveal a zippered seam which could open a huge pocket across the full width of the back of the jacket, extending down to the lowest seam at the bottom, measuring about thirteen inches wide and twenty inches deep. Soames told the tailor these pockets would avoid the stigma of carrying clumsy portfolio bags when traveling with manuscripts for clients. He didn't mention they were also great for concealing large papers to spirit away from unsuspecting owners. The pockets in his finer suits were best when only a few leaves of papers were carried, but his nice sporting tweed jackets could conceal quite a bit more without becoming too lumpy. Similar pockets in custom-tailored raincoats were bigger and very useful.

In fact, he wanted to have several similar items made for a friend as well, and Professor Rowe was only too happy to present himself at the shop on Saville Row to have his own manuscript-pocketed garments made. Anything to please his dear boy, Soames.

About 80 percent of the owners Rowe made his appraisals for ended up introducing themselves to Soames. Most sold their complete lists to him. Only a few held on to a family treasure or two, usually for a future sale in a year or so. None of these grandees wanted their names attached to the items going forward, because they didn't want their fellow club members to know they were flogging the family treasures to pay the bills. Therefore, if Soames later put things up for sale at the major auction houses, the documents were always listed as "Property of a Gentleman." Over time, Soames listed so many properties of so many gentlemen, that the specific provenance of any one item would have been conveniently obscured, and even the original owners would have no clue the auction lot had originally belonged to them.

This modus operandi worked a charm for manuscripts, which by their very nature are one of a kind and of varied sizes and conditions, each of which can be further modified by discreet trimming to a new size, or by a strategic tea stain or simulated wormhole making them appear different than they were when they were stolen. Printed books were more difficult to mask because they usually have easily recorded bibliographical details such as publisher, date, bookplates, and bindings. But over time Soames and Rowe extended their activities into these more exposable areas as well. They needed to ramp up the flow of treasures to sell as more and more of Soames's family inheritance disappeared.

The current get-together coincided with a particularly bad set of circumstances for Soames. First of all, his inheritance was now completely gone: there was nothing left to dip in to when he ran a little short; he was all dipped out. Secondly, one lender had discovered the goods used as collateral for a substantial loan to Soames were also used as collateral for loans from other lenders as well. While this enlightened lender probably suspected some of Soames's business was trafficking in stolen goods and didn't want to expose him, he did indeed now want his money back—immediately, or else. Finally, mortgage payments and rents for his farmhouse, London house, and bookshop were all about to go one month late when December's bills went unpaid, so he needed an urgent solution.

Rowe had started reluctantly on this slippery slope of supplying items for Soames as a kind of lark for his deliciously attractive young lover. The first purloined items sold had simply paid for an April holiday villa for them both in Tuscany, a few years before. It was well worth it for the older man who returned from Easter break with a healthy tan and a new vigor poured back into his loins. After that, it was more of a game—because it was so easy to dupe these clueless degenerated aristocratic families—and the young man was so proud of the old professor as a good provider. He was actually proud of himself as well.

But lately Soames's desperation had become all too noticeable to Professor Rowe. While he himself had plenty of money from his teaching, books, and lecture fees, the young man was swimming fast to keep from drowning. When he thought of the expense of this Gloucestershire retreat in Upper Slaughter, that mews house in London, and all the bespoke clothing, the old professor could only thank the Lord for his own lesser mortgage-free existence, and worry about how all this might be likely to end.

This Thursday, those concerns finally came out of the closet and into the kitchen table conversation in the charming stone-walled old farmhouse.

Soames began, "I do have to believe the gods are still smiling down on me—because at this moment of my greatest need, they have also presented our greatest opportunity."

"What do you mean, my boy?" asked Rowe.

"Those Vavasour papers. I mean, between what I already stole and what you've told me still remains, that collection would put 'PAID' to all my bills and probably set us up for life, with a new villa on Lake Como as well."

"Hmmm," said Rowe. "Haven't we taken too many chances on that one already?"

"I do admit I made a misstep with the vicar...but we have to prevail somehow. As far as I know, I don't think either White or the Hamilton girl fully understand what they have."

"True."

"By my measure, the *Macbeth* manuscript I have already taken could bring things to a ridiculously high level—it's possibly a million-pound item or more. And the other new specimens will add fuel to the debate about Shakespeare authorship. So they would set off a bidding war between the British and American museums, the Folger, the RSC, and the University of Texas, and so on. All together, who knows where the bidding could take this?"

"But even Master White and Miss Hamilton might deduce these things came from their papers," said Rowe. "We've already taken in a good haul from them. Shouldn't we be very discreet and careful dripping all that out into the rare manuscript world and leave well enough alone? I don't think they suspect anything yet, and if we retire from the field and leave them alone for all the future fanfare about the items they still have, we might just be able to slink away and carry on elsewhere."

"How can we leave that much money on the table—it's probably equivalent to the gross national product of Trinidad and Tobago, for Christ's sake," said Soames. "And unlike you, I'm about to be ruined as soon as December comes around."

"Well, you let your high jinks go too far. Can't you just sell this place, for example? I don't think you come up here very often and it must be worth a fortune. You already have a nice place in the city—why in god's name do you need this, too?"

"Thanks very much for the lecture, professor. I don't think there are too many people seeking trophy holiday houses in Gloucestershire just now. Although there probably will be takers in the spring. But I need a way to stay above water until then and I don't see anything better."

"Can you take out a loan on it now?" asked Rowe naïvely—property mortgages were anathema to him and something to consider only in the most desperate of times.

"I already have a loan on it. Three loans, in fact."

"My goodness—this is dire."

"I'll tell you how dire: we're going to get ahold of those papers—all of them. I don't know just how at this moment. But we're not going to leave here today without some sort of plan. I'm going to call the Hamilton girl tomorrow and firm up plans to see her about their inventory on Saturday evening. And you should see Stephen as well. We have to move fast. Eventually, we'll probably just have to take the damn things."

"My dear boy, I can't see how we can expect to do that and get away with it."

"It may, unfortunately, mean that we grab the papers and then make damn sure there are no witnesses to tell the tale."

"What do you mean?"

"I mean," Soames continued, "I don't think Stephen White and Margaret Hamilton have shared their discoveries with anyone else. I don't think they have finished making their own study and inventory of them. And I don't think they have alerted other parties about what they have found in any detail. Therefore, if those two were to exit this drama, we would be free and clear just to take over the papers. I could forge a bill of sale for one hundred thousand pounds proving I bought them. We might have to be discreet for a while, but I could make enough private sales to tide things over for the next year or so. Then the fog would eventually lift and we could be at the focal point of the most important manuscript discovery of the past hundreds of years. I mean, we'd have to give pride of place to the Dead Sea Scrolls and the Rosetta Stone, I suppose. But otherwise, this would be it."

"They would have to 'exit the scene?'"

"Yes, I'm afraid that would have to be an essential part of the plan. No witnesses. No one to explain every detail of the early discovery stages—that would all have to disappear."

"And you'd achieve that by..."

"Come on, professor. Don't be coy with me—it doesn't suit you. We will have to permanently remove Mister White and Miss Hamilton from this story. Perhaps they have a terrible car crash when their brakes fail, or they fall victims to some sort of pestilence or attack. Any way you like, but they have to be gone," concluded Soames.

"We can't take on murder, for god's sake. It would be better for you just to suffer the consequences of your extravagance. History is full of people who were ruined and then rose again to make another fortune. You don't have to get even deeper into an impossible situation, you know. They no longer imprison people for debt in this country."

"Well, just listen to you, you horny old crow! You who like private villas in Tuscany, first-class seats on British Airways, and the warm glow of all those television cameras for your interviews. I'm not going to be the one who takes the fall on this one, mate. If I go down, you're coming with me. And perhaps I can get some relief by giving evidence about your career of stealing treasures from the unsuspecting aristocracy and great libraries of this nation, while I was forced to be the poor book dealer duped in to buggering you and monetizing your ill-gotten gains. Maybe I'll get extra marks for preventing the embarrassment of the Queen, who is on the verge of giving you your knighthood or even more. Perhaps she'll make you the Lord of Misrule?"

Rowe couldn't even comment on that diatribe—he was stunned.

"It's ironic that all this is tied up with *Macbeth*, isn't it. Well, I can say that it's you who is 'too full of the milk of human kindness' and that if this is to be done, then 'twere well it were done quickly.' We just have to come up with the specifics of the plan."

The silence in the room was deafening. On the one hand, Soames had already accepted the worst and was just looking for a specific plan to do it. And on the other hand, Rowe was just now understanding what their game had come to.

There was already one man killed by accident.

And now, it had come to murder.

~

While Soames and Rowe were unraveling that Thursday, Margaret's team in Sarajevo discovered a lead on Mister Juric. There had been a lot of meetings going on in the main government building the day the intense shelling started and one driver recognized Juric's picture. He said he might have dropped him off near there before the firing started. Aid workers were going through all the rubble now that the fires were all out. So they might know more soon—but not good news. Margaret and Stephen decided to call the children's caregiver with the update and then go over to visit the children after school.

The Jurics had rented a semidetached stucco and tile-roofed house in the village. It was set back from the busy road leading downhill to the British Rail station, with a front garden shielded by mature trees. It was close enough to St. George's School that Stephen could just walk over for the arranged time at 4:30 p.m. On her way from the vicarage, Margaret stopped at the bakery and bought half a dozen of their prized lemon tarts as a treat. They came up to the house together and rang the bell on time. Denis Juric opened the door to welcome them.

"Hello, sir," he said to Stephen.

"Hello, Denis. I'm not here as your headmaster, by the way, but as one of your parents' friends, all right? So please do relax. This is Margaret Hamilton."

"Hello," Denis said. "You're Mister White's girlfriend, aren't you?"

"Denis!" boomed a stern voice from inside.

Margaret reddened slightly, but answered, "That's right, Denis. How did you know that?"

"From the funeral, miss. I saw Mister White with you there. I'm very sorry about your father. Please come in."

"Thanks," said Margaret, taking Stephen by the hand and stepping inside. She knew the boy wasn't being rude, but she was startled by his directness.

"This is my sister, Mia," said Denis, motioning toward a brown-haired, big-eyed little girl of about eight who looked up at them cautiously. She was dressed in a brown school uniform and sat surrounded by books and school papers spread out on the carpet in the lounge.

"Hello, Mia," said Margaret, as the girl shyly returned to her work.

"And Mrs. Quick is just through here, in the kitchen," said Denis, leading them on.

Mrs. Quick was just heating a small piece of meat on one of the stovetop burners and it was crackling softly. "Hello, there," she said smiling up at them. She was a prim and erect woman of about fifty, neatly dressed in a brown cardigan and matching tartan plaid skirt, with reading glasses hanging on a chain from her neck. "Denis is very direct, I've discovered. Says whatever is on his mind."

"Yes, same at school," said Stephen. "Well, Mrs. Quick, may I introduce you to Margaret Hamilton, Vicar Hamilton's daughter?"

"Oh yes." Mrs. Quick turned from Stephen to Margaret. "Hello," she said, offering her free right hand to Margaret.

"Are you cooking for tea?" asked Margaret. "Can I help?"

"Oh no," said Mrs. Quick. "This is just for Billy here," pointing to a wire-haired fox terrier on the floor. Her dog was sitting bolt upright and staring intently at the frying pan on the stove. "Aren't you a good boy, Billy? Yes, yes, aren't you now," cooed Mrs. Quick to the dog. "I've made a few tea sandwiches for us."

"Really," said Margaret, thinking how odd it was that she made tea sandwiches for the humans and cooked meat for the dog. "I've brought us all some lemon tarts from the bakery as well."

"Thanks for letting us stop by," said Stephen.

"Glad to see you," said Mrs. Quick. "Denis, would you and Mia please wash your hands and join us at the dining table?"

The boy turned around and called, "Mia, come on and wash up for tea," as he went back toward the lounge.

"How are things going?" said Stephen.

"As well as can be expected. We'll have a chat about it after tea, shall we?" said Mrs. Quick, as she led them through a swinging door and into the dining room. There she had the table set with five places and a plate of tiny tea sandwiches in the center. Stephen and Margaret sat down as the kids scampered in and Mrs. Quick came back with the hot water.

They started with some small talk, asking the children how they were getting on at school. Mia was very quiet, but Denis spoke up about how much he enjoyed the outing to Stratford. "My mother was really interested to hear about it. She did some acting of her own in school and thought it sounded wonderful. We talked about making a family trip up to Stratford to see a show later this fall."

"And I understand you're doing well at football this term?" asked Stephen.

"Yes, sir—much better than cricket. We used to play football at home all the time."

"Well, don't give up on cricket. We'll need you when we get to the spring to summer term!" kidded Stephen.

"Mia, what's your school like?" asked Margaret, gently.

Mia kept her eyes on her tea sandwiches and shrugged her shoulders to the question.

"She's a quiet one," said Mrs. Quick. "But we do have nice chats with the bedtime books, don't we, Mia?" That at least elicited a concessionary nod instead of a shrug.

"Mia, they brought us some of the lemon tarts from the bakery where Mother takes us," said Denis to his sister. "You know, the store with the big glass cake counters and where the big girls all wear white hats?" That got her to crack a smile, looking back at him.

"In fact, let me go and bring those in now," said Mrs. Quick, standing and heading into the kitchen.

After the sandwiches and the tarts, Stephen said to the children, "I've been in touch with your dad's embassy. They're continuing to try to find him and your mother." The kids were reading Stephen's face carefully. "Margaret is also helping," he continued. "She works with the BBC—"

Margaret interrupted. "Yes," she said. "For work, I have to be in touch often with a team in Sarajevo now. I've told them we need to find your parents. So they're asking around along with the embassy, too."

"We just wanted you to know all that is happening," said Stephen.

"That's good to know, isn't it, children?" said Mrs. Quick. "With all that going on, we'll hear some news soon."

"Like whether they're dead," said Denis.

"Or not," parried Mrs. Quick, used to dueling with him by now.

Stephen had too much respect for Denis to lob back platitudes and reassurance, but after some silence, Margaret soldiered on. "Mia, I saw you had all those animal books out in the lounge around you. Have you been to the zoo here? The one really close by?"

Mia turned and made eye contact with her for the first time, not knowing whether to show interest or not.

"Well, it's not an ordinary zoo," continued Margaret. "It's where the London animals go for breaks. All the animals are running free. There are no cages. You can even walk among the ones that aren't too dangerous, and get very close to the others who roam about in their own big fields. Did you know?"

Mia almost replied, but then turned to Denis.

"We did go to the zoo in London when we moved here," said Denis, "but then we heard it was to be closed."

"I heard that, too," said Margaret. "But that was a false alarm. The politicians were arguing about their budgets and one side threatened to close it—get rid of all the animals and fire the staff. The zookeepers even offered to pay for it all themselves, with help from a public appeal. But then something unexpected happened and saved everything."

"What happened?" said Mia, speaking for the first time.

"Well, we helped Kuwait early last year when they were threatened by Iraq. The emir of Kuwait heard about the situation and simply sent all the money needed to pay for the zoo and all its expenses as a gift from the children of Kuwait to the children of Britain."

"Really?" said Mia.

"Don't expect that to happen for us," said Denis.

"Well, we can jolly well go to the zoo," said Margaret. "No matter what. Let's have a picnic lunch there on Saturday— all right? I'll take you, and that's a promise. It doesn't help to make everything even worse than it is, you know, Denis—no matter what."

After they finished their tea, Mrs. Quick escorted the children off to finish their homework and came back alone to join Stephen and Margaret at the table.

"You seem to doing a wonderful job, Mrs. Quick," said Stephen.

"Yes, indeed," agreed Margaret.

"Well," responded Mrs. Quick, "I'm trying to keep everything going along as normally as possible. Off to school, play outside after, settle down for tea, do your homework, have a light supper, take your baths, and then bedtime stories—you know. Denis comes in to watch television with me or talk for a half hour or so after I put Mia to bed. But obviously, they're very upset beneath the routine. Last weekend was a lot trickier with all the time to fill, I can tell you. So thanks for offering the picnic, Margaret. Mrs. Juric asked me to come for a week at most—but now it's been two weeks since I heard from her. I keep the news off the radio and television in case there are stories about Sarajevo. We'll have to come up with a longer-term plan, I think, unless we hear something soon."

"Mrs. Quick," said Stephen, "I've spoken to one family at St. George's—with children of about the same age as Denis and Mia. They may be willing to take them into their home for a few weeks. Or even longer if necessary. How does that sound?"

"That would be better, I think."

"And meanwhile the embassy asked me to make sure you have everything you need for the children, and to let you know they will reimburse any and all of the expenses you have. Just keep a list."

"Oh, that's good to know. I've been going shopping day to day—and I will again tomorrow." She laughed. "All these little things have to be done right in the face of the ominous big picture."

"I get the feeling the embassy is also very much in the dark about what's going on at home," Stephen said. "Margaret's team is really stretched as well. It's chaotic."

"Yes," said Margaret. "Yesterday I heard they have a lead they're following up on. And I gave them the name of that village you gave us where there might be family. But I haven't heard back yet with anything else. They did warn me the news might not be good when it comes."

"The picnic idea will be very helpful," said Mrs. Quick. "I have to drive back over to my house, check on everything, get a few things for Billy, and tend the plants and so on. It would be a good break."

"Fine, then. I'll drive my father's car from the vicarage and pick them up here at ten on Saturday. I'll take care of everything for the picnic. I'll load them up on books, toys, and videos at the zoo shop and have them back here between three and three thirty, all right? I have something to do that night in the city, but the zoo is unique and will surprise them, I think."

And a good surprise will be better than dread, thought Margaret.

At least for a while.

PART FIVE

PART FIVE

1603. Queen Elizabeth hung on tight until the very end, and gave the nod for the succession to her cousin James VI of Scotland only on her deathbed. Early the morning of March 24, Elizabeth died in Richmond and a rider headed north to Edinburgh with the news. Then her body was moved to Whitehall in a river procession of barges draped in mourning black. There she lay in state awaiting burial for over a month while her old court went on as usual.

At last, on April 28, a funeral procession of fifteen hundred mourners marched with her hearse to Westminster Abbey. On her coffin was a painted wax effigy, so lifelike many thought it was her body, still unchanged by death, and another legend about her spread. She was entombed with her own coffin literally sitting on top of the coffin of her sister, Queen Mary, "partners of the same throne and grave."

On May 7, seventy-year-old Sir Henry Lee led a troop of sixty men who rode out from London to welcome James arriving from Scotland. They wore golden chains or scarves decorated with the motto *"Constantia et fide"*—"Constant and faithful." The new king knew Sir Henry well and spoke "lovingly" to him, well pleased at the reception.

In July, Sir Henry was at the Order of the Garter installation with King James, and in September, when the court was at Woodstock most of the month, James and his wife, Queen Anne of Denmark, went to visit Sir Henry and Anne Vavasour at his country house three miles away, with the Dutch and French ambassadors in tow. James loved to hunt, and he asked Sir Henry to become a mentor on chivalry to his son Harry, the Prince of Wales.

~

1605. Sir Henry had a full-size portrait of Anne painted by Jacobe de Critz, one of the family of Flemish artists he patronized at court. Anne is resplendent in a bejeweled ensemble and mysteriously holds either a glove in her left hand, or possibly the hand of an ailing Sir Henry, who might have been lying just outside the main image area of the portrait, on a daybed.

~

1606. Sir Henry was ill and missed the Garter installation and feast in April, but he recovered and was at court during the summer state visit of Queen Anne's brother, King Christian IV of Denmark and Norway. The last week of July, both he and Shakespeare (who, as one of the King's Men players, carried the rank of Groom of the Chamber at court and was issued red cloth for his livery) were probably in attendance for the public procession of James and Christian into the City of London. A week later, King Christian was admitted into the Order of the Garter. He celebrated his installation the same evening at Hampton Court, where he viewed a shortened performance of a new play by Shakespeare called *Macbeth*. Songs and jests were added and the script was trimmed to fill no more than two hours in the evening's well lubricated festivities on the eve of Christian's departure for home. However, the drinking didn't dampen the interest of the royal guests—they were transfixed by the play.

~

1607. Edward Vere, Anne's bastard child from her days as Gentlewoman of the Bedchamber for Elizabeth, was knighted for his military service by King James. A scholar as well as a soldier, he was famous for spending "all summer in the field, all winter in his study."

~

1608. James's wife, Queen Anne of Denmark, visited Anne and gave her an especially fine jewel. Sir Henry, now aged seventy-five, was energized by his sweetheart's recognition and decided to go to court again, one more time. Anne and Henry's bastard son, Thomas Lee, won a royal appointment as a Yeoman of the Armoury; and Anne's younger brother Thomas Vavasour became a favorite of King James and was given both the office of Knight Marshal of the Household and a princely stipend. He built a fine residence called Ham House on the river at Kingston-upon-Thames.

~

1610–1611. Sir Henry prepared tombs for himself, his family, and Anne at the chapel of his estate at Quarrendon, Buckinghamshire.

He died in 1611, a month before his seventy-eighth birthday. His instructions ordered a magnificent funeral. Anne was left alone at age forty-seven, but was well cared for by a rich inheritance assured by Sir Henry and the attentions of her two grown sons, Edward Vere and Thomas Lee who both had successful careers. She moved to a fine house in Surrey, two miles from the beautiful Ham House estate of her younger brother, Sir Thomas Vavasour.

~

1612–1621. The Lee family heirs have repeatedly tried to sue Anne for her inherited treasure, but she always prevailed. In August 1618, the heir of Sir Henry—a distant cousin, but the nearest legitimate heir—attempted to fight Anne on different grounds as described in this letter:

> *Mrs. Vavasour, old Sir Henry Lee's woman, is like to be called in question for having two husbands now alive.*

Anne had remarried, to John Richardson of Durham, but apparently old John Finch was still living. At first the bigamy case went badly for Anne. In February 1621 she was condemned to pay a fine of £2,000 (an incredible sum at the time), with the King's interest in the fine—about half—being granted to the heir. Corporal punishment was also to be administered. However, with James I still on the throne, a royal pardon was issued "to temper the severity of the law with our royal mercy, and grant her dispensation from public penitence or other bodily penalty." James wasn't about to let his old friend's mistress be disciplined in public, and he knew she had plenty of money.

~

1622. Anne was asked to send her shortened version of the script for the 1606 performance of *Macbeth* to John Heminge, who was collecting materials for a memorial edition of Shakespeare's plays, known today as the First Folio. Anne's manuscript was the only copy of that play that Heminge could find.

~

1622–1654. Anne lived another thirty-two years, as a very rich old lady of the old school, fighting off the legal efforts of her figurehead first husband, John Finch, to get her money. In particular, she was a great patron of her village church.

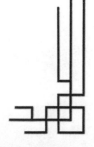

Epigram. Upon the Queen's last remove, being dead

The Queen's removed in solemn sort,
Yet this was strange, and seldom seen,
The Queen used to remove the Court,
But now the Court removed the Queen.

Lines by Thomas Dekker on Elizabeth's death and James's succession

Never did the English Nation behold so much black worn as there was at her Funeral. ... Her hearse (as it was borne) seemed to be an island swimming in water, for round about it there rained showers of tears.

Oh what an Earth-Quake is the alteration of a State!

Upon Thursday it was treason to cry "God save King James, King of England," and upon Friday high treason not to cry so. In the morning no voice heard but murmurs and lamentation, at noon nothing but shouts of gladness and triumph. Saint George and Saint Andrew that many hundred years had defied one another, were now sworn brothers: England and Scotland ... are now made sure together, and King James's coronation is the solemn wedding day.

—Thomas Dekker in his pamphlet
"The Wonderful Year 1603"

Captions on 1605 hunting trophies at Sir Henry's estate in Ditchley

August 24th, Saturday
From Foxehole Coppice rouz'd, Great Britain's King I fled,
But what, In Kiddington Pond he overtoke me dead.
August 26th, Monday
King James made me run for life from Dead man's Riding;
I ran to Goreil Gate, where Death for me was biding.

From a letter about Queen Anne Denmark's gift to Anne Vavasour in 1608

The Queen, before her going out of the County, dined with Sir Henry Lee at his Little Rest, and gave great countenance and had long and large discourse with Mrs Vavasour; and within a day or two after, sent a very fair jewel valued above £100; which favour hath put such new life into the old man, to see his sweet-heart so graced, that he says he will have one fling more at the Court before he die; though he thought he had taken his leave this summer, when he went to present the Prince with an armour that stood him in £200.

—Letter of John Chamberlain
to Dudley Carleton

Inscription engraved on Anne's tomb in the "lost" chapel at Quarrendon

Under this Stone intombed lies a faire & worthy Dame
daughter to Henry Vavasour, Anne Vavasour her name
Shee living with Sir Henry Lee for love long time did dwell
Death Could not part them but that here they rest
within one cell

Naughty epitaph about Anne and Sir Henry, as reported by Aubrey

Here lies good old knight Sir Harry
Who loved well, but would not marry,
While he lived, and had his feeling,
She did lie, and he was kneeling,
Now he's dead and cannot feel
He doth lie, and she doth kneel.

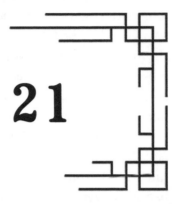

21

On Friday morning, Stephen and Margaret both wanted to be in London early, so they took the 0700 morning train down to King's Cross. Walking out onto the Euston Road, Margaret gave him a light kiss on the cheek and headed west for a quick check in with the Bosnia team at the BBC. Meanwhile, Stephen joined the wave of people marching south into Blooms-bury. He wanted to be at the British Museum at opening time to see the Heminge papers retrieved from storage and compare them with what they had seen in Stratford. Then they would both be together again at a late morning meeting arranged with an Elizabethan expert at the museum, to talk through Shakespeare's supposed handwriting treasure, the play-doctored manuscript of *Sir Thomas More.*

Stephen stopped for a takeaway cappuccino and killed a little time peering into the windows of secondhand bookstores until the museum's gates opened. Once settled in at the Manuscripts Students' Room, it took only a few minutes before he found one bold signature on a short note that confirmed Anne Vavasour's letter from Heminge was genuine. So there was some kind of connection there—but what?

Margaret arrived with a visitor's day pass just before 11:00 a.m. and they were ushered into a small meeting room behind the service desk. She told Stephen there was nothing new to report on the Jurics yet, but everyone in Sarajevo would keep looking. Soon a bearded and bespectacled young man who introduced himself as Doctor Bowen, not much older than Stephen and Margaret, joined them across the table with a small portfolio bag.

After assurances that Margaret was not there in some official BBC capacity, but simply as the owner of a hoard of papers unearthed from her family's tomb, the meeting was ready to begin. Bowen was sharp enough to immediately offer another meeting with people up the chain from him at the museum, if Margaret wanted to have a discussion about having the staff take a look at her papers.

Bowen unzipped his portfolio and took out a massive two-inch-thick block of clear plastic laminate, somewhat smaller than a tabloid magazine, in the center of which was encased a single sheet of paper measuring about 9½ by 12 inches. Around the edges were six substantial brass screws, smooth on both sides and without convenient slots for unscrewing, which hinted there were probably two clear plates, fastened together, holding the precious parchment within. Stephen thought you could probably set a bomb off on top of the thing and there would be no damage to its precious cargo.

"This is one of the pages thought to include Shakespeare's own handwriting in the manuscript of the play," explained Bowen. "Another page is on display downstairs in one of the museum's 'greatest hits' exhibits, oddly enough next to Lennon and McCartney's handwritten lyrics to 'I Want to Hold Your Hand.' Some sort of Shakespeare-meets-the-Beatles pairing, I suppose. But at any rate, we'll have to make do with just this one sheet."

"Good lord," said Margaret. "At least it looks very well protected."

Bowen laughed. "That's for certain, Miss Hamilton. It's from the manuscript for a play that was never approved by the censors called *Sir Thomas More*. The document has been dated to the mid-1590s. First, there is the base script, primarily written in the autograph hand of a gentleman called Anthony Munday who was a writer and professional scribe very active at the time. Approved scripts were in much demand among the acting companies of the time, but the general topic of this play—the rise and fall of Sir Thomas More and his conflicts over religion with King Henry VIII during times of civil unrest—was just too hot to handle as far as Elizabeth's censors went. They were very wary of material that could spark dissent in their own day, especially about matters religious. But then this manuscript shows four or five 'play doctors' having a go to desperately rework the script so it might be approved and get into production. They ultimately did not succeed, but that's the background. Shakespeare is thought to be one of those play doctors. His supporters believe he wrote 142 lines for a crucial speech by the lead character, Sir Thomas More. That block of handwriting is referred to as being written by 'Hand D' among the others all working on the script."

"But I thought there were no examples of Shakespeare's handwriting. So how could people claim that?" asked Margaret.

Stephen said, "Correct me if I'm wrong, Doctor Bowen, but, when all is said and done, almost everyone agrees that there are six genuine handwritten signatures of Shakespeare, on his will and various deeds and leases. That's the starting point."

"But, how can you get from six signatures to these lines?" said Margaret.

"That's a good question, Miss Hamilton," said Doctor Bowen. "And there is an explanation...quite a good story, actually. So here goes. The first real work on this play was done in the 1840s, when a Reverend Alexander Dyce spent a great deal of time making a thoughtful transcription, including all its crossing outs and adding ins, from a manuscript buried here in the British Museum."

"Watch out for those vicars," said Margaret. "Just kidding, Doctor Bowen. It's an in-joke."

"Yes, well, it was a difficult manuscript, but over the years the work was noticed, and eventually people began to put forward theories about it—including one that proposed those 142 lines were written by Shakespeare. All of this discussion was bubbling around during the years leading up to the three hundredth anniversary of Shakespeare's death, when his tercentenary celebration came up in 1916. That's when the Oxford University Press was working on compiling a celebratory book called *Shakespeare's England*. They'd invited the leading scholars of the day to contribute a chapter each on topics as diverse as religion, science, agriculture, sports and pastimes of the period, and so on. Two volumes and about three dozen separate sections on aspects of Elizabethan life. It first came out during the Great War and then again in later editions."

"Yes, I have one of those copies from 1926. It's a great set," said Stephen.

"Then several of those scholars decided as a companion effort to really take a close look at these lines in *Sir Thomas More* and render a definitive opinion—and that's what they did. The old turn-of-the-century scholars were a special bunch. They had each spent their whole lives exploring some arcane corner of their chosen fields. They first determined there were actually six examples of Shakespeare's writing that were definitely his, beyond the shadow of a doubt—those are the six signatures Mister White just mentioned. And there were thousands of other supposed Shakespeare scribblings that could not be certified as genuine. I mean, there were lots of forgeries and so on that were put forward through the years, so they set all of those aside and just settled on the six signatures."

"Six?" asked Margaret.

"Yes, six. There are the three signatures on the various pages of his will, although those are obviously a bit shaky since he was already old and suffering through his final illness. And he abbreviated the spelling of each one of them to keep it quick. Then there is one signature on a sworn deposition in a legal case; he was much younger, and presumably more healthy, but that had to be signed in a very constrained area across the tape attaching a seal to the sworn testimony, which meant he had to fit his name to the width of the tape. I think that one is over two lines: you know, 'William' on top and 'Shakespeare' below—not exactly the most natural way to scratch your handwriting. And then the final two signatures are on papers for buying a house one day and then taking out a mortgage on it the next. One was across seal tape again, so it was tight for space. But the other was free of any space constraints, so that's probably the most natural example. He even wrote 'by me William Shakespeare' with a curly flourish after it."

"That's it?" asked Margaret.

"That's it."

"So how do they get from that to this writing on the old play?"

"Well, three or four of the scholars split up the work and tackled the question, each from a different angle. All of the resulting evidence is circumstantial, but it does all point to the same conclusion. And I, for one, believe they are probably right, that this play contains an example of his writing."

"I'm sorry, I don't see how they could do that. You know, I am supposed to be an investigative journalist," insisted Margaret.

"Okay," Bowen continued. "The first scholar was Sir Edward Maunde Thompson, principal librarian at the British Museum. He had just written a paper called 'Shakespeare's Handwriting' for that tercentenary book, *Shakespeare's England*. He simply chopped up each of the letters in the six signatures, so he had six capital Ws and six capital Ss, and then six or more examples of all of the lowercase letters in the signatures. And he put them all next to one another, side by side, and then made a forensic description of each set of letters—and, you know, the letters all shared the same sort of quirks about them. And he had a fair share of all the alphabet letters represented there, so that was a good start."

"That seems very sensible," said Margaret.

"The second scholar took the manuscript of *Sir Thomas More* and studied each of its passages to determine who annotated them. He identified about six or seven individuals writing on the pages, each with a distinctive handwriting style, and he actually was able to say who several of the individuals were, because he knew other examples of their handwriting on things that were under their names. One he labeled 'Hand E' and identified as Thomas Dekker, a playwright of that time. 'Hand S' was Anthony Munday, the copyist who worked for all the playwrights producing fair copies of finished scripts and so on. Also very easy to identify was the handwriting of the censor, Edmund Tilney. He was the Master of the Revels responsible for licensing plays to be performed. He kept putting in comments like 'No' or 'Must be changed,' and so forth. One other set of lines the scholar could differentiate by handwriting style, but he didn't know the writer by name, so he labeled it as 'Hand D'—and that's the one they think might be Shakespeare."

"How did they argue that case?" asked Margaret, with furrowed brow.

"Well, the passage in question is 142 lines of a long speech at the beginning of the play. 'Hand D' doesn't appear anywhere else in the document, just in this one place. First of all, it matches up with the work of the man who chopped up the six signatures. I mean all the letters—the capital Ws and the small e's and so forth—all match up with the signatures that had been chopped up."

"I see," said Margaret, impressed with the practical approach.

"And then another scholar weighed in from a totally different angle," continued Bowen. "This man was an expert on Shakespeare's style. The play *Sir Thomas More* follows the arc of More's career, just like in the film *A Man for All Seasons*. At the start, a raging mob wants to overturn the King, but Sir Thomas steps in front of them and delivers this speech that calms them down and saves the day. This makes Sir Thomas well loved by King Henry VIII, who advances him along, right up to being chancellor. But then Sir Thomas won't approve of the King's desired divorce to marry Anne Boleyn, so he goes out of favor and eventually is tried and executed—that's the play. Obviously, Queen Elizabeth is the daughter of King Henry and Anne Boleyn, so this play is never going to get approved for production in front of the London mob of 1596. But these 142 lines in 'Hand D' are the speech Sir Thomas More makes to calm the crowd. In other words, it's the critical speech to demonstrate the greatness of Sir Thomas. This third scholar argues all these hacks dragged in Shakespeare to add his magic to this crucial turning point for the play."

"And is it that good?" asked Stephen. "Could it credibly stop a mob?"

"Yes, actually," said Bowen. "The scholar compares the speech to others where a Shakespearean orator controls a mob—think of Marc Anthony calming the crowd after Caesar's assassination in *Julius Caesar* with the 'Friends, Romans, countrymen' speech, or others from the early plays *Henry VI* and *Henry IV*. Anyway, the scholar says the author shows real insights and wit playing to the humors of the crowd—he simply understands angry people. And he has a profound belief in the rights of kings and those in positions of legitimate authority, as did Shakespeare. So whoever wrote the lines did indeed display the necessary passion in the oratory. He warns the mob of the chaos they would set in motion if they overthrew the very order ordained from heaven which allowed good Englishmen to live in the peace and order that every one of them craved for. It's a very emotional connection."

"That is very interesting," allowed Margaret.

"Yes, and the scholar finishes his bit noting that those lines appeared to be written quickly, in the free flow of an author composing, with fast crossing outs and revisions—nothing like the careful lines of Anthony Munday, the so-called Hand S, who was obviously only a plodding copyist, on this project at least.

"Just let me finish telling you about the last scholar, Mister White and Miss Hamilton. And he was probably the most arcane and microscopic of them all."

"That should be pretty amazing," she said.

"This last poor bastard made his life work studying the typographical errors made by typesetters trying to read the hand-writing of Elizabethan playwrights when printing their plays," began Bowen.

"You're joking," said Margaret.

"Really. It was his life's work. He knew, for example, that an apprentice in the Jaggards print shop set parts of *Macbeth* in the First Folio, because he always made the same mistakes. The scholar had pretty much figured out what materials were used as sources to set each play in the First Folio collection. Half a dozen were from fair copies of scripts made by a scribe called Ralph Crane who wrote very clearly and standardized all the stage directions a certain way. But others were from scripts that looked like *Sir Thomas More* where many people had written all over them. For the First Folio, the source material for *Macbeth* was so confusing that one of the stage directions—I think it was 'ring the bell'—appears in the dialogue to be spoken, so a character actually says 'ring the bell' in the middle of his speech because the typesetter accidentally made the stage direction part of the speech."

"I read about that," said Stephen smiling, "but I didn't understand some poor apprentice actually was known to have made the mistake."

"Anyway, this last scholar knew which of the First Folio plays were likely set from manuscripts in Shakespeare's own handwriting—he called those 'fair papers.' Other plays were set from copies by someone else: a stage manager, or something. Those were called 'foul papers.' And Shakespeare's handwriting obviously had some quirks that caused typesetters to make the same mistakes frequently. Apparently Shakespeare's e's and o's could easily be mistaken for each other—so could his c's and i's. The letters m, n, and u also caused misprints when they were followed by e, o, or i.

"I mean, this micro-babble goes on and on—but the last scholar's conclusions are that all of those quirky letter formations that resulted in so many misprints by typesetters working from Shakespeare's handwriting—those same quirks are in the letters of the 142 lines written by 'Hand D' in the manuscript of *Sir Thomas More*. So all of these different lines of analysis point to the same conclusion: 'Hand D' in *Sir Thomas More* was penned by Shakespeare."

"Blimey," offered Margaret. "I had no idea what these people did—it was crazy. How could they know all that?"

"And the sad thing is that we don't have old scholars like them today. Today, we have literally millions of old documents that only a few hundred people can decipher," Bowen concluded.

"Good god," said Stephen. "I'm even one of those few people—but I'm so inept compared to those earlier scholars that I'm like the monkey banging out Shakespeare on the typewriter. There are just as many answers to mysteries out there that we will never recover. Margaret, that's why your papers from Anne Vavasour are such a miracle. Not only are they rare, but also they are in fine condition—and somehow they fell into the hands of people who can at least work out what they say. There won't be many others that fare so well."

"Stephen, I'll never laugh at your love of classics again. And I must say it provides a welcome respite from the modern world. That story is just amazing, Doctor Bowen," Margaret said, turning to the librarian. "Thank you so much for taking us through it. And if there turns out to be anything of real value in the papers we've found, we'll be sure to follow up with you about that further appointment here at the museum. Thanks so much."

"And thank you for the photocopies of the pages with the Hand D speech," said Stephen. "They'll be very useful for us."

"No problem," said Bowen, zippering up his portfolio.

~

The fresh air out in the museum's courtyard fronting Museum Street was a welcome relief from the sealed manuscript rooms, but what an education I've just had, thought Margaret. "Stephen, you went quite quiet there for a while. Was I being too much of the reporter or something?"

"No, Margaret, I was just sidetracked while Doctor Bowen was talking. I mean, I already knew a bit of what he was saying—and it was great to hear the whole story—but I was totally distracted by something else."

"What was it?" she asked, stopping for a moment and looking over at him.

"Well, I think there is some of the same 'Hand D' handwriting in your papers, Margaret."

"My god," she said. "Is it possible there could even be another surprise with all this?"

They just stood there awhile, watching school buses unload their charges for field trips.

~

That night, back at home in the village, Stephen was able to confirm the Vavasour papers did indeed include contributions made by the owner of Hand D.

"It's true," said Stephen, "the handwriting known as Hand D is all over the manuscript of the Ditchley masque that Sir Henry and Anne put on for Queen Elizabeth in 1592."

"Are you sure?"

"I think so. Actually, it makes some kind of sense. The year 1592 was about the time Shakespeare wrote his long poems *Venus and Adonis* and *The Rape of Lucrece*. He did that because the playhouses were all closed because of plague and writers needed money. He would have been desperate for work. Since Sir Henry had the Queen to entertain for two days just then, he was one of the few rich people in England who actually needed some drama written. They had months to prepare, so they would have hired lots of talent to help in a big way."

"Has anyone hinted that Shakespeare might have had a hand in that?" asked Margaret.

"No, nobody has," replied Stephen. "In his book, Chambers thought the principal ghostwriter was Richard Edes, a scholar from Cambridge. But then no one has put much effort into studying the text of the entertainment that has been available until now—and I know that manuscript is incomplete. So your copy may be much longer than what anyone has seen of that work before. There's also some of the same handwriting on the scroll, and that's from fourteen years later, so it looks like whoever Hand D was became a friend of the family with our favorite couple."

"What do we do with that?"

"I don't know yet. I think we should calm down and think it all over. And I think we should go ahead with Soames and Professor Rowe to get the rest of their input. I've arranged to see Professor Rowe tomorrow with my inventory. He might also have had some insights into the scroll and Heminge, so I want to see what he says. Then you and I can compare notes on Sunday morning, after you've had your dinner with Soames. But I wouldn't say anything about the scroll or the Hand D thing to him yet—he would go absolutely bonkers."

"All right. Then I want to get the lot into that bookseller Maggs for an authoritative estimate. While we're waiting for that, we should go together to meet with our new detective and all get on the same page. Okay?"

"Sounds like a plan," said Stephen.

~

Up in Horton-cum-Studley that evening, someone else was thinking about the same Saturday meetings as Stephen and Margaret. Hugh Rowe was at home alone, slouched into his favorite leather chair in his study. The professor was angled comfortably to catch the heat spreading out from the gas grill in his fireplace, with its burners hidden behind a sculpture of orange and black fake coals reminiscent of the old coal fires he remembered from when he was a boy in his parents' row house, seemingly a thousand years before.

His previous day's visit in Gloucestershire with Soames ended badly. He hastily repacked his overnight case and fled to his car in the driveway at six thirty, just as the light was failing. Soames was in the blackest mood and deaf to any arguments for a reasonable resolution to his financial crisis. Soames was staring off intently into space and playing out scenarios of theft and murder silently in his imagination. He didn't even seem to notice the professor fleeing the scene.

Rowe reflected on how all of this had started. Out of the blue, Stephen's photocopies had arrived in the post. He could see what they were, and guessed what else just might be with them, and he had called Soames with the good news. Then, Soames found the article about the discovery in the *Village Advertiser*. And when Soames broke into the vicarage in Margaret's village, he thought he was alone in the house—until he heard sounds of the vicar tinkering around in his kitchen. Soames had already looked through most of the papers in the dining room, and all he had to do was wait for the old man to go up to bed, or even just fall asleep in his chair. Then he could have simply taken the things he had already selected, and left the scene without a fuss. But that had not happened. Apparently, patience was not one of the arrows in Soames's quiver. Instead, the stupid boy decided to bludgeon the old man on the head, knocking him senseless from behind and shriveling him down into a heap on the kitchen floor—a blow from which the vicar never would recover. And the booty taken that night was the script of *Macbeth* that Heminge sent back to Anne Vavasour after the First Folio was published. When he saw it, Rowe knew it was a priceless maximal copy of the play—the full-length master version, not the abridged one put hurriedly into Heminge's great book, but one marked with all the crossing outs and amendments added.

Now, if Soames was to have his way, Stephen White and Margaret Hamilton would both be dead by Sunday. Soames had spoken one scenario in which he planned to stage the scene as a murder-suicide in the middle of the night between Saturday and Sunday—first killing Margaret and then killing Stephen and leaving him holding the proverbial dagger in his hand.

Rowe's thoughts were racing.

Those two are such innocents. The boy is a good scholar, and he's obviously starting to make his own way in the world. And he's managed to have that beautiful gel along with him. She couldn't be finer—not like that cowering wimp who used to come with him to my study for tutorial. This gel is wonderful. People think gay men can't appreciate women, but it's not true. This one is very pretty and feisty; wouldn't put up with my nonsense, and just pushed back at me—charming. If I had had any exposure to females at all before I was eighteen, I might have fancied her myself. But then I was always naturally one for the boys. And Soames was the most beautiful of them all. Sublime. But that was long ago. Now he seems like a twisted old fiend—even older and deader than me, for god's sake. I can't allow all this to happen, Rowe thought. But how can I stop this demon from his plan?

Of course, it would help if the manuscript of *Macbeth* is absent from Stephen's inventory. After all, Soames grabbed it right in the early days, before Stephen could have gotten very far with his damned cataloguing. He might not know he ever had it. Unfortunately, Rowe thought, it's mentioned in the Heminge letter, so it would be a bit hard to explain how it had suddenly surfaced separately from all the rest...although the *way* it is mentioned might not be understood by Stephen's just reading it. It's very cryptic.

Well, there may be another way: perhaps I could offer Soames everything I have—my house, papers, and bank accounts—and then kill myself? That would help, but probably even that would not stop his will to profit from those incredibly valuable papers.

Then the solution came to him—and he thought it felt right. It was the only answer. Pouring a final glass of brandy from the cut-glass beaker in his study, Professor Rowe decided he should sleep on it and confirm his final decision tomorrow first thing.

After all, he always did his best work in the morning.

22

Saturday was busy for Margaret ahead of her dinner with Soames. At 10:00 a.m. she pulled into the driveway of the Juric house, with everything needed for the promised picnic at the Whipsnade Zoo packed up and stowed in the boot of her father's car. And she had brought along an old brochure she had about the zoo to show Denis and Mia on the drive over to Dunstable Downs in Bedfordshire.

The children were ready and seemed to be relaxed and also happy about escaping the regime of Mrs. Quick, who smiled and waved goodbye to them all as Margaret drove the car away.

"Do you know about this zoo?" asked Margaret. "As I told you, it's run by the same people as in London—the Zoological Society, but it's up here in the middle of the countryside. It's very large, hundreds of acres, and an 'open zoo,' where the animals run around and live normally. When they get tired in the city, they bring them here to relax—or to breed. And we can drive all through it and even get out of the car and walk about and so on. It's very special."

"That was a good story about the emir of Kuwait, Miss Hamilton," said Denis. "I didn't used to be so negative, you know."

"Please don't call me 'Miss Hamilton,' Denis. It makes me feel ancient. Call me Margaret. And it's a blessing to be realistic—just don't go too far with it. Leave some room for hope—at least that's what I tell myself, anyway."

After a pause, she continued, "My favorites at Whipsnade are the rhinos and the tigers. But I do like the sea lions as well. They have a lunchtime show at their pool at feeding time. They do tricks and dive into the water. It's great fun and I think the animals like to have the people there cheering. Mia, I think you'll like the sea lions. You can look at this brochure as we drive over." Margaret handed the book to Denis to pass to her in the backseat.

~

Half an hour later, they came up to the gates of the park. Margaret paid at the gate, and was given a guide map, which she handed to Denis.

"Let's drive around the perimeter and get a feel for the place. Denis, I'll go around to the left and you can tell us what we're passing by on the map. Okay?"

"Okay," said Denis. "It looks like we go past something called the children's zoo on the left and then up by the birds, wolves, and Indian rhinos."

"I'll go slowly, and call out when you see something," said Margaret. Both of the kids sat up straight and looked very sharply out of their windows.

"Oh, there are the rhinos," said Mia.

Margaret thought Mia's English was actually very good, which was a blessing. She pulled over to the side of the road. "We can get out, and stand by the fence near them, if you like," said Margaret slipping off her seat belt and opening the door. "Come on."

Leaning on the fence, they all watched the rhinos out in front of a little shelter in their huge compound. Then Margaret continued, "Mia, those are the very rare ones—the great Indian rhinos. When I was last here with my cousins, there were less than a thousand left in the world. But they were breeding them here. I don't know if there are more now or not—but they are very rare. We can find out how they're doing when we stop at the shop and visitor center later."

Mia ran a little way along the fence from Margaret and Denis to get a better view.

"Isn't it funny," said Denis to Margaret, "that people can build a place like this and be so kind to the animals when, where we used to live, the same sort of people are killing each other?"

"I don't know what to say, Denis. I haven't got any explanation either. I have to travel sometimes to trouble spots around the world for work, and I just can't believe what goes on. I keep thinking people will come to their senses—but here we are."

"Do you think they will find our parents?" Denis asked. "I mean, we should have heard something by now, don't you think?"

"We should know something soon, I hope. Along with your embassy, my friends down in Sarajevo are looking into it, and I'll hear from them on Monday about other things. But maybe they'll have some news on your parents as well. It may not be good news, Denis, but we'll have to wait and see. But I know your parents must have been very glad to get you and Mia settled in our village, where things aren't perfect, but it's at least safe now. That was their plan—and it was a good one for both of you. Remember that and make it work. And you've got to help Mia too—and not just keep her aware of the worst. It's very tough not knowing, but we just have to carry on. I wish I could fix things, but I can't."

Denis was glad Margaret was straight with him. It was a relief to get some real advice on what he and his sister were facing.

The rest of the visit went down very well. Mia even became a bit of a chatterbox at the children's zoo, where younger kids can be hands-on with the animals. She giggled constantly while holding a baby penguin handed to her by a young female zookeeper, and that seemed to break the last dam of her reserve, because after that her comments flowed freely as they ogled the Siberian tigers and watched the sea lions leap high into the air before landing in the water at the feeding show. After that, the three of them had their own lunch sitting on a blanket next to the parked car by a herd of grazing Thomson's gazelles. And then they went through the visitor center and gift shop, leaving with books, videos, and a stuffed penguin for Mia.

The mood was pretty merry on the drive home. "You should think of that as your first visit of many," said Margaret. "We only saw a fraction of the place. We didn't even get to the zebras or the birdhouse, where they fly all around you—oh, and the butterflies are the same—and land on your shoulder."

"Thank you for taking us, Margaret," said Denis.

"Yes, thank you," said Mia, from the back, smiling, clutching her penguin.

When they got back to their house just after three in the afternoon, Mrs. Quick was waiting, and Mia sat down with her to talk about the visit, leaving Margaret with Denis for a moment.

Margaret turned to him. "I'll let you know what I hear from my colleagues on Monday, Denis. If I can't come over, I'll call you at least. All right?"

"Yes. Thanks, Margaret," he said.

"And Stephen is also all over the embassy to find out more. So you and Mia aren't all alone in this."

"That's good to know," he said. "I do like him...and you."

Margaret smiled.

~

Driving away from the Jurics', Margaret realized she'd had enough of her journalism career. It had all seemed very grand to travel the world and write up stories to educate the public about injustices and suffering in the world. But now she knew that the public was not much interested, thank you very much, as long as Tottenham Hotspur was bashing Chelsea that night at football. Her purpose had been admirable, but her path was wrong. Nevertheless, she *still* wanted to make a difference.

She could make a difference with these two kids, Mia and Denis, and will, she thought, if their family doesn't reemerge somehow.

Maybe this was where Anne Vavasour might come in. My saucy, independent-minded ancestor has already brought me back from the brink of abandoning Stephen. Perhaps she can help me again with her treasure trove. Imagine what could be done with the money. The flow of refugees into Britain from the Bosnian war was swelling. It certainly wasn't just the few poor souls in Hampstead. Under the current British policy, legitimate refugees could settle in, with a helping hand from the government and various charitable organizations, and weather out the storm. Then, when the trouble at home was over, they could decide— themselves—whether they wanted to return to their native land or stay and assimilate into Britain. Germany might allow them in, but not let them put down roots to become tomorrow's Germans. There they'd have to clear out in eighteen months and go home— or somewhere else. My beloved France might grant asylum, but realistically that was more likely to be reserved for fleeing dignitaries and artists rather than the ruined poor.

Based on her time at Shelter from the Storm, she knew the refugees needed more than a flat and an allowance. They had to have some kind of welcoming mentoring to really help them with healing and fitting in. Britons themselves needed to be educated on how to welcome and save these people. The British love to support charities. Surely some of them could be mobilized into an active force to help with that. People of all ages...kids helping kids, teens helping teens, and adults befriending adults, all trying to make sense of a new life hundreds of miles away from the one they knew. Perhaps this money could be put to work to help make that happen. Wouldn't that be good? She would talk to Mrs. Arnold, the patron for Shelter from the Storm, with all her government connections, about this later. Maybe Margaret could help that charity grow by starting new chapters all around Britain. That would be worth doing.

Next, however, Margaret had to focus on her dinner in London that night with Soames while Stephen was sounding out Professor Rowe up near Oxford. As the main talking point, she finally had a copy of Stephen's hard-fought inventory, listing all of the 146 items in the Vavasour trove along with an annotated description of each piece so Soames would know just what they were talking about. Then hopefully he'll be able to give an informed opinion about value, as well as some commercial guidance on how to proceed to best advantage. With any luck, by Monday or Tuesday they should be able to update Detective Harris and start working with him on solving her father's murder.

~

About the same time Margaret was heading into town for dinner, Stephen was noticing there were no tourists in sight at Horton-cum-Studley on this early October Saturday. Not even one of England's prettiest villages could take the gloom off its cold gray day there, although there was an enervating fresh mist of moisture carried on the breezes from the brook running near Professor Rowe's house. Stephen smiled as he remembered his mother's admonition for the English winters: "Damn the electric bills—light the house, and then add plenty of fresh flowers."

Professor Rowe's housekeeper was apparently from the same old school, because the house was ablaze with lights, and vases of imported flowers from the supermarket adorned the hall and study, where the old man was waiting for him.

"Good afternoon, professor."

"Hello, Stephen. Where's your pretty gel?"

"Oh, Margaret's not with me today, sir. She's busy in the city, so it's just me today, I'm afraid."

"That's fine. Would you like some tea? Mrs. Wells is in the house just now and bringing us a nice tea will be her last official act this weekend." Professor Rowe reached over to the wall and pressed an ancient buzzer, which sounded in the kitchen, a tribute to the wiring of a bygone age in England when servants hovered at one's beck and call.

"How did you get on with all those papers?" Rowe asked Stephen.

"Very well, sir. It took me quite a while—a month, actually—but I've managed to go through them all and write up an informal descriptive inventory. It's not done properly, in the formal way with all the bibliographical detail, but I have tried to include enough details so an appraiser won't have to charge poor Margaret a full fee, as if they had to start from scratch with the collection. There are one hundred forty-six separate items and I've sketched out a brief summary of the appearance and content for each one."

"That's marvelous, my boy. I'm proud as Punch that my former student could still wade through all that, even after you'd escaped from school and gone out into the modern world. Perhaps there's hope for classical English studies after all."

Stephen opened his briefcase and extracted his inventory, which was contained in a one-inch-wide three-hole-punch binder bought for less than two pounds from the Ryman's stationery store in his village. "I'm afraid it looks just like a school report, professor. But I hope it will be quite a bit more illuminating than that," he said, opening the binder and walking it over to the professor in his chair.

Mrs. Wells appeared at this point, with her tray laden with teapot, cups, saucers, milk and sugar, and the obligatory plate of

Huntley & Palmers biscuits from the supermarket. Stephen eyed the oval ones with red jelly medallions above the vanilla crème filling. They had been his favorite as a child, and now they were tempting him to become even more comfortable in the role of schoolboy with his old professor. But he chose to stay on edge.

Rowe took the binder and set it down on the table next to him. "Very good. We'll have a look at that in just a moment. Shall I be mother?" he said as he took upon himself the task of pouring tea as Mrs. Wells exited the room. "Thank you, Mrs. Wells. Have a good weekend," said the old man to her back. The door closed silently and Rowe handed Stephen his tea. "No milk or sugar, I seem to remember," he said.

"That's right. Thanks."

"Sir Henry Lee and his mistress, Anne, were two remarkable characters," began the professor. "And to think he was able to live with her so properly. I mean, he waited until his sainted wife and children were all dead before he took up with Anne in any public way at all. Who could fault him for that? He even seemed to get Queen Elizabeth's tacit approval for her, with that Ditchley masque and portrait and all that. And Elizabeth was not a monarch to forgive past grievances—she was like her father in that. You know, it's made me think that perhaps that scoundrel Aubrey was right when he reported Sir Henry might have been a natural child of Henry VIII, and so half brother to Mary and Elizabeth. Usually you can disregard almost everything that Aubrey said, but that point would explain a lot, don't you think?"

"Yes, sir. Aubrey may have been right, for once."

"Well, let's see what you've got here," said Rowe, lifting Stephen's binder.

The conversation continued for the best part of two hours as the professor paged through the binder and looked up at Stephen above his reading glasses, peppering him with questions. At one point near the middle of the inventory, Rowe scanned ahead, quickly looking over all the remaining items. The old professor kept his poker face as he noted there was no mention of the scribbled and crossed-out full script of *Macbeth* that Soames had stolen—so perhaps Stephen never even knew he had it. "And this is everything, Stephen? Nothing not yet in it?"

"Yes, sir, that's the lot," Stephen answered. "I did have one question about that Heminge letter, however. I think it's there as item eighty-five."

Rowe turned to it and read Stephen's brief description. "Yes, it's rare to find a Heminge letter. I must say, I can't think of another one. Of course, his name is all over the payments and receipts the King's Men received for their plays at court. The payments to the company were always made to Heminge and those court registers are some of the chief ways we know which plays were played where and when."

Stephen said, "There was a reproduction of his signature in Halliwell's life of Shakespeare from the 1840s—and that was a very useful start in validating the identification. But then I actually saw two more of his signatures up in Stratford, in the Royal Shakespeare Company's collections, and another scribbled one at the British Museum."

"Yes, he was a very active businessman, with signatures on various leases and lawsuits from the time. Ran an alehouse too, you know—as well as acting in the plays."

"Yes, sir. But it's that reference in the letter that puzzles me. He's thanking Anne for 'the cut that woke the Dane' and then sending her back something. And then he wrote he had 'pry'd it back from J's' or something. Would it be some copy of *Hamlet*, do you think? You know, Hamlet the melancholy Dane?" Stephen asked.

Rowe was disturbed. He simply couldn't help himself by not answering a clever student's question, even if he would be getting perilously close to the neighborhood of his own felonious activities with Soames. He loved to show his students how much more he knew than them.

"No, dear boy. It wouldn't have been *Hamlet*. I think the answer is in this rather remarkable prompting scroll you have right at the beginning as item two—just after the Burghley letter."

"The lines for Lady Macbeth? You recognized it as a prompting tool?"

"Yes, that's the one. In fact, together with the copy of the Ditchley entertainment for Queen Elizabeth, it's the diamond in the crown for this collection."

"But how would that be related to the Heminge letter?" asked Stephen.

"I think you'd have to go back to the context and setting for when the play *Macbeth* first appeared—I think Chambers tentatively dated it to 1606. Am I right?"

"Yes, sir. He says he thinks it would have first appeared early in 1606. But he's not quite certain of that in his commentary. Others say August 1606."

"You are a good student, Stephen—I couldn't be prouder. Well, let me tell you. It was August, I believe. All the hacks point out that Shakespeare wrote his Scottish play to pander to King James I, who was also King James VI of Scotland, as every schoolboy going unwillingly to school would know. *Macbeth* is all about Scotland and also much about witchcraft, which was a well-known area of study for King James, who prosecuted witch hunts in Scotland and even wrote a book about witches called *Daemonologie* in 1597. What the hacks never mention, however, is that while James was *interested* in witches, his wife's brother, King Christian of Denmark, was positively *obsessed* with them. While he was on the throne of Denmark and Norway, more than fourteen hundred of his loyal subjects were burned at the stake as witches. I think he's been called the 'Witch Hunter King.' And then it so happened that King Christian and three hundred sixteen of his court came to visit James and Queen Anne of Denmark in July and August 1606—this is some of the material I was freshening up on before your visit. There aren't too many records of this visit because, by all reports, it was a continuous drunken bacchanal. I actually hoped our conversation might come to this point today, because I put aside something to read to you about it."

The old professor stood up from his chair and stretched briefly before walking over to one of his bookshelves lining the study. He picked out one leather-bound volume with a book-mark. "This is *Nugae Antiquae*, a collection of antique nuggets, if you will, from the antiquity of King James's time, among others. I want to read you this from a letter written by Sir John Harrington in 1606: '*My good friend, In compliance with your asking, now shall you accept my poor accounte of rich doings. I came here a day or two before the Danish King came, and from the day he did come until this hour, I have been well nigh overwhelmed with carousal and sports of all kinds. The sports began each day and in such manner as well nigh persuaded me of Mahomets paradise. We had women, and indeed wine, too.*'"

The professor continued, "He goes on a bit and then comes to this description of one evening's entertainment with a play or masque of some sort: '*One day, a great feast was held, and, after dinner, the representation of Solomon his Temple and the coming of the Queen of Sheba was to be made, or (as I may better say) was meant to have been made before their Majes-ties, by device of the Earl of Salisbury and others. But, alas! As all earthly things do fail to poor mortals in enjoyment, so did prove our presentment thereof. The Lady who did play the Queen's part, did carry the most precious gifts to both their Majesties; but forgetting the steppes arising to the canopy, overset her caskets into his Danish Majesties lap, and fell at his feet, tho I rather think it was in his face. Much was the hurry and confusion; cloths and napkins were at hand, to make all clean, His Majesty then got up and would dance with the Queen of Sheba; but he fell down and humbled himself before her and was carried to an inner chamber.'*

"The letter then ends with reports of how ladies later portraying Faith, Hope, and Charity stumbled around flubbing their lines before being sick and spewing in the lower hall. The evening was then concluded by another lady playing Victory, who had to be led away and put to bed and Peace who was unable to pull off a triumphant finale. I'm not sure Harrington ever actually sent this letter—it seems almost treasonous. He might just have kept it and shown it to friends as a jibe against James. But there are other reports that much of the state visit was a total drunken shambles."

"That was quite a party," said Stephen. "But how do you think it connects with the Heminge letter?"

"Well, I think Master Heminge was talking to Anne about *Macbeth*. The Chamber and Revels accounts show that Heminge was paid for putting on three plays before James and the Danish king. Two at Greenwich and then one at Hampton Court specifically noted as taking place on August 7. Early that day, King Christian was installed in the Order of the Garter. Sir Henry may even have been there because he had been too ill to go to the usual annual installation and dinner in April 1606, but he'd recovered. Then that evening they had the play at Hampton Court. I think that was *Macbeth*. It was a bit of a finale for the visit, because Christian went back to his ship for the trip home within a day or two afterward. Anyway, I believe that Anne Vavasour helped cut the play down and made certain improvements to some of the speeches given by Lady Macbeth, as shown on your scroll...at least in the copies I had. Her education and examples of extant poems attributed to her show she well may have been up to that challenge. And after Elizabeth was gone, she probably came back to court—in fact, James and Queen Anne seemed very fond of her. The Queen gave her a fabulously valuable jewel after chatting with her at Lee's house all of one day in 1608.

"Anne might have even played the part of Lady Macbeth in that performance, you know—just like the poor gels who acted in the *Queen of Sheba*. And that might be why she had that scroll. All the ladies at James's court were prancing around acting in the masques Inigo Jones put on for entertainment. It was only the public playhouses that required men to play the women's roles. Anyway, this would, perhaps, have been the first time that play had been performed at court. Also, it was clearly abridged from a longer version, now lost—probably because King Christian didn't know English very well. But he would have been able to appreciate the witches round their cauldrons, all the blood, the drunken porter, and the songs—so all that was lobbed in. Someone also wisely cut the scene about Lady Macbeth lamenting her lost child—one of those marked out on the scroll. The whole state visit was meant to celebrate the birth of a new child for James by Christian's sister, but that baby by Anne of Denmark did not survive and its unexpected death cast a pall over all the proceedings.

"You mention some of the pasteovers on your scroll were written out in an italic hand, and I would guess those are very similar to Anne's own hand. I think she rewrote those speeches to a degree and Heminge was complimenting her that the speeches were so good—with her "cuts" pasted over the original words—that the players managed to keep the Danish king awake during the whole performance, although they had wisely shortened it down to probably just under two hours. So it was 'the cut that woke the Dane.'"

Stephen was amazed by this analysis. "So Heminge is saying her rewrite, plus all the subtractions and additions, made something good enough to keep King Christian IV awake during the bacchanal? That's brilliant, professor."

Professor Rowe smiled, basking in the praise in spite of all his troubles. "And when he wrote he 'pry'd it back from J's,' I would think he meant he took the manuscript she had loaned him back from Jaggards, the bounder doing the typesetting and the printing for the First Folio, who usually would have trashed the rough copies. And then he must have sent it back to your Anne."

"That's a wonderful read on the line, professor," said Stephen, truly impressed.

"You flatter me, dear boy. I would love to take a close look at that scroll, by the way."

"I think it will be really interesting to see whatever was underneath the patches that Anne pasted on to it. But we thought we should wait until it was in the hands of experts before trying anything."

"Very wise. The conservationists will tell you which way to go with that," said Rowe.

"This has been very enlightening, professor, and you've been very generous with your time. But there is just one area of questioning I promised Margaret that I would ask you about. I hope you don't mind or think me too impertinent for doing so."

"Nonsense. Fire away, dear boy," said Rowe, secretly steeling himself for the next turn in the conversation.

"Sir, looking back now, I realize that the photocopies I sent you included sections where the secretary hand being shown was a virtual match with a rather famous swatch of secretary hand well-known to paleographic scholars—"

"You mean the famous Hand D from the play *Sir Thomas More*?" interrupted Rowe.

"Yes, sir," said Stephen, unable to suppress a smile at the old don's expertise. "That's the one. It's really all over the copy of the Ditchley entertainment we have."

"Yes, I did recognize it. Actually, it almost gave me another heart attack. In fact, I'm quite convinced you really have a treasure trove for Miss Hamilton, you know. Even though I did at first seem quite dismissive of them—I think I told your gel they were only 'family papers'—I was quite wrong, now that I've thought about it. And the Ditchley entertainment does make sense for the young Shakespeare to have a hand in, if he was indeed Hand D. It was performed in September 1592, and Sir Henry had probably had all sorts of people working on it since the spring. After all, this was going to be his best chance to really state his case for loving Anne Vavasour to Queen Elizabeth. Anne was the very same wench the monarch had locked up in the Tower a dozen years before. And Elizabeth would not have forgotten that: since she had to remain celibate, she bloody well didn't want her maids bonking in the hallways, and that's exactly what Mistress Vavasour did with Oxford—and the poor gel was only sixteen or seventeen, I believe."

"Margaret's fear, professor, was that anyone who might have recognized Hand D could well have a motive for robbery, and perhaps you've heard that many believe Margaret's father's death—Vicar Hamilton—could have been foul play, whether planned or by accident."

Professor Rowe chuckled and slowly shook his head before saying, "Well, that's not my game, dear boy. I'm no saint, but I'm not that sort of criminal either. Quite frankly, even though Vicar Hamilton must have been 'old,' he was probably a lot younger than me. So I don't think I could be a credible suspect for doing him in, if you'll pardon the expression—no disrespect intended."

"No, professor, I can see that. But I just had to ask, you understand. You were probably one of the few people who might have recognized Hand D."

"I'll take that as flattery, Stephen. Rest assured, I would never have harmed a vicar—not when I'm so close to going to meet my maker. The thing is, your treasure trove has been quite a blow to me, and I was in denial when I first spoke to you and

Miss Hamilton. You know, my whole career has been a rigorous defense of the 'Stratford man' as the author of Shakespeare's works and I have very publicly ridiculed the proponents of the Earl of Oxford as a candidate author, or Sir Francis Bacon, or Queen Elizabeth or even the Tooth Fairy. I've said the works are all by the 'Stratford Man' and only he. I've said it in print, on podiums, and even on television—said it so often I can't take it all back. And yet now, it's clear to me that while Shakespeare was the magisterial maker of all the plays, he had quite a lot of collaborators. So in many ways, your collection has been my undoing, professionally. Actually, I still am reeling from that and, in fact, I have not yet figured out how to deal with that at this stage in my life. Quite devastating actually. But I'm not your robber and I'm not the vicar's murderer."

But Rowe left unsaid just how astonished he was to have been the robber and murderer's accomplice. And if events continued to unfold according to Soames's new plans, Stephen and Margaret, this attractive young couple, would also become his victims. And that simply could not happen.

"No, sir. Sorry I asked. I can see it wouldn't possibly be you."

Stephen said his goodbyes and promised to keep Professor Rowe informed as he and Margaret moved forward to value the collection. As he started down the driveway, a cold chill went down his spine as he realized what must have been the truth: the villain must be Soames. He was the only other person he had shown some of the papers to. And the only other person who might possibly have understood whose handwriting was shown—although he didn't think Soames had studied paleography that closely in school, so that's a mystery.

But Margaret was seeing Soames tonight. He must warn her immediately, he thought. Thank god the BBC gave her one of those new alphanumeric message pagers so she could be reached at a moment's notice, in case some sort of catastrophic story broke. Now he'd just have to drive to one of the pubs in Horton-cum-Studley, call her office, and have them get word to her. Thank god there was always someone there at the BBC, answering the phones.

She could be walking into a deadly trap, for god's sake.

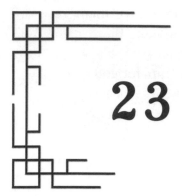

23

It's a bloody business, thought Soames. But thank god I have found a way out of my mess—again. It's a shame, although it can't be helped.

Soames was not the sort of bleeding heart to be upset by any qualms about his intent to kill Margaret that very night, after checking out a fancy restaurant for his future use. For her nightcap, just before he was to allegedly drop her off at King's Cross for the train, Soames was planning to add the contents of the small vial in his right-hand side pocket. That should give them just enough time to pay the bill and stagger her back into the passenger seat of his car for her last ride home. His plan was then to divert her over to her flat—since by then she surely wouldn't feel up to traveling anywhere by train. He would then call Stephen and explain that she had taken ill and that he had now just left her in a bit of a heap at her flat. Knowing Stephen, that would set him off racing into London to the rescue. And when he arrived at Margaret's flat, Soames would complete his plan to compose the couple into their murder-suicide tableau. Margaret would seem to have been killed by hotheaded Stephen who was blindingly outraged at the sale of her papers to Soames that night for a supposed £100,000. And Soames would have the supposedly signed bill of sale. Then Stephen would be consumed by remorse and decide to join her in the afterworld himself.

It was all such a tragedy, thought Soames, and a truly Shakespearean *Romeo and Juliet* one at that, appropriately enough.

Margaret had quite different expectations as she started to travel across London from her flat to join Soames briefly at his mews house before going off to some restaurant he seemed to be excited about. Afterward—if it should be early enough—he'd be dropping her off at King's Cross for a late train home. She certainly wouldn't be the only one to have lingered for a Saturday night dinner in London before escaping home to the country for the rest of the weekend. And if for some reason it went later, she could simply go back to her flat and go up to join Stephen Sunday morning.

She hailed a taxi, stepping out of it just at the side entrance of Harrods, just around the corner from Soames. True to form, the headlines on the signs for the *Evening Standard* outside the entrance to the tube station had nothing to do with the cataclysm in Bosnia and everything to do with Princess Di. Soames lived very nearby in a dollhouse mews house behind Ovington Square, just fifty yards away from the chic shops along the Brompton Road. It had the impossible luxury of providing its own inside parking space for Soames in what used to be the stables underneath an entire floor of luxury living space upstairs. She rang the brass-ringed doorbell and was buzzed in to the entry hall beside the stairs.

"Come on up," bellowed Soames from above.

"Coming," she replied, ascending the black and white checked painted stairs. "This is quite the place you have here," she said noting the stained-glass landing window halfway up.

"Yes. Hello, Margaret. Lovely to see you again," said Soames, kissing her lightly on the cheek in the continental style. "I snapped it up about four years ago from an aged aristocrat who had it as his pied-à-terre. He was selling all his books—and this house—to try to make the taxes on the family seat up north. I think he actually succeeded, only to have his heirs get rid of all that as well a year or two later."

"How sad."

"That was the fate of most of our landed gentry, of course—but only a very few of them hung on as long as that dear old boy. It would have been better, I suppose, for him to keep this place and let English Heritage take the stately home, but he was a traditionalist, for sure. Since then, I've had fun fixing it up, and lots of help from the Knightsbridge decorating crowd, who gave me quite good discounts as long as they could photograph it all and bring the occasional client over for convincing."

"Yes, it does look like a page from *Country Life* or even *Hello!* magazine."

"Funny you should say that. Both of those have called, but we just haven't worked out a date for a photo shoot yet." He laughed. "Would you like a drink?"

"No, I'll just wait for the restaurant, if that's all right."

"Yes, fine. I think you'll like it—it's a new one of Sir Terence Conran's group. Mandy and I are quite the regulars at Bibendum around the corner here, but I haven't been to this new one myself yet. It just opened."

"I thought Conran was a designer. I mean, he has a big store around the corner from the BBC on Tottenham Court Road."

"Designer, architect, and restaurateur, as it turns out—a veritable Renaissance man. Although he doesn't call them restaurants. He prefers 'gastrodomes,' as the French say."

"Palaces of fine foods?" asked Margaret, suddenly opening up the fluent French part of her head for this conversation.

"Yes, that's it. So at Bibendum, besides the restaurant, they have a bakery, flower mart, and cooking shop with two hundred-pound stew pots and so on. He calls all that a 'gastrodome'—some kind of temple for the foodies, I suppose," said Soames. "I think he means to educate us British on fine foods."

"Good luck," said Margaret, chuckling.

"Well, let's go see this new one – it's called Pont de la Tour and it's down by Tower Bridge in an old renovated riverside warehouse. Conran, the architect, did the renovation as well. I thought it might be a fun setting for our chat—and I have to check it out anyway to see if I should take some of my posher clients there."

"That's a hard lot you have there," said Margaret, kidding him.

"Just let me finish up getting ready, and we'll be off. I thought I'd drive us over and then I can drop you off for your train. They advertise their valet parking service, so let's put them through their paces," said Soames as he turned and walked down the hall. "Sit down for a moment. I'll just be a minute."

Margaret surveyed the picture-perfect surroundings. Behind the sofa, a library table, with two brass lamps fashioned from statuettes of Wellington and Nelson, framed the fireplace and hunting scene above the mantel. On the table were a short stack of coffee table books and an oversize leather portfolio, lying flat. Without thinking, Margaret reached down and lifted up a corner flap of the portfolio, revealing a small stack of manuscripts within.

Good lord, she thought, staring wide-eyed down at the old writing. They are just like the ones at home. She backed away from the table, much surprised, with the back of her hand instinctively now up across her mouth as if to stifle some spontaneous gasp of surprise. Hold on, now, she continued thinking to herself. You know, he is a manuscript and book dealer, for Christ's sake. I mean, that's why we're going out tonight. Of course, he'd have things like that lying around. That's what he trades in all day, you idiot.

In spite of the attempt at reassurance, she felt suddenly quite off her guard and sat down quickly to compose herself before

Soames came back. She succeeded in that, to a degree, and he reappeared quite shortly and said jauntily, "Off we go. We just go down the stairs again and then through the back into the garage. We should be at the restaurant in about fifteen or twenty minutes, as long as we stay clear of the main roads."

True to plan, Soames kept his Jaguar clear of the Brompton Road and started threading his way along the squares and back roads until they came out onto the Embankment by the Thames. Then it was over Waterloo Bridge to the South Bank and into a warren of dark commercial streets that were totally devoid of any traffic, whether pedestrian or cars. Margaret thought that it was suddenly getting all a bit creepy.

"Old Conran is the development pioneer in this part of town," said Soames, explaining the unlikely setting they found themselves going through. "I don't think he would have much luck with these old streets full of livery garages and warehouses, but he might just attract the more adventurous expense-account people over here to the river's edge. And those are just the sort of people looking for the next new thing."

"Yes, rather like you," teased Margaret.

"Oh yes. You're on to me now, Margaret." Well, he thought, no—she isn't on to me at all now, is she?

~

Pont de la Tour was a welcoming oasis of splendor compared with the dismal empty warehouses that were its neighbors. But all of those became invisible when Soames and Margaret were seated at their table with an unobstructed view of the river and a backlit Tower Bridge.

It was a setting more akin to Paris than to London—more like looking out at the Seine instead of the plodding old Thames—and even the food fit the setting, thought Margaret as she finished the pea risotto with mint. But the conversation was more than a bit unsettling. Soames had been very intent on understanding the inventory and she had explained some questioned areas as best she could while also suggesting he follow up with Stephen. But Soames had been quite thin on the sales-advice side, almost as if that would be nothing for her to worry about. He had also been quite keen to keep the copy of the inventory, which he had scribbled all over attentively as he read. It was unsettling in the extreme to Margaret, who decided she would not be leaving the restaurant with him as planned. At some later date she'd have to come up with an explanation, she supposed, but just call it a sixth sense for now. She was going to ditch him.

The meal ended with Soames ordering two cappuccinos; before they came, she excused herself to go off to the ladies loo. As she went down the short corridor past the gents, she saw a door marked Staff Only. She checked behind her and then tried that door which opened heavily. Inside that restricted space, she could see part of the kitchen down to the right, but to the left was an outer door, which brought her out onto an alley just off the street on the back side of the restaurant, away from the entrance and valet parking. There was a light mist falling—not enough to call it rain, but just enough to give the darkened streets the look of some dark Sherlock Holmes adventure, she thought, somewhat unsettled. She pulled her jacket collar up and hurried westward along the street, running parallel to the river. She kept close to the buildings, so she could duck inside a doorway if any headlights came in sight.

Meanwhile, Soames waited until he had to ask the waitress to go back to the ladies and check on Margaret. He didn't want her cappuccino laced with chemicals to get too cold, after all. But the report came back that there was no sign of her by the toilets or the doorway, and he moved quickly for his car. Why had she left? Was there something he'd said that set her off? Where the bloody hell had she gotten to?

~

Soames nearly knocked the valet-parking attendant over as he leapt into the car, quickly remembering himself and handing over a five-pound note to make up for his rudeness. He didn't want to be too memorable if anyone later came checking up on his evening out with Margaret—because he was confident that he could now find her, and confident that he could complete his plan somehow, even though the opportunity to anesthetize her at dinner had disappeared. But the streets were just as deserted as when they arrived, and were even more cloaked in inky darkness by the mists surrounding the occasional lit lamppost he came upon as he careened around the blocks at high speed. Soon he realized it was pointless, and she had gone. What now?

He stopped to channel all his attention into modifying his clever plan—and that's when he noticed Margaret's newfangled alphanumeric pager on the passenger seat. She'd showed it to him on the way over. BBC reporters all had them and it was just the sort of status symbol he should have as well, she had laughed.

Soames saw the tiny screen was flashing "One message received." He pushed the Show command just below and a text message from the BBC call desk displayed: "Get away from Soames. Dangerous. Stephen to be at your flat at 11 p.m."

Soames stared at the pager. What the hell should he do now? She must have gone to her flat—Welbeck House by Selfridges, wasn't it? He knew he should just head over there. He could just ring the bell and say he came to make sure she was all right. She wouldn't know Stephen was on his way, so perhaps he could still complete his plan.

He steered himself at speed across the quiet streets of ten p.m. Saturday London, from the docks across the river into Mayfair, and parked in the drop-off zone kept clear in front of Welbeck House. The lights on the ground floor were blazing out the windows of John Bell & Croyden, the all-night chemist on the corner that stayed open dispensing prescriptions to the well-heeled needy at all hours.

He was just walking from his Jaguar toward the doors of Margaret's building as a taxi pulled up, and out came Stephen, at a run.

"Stephen, old man, good to see you. Margaret disappeared from me at the restaurant, and—"

Soames didn't have a chance to finish his sentence because Stephen lunged forward and hit him on the jaw with a punch that would have felled a heavyweight. It had all the might of his strong right arm, propelled by the full weight of his body flying forward. Soames went down on the pavement in a heap, flailing for a few moments to bring his hand up to his jaw, before his eyes rolled back in his head and he passed out.

"You fucking wanker," Stephen said through his clenched teeth. "If you've hurt her, I'll kill you." Then he vaulted through the doors and into the entrance hall.

The doorman came into the birdcage lift right after Stephen, clanged the door shut, and started its smooth ascension. "She just came in ten minutes ago, sir—looking a bit wet."

"Really?" said Stephen. "She's all right?"

"Seems so, sir," the man said, pushing open the gate at Margaret's floor.

He rang the bell, saying "Margaret, it's me," and she let him in straight away, just managing to close the door as he hugged her.

~

Back downstairs, the doorman managed to help Soames up and back into his car. He took a minute, just sitting behind the wheel to focus before he drove off, pretty sure that his jaw was broken.

Pulling up to his mews house, he saw the upstairs lights were on. He opened his garage doors with his remote and parked the car in its place. Upstairs he heard some shouting going on—what the hell? As he reached the top of the stairs and walked into the main room, the shouting stopped and he became the center of attention for the warring Mandy and Rowe who had somehow managed to become his unexpected welcoming committee.

Mandy just threw an ashtray at him and spat out "You stupid buggering bastard," as she pushed by him and down the stairs. "I better not have picked up any of that old fart's germs or you'll be dead," she ended, smashing the door behind her.

Soames stepped in and turned his attention to his second surprise visitor. Professor Rowe was standing in front of the fireplace, framed by the tall table lamps of Wellington and Nelson. "What the hell are you doing here?" said Soames.

Rowe paused for a breath, recovering from his unexpected verbal fisticuffs with Mandy. "Well," he started, "I believe I have a solution to your predicaments...so I came down to share the good news. I tried calling, of course—but it seems you were out, so I just motored myself down." He walked over and lowered himself into one of the upholstered chairs facing the matching sofa.

"A solution, you say?" Soames stifled his surprise, slipped out of his coat, and moved on his best behavior over to sit down on the sofa facing the professor, while cradling his hurt jaw. "Well, I'm all ears, I must say," he said, waiting.

Rowe reached into the left side pocket of his tweed jacket and took out his small notebook. "Yes, I've been thinking about the tangle of your financial affairs, and have a few suggestions. The first one addresses your smart country house. One of my old colleagues, now retired from his university post in London, is struggling with the completion of his magnum opus—which is, as I understand it, a multi-volume treatise on the lesser metaphysical poets—you know, not John Donne, but perhaps Andrew Marvell and the others. Anyway, my friend's London house has been filled suddenly with his daughter and her children, who are apparently fleeing his son-in-law, and a messy divorce is certainly about to ensue."

"Why are you telling me all this, for god's sake?" said Soames, very annoyed.

"Well, I rang my friend this morning about his sad plight, and mentioned I might know of a haven where he could distance himself from the soap opera unfolding before him in London, and finish off his metaphysical musings in peace. I described your place in the Cotswolds as heaven itself—although I mentioned it would be very pricey—but instantly available, probably for six months or more as a short-term let. His response was joy, along with the comment that the price was no issue for him, as long as he could go there *now*. So he could carry your costs for that part of your obligations for a while."

"Really? Why on earth would I want him in my house?" asked Soames.

"Well, I thought it would buy us some time while we made ourselves busy to raise new income for a more permanent solution. And I also made a short list of some of the items I thought we could procure together in the interim to raise other funds for you."

Soames stood up from the sofa and walked over to his cocktail cabinet. He reached inside for a bottle of pricey Napoleon brandy and two snifters, hoping to help the throbbing in his face. "Very thoughtful of you professor. Care for a nightcap?" But then he went quiet for a moment before his attitude turned cold. "And afterwards perhaps we can go through my closets," he hissed. "Who knows, we might even find some evening clothes or riding outfits to sell at the used clothing shops in Camden Town?"

"Well, my boy, I think we can set our sights higher than that," responded the professor, looking down at his notebook, about to continue. But Soames cut him off.

"Listen, you old bugger, why should we have a jumble sale of my belongings when, within our reach, as Dr. Johnson once said, are riches beyond the dreams of avarice? These Vavasour papers are not only the answer to my financial problems, but also the means for lifelong luxury. All that stands in the way is a small amount of unpleasantness before fame and salvation. And while we're setting the course straight, please tell me just what were you chatting about with Miss Mandy a few moments ago?"

"Miss Mandy?" said the professor, putting his notebook back in his pocket and turning upwards to look Soames right in the eye. "Well, I told her that you were taken, and always had been, by me and no doubt by a long line of other horny older men. So I told her, using the words of my young students today, to fuck off."

Soames looked away from the professor's stare and poured brandy into one of the glasses. "That's really too much," he began slowly, taking a swig. "You've blotted your copybook, old man. In fact, I think we are done and dusted. If you think I'm going to walk away from Miss Hamilton and her bloody papers, you're bonkers. So just forget the nightcap, and buzz off. I don't think we have anything else to talk about. I'm done with trudging through another series of small acquisitions with you, and the subsequent annoying sales transactions. I'm moving on, and it's time to say goodbye."

Professor Rowe lowered his gaze and moved his hand over to his other jacket pocket. "I'm sorry to hear you say that, dear boy. But I do agree, reluctantly, that it is now time to move on."

~

Five minutes later, Professor Rowe had recovered himself to the point that he had poured his own brandy and moved out of the lounge and into the fine en-suite bathroom adjoining Soames's master bedroom. At least he still had his aim. He was glad he had managed to put two bullets right into Soames's bull-headed face, and the noise of the shots had not been as loud as he had feared. Very sorry about the mess, but they can do quite a lot these days getting stains out of upholstery, he thought. He drank the last of the brandy and felt its warmth going down.

Now it was time to take just a moment for himself, he thought. He put his gun on the edge of the bathtub and turned on the taps, taking the time to get the combined flow to his preferred temperature before slipping in the plug of the bath. Then he stepped back into the bedroom, and slowly undressed, leaving all of his things arranged neatly on the bed before coming back to the rising water. He had already placed his note on the desk in Soames's front lounge, together with Soames's portfolio with the Vavasour papers stolen from the vicarage. Now he could just get into the bath, and relax into his thoughts.

Of all the men and boys he had known, Soames had been the love of his life, and such an unexpected one, appearing on the scene long after he thought he had passed his prime. The boy seemed fresh, adventurous, and even joyful at the start—especially on that first spring trip to Italy. Rowe remembered not only did all of his own dormant physical machinery seem to perk up, but he had managed to become almost priapic in the heat of their new passion. Then their first capers together to purloin and sell rich papers were simply larks to laugh over later—not money-grubbing thievery. How that had all changed. The twisted man in the mess on the sofa was nothing like he had been—that boy had died long before. He tried to help him tonight, but Soames was just too far gone.

And what would be ahead for himself now, thought the professor? There would be the commotion about the shooting, the revelations of the thievery, and the dismantling of his "distinguished" academic life, much of which actually did deserve to be remembered as "distinguished" after all. But all of that would be cut out of him while he watched, like someone being hung, drawn, and quartered back in the day. No, that wasn't the way, he reflected, just as he had said in his note. He would take all that up with his judges in the next world, and not here.

With his left hand, he tugged a heated towel down from the rack just above him, and stretched it over his head. Then he reached with his right hand for his pistol.

Try to be tidy, he thought. And now, it was time to go.

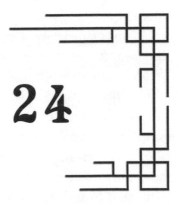

24

Back at Welbeck Street, Margaret wrapped a bandage around Stephen's bleeding right hand. They shared a bottle of wine and talked through their hopefully unfounded fears about their old classmate Soames. If she ever saw the bastard again, they came up with a story she could tell him about why she had left (female problems, and embarrassment at having to get home right away)—that was the best they could do.

Stephen then told her about his conversation with Rowe and how, at the end, he made very candid comments about his own incapacity for theft and murder, which were totally credible. They agreed to call Detective Harris and update him on everything in the morning.

Very late, Margaret took care locking the door, and even put a dining chair up against the doorknob. Christ, she thought. How can we live like this?

~

They had slept in, in spite of their troubles, and were awakened by the telephone just after 11:30 a.m. Sunday morning. It turned out they wouldn't have to call Detective Harris or need any alibis, nor any strategy about how to deal with Soames and Rowe in the future.

It was Detective Harris himself calling to deliver the message that Soames and Professor Rowe were dead—found a short time before at the mews house in Knightsbridge when a cleaning lady arrived to tidy up. She had been used to Sunday duty cleaning up the morning messes after big nights out, but the sight of Soames and Rowe dead from gunshot wounds had her calling the police right away, crying and screaming. It looked like they had had a fight, because Soames's jaw was broken, but then Rowe apparently shot him dead, and, perhaps after a moment of reflection, blew his own brains out as well.

The detective didn't have time to go into any more details—he just wanted them to be at ease in the event they feared they were in danger. He said he wasn't happy Margaret and Stephen had had more meetings with Soames and Rowe on their own, after he had spoken to Margaret. But all that didn't seem to matter now. They should just say prayers of thanks that they had escaped those two and been so lucky.

Anyway, he wanted them to come in to Scotland Yard for a debrief on Tuesday morning. Margaret agreed straightaway, hung up the phone, and told Stephen the story. He told her Harris had got the bit about Soames's jaw wrong: he had done that.

~

The rest of Sunday played out as one long recovery, starting with a walk over to Marble Arch and then continuing on through Hyde Park over to the Serpentine. Then they walked right around the lake to see crazy young men at the Lido running out from the changing rooms in their Speedos and jumping in to the swim lanes for brisk freestyle swims across the shallow waters with their white swim caps shining. At the other edge of the park, the cavalry from the barracks there were riding in formation on the sandy lanes of Rotten Row along the Knightsbridge side. It was mad how the everyday world continued all around you when you'd been shaken to the core by tragedy, Margaret thought. There was no making sense of it all, and the strange limbo ended with Stephen heading back to the normality of another Monday at St. George's.

Monday was different for Margaret, at least, because she decided to hand in her notice at the BBC that day. Her boss couldn't really understand her decision. It was all going so well for her, except for the recent loss of her father. How could she throw away a successful career all her colleagues dreamed of? She didn't really answer, except to say her dreams seemed to be changing, and she felt a massive sense of relief as she walked out of Broadcasting House at lunchtime. But it wasn't really a final break. Her boss had ended by saying she could come back, if she reconsidered, and he would check in with her again in the new year. But for right now, she just had a few more days to work out her transition out of the team and she would be rid of the place— and selfishly rid of the siege of Sarajevo, although she knew she was shirking doing the play-by-play commentary on that reality. But the rest of the population of Europe didn't want to hear it anyway, so goodbye to all that for now.

~

Stephen made a day off out of their Tuesday appointment at New Scotland Yard. Walking in, they had a sense of all the people who had passed through those doors and never been free again—but they were going in the opposite direction—to find freedom from the sinister threats that had plagued them for weeks.

Detective Harris put them at ease with the offer of tea and the same obligatory small plate of biscuits that Rowe had served them back in September. He repeated that he was angry about them continuing their freelance investigation, but he decided he wasn't going to lecture them about that now, as long as they knew they had been stupid and almost gotten themselves killed.

So he explained what he knew. "The professor left a suicide note, and the ending is quite personal to you, Miss Hamilton," said Harris. "So I'll read you a few lines." He slipped on his glasses and read out the words Professor Rowe had left behind: "At this point I have decided not to face earthly interrogations and punishments for my crimes of filching antique treasures from oblivious modern keepers. Instead, I will face my judgment in the next world. And I am taking my accomplice with me, to prevent any more victims being added to our case file."

"Oh my god," said Margaret. "He seems so calm about it all. It's eerie."

"Perhaps he was," said Harris. "He then left a short list of their conquests. It's a kind of 'greatest hits' going back five or six years. Most we had absolutely no idea about. They were very good at what they did. Here's the end of his note, with his message to you. He wrote: 'Please return the attached papers of Anne Vavasour to Margaret Hamilton, with our sincerest apologies.' Then he signed it, and that's it."

They sat quietly for a few minutes before Harris continued to give his own commentary. Both Rowe and Soames Bliforth had been at the epicenter of a long trail of thievery and deceit. Soames had been the driving force, feeding an insatiable hunger for more and more wealth, needing much more than even the riches that had come to him from his inheritance. The detective had seen it all before—the same frenzy that drove an art thief to risk all for an impressionist painting to hang in a dark corner of his bedroom. It was a disease that somehow perverted the appreciation of beauty and rarity into an all-consuming need to hoard the artwork itself.

Professor Rowe was only the besotted lover who relished the pleasure he could give to Soames by providing the treasures—certainly something he could never achieve in other forms of lovemaking they might try. He didn't value the art himself—only the reaction the fine things provoked in young Soames. That at least was something he could be sure of; and yet he was only as good as his last theft, so he had to keep stealing at an ever escalating rate just to keep up the attentions of Soames, who could have gone in many other directions at any time.

Margaret's Vavasour papers were just the sort of miracle that might have kept Soames interested in Rowe for another ten minutes. And perhaps Rowe had underestimated just how desperate Soames would become in his quest to own and control them. Past treasures had only justified danger and theft, but the Vavasour trove allowed murder as well. And that had been their undoing.

About two months before, Scotland Yard had been alerted about this unlikely couple—the avaricious former student and the smitten professor—by complaints from two victims, who had come forward, by chance almost simultaneously.

The first to complain was a librarian at a small college up in Northumberland. Professor Rowe had visited there for several days last winter, evaluating a collection of local manuscripts from the medieval monastic period and, although there was no formal catalogue of the library's holdings, two choice items had seemed to go missing. One was an illuminated manuscript sheet with a particularly randy illustration of devils tempting an abbot, and the other was a fifteenth-century map of the northern coastline facing Ireland, replete with dragonlike sea monsters threatening some bold mariners afloat. The librarian missed them only because she had been planning to feature them in a lobby exhibition to tempt the students into using the library this fall.

The second victim was a man working to tidy up his grandfather's country house before an estate sale to benefit the heirs. The young man couldn't locate certain treasures in the library, ones that he had often looked at as a boy on his grandfather's knee. He thought some mischief might be involved because his grandfather had written him about his excitement at the visit of Professor Rowe of Oxford, who actually deemed to stay for an entire weekend some months earlier, studying in the library for an upcoming book he was preparing. Now those items had disappeared.

Detective Harris had then worked behind the scenes and discovered links between these missing treasures and the sales of Soames Bliforth, bookseller. Over the last few weeks, the detective had found additional grieved librarians and manuscript owners to come forward, and a significant ironclad case against the pair was being developed.

When Bliforth seemed to be about to run out of the money he needed to fuel his bookshop, mews house, and country house in Gloucestershire, his actions took a much more desperate turn, and sadly that first manifested itself in the incident at the vicarage that involved Stephen and Margaret in this whole affair. Ironically, the police were just about to move in when Margaret's background checks came up. Of course, telling them all this was 'off the record,' as they could understand, but the detective thought they deserved to have the full story.

Once Harris and his team were aware of the Vavasour papers, they were willing to delay arresting the pair slightly, in the hope that taped conversations might reveal some of the international connections Soames had been using to launder his stolen goods through a worldwide stolen-documents network. And that delay had almost turned fatal for Margaret and Stephen.

Now the police and judiciary would simply proceed to recover damages from the estates of both Soames and Rowe for all of the documented earlier thefts and transactions. Because of that, there really was no need to include the Vavasour papers in the legalities going forward—which otherwise would mean the police would have to retain possession of the papers stolen from Margaret and Stephen indefinitely. So the detective was happy to slide across the table a stack of papers and journals recovered from Soames and Rowe; these simply would not be needed as exhibits in the proceedings.

Margaret and Stephen had a few questions, which caused them to linger another ten minutes. For example, they learned the theft of the church crucifix and candlesticks turned out to be totally separate from the assault on Vicar Hamilton. One of the workmen drying the vaults had just been caught trying to sell them.

Once the ninety-minute interview was over, they exited the building and with the bundle of papers under his right arm, Stephen hailed a taxi with his left to drop off their bundle at Margaret's flat.

Spreading the recovered items out on Margaret's table behind the sofa, Stephen's eyes went right to the thickest manuscript, which was indeed the maximal copy of *Macbeth* that Heminge referred to in his letter—with all the crossing outs that made it 'the cut that woke the Dane.' Stephen hadn't even been sure he'd ever seen it, because it was one of the things taken by Soames on the night he assaulted the vicar, long before Stephen had any sort of handle on the full list of what they actually had found. Heminge had not had the time to rebuild the full play for placement into the First Folio, so he just used the cut-down version, telling the typesetters to ignore all the crossed-out sections of the longer version it contained. Perhaps he planned to include a longer one in the next edition of his Folio, if there was to be one. Sadly, his own death intervened, along with the loss of any other copy of the full version of the play. Only the short version survived, as printed in the First Folio—until now, when the Vavasour trove could reintroduce the public to Shakespeare's complete telling of the play.

What exactly to do with all this would be Margaret's decision—after she had the time to consider all of her options
properly, and now that she was almost clear of the BBC. Meanwhile, Stephen would be happy to carry the returned papers back
to the village, add them to his inventory, and deliver them to the
safety deposit boxes of the local bank.

~

Later the same day, Margaret heard bad news from the BBC team
in Sarajevo, which the Bosnian embassy in London confirmed at
the end of the afternoon. Mister Juric's remains were identified
in the rubble near the Bosnian government building in Sarajevo
that had been the target of repeated shelling by the besieging
forces attacking the city. And the BBC team were tracking reports
that Mrs. Juric had probably never connected with her husband
before his death. She might have traveled towards her family's
village to the south, near Mostar, and travel anywhere now was
very dangerous. So she might have been caught up in something
during the journey. They would keep going on that lead.

That left Margaret and Stephen with the task of telling the
children and making some plans for keeping them safe in the
village for the foreseeable future, at least until they discovered
the fate of Mrs. Juric.

"All right," said Margaret. "We should telephone Mrs. Quick
with a heads-up, and then go over and tell the children."

"Bloody hell, that is going to be awful."

"You know, Stephen, what if I just moved them over into the
vicarage with me now for a while? I have it until the end of the
year and have to be out there going through things anyway. I
mean, I don't think the BBC will need me to come in and work
out my transition very long—not after my boss hears all this
about the Jurics. Everyone on the team there will all want me to
be with the children. And Mrs. Quick, or even another family in

the village, wouldn't be the right answer for the first few days and weeks after news like this. I mean, I want to do it. They at least know me a little and I want to take them through this."

Looking over at her, Stephen knew she had already decided and that was that. And besides she was right. "Yes, Margaret," he said. "That is actually the right thing to do, and I will back you up with it—all the way. They know me a little, too."

~

The next few weeks were a heartbreak. The final word came in that Mrs. Juric was dead, along with several others who had been taken off a bus with her at a roadblock just outside her home village. The embassy organized a funeral and memorial in London, and a special interfaith service was held in the village at St. Mary's, with the St. George's schoolchildren attending, as well as Mia's classmates and teachers from the village junior school. Denis and Mia were out of school for two weeks, spending all their time with Margaret, but then they began to carve out a new routine.

Stephen was never very far away from those three, and he began to spend less time at his school, encouraging Mrs. Boardman to gradually take over. He had been thinking he could do a better job with his inventory. In fact, after he added the stolen items just returned, it could be the core of a catalogue for the whole collection, along with a note about its discovery and significance. And, quite frankly, he was thinking a new book about Sir Henry Lee and Anne Vavasour might be another good project for his literary debut. He already was the world's leading living expert on the pair, so how much trouble could it be to simply tell their story properly to the world? Besides, all that would keep him busy as he gave up his teaching career. Then the book about Byron, Keats, and the Shelleys might come next.

As for the Vavasour papers themselves, Margaret thought, they had sat comfortably next to Anne and Sir Henry for almost

350 years, so there really wasn't any need to rush them to market. She would have Maggs and Company appraise them. Stephen could consult the papers while writing his book, and when the moment was right, she could make sure they went to some place that could provide access to any curious scholars and the public. Actually, it was almost a certainty she would choose the British Museum—or its coming spin-off, the new British Library, which had been under construction forever. Perhaps displaying the trove could be part of the new library's launch?

All of these things suddenly were less of a headache for the couple and just fantasy fodder for thinking about what their future together might bring.

Long term, Stephen thought finishing the school year in the village, followed by a quiet summer in the English countryside would be right for them all, with some excursions around the country to help heal Denis and Mia.

After all, Anne and Sir Henry had lots of choices and found a simple life in the country was just right for them, didn't they?

Epilogue

Anno Domini 1654 was a dour time in England, with King Charles I having been executed five years before and Oliver Cromwell presiding. All forms of religious worship were tightly regulated. Even the everyday prayers in the beloved Book of Common Prayer were banned in favor of a dry new text called A Directory for the Public Worship of God.

For burials especially, simplicity was mandatory, even if the deceased was a colorful Elizabethan.

Yet, in spite of all that, a ninety-year-old widow named Anne Vavasour was about to be buried in the old style. Decades before, she had prepared her vault under the village church floor in front of her memorial. Ever since, she had been the primary patron of the parish, contributing mightily.

As a result, once again, Anne Vavasour was about to have her way. Lady Frances, Anne's dutiful great-niece, was ready to oversee her interment according to her wishes, with the old, familiar Catholic prayers, and making sure her ebony boxes with her papers were sealed up along with her and Sir Henry Lee, who was already there waiting.

Anne died at an unheard-of age, and none of her own generation, and few of her children's generation, were still living. But Lady Frances was determined to make sure everything went smoothly and was now waiting for her brother and sister to arrive with their families before the church ceremony at five o'clock in the evening.

Earlier that day, Frances visited the minister and walked with him to the church to make sure all was ready for the burial. In this blustery January, it was a blessing the interment was taking place inside the church and not in the windswept churchyard. Anne built her memorial and vault more than forty years before, on a wall of the Lady Chapel, off the Norman nave of the church. After construction, and after Sir Henry went in, it was never reopened. Above, the memorial stood like an altar, decorated on its long lower front panel with a sculptured image of Anne, painted in a white cap and red dress, kneeling in humble prayer before a lectern with an open book. Armorial crests adorned either side of this tableau, and the top was marble. Just in front, three large slabs of the church's stone floor had been taken up and stacked to one side, exposing the entrance to the burial vault.

Later that afternoon, when the full funeral party gathered, the minister led the small procession of about twenty souls by torch-light on the short walk across the green and churchyard into the softly lit church. By four thirty, it was already dark, and the timing gave a privacy that was a deliberate choice by Lady Frances. No tolling of bells was needed to attract the attention of the village for these private rites. Also, without a crowd of onlookers, there would be no need to explain the special service, the Catholic prayers, or to provide a public funeral feast and costly gifts. This was to be a simple family affair, just for their matriarch, her living kin and longtime servants. After the burial, all would return to Lady Frances's house for the private funeral feast.

Finally, at the right moment, the minister was bold enough to lead the small gathering in the old prayer Anne had requested. "Almighty and everlasting God, we humbly entreat thy mercy, that thou wouldest commend the soul of thy servant, for whose body we perform the office of burial, to be laid in the bosom of the patriarch Abraham; that when the day of recognition shall arrive, she may be raised up, at thy bidding, among the saints of thy elect." More scandalous still, some holy water was even dripped lightly onto the coffin, although any hint of incense was suppressed. Prayers ended, the family and servants watched as the workmen angled Anne's coffin down into position on the northern side of the vault, next to the other coffin already there. In her final duty, Lady Frances then gestured for two hall boys from the house to bring forward the small ebony chests to be placed next to Anne. Such boxes were no surprise to anyone. Indeed, there were similar sad small caskets in all of the other vaults inside the church.

By five fifteen, the family was following the torches, retracing their steps back to the house for the feast as Lady Frances's steward watched the workmen rebrick the manhole, shovel the rubble back into place, and position the slabs back onto the floor. The adults chatted quietly, and the children whispered excitedly with their cousins.

That night, inside Lady Frances's home, there was good food and fine wine, along with family stories about Anne's long life— stories that surprised the youngest of the family who learned their old "black sheep" was not as dull as they'd thought.

AUTHOR'S NOTE ABOUT THIS STORY

To make people and places from the past "come alive," historical novels often blend fact and fiction. So, what is "real," and what is "made up" in *The Vavasour Macbeth*?

I've written the answers in three sections: first, for the modern-day action; second, for the story of Sir Henry Lee and Anne Vavasour; and, third, for a brief discussion of some facts and problems around Shakespeare and his much-loved play *Macbeth*.

Fact or Fiction?

1. About England in 1992. Although Stephen and Margaret never existed, their characters and backgrounds are composites of bits and pieces from real world people whom I encountered or knew well during the many years I spent in England.

The village where Vicar Hamilton, Margaret, and Stephen all lived is based on the commuter town where my family and I stayed for several years, and Stephen's school is very like the one I attended as a boy in Hampstead in the 1950s and 1960s, including the cricket practice in the batting nets.

Since my job in the '80s and '90s was based in London's Soho Square, travel from the village by train to King's Cross was a regular event for me, as was walking in the neighborhoods near the BBC's Broadcasting House and the British Museum. Although The Pillars of Hercules pub where Stephen and Margaret chatted has recently closed, you can still enjoy memorable high-priced dining on Surrey Snails at Soames's favorite perch, L'Escargot on Greek Street, or sample the pea and mint risotto at Sir Terence Conran's posh riverside restaurant Pont de la Tour over by Tower Bridge.

Book lovers should note that although the British Museum was indeed the repository for most of Britain's rarest books when Stephen went there in 1992—including the Elizabethan State Papers, and the letters of the Earl of Oxford and Sir Henry Lee—that all changed with the opening of the British Library in 1998. Today's home for those items lies about a half mile north at the library's new campus located just between Saint Pancras and King's Cross stations. And, sadly, most of the rare bookshops next to the British Museum have closed by now after high rents and internet bookselling cut into their trade.

Margaret's apartment on Welbeck Street, behind Self-ridges, is, in fact, in the building I grew up in back in the day. And, if you go museum-hopping in London, make sure you include a visit to the Tudor section of the National Portrait Gallery to say hello to Sir Henry Lee's portrait and, next to it, Queen Elizabeth I's picture showing her standing in splendor on the carpet map of Oxfordshire to memorialize the Ditchley entertainment put on for her and the court in 1592. Make sure you have lunch there, too, in the wonderful Portraits restaurant on the top floor of the NPG, with its unique panoramic views of Westminster's rooftops, domes, and battlements.

If you investigate Oxford, you'll find the university continues to offer popular degree courses in both Classics and English (Stephen), and English and Modern Languages (Margaret), and those degrees often land their graduates in teaching, journalism, and writing careers. And walk around the stately grounds and cloisters of Magdalen and Brasenose Colleges, both of which would be likely homes at Oxford for the students lucky enough to be studying for their degrees in languages and classics.

Finally, if you go to Stratford-upon-Avon in search of Shakespeare, you should be able to find a hotel like the one described near Trinity Church and the imposing Shakespeare Memorial Theatre, where the Royal Shakespeare Company does indeed run school workshops to let students experience what it's like to perform one of Shakespeare's plays.

2. About Sir Henry Lee and Anne Vavasour. Unlike fictional Stephen and Margaret, Sir Henry and Anne are very real historical characters.

Sir Henry Lee. The details of Sir Henry's story are all true as told in the book. Officially, he was the son of Anthony Lee and Margaret Wyatt, born in 1533. However, in the 1680s, the sensationalist antiquarian and biographer John Aubrey included in his notebooks (later published as *Brief Lives*) the rumor that Sir Henry was the "supposed brother of Queen Elizabeth," implying he was actually an illegitimate child of King Henry VIII.

His more scholarly biographer, Sir Edmund Chambers, later thought this connection "unlikely," although he did not totally dismiss the possibility. Instead, he allowed that Sir Henry was extremely "lucky." First, when he inherited his family's properties at age fourteen, he left his schooling by his uncle Sir Thomas Wyatt, and went directly into the service of the king. No doubt his manly skills of hunting and riding in knightly splendor had their beginnings in those days. As he grew, he seemed immune to the dangerous twists and turns that bedeviled the English aristocracy and gentry as King Henry went through six wives and made a chaos of state religion, alternating between Roman Catholicism and Anglicanism. Then, his immunity continued as King Henry's children Edward, Mary, and Elizabeth followed their father onto the throne. Through it all, Sir Henry remained on center stage, unwavering in his service of whichever monarch happened to be in power. He even made a smooth transition as power shifted from the House of Tudor to the House of Stuart when James VI of Scotland came to London as King James I of England after Elizabeth died. And it was very unusual for a "commoner" knight to be admitted to the Order of the Garter as something of an equal of the aristocrats and monarchs who were the ones usually honored as Garter knights, such as King Christian IV of Denmark and Norway.

In 1590, when he was a widower about age fifty-seven, he did indeed retire as Elizabeth's personal champion at the joust, and he invited Anne Vavasour, then about age twenty-seven, to join him as his mistress and *de facto* wife, a situation which would have been well known to Queen Elizabeth, who had banished Anne from court about nine years before. And historians agree that his Ditchley entertainment of the queen and court in 1592, with its famous commemorative portrait of Elizabeth standing on Oxfordshire, was designed to seek the tacit approval of Elizabeth for his unusual housing arrangement, which he did achieve. Furthermore, it is true that King James I and Crown Prince Harry were frequent guests of Sir Henry for hunting at Ditchley, and James's queen, Anne of Denmark, liked to chat away there with Mistress Anne, commemorating one well-documented visit by sending a precious jewel to Sir Henry's "dearest dear" as a token of their friendship.

I could not verify that Sir Henry (and Anne) were at the special Order of the Garter investiture service for the queen's brother, King Christian, which took place on August 7, 1606, but it is at least plausible since Sir Henry was a current Garter knight and was frequently in the company of the King and Queen. In addition, he had missed the annual Garter ceremonies in April of that year due to an illness that he had recovered from by summer, and he may have wanted to reassert his place at court. The actual attendees of King Christian's investiture are not listed in the record of that event in the Garter archives at Windsor Castle, but it is noted that the royal party retired for the evening to Hampton Court that very day, and many Shakespeare scholars believe the first performance of *Macbeth* took place on the same evening, although others disagree. It is, of course, fiction that Anne actually edited and performed in that performance, but I like to think it is perhaps just within the realm of possibilities.

Anne Vavasour. I did have to take more liberties with Anne's own history, because she has not attracted the same degree of biographical attention as Sir Henry through the years. Quite simply, all the biographies are about him, and not about her.

As a result, I had to speculate that Anne would have been tutored according to the precepts of Roger Ascham, Queen Elizabeth's own tutor. This is plausible, however, since the Knyvet family who sponsored her to court made careful plans for Anne to be shaped as a companion to the queen, and Ascham's techniques had just been published when Anne began her schooling as a child.

It is, however, sadly true that in 1581 Anne did give birth to a boy in the "maidens' chamber" provided for Elizabeth's closest attendants at court. She was seventeen years old, and instantly became the delicious scandal of the season. Making it even better was the fact that the father was the pretentious Edward de Vere, the Earl of Oxford, who was then estranged from his wife Anne Cecil, the daughter of Elizabeth's chief minister, Lord Burghley. As a result, the earl was mocked and Anne was roasted and ridiculed as the Monica Lewinsky of her time. Meanwhile, the Knyvet family remained fiercely loyal to Anne, and took revenge on the Earl of Oxford by inflicting a wound on him during a duel. That kept Edward de Vere lame for life.

Nine years later, when Sir Henry retired in 1590, he completed Anne's rescue from what must have been a difficult life as an unwed mother, treating her as his wife with love and luxury for the next twenty years. And when he died, at almost age eighty, he tied up his considerable fortune so Anne could have the use of it (and several of his estates) for the period of sixty years, or until her death, the exact date of which is not known but is rumored to be 1654. He had no surviving close relatives.

Anne would have still been in her forties when this bequest occurred in 1611, and for years she fought off the unsuccessful attempts by distant family members of Sir Henry to grab the money, as legal records attest. But, no one has followed the trail of Anne and her money past the 1620s, when she was fined for bigamy. I did, however, find the path for learning more, starting at the imposing National Archives facility at Kew outside London and at New College, Oxford—and I may resume following Anne's trail at a later date. That process will not be easy, however, since the relevant legal documents are composed in both Elizabethan English and Latin, and most are written in the difficult-to-read secretary style of handwriting. And I have already learned it is an expensive business to hire today's paleographic scholars to translate and inter- pret these records since the files sit all mixed up and out of order in boxes undisturbed for the last 400 years or so.

But both of Anne's illegitimate sons did well. Edward Vere, her scandalous son by the Earl of Oxford, kept in close touch both with his mother and the de Vere family, and went on to distinction as a soldier. He first surfaces in records at the University of Leyden at age fifteen. Two or three years later, he served in the Netherlands under the command of Sir Francis Vere, the Earl's cousin. He was knighted by King James I in 1607 for his military service and was a witness to the will of Sir Henry Lee in 1611. Later he was a renowned scholar and Member of Parliament for Newcastle-under-Lyme in 1623. A letter from the period describes him as a soldier and scholar, noting he was "all summer in the field, all winter in his study." Unfortunately, he was killed when he was shot through the back of the head with a cannonball after showing the Prince of Orange around the fortifications at the Siege of 's-Hertogenbosch in the Netherlands in 1629. English troops were supporting the Dutch there against the Spanish.

And Thomas Freeman Vavasour—Anne's natural son with Sir Henry—became a Yeoman at the Tower of London by 1607, went on to be knighted by King James, and received an annuity of forty pounds per year in Sir Henry's will, as well as some silver-plated pieces that had been given him as a gift at his christening.

Finally, I have to admit that it is pure fiction that the location of Anne's tomb is known, or that any buried manuscripts were discovered there. Sadly, all of that is fiction.

3(a). About Shakespeare. In most bookstores, Shakespeare is the only author with his own section. Schoolchildren throughout the world have been made to read one or more of his plays, all of which have been translated into every language. Probably everyone reading this now has seen at least one or two of his plays performed. And each year, scholars grind out hundreds, if not thousands of articles about him.

That's why many people find it surprising to learn that there remain questions about who actually wrote the works attributed to "the Stratford Man" William Shakespeare. It was no accident that Sir Edmund Chambers entitled his masterful 1930 two-volume biography of the bard *William Shakespeare: A Study of Facts and Problems*. Indeed, the topic of the "Shakespeare authorship question" is perhaps the most curious and colorful corner of English literature studies, filled with insane conspiracy theories, name calling, and loud shouting.

The main stumbling block seems to be that the few solid facts remaining from the records of Shakespeare's life are not what one might expect to be the pedigree of the world's greatest author. He was neither well-born nor well-educated. In fact, he was the son of what might be called "middle class" parents in a small country town. His father signed documents with an "X," and although in mid-career John Shakespeare rose to the high office of bailiff in Stratford, he then encountered difficulties and, at the end, avoided church because he was in danger of being arrested there for his debts.

There is no record of William's schooling, but speculation continues that he probably went to the local school in Stratford, which would have been a very good start. However, there are reports that he was taken out of school early so he could help out at home, which Chambers thinks may have been true, based on his father's difficulties. William appears next in the local records applying for a marriage license when he was eighteen years old and christening his first child six months later. Twins followed in 1585 when he was aged twenty—and then things go quiet for a little over seven "lost" years, about which many unsubstantiated theories have been constructed to help explain his later achievements.

He next seems to be mentioned by a satirist in 1592 as an actor called "Shake-scene" in London, and in the following year his actual name starts appearing regularly in the lists of players and authors active on the Elizabethan stage. *A Comedy of Errors, Taming of the Shrew, Romeo and Juliet,* and *The Merchant of Venice* all most likely appeared (along with several others) between 1592 and 1597.

It is universally agreed that the sonnets, longer poems, and plays attributed to him show great familiarity and skill with the technicalities of the legal profession, and also provide startling insights into the characters, behaviors, and oratory of soldiers, aristocrats, and rulers. Oddly, while some of his fellow writers had academic and professional credentials—for example, Christopher Marlowe had six years at Cambridge and Thomas Dekker was a lawyer—Shakespeare had none, which is a problem for many.

In spite of all that, he must have been doing well financially at his writing because by 1597 his name is also back at home in the Stratford records as having to pay a fine related to his purchase of one of the finest houses in the town, which was called New Place. Then, for a dozen more years he wrote more of his greatest hits—including *Julius Caesar, Twelfth Night, Hamlet, Othello, King Lear, Macbeth* and more—apparently dividing his time between London and Stratford. Around 1610, biographer Chambers writes that he seemed to return to his hometown more permanently, and there he is actively recorded as paying fines, pursuing people to repay their debts to him, and making land transactions while writing about one play per year until 1613, followed by two years of silence. Then, in 1616, came his final illness, will, and death. No letters or correspondence from him have ever been found; no one wrote down stories about visiting or interacting with him; nor were any books ever mentioned among his belongings.

As a result, several differing opinions as to the *real* author of Shakespeare have been expressed over the years. Most people seem to accept "the Stratford Man" William Shakespeare as the author, while admitting that it is remarkable his writing scaled such heights from his humble beginnings. I tend to agree with this, even though the achievement does seem amazing. One distinguished professor said that it was as if Shakespeare arrived here on a spaceship from another planet, and then transformed his period drama from wooden religious morality plays into full-scale psychological stream of consciousness exposés of the inner workings of our minds.

Others have doubts. Henry James said he was "haunted by the conviction that the divine William is the biggest and most successful fraud ever practiced on a patient world." Along with Mark Twain, James thought the well-born, well-educated, and highly credentialed Sir Francis Bacon was just as likely a candidate to be the true author. Sigmund Freud thought so as well. Yet others have argued that Edward de Vere, the seventeenth Earl of Oxford— and Anne Vavasour's seducer—is the true author, and a society called "The Shakespeare Fellowship" began publishing mountains of material to support this view back in 1922. Several books by members in support of de Vere by the American Ogburn family, parents and son, have more recently contributed over 2,000 pages of explanations, and the debate continues. Personally, I think the most damning evidence against Oxford as Shakespeare are the few poems that are factually known to have been penned by him, since they are not nearly up to Shakespeare's mark.

Then, there are the ongoing investigations in search of Shakespeare's handwriting. In *The Vavasour Macbeth*, I describe the only proven examples of Shakespeare's writing—the six signatures taken from his will and a few real estate related transactions. I also explain the excitement that really does exist around the manuscript of the old play *Sir Thomas More*, which many believe contains 140 lines of text written by Shakespeare himself amid all the other improvements attempted by the collection of play doctors trying to whip the play into good enough shape to be approved by the censors—which ultimately did not happen.

I included all of these uncertainties to suggest to you, the reader, just how important and valuable the fictional examples of Shakespeare-related materials from Anne Vavasour's tomb would be today—certainly valuable enough for murder. And, having seen some of the mountains of unread Elizabethan period manuscripts stored in various archives and libraries in Britain, I can promise you more documents and facts about Shakespeare might very well surface someday, so stay tuned for that.

3(b). About Macbeth. We are very fortunate that in 1623, seven years after Shakespeare's death, two of the bard's friends and fellow actors—John Heminge (or

Heminges) and Henry Condell—decided to collect and publish thirty-six of his plays in a large oversize edition that has come to be called *Shakespeare's First Folio*. While most of the plays in that collection did have earlier solo editions, *Macbeth* did not—and the version of the play in the *First Folio* is the only version to have survived.

Describing the surviving text of *Macbeth*, Sir Edmund Chambers called it "unsatisfactory" because of "rehandling" and "interpolation." In other words, someone had been fiddling around with the text. Noting that it is exceedingly short—2,106 lines compared to *Hamlet's* more than 4,000 lines—he goes on to explain how it shows signs of being abridged and adapted from a lost version which perhaps was longer and more complete. In addition, two songs have been lobbed into the scenes with the witches (only their titles are indicated in the *First Folio*—you have to look elsewhere in search of the complete words to the songs). Also, a stage direction to "ring the bell" has been incorporated into the spoken lines of the play, possibly due to typesetter confusion. Finally, some readers—such as Samuel Taylor Coleridge—believe that someone other than the original author added the scene with a drunken porter mumbling around while answering knocking at the castle's gate after King Duncan's bloody murder as comic relief.

Because of these observations by reputable authorities, I decided to make the missing longer version of *Macbeth* the most important fictional document discovered in the tomb of Anne Vavasour. To bolster this invention, I also had Margaret and Stephen come across the real surviving prompting scroll for *Orlando Furioso* (a play contemporary to *Macbeth*) from the papers of period actor Edward Alleyn. That real scroll does show evidence that a longer version of *Orlando Furioso* was lost compared with the shortened version, which is the only one surviving today.

Finally, there is a lot of uncertainty about when each of Shakespeare's plays was first performed. Queen Elizabeth I's Court Calendar and the payment records of her Treasury and Office of the Chamber and Revels show acting troupes being paid for putting on performances on certain dates, but the records do not always note the name of the play. In *The Vavasour Macbeth,* I have sided with the experts who theorize that *Macbeth* was first performed during the summer of 1606 as an entertainment during the state visit of King Christian IV of Denmark and Norway, who was the brother of King James I's wife, Anne of Denmark.

Like James, Christian was fascinated by witches and actually had more than 1,300 of his Scandinavian citizens burned for that offense at home during his reign. The actors probably would have been told to keep the performance short—just under two hours—because Christian and his court did not speak fluent English. But they would have all appreciated the scenes with the witches, the songs, the drunken porter scene, and all the blood connected with the murder, the battles, and so on. Another reason to be quick was the fact that there was prodigious drinking on all sides during that visit, and things tended to be moved along quickly during the entertainments. After his four-week stay, King Christian and his court left for home on their ships a few days later, to everyone's relief.

So, as you can see, there is indeed fiction about the *Macbeth* treasures described in the novel, but not wildly improbable inventions.

Additional information. If you want to know more about all of the history and problems in *The Vavasour Macbeth* and around the whole "Shakespeare authorship question," here are some recommendations:

Further reading:

1. *Anne Vavasour and Sir Henry Lee,* by Bart Casey (New York, Post Hill Press, 2019).

> This is a short ebook telling the complete non-fiction story of the lives and romance of Anne Vavasour and Sir Henry Lee.

2. *Sir Henry Lee,* by Sir Edmund Chambers. (Oxford, Clarendon Press, 1930).

> This is the same biography that book character Stephen requests through an inter-library loan to find out more about Sir Henry Lee and Anne Vavasour. You'll probably have to get it the same way, by asking your local library to order it from a nearby university's collection, which they can do for you.

3. *Sir Henry Lee (1533-1611): An Elizabethan Courtier*, by Sue Simpson. (Surrey, England, Ashgate Publishing, 2014).

> This biography retells the story of Sir Henry in a more modern style with illustrations.

4. *Shakespeare's Lives*, by S. Schoenbaum. (Oxford University Press, 1993).

> This masterful summary of the evolution of the many diverse and often wacky theories about the "Shakespeare authorship question" was written by the Distinguished Professor of Renaissance Literature at the University of Maryland. It was widely praised and became an international bestseller.
>
> Reviewing it for the British newspaper *The Sunday Telegraph*, Frank Kermode wrote, "It is not often research as vast and minute as Schoenbaum's produces such good fun."

5. *Will in the World: How Shakespeare Became Shakespeare*, by Stephen Greenblatt. (W. W. Norton & Company, 2004).

> Harvard professor Stephen Greenblatt makes the best possible case for how Will Shakespeare, the boy from Stratford, could have become the real Shakespeare—without a university education or a legal degree.

Further movie viewing:

6. *Shakespeare in Love (1998)*.

> Winner of seven Oscars, this fictional comedy is about a young Shakespeare, out of ideas and short of cash, who meets his ideal woman and is inspired to write one of his most famous plays, *Romeo and Juliet*.
>
> This farce probably comes close to the truth about the collaboration of the Elizabethan writers desperate to produce popular plays to pay the rent.

I particularly like the pub scene in which Shakespeare tells Christopher Marlowe he is working on a play called *Romeo and Ethel, the Pirate's Daughter,* about a pirate. Marlowe suggests it might be better to make it about an Italian boy who's always in and out of love and who falls for his enemy's daughter...or something.

And the rest is history.

Acknowledgments

For the first journeys into this project, I would like to thank the late professor Betty Bandel of the English Department of the University of Vermont graduate school in the early 1970s for driving me farther than ever into little explored territories around the facts and problems surrounding Shakespeare.

Then, more importantly, I am grateful for the navigational sense of my wife, Marilyn, who insisted we turn away from the well-worn highway pursuing Master Shakespeare, to go instead down the small country lane leading to the virtually forgotten story of Anne Vavasour and Sir Henry Lee.

As we amassed more and more information about *that* story over the years, we were lucky that our three children are all excellent writers and critics. Matthew, Lauren, and Michael never failed to give us excellent feedback on ideas and drafts as the story took shape.

Research forays into primary manuscripts and other obscure sources were always at the heart of the information gathering parts of this project, and I would like to thank the following resources for giving me access to rare materials:

- In the UK: The British Museum, The British Library, The National Archives in Kew, the Buckinghamshire County Museum, the Centre for Buckinghamshire Studies, the National Portrait Gallery, the Victoria and Albert Museum, the library at Westminster Abbey, and the Royal Archives at Windsor.

- In the USA: the New York Public Library, the Morgan Library and the Harvard University Libraries.

Many individuals were extremely generous in sharing their knowledge, resources, and advice with me along the way. I would like to thank Mr. Peter Bateman, Clerk of the Armourers and Brasiers' Company in London for sharing his knowledge about the story of Anne Vavasour and Sir Henry Lee, and for allowing me to reproduce the cover images of their portraits on the cover of this book. Mr. Miles Young, Warden of New College Oxford, helped me understand the experience and training Oxford students such as Margaret and Stephen would have had at that wonderful university. Mr. Richard Bonner-Davies generously refreshed my schoolboy familiarity with cricket enough to avoid the most serious mistakes. And British researcher Susan Moore was brave enough to dive into boxes of ancient documents at the National Archives in Kew and to re-surface with understandable translations and summations of previously unpublished Elizabethan English and Latin documents she had resurrected relating to the adventures of Anne Vavasour and Sir Henry Lee.

When the final draft was taking shape, I am indebted to my early readers who provided invaluable feedback and suggestions on how to improve the storytelling—especially Laird Stiefvater, Angela Johnson, Garth Hallberg, Chuck Guariglia, Tom Vincent, Linda Jackson, Sheila Morse, Peg Brown, Karla Kirby, Ian Latham, and Virginia Doty.

And finally I want to thank the publishing team who worked so diligently with me from the earliest stages of development through to the end: my editors Paul DeAngelis, Trent Duffy, and Madeline Sturgeon; my agent Lynne Rabinoff; and the entire professional staff of Post Hill Press in New York and Nashville who delivered the final product.

For all of this help and encouragement along the way, I am truly grateful.

Bart Casey
Brattleboro, Vermont, USA
2019

About the Author

Bart Casey grew up in London, studied Literature at Harvard, and trained as a professor before switching to an advertising career, living many years amidst the settings for *The Vavasour Macbeth*. His recent biography of Victorian Laurence Oliphant was chosen by Kirkus for its *Best Books of 2016*.